THE SONG OF THE SLEEPERS
BOOK ONE

AN

EXILE

OF

WATER & GOLD

JOSHUA WALKER

Praise for *An Exile of Water & Gold*

Walker intricately weaves together epic fantasy and a dash of mystery, creating a mesmerising tale where characters are forced to seek the meaning of freedom in the intriguing, rich world of Q'ara.

Livia J Elliot, Author of *The Genesis of Change*

A masterclass in fantasy. The world that Walker brings us is full and fantastic, showing us a beautiful and complex universe. The story is masterfully woven, giving you mystery and lore, mixing the everyday struggles of its peoples with the extraordinary struggles of kings and nations.

Isaac Hill, Author of *The Dragon Legion*

Walker has already placed himself among the elite cadre of top fantasy authors. His worlds are exquisite, his twists as sharp on the plot as they are on your guts, and his characters so real you feel like they're about to reach through the page and throttle you.

Jonathan Weiss, Author of *The Flux Catastrophe* series

Walker's rich imagination and powerful storytelling will leave you struck with awe and wonder.
Esmay Rosalyne, *BeforeWeGo Blog*

An incredibly unique blend of environmentalism and fantasy that will keep you thinking long after the final page.
Kris, *A Fictional Escapist*

This isn't just an epic fantasy novel, this is a tale of love and purpose.
Graham Blades, *The Wulver's Library*

A grand epic fantasy tale brimming with magic, tragedy, and the discovery of oneself in an unknown world.
Kristen Shafer, *SFF Insiders*

Edited by Sarah Chorn, https://sarahchornedits.com.

Proofread by Isabelle Wagner, https://theshaggyshepherd.wordpress.com.

Cover art and design by Jeff Brown, https://www.jeffbrowngraphics.com.

Map design by Joshua Hoskins, Noctua Cartography (@Noctua_Maps).

Chapter Headings by Anna Maslennikova.

ISBN 978-0-6486427-4-9 (paperback)

ISBN 978-0-6486427-5-6 (hardback)

ISBN 978-0-6486427-3-2 (ebook)

To the two Mr W's:
The first is my dad, who compelled me to read.
The second is my high-school English teacher, who compelled me to
write.
I am endlessly grateful.

Contents

A Note on the English Language

Dear reader,

Before we begin, I thought I should let you know that I am unabashedly Australian, and a result you might find some spellings in this book that you do not agree with.

Firstly, our main character, Drift, is an unexpected **traveller**, and because of this, he hasn't packed **pyjamas** for the journey. They are after all, clothes that are designed to keep one **cosy,** a feeling which Drift sadly does not have much experience with.

Additionally, you may see buildings with several **storeys,** fire that **smoulders,** and **sceptics** aplenty. After all, my characters are often in **dialogue** with the kind of folk who are (frustratingly) morally **grey.**

I promise, I'm not an **arsehole,** but I won't **apologise** for writing in British English. It is after all the superior form, my **defence** of which is totally justified.

Josh

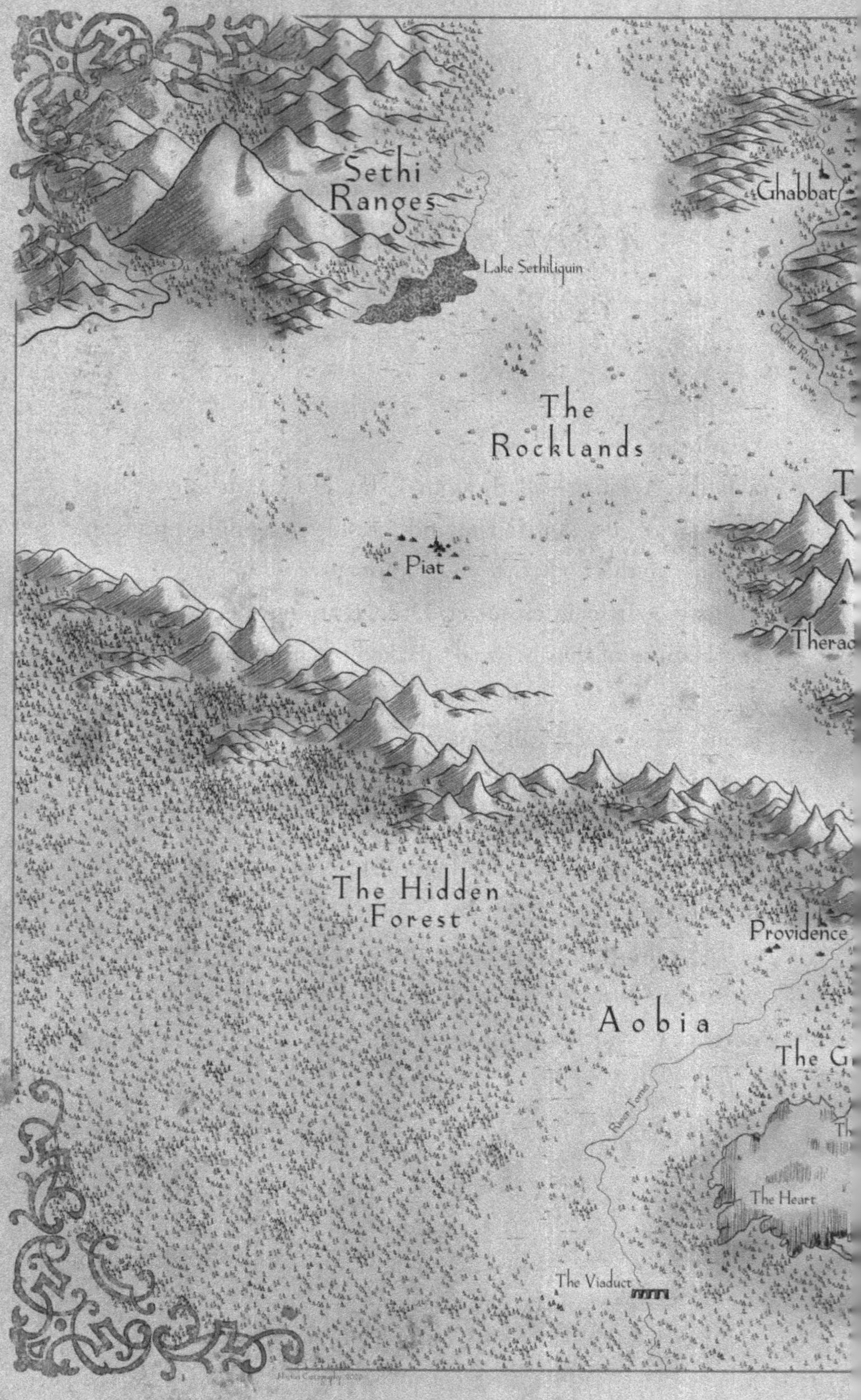

Sethi Ranges
Lake Sethiliquin
Ghabbat
Ghabbat River
The Rocklands
Piat
Therac
The Hidden Forest
Providence
Aobia
The G
Rhion Tower
The Heart
Th
The Viaduct

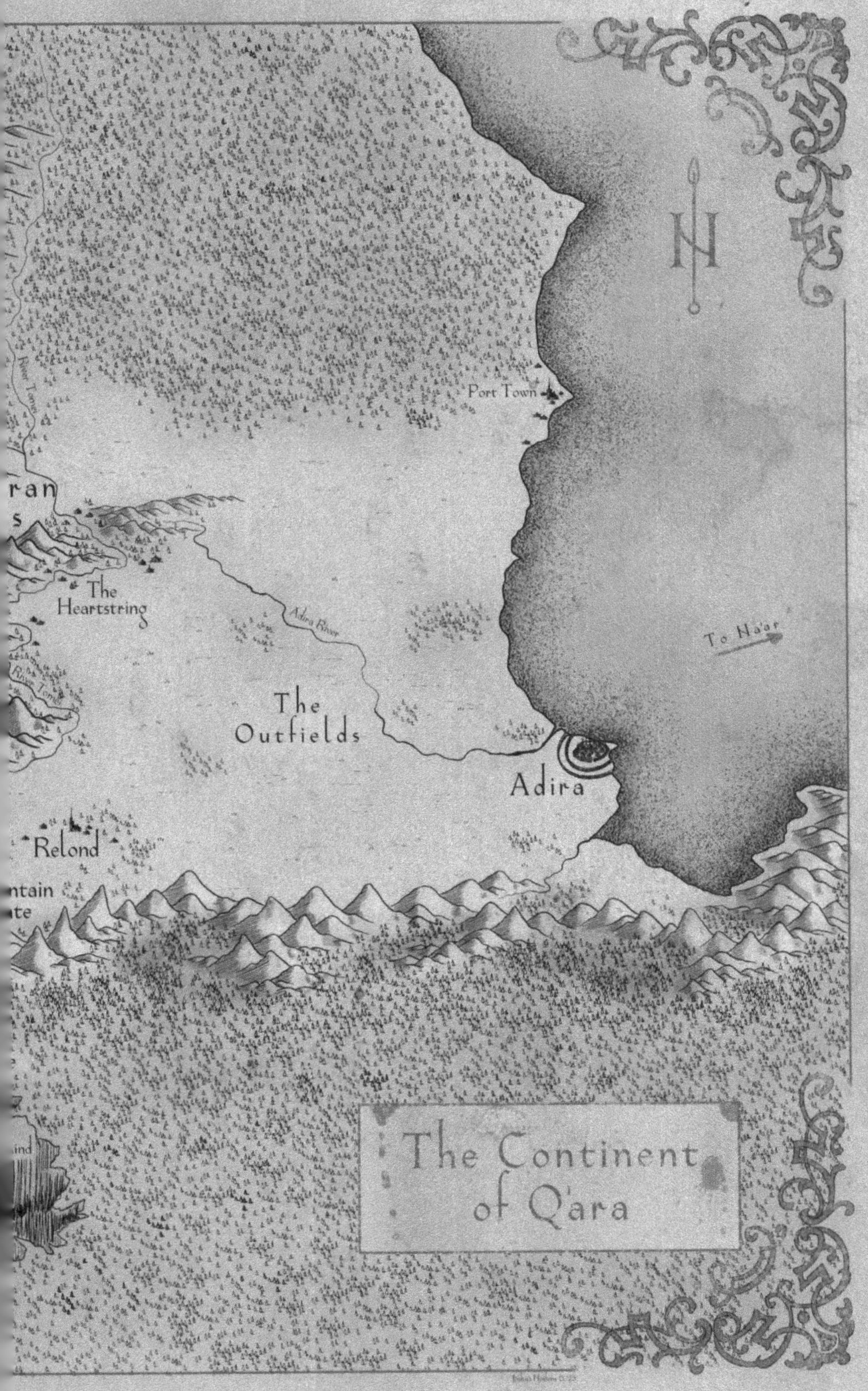

Port Town
ran
s
The
Heartstring
Adira River
To Ha'ar
The
Outfields
Adira
Relond
ntain
te
nd
The Continent
of Q'ara

PART I
An Exile of Water

"The fall of dropping water wears away the stone."

- Lucretius

ESME

Esme, heir to the throne of Adira and all-round smartarse, hummed as she walked the lonely palace halls to her father's study. It was nearly midnight and he hadn't come down for supper. A curious case, she supposed, but nothing too far-fetched. Her father was King Terrens, though he was known to her and her stepbrother Sefil as 'the Overworker'.

"He sought a throne not made of gold…

But a throne of por–ce–lain, hmm, hmm…"

The week had been filled with comings and goings, and despite her attempt to force some food into her father, she knew that the moment she'd walk in, he'd reject the offer to eat with her. Aobian ambassadors from the Great Tree as well as members of the governments of Piat, Ghabbat, and Sethi were visiting. Negotiations were underway, preemptive actions being taken to ensure that there would be alliances in place across the continent of Q'ara after word had spread of some terrifying inner workings happening in Therador, the tyrant-led empire at the heart of the Theradoran ranges.

"He said, 'I'll go with glee, to the privy,
In the chamber where secrets unfold—Ha!"

She stifled a laugh at the song as she skipped down the hall. At the end came the yellow light from her father's study. She might have been singing about a made-up prince who ejected golden nuggets from his rear, but it wasn't so far from the truth. *Rainol.* The other most sour aspect of their week. The prince of Therador, son of Emperor Jurin, had proposed to her again. The Most Vile and Pernicious Rat was no match for her ability to say no for the tenth time, however. There could be no alliance with Therador. They'd had their days of armistice after the war, and yet again, they'd turned to secret projects, shielding their strange experiments from the outside world.

"A strain, a push,
From forthwith my tush!"

This had started a century ago when members of the Theradoran High-Church had discovered a way to use a power that did not belong to them. A power that predated humanity's time on the continent of Q'ara. She had never discussed with anybody what exactly this was; she only knew it by name: Luminosity. Sleepers in the Great Tree known as Aobia wielded it, but nobody knew what its limitations were, just that it came from the Tree, a result of the spiritual connection the people there shared with their home, which towered above the surrounding world.

But the rumblings in the meetings she and her father had attended this week suggested that Jurin and his Priests of Dirt were close to finding a way to use Luminosity for themselves. It might not be long until they would sabotage the peace that had been upheld for more than fifty years across the northern part of the continent.

"A golden nugget!"

She sped up as she reached her father's study door, which was ajar. Unusual. Out of the corner of her eye, she thought she saw a flash of light illuminate her from behind, the direction from which she had come. When she whipped her head around, however, the hall was dark.

"In my bowl…"

She rested her hand on the doorknob, which was made of polished whitestone. It would annoy her dear dad, but he needed to take a break. And she had a line to finish.

"Of Por-ce-laaaaaiiiiin!"

She struck the door open dramatically, kneeling with her eyes shut and raising her hands to the heavens as she sang her final note. "Ta-daa!" she called, though her father sat with his back to her, hunched over his desk.

"Oh please, Father. Won't you eat something before you work yourself dogged through the night?" She made her way to him, put a hand on his shoulder, and peered around to see his face.

But there was no face. Just a hole where the gentle smile of her father had once been.

She screamed, instinctively removing her hand from his shoulder. "Father…" she breathed. "Father! Father!" She was crying now, sobbing at the hollowed-out skull that had once worn her father's face. Dead. All that stared back at her was a mixture of pulverised flesh, blood, and brittle bone. She retched, unable to scream her father's name as she vomited all over the desk. She was no child—damn it, she was nearly twenty-three—but she couldn't control the eruption that spilled over her lips and ran down her white bedgown.

Everything here was stained now: her clothes, the floor, her *life*.

All their lives.

Clambering feet began to sound from afar, like a stampede of bulls. Guards arrived at the door of the study to see Esme choking down vomit. Streaks of tears blurred her vision, making it impossible to see the oxidised red goop on the floor beside her father's chair. "No … No! Don't touch me!" she yelled as guards pulled her away from the scene. She thrashed, struggling out of their grip, before her foot slipped through the pile of what had once been the King's face on the polished stone floor, sending bits flying.

"Princess!" The head of the guard, Mirthorn, was here now. He scooped Esme up. "Princess, he's gone." His pensive eyes never changed. This man had watched over her since she'd been a child and had worked for her father since he'd been but a boy. Through every tribulation, however, his expression was always the same. Stern, unwavering. Grounding.

"He's gone now," he whispered, pulling her into an embrace.

Esme heaved a lengthy, strained sigh, the kind that was so disrupted by torture it barely sounded human. And then she cried, long into the night, in the crevice between Mirthorn's body and the destruction in the room beyond.

DRIFT

AFTER A DAY'S HARD work, Drift's body was as tired as his mind as he trudged through the streets of the Heart, the Great Tree of Aobia's main industrial sector. His silver-blonde hair was tied back into a messy bun that had once been tightly kept and his dark green work garments were stained with dirt and damp alike. His last four hours working below the Great Tree had involved a rigorous schedule of feeding the River Tomei's algae blooms the proper nutrients. He hoped his colleague, Nida, would return to work soon to fulfil her responsibilities, but her mother was dying, so Drift had been handed twice the amount of tasks for the past few weeks.

He took a step through the swinging door of The Minister's Secret, the bar his friend Vex ran with his only employee and confidant, Ame. Tonight, Vex was in the middle of serving a group of women while Ame was pacing between tables, running food and filling mugs of roughshod ale.

A glass of wine or two would be enough to loosen Drift up before he went to meet Tarri in the Heart's botanical parkland, where they had agreed to meet for a picnic supper under the Great Canopies and the mottled view of the starry sky. The two hadn't crossed paths in over a week and his heart ached to see his betrothed. Apart from his incessant exhaustion after work, Tarri was working hard on a special project, having just acquired an important new client.

The inside of The Minister's Secret was a combination of old, beautifully branchrendered walls and hanging lanterns that illuminated the room with a cosy yellow glow. The building was one of the oldest establishments in the Heart, named after an ancient minister who had lived in the district and paid a tidy sum for a family of branchrenders to mould the tavern out of the very limb of the Tree, against the approval of the Magisterium. It was Drift's favourite locale, where he could often find a small table tucked into a corner to gather his thoughts, drink, or stifle his endless worries with Tarri and his friends.

He approached the bar, where Vex was cleaning up the mess from a spilled mug of beer with a rag. Beside him was a group of ladies, who had done themselves an injustice with the fruity mixed drinks Vex had set out for them. One of them was wearing the traditional sage that was worn by an up-and-coming bride, her hair coloured a similar shade. Drift smiled at the ladies as

Vex moved over to him. As he opened his mouth to speak, the bride-to-be squawked, "One more, bartender! Then we'll be off!"

Drift smirked as Vex ducked away and pulled a cork out of an elegant bottle of straw-yellow wine. It wasn't the strong stuff, but he wagered Vex wasn't concerned that the ladies would be aware of that. For this early in the evening, they were more exuberant than any male Drift had ever seen in the tavern, even after dove-racing nights. He looked at the bride-to-be while Vex poured her last glass and felt an odd tension in his chest. This person was here to celebrate with her closest friends, maybe her mother, too. And tomorrow, she would continue to celebrate the best day of her life. Tarri's anecdote ran through his head: *"You might not think about what will happen the day you get married, sweet dove, but I have clutched all ideas for it since the day I could speak."*

Tonight, however, he *was* going to think about that day. Not only would he think it, but he'd suggest it. Tonight, he was to propose to his love of seven years. An incredibly long courtship, Drift knew.

"Okay," Vex said with a quick exhale, interrupting Drift's thoughts. "What can I get you, Drift? Actually"—he leaned in close—"talk to me a moment. I need a break from these ladies. Complain about your drink as I hand it to you. Anything for a break!"

"I thought she said it was her last glass?" Drift asked, a wry smile curling the corner of his mouth.

"She said that the last three glasses, Drift!" Vex hissed. "And I've no doorman tonight. If I want someone removed, I'll have to do it myself." He shook his head. "I won't be the one to interrupt the poor lass's dream."

"Well, I'll do it then," Drift said, crossing his arms. "Maybe she won't be the only one to have her dream broken tonight."

"No," Vex said, smacking a sweaty hand on his forehead. "*No.* You're not going to run from this again, are you? This is ridiculous, you know. Seven years, Drift? If it was me, I wouldn't have stuck around that long."

When Drift didn't say anything, Vex seized the moment to continue. "Tarri was here, asking after you earlier. Why don't you just do it here? Surrounded by friends and patrons who know you?"

"That's romantic," Drift said sarcastically. "But no. I told her I wanted to come by for a drink with you and then the two of us could head out for supper in the park."

"Ah," Vex said, his eyes going dreamy for a moment. "That's more like it. It's a nice night for stargazing. No breeze to stir the canopies." The Great Canopies above them, at the top of the Tree, were always an obstruction between the people of Aobia and the Sky. But if there was no breeze, one could stargaze well enough through the gaps between the Great Leaves.

"You know," Vex said, drying a clean glass with a cloth, "for what it's worth, I think you've hit the nail on the head. She'll love it, Drift. Now—let's celebrate. What do you want to drink? Apple wine?"

"I suppose," Drift said, scratching his arm. The more the minutes inched closer to leaving the bar and going to see Tarri, the less confident he felt that he was doing the right thing. He'd done it more times than he could count now. Self-sabotage. 'I'm not good enough' and 'what does a girl like her want with a dirty scrub like me?' Drift knew the drill. Somehow, stopping it before those thoughts took over only got harder the more it happened.

Vex smirked. "It's almost like you can't accept the good things that come to you." His friend looked squarely at him. "Sometimes I worry your … eccentricities are getting out of hand."

"I want to marry her!" Drift protested. "And you called them paranoias last time, Vex. Then you apologised and told me you didn't mean what you said. So, which is it?"

"I don't know, Drift," Vex said, his agitation rising. "Nobody else spends their days pretending they're living in a world where their every move is controlled by the Magisterium or thinking they don't deserve love and they can't possibly lead a happy life. The Sleepers might govern our home in this tree, but they don't read our minds, Drift. Whether they *can* or not is a moot point. They don't have time to worry about what you or I think. And don't get me started on the name thing—"

"I know who I am, Vex!" Drift snapped, his cheeks flushing.

"Naming rituals?" Vex put up his arms. "By the canopies above, Drift! After all those dark centuries, our people have moved past it and created a better world. Why can't you just live in it?"

Drift grimaced. "Flow believes me," he said.

"Flow's a fool," Vex said, pouring Drift's wine. "And if he isn't quieter about that stuff, it won't do well for him in his current job either."

Drift snorted, taking the glass of light green wine. "You know, Vex, Flow is in a better position than all of us. He's out there right now, exploring the world outside the Tree. Why should I have to live in this one tree all my life? Because that's what gets me caught up. Maybe I doubt myself. Maybe I think I can't possibly commit to a person for the rest of my days and live to tell the tale. But the greatest reason I stop myself short of every good thing that comes to me ..." Drift held Vex's gaze. "I'm scared of being a prisoner, Vex. All of us Aobians living in this tree we call home, unable to see anything outside of it. What kind of life is that? Will marriage not simply make me more cynical? What justice is it if I become resentful of the one I love, because she decided long ago that she was happy to settle?"

"She wants to settle with you, you idiot!" Vex barked back. "That is not a prison sentence, Drift, and it's deplorable that you think that way about her. Do you think that way about me? Anyone else?"

Drift's breath came fast and hot. "My father thought that way. He lost everything—*everything*—because of the ones who govern us. Your prime minister and her gaggle of glowing geese in the Mind took my mother, Vex. I thought you'd understand after all this time we've known one another."

Vex stopped wiping the cup that he'd had in his hands. "Look," he sighed. "I understand, Drift. I've always been here for you. Please believe me when I say I just want you to be happy. Your father would have, too. And your mother."

Drift's eyes were wet with emotion and he sniffed lightly. "I know. I'm sorry."

"Nah," Vex said, stepping out from behind the bar. "Come on. Grab a seat and I'll get you some more wine." They found a table together and Vex threw his drying rag over his shoulder. "Let me see if Ame can keep the bar going by herself for a while. You know, your father would've loved Tarri, Drift." There was a twinkle in his eye when he said it.

Drift blinked back tears, only half getting the words out. "Yeah, he-he would've." He smiled at his friend and watched him go back to the bar.

The door to the tavern swung open, letting in a familiar face. The person unfurled a long, green travelling cloak from his shoulders as he approached Vex at the bar. Flow was an old friend of Drift's and now an ambassador between the Magisterium and the human King of Adira, Terrens. Drift was envious of him. He had the perfect job. A way to see the outside without being exiled. The kind of job that someone generally kept until they retired or died. Flow's only colleague, and Drift's ideological nemesis, Stag, certainly embraced the latter reasoning.

"Strongest thing you've got on hand, Vex," Flow called as he approached the bar. He waved at Drift. Something about him didn't look right, Drift realised as Flow struggled to lift his glass without spilling it.

"You're shaking. Is everything all right?" Drift stood with his nearly empty wine glass, abandoning his new seat and walking over to where Flow leaned on the bar. "You weren't away for long," he commented.

"And aren't I glad for that," Flow said, looking stricken. "Barely made it home alive." His glass wiggled and Drift took it from him, setting it down on the counter.

"What happened?"

"Shouldn't say …" Flow murmured. "Someone might be listening." He spun a finger in the air, pointing upwards in the direction of the Mind, the upper branches of the Tree where the Sleepers of the Aobian Magisterium, the blessed people who governed Aobia, lived and worked.

Vex snorted. "This again. Just as bad as each other." He strode off to another customer.

"And you won't have to hear a single thing about it. They've asked for my silence on the matter." He threw down the rest of his rice wine and tapped the glass onto the countertop, rolling a handful of coins alongside it. "Another, Vex? I'll pay ahead."

Vex looked at him. "Why don't you go sit down? I'll bring it over in a moment."

Drift followed Flow to the same empty table he'd been at moments before. "You can tell me what happened, Flow."

Flow eyed him, then ran his hand through his short, white hair. Flow had cut his hair before his most recent trip away from Aobia. He'd dyed it black to see what that was like and the Sleepers had requested he cut it off once it regrew, for the job, of course. All Aobians looked the same: taller than humans, silver-haired, and longer-lived, too. In addition, the Sleepers were Luminous and their hair shone with a glow that only could be described as transcendent. It was said that Sleepers were people chosen by the Tree itself to receive a Blessing that gifted them with Luminosity. Drift wasn't sure he believed it, but he never had a different explanation for how they got to wield Luminosity, the powers of the Tree.

"You must be careful," Flow said. "I can't be to blame if you get caught. It's confidential, Drift."

"I won't think about it," Drift promised. "I have too much on my mind, anyway."

"Fine," Flow sighed. "It's trouble in Adira. I was with the Adiran nobility all last month, but in the last nine days I've travelled nonstop to get back home. Back-breaking pace, if you ask me. Even Stag said he's never travelled that fast." He took a moment to roll around the next words in his mouth, as though they were stiffer than the rice wine he'd just finished. "Turns out the King of Adira is dead."

"What?" Drift sputtered. "He wasn't that old for a human."

"No, Drift." Flow shook his head. "He was killed in the night. And right after meeting with a new ambassador from Therador. Authorities tried to capture the man but there was no sign of him once we'd caught on to the king being … well, dead." Flow looked away. "And then they tried to contain Stag and I as suspects because a guard swore he saw someone with Luminous hair running from the room and through a stairwell out onto the streets below."

"But you're not a Sleeper." It was a statement, not a question.

"No, but most humans don't understand that. They see us and the Sleepers as one and the same."

"I …" Drift began, but he didn't know what to say.

"We've been at peace with Adira for centuries," Flow said. "There have been two generations of peace since the war and we've lived through one of them. I think it would be unlikely for them to continue a strong alliance with us if they suspect that we killed their king."

"But then again, we treat their water. We supply rice, vegetables, and farmlands on the fringes of the valley. They need us."

Flow snorted at Drift's comment. "None of that stuff is enough. They can find other ways to access food, Drift. Anyway …" He spun his empty glass on the table. "Consider me spooked after what happened. I came back, met with Staril and her advisors, and they insisted I stay here and catch up on paperwork. I can't tell whether I'm being let go after rousing suspicion or if they are just giving me time to recover." He shrugged. "Besides, I have a mound of work to do here, tax forms and trade documents. Finding ways to get the humans to pay their dues on time."

Time. Drift glanced up at the bronze clock that hung above the bar. "Damn it!" he muttered.

"What is it?" Flow asked.

"You reminded me—there's somewhere I need to be." He stood, pulling his coat over both arms. "We'll catch up again soon?"

Flow nodded. "Of course."

"Right," Drift said, nodding to his friend. "I've got to go."

If he was going to break Tarri's heart, couldn't he at least be there at the time he'd promised? He hated to think that she was waiting for him, all alone in the park, with supper packed and ready. He ran out the door and didn't look back.

TARRI

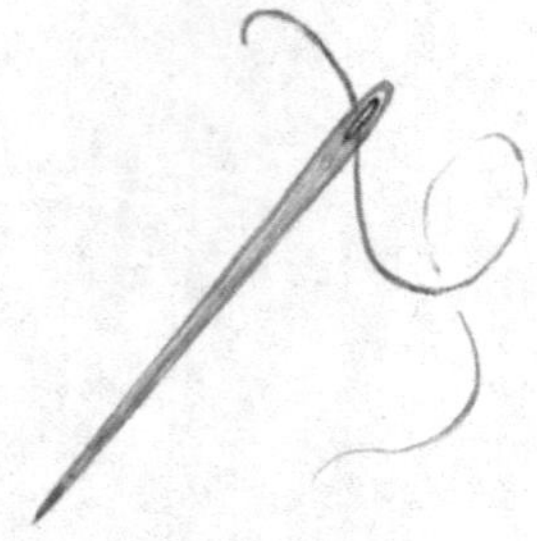

TARRI SAT IN AWE of the sky, blooms of stars like flowers in the night peeking through the Great Canopies above her. The Great Tree of Aobia was her home, and yet it also served as a bridge to the celestial planes above. The gods and who knew what else. Here in the Tree, she towered above the human lands below. The Tree sat so high above the ground. From the edges of its Canopies, it was said that one could see the Mountain Gate and sometimes even the land of Adira in the far northeast of Q'ara. She was safe here.

She was sitting on an ornate iron park bench in the Heart's Botanical Gardens. Beautiful arrays of Luminous plants poked out of the branchground all around her, sculpted into pathways, hedges, and magnificent garden beds. Holding her hand up in the moonlight before her, she smiled at the opalescent blue and purple lights that washed over her as the Great Canopies, hundreds of metres above, gently swayed in the breeze. Aobians lived fairly low in the Tree, for all it was worth, where the limbs were the strongest and the trunk was more easily accessible to reach the forest floor if need be.

"I'm sorry I'm late," came her favourite voice from close behind her. Drift turned her around and scooped her up into his arms, planting a long, slow kiss on her lips.

Once they broke away, Tarri pulled herself back into him, nudging her nose against his for a quiet moment. "You always know where to find me, don't you?" Tarri asked. Her blue eyes were like ice under the clear sky. Her cheeks were puffed because it was warm, though the air had begun to take a cold turn now that the darkness had set in. Her shoulder-length silver hair was tied up around her head, as opposed to how she usually kept it, curled and hanging down. She leaned into him for warmth.

She breathed in his scent, the smell of another hard day tilling soil and feeding algae down by the River Tomei, which ran alongside the Tree's base on the forest floor. Despite the dirt and grime, she liked his smell. She'd felt the need to distance herself her whole life, especially as an orphaned child. She recalled her mother's words of wisdom to her one day, before their life had been changed forever. The first day she'd met Drift. The second … still made her shudder.

But her mother used to say that her need to distance herself would mean that nobody would ever love her like she loved them. That was to say, she would never be able to give enough of her heart to do love justice. Sitting here now, she couldn't help but think that this had turned out to be false. When she was near Drift, she didn't feel the need to run or grow defensive. She felt, in fact, quite the opposite. She wanted a house filled with children, a home to outlast their generation. Mother would've been proud if she could've seen the person Tarri had become.

"Shall we … eat?" Drift asked, coughing to interrupt her daydreaming.

When she stepped back, she searched his eyes as she always did, swimming in them, thinking about what he held in their pale blue oceans. Only tonight, something was … different, like a dark cloud filled the skies. Seven years she had courted him and she had known him longer still, at least half her forty summers, but she'd never understood the darkness in him. The melancholy. Maybe it was because they were practically children, unlike the humans, who were halfway through their lives at the same age. She suspected this was not the case, however. Tarri was never wired with the same introvertedness as her dear Drift. Despite the challenges she'd grown up with, the life she'd had to carve out for herself after her mother…

Now that they stood apart, another thing became apparent. Drift had stopped tensing his shoulders, his body going slack with contentment. Why did she feel relaxed when she was in his arms, but he was relaxed outside of hers?

They walked a little ways from the iron park bench to a nearby patch of grass that had grown over the massive branchground. There stood a twig poking out of the branchground the size of a tree below them on the forest floor. It had two Great Leaves poking out of its ends and was soaked in moonlight. Beside it was a small water display, a lily pond with a glowing yellow fountain in the centre that was powered by Luminosity. She laid down the supper basket she'd brought and got out the long, wooden board she'd packed that was topped with Tree-grown blackberries, soft goat's cheese, and slices of walnut, mushroom, and olive rillette.

"How was your day, my love?" She passed Drift a plate and a mug before taking out a jug filled with cold jasmine tea from her basket.

Tonight, the air was so still, even the lily pads on the pond's surface beside her didn't stir. Drift heaped a lump of goat's cheese onto a cracker, chewing as he spoke. "I'm exhausted, Tar. My feeding schedule at work is still twice what I would normally be required to do."

Tarri frowned, sipping some of the jasmine tea. "When will Nida return from her leave?"

Drift shrugged. The moonlight made his tired eyes even more obvious. "I dunno. Her mother's on the way out. That's how these things go. Can't force someone to come back to work when their life is falling apart."

Tarri nodded. Drift had been so busy for weeks now that they'd been like ships in the night. Though he worked in a team of able-handed engineers down at the Water Management Facility on the ground, several hundred metres below the Tree, he had been given a lot of his colleague Nida's responsibilities until she could return to work. His superior, Sedulus, to whom he reported, was chronically overbearing and would not hesitate to lump more tasks on Drift's shoulders if he was to complain.

They ate in silence, which was usually comfortable, the perfect result of their companionship. This time, however, the silence was harder, the kind that tugged at the corners of her mouth, prodding her to speak. "Well," she began between bites of food, "my day was entirely positive!"

Drift furrowed his brows, looking down at the food, but seemed to reset his expression as he lifted his head. "Well, don't stop there." He smiled. There he was. Her Drift. "What happened?"

"I ..." She could barely contain her excitement. "I got the contract, Drift! Signed on paper with a real pen, connected to a real hand—a glowing hand, to be precise—belonging to Lady Nischia!"

Drift's eyebrows rose. He was impressed. "The Sleeper! That's wonderful, Tar!" But instead of leaning over to hug her, he went back to his food, devoid of words.

She lowered her eyes. "Thank you. I, um, thought you'd be more excited for me than that, if I'm honest."

Drift sighed, dropping his piece of rillette back onto the board. "I'm sorry, my love. I shouldn't let my day affect yours. I've just been knocked about, as you know."

"Yes, well, I haven't seen much of you these past weeks." She cleared her throat. "I know how busy we both are, but you already live a long way from my house and we've been too exhausted at the end of the day to even bother writing each other, I just—"

He leaned in and picked up her hand. "I'm so sorry, Tar. I was thinking that, well, perhaps …" He trailed off, searching for the words. She felt her cheeks burn. He'd never been this lost with his own tongue before. Maybe, just *maybe,* he was thinking the same thing as her. Maybe he would propose and they could begin their process of merging homes and hearts more fully. The desire in her burned like an endless flame.

"Maybe we could, I don't know, pick three regular nights a week to spend time together, no excuses?" His eyes twinkled in the moonlight, hungry with anticipation for her response. Tarri felt her heart sink.

"Drift, I—" She was going to say it, damn it. Roots below, she couldn't handle this anymore, this irrational fear of being close to her, this lack of self-belief that so often derailed their most special moments together, this—

"I would like that, my love. Maybe we can pick every alternating day. Some weeks we see each other three times, others four. Once the work settles down, maybe we can go back to the way it was. Find time every day." She forced the words to come out gaily, but she hung her head with sorrow. She'd let herself down again, held back what she wanted to say. *Let us live together, let us get married. Seven years, Drift, and I still hang on tenterhooks, unsure of whether you feel the same as me.* His fear of himself was too much, sometimes, transforming her own insecurities into new beasts, alive with a tempest she did not have the skillset to stifle.

"That sounds lovely, Tar." Drift threw back the rest of his tea and patted his hands on his pants before standing. "Well, I think on that note, we should hail a cabriolet and get home. The gods above know I need my rest and if you landed your big contract with that Sleeper, you do too." He cupped her cheek in his hand, lifting her face to meet his. She wanted to hold back, keep her head down. She wanted to cry. She wanted to scream his name, shove him into the twig-tree behind them, push him into the little pond, just for him to ask, "Will you?"

"Yes," she whispered, closing her eyes and letting him kiss her. "We need our rest, my love."

Drift grinned at her, offering a hand to help her up. She looked at how black and dirty his work clothes were. Even in the darkness, she could tell. She'd *made* those work clothes for him, after all. "Look at you, Drift!" she chided him, almost playfully. "Best give me these in two days' time when we see each other next. I'll wash them for you."

"Or you could take them now," he winked. "I'd just have to get myself home in skin alone."

"Oh, shut up, you lout!" she laughed. "Now, help me pack this basket."

Drift chuckled. "What I wouldn't give to take your clothes and wash them overnig—"

She slapped him across the neck. "Stop it!" Now they were both giggling like children as they scrambled about to collect scraps and plates and mugs and put them back where they belonged. This was how he could make her feel. Why couldn't she make him feel the same way?

When they finally made their way out of the gardens, standing at the roadside, Drift gripped her shoulder, holding her gaze. "You're going to do great with this contract, my love. This Sleeper has no idea what wonderful things you will make her."

She felt a tear prick her eye. "Thank you." For much of her career as a tailor, Tarri had spent time completing small projects and contractual work for various industry moguls with the help of her two assistant designers, Apris and Rela. But in the last few years, she'd finally made enough headway as a custom tailor to win over the hearts of more important people: first, the clerics and assistants who worked for Sleepers in the Mind, and now, a Sleeper herself. One day, gods willing, she would open a second shop in the Mind, where the Sleepers lived and worked, and she would cater to them as well as the common people. She would raise those who worked for her up from their current lives and make a difference in this tree.

"You know, I didn't doubt that you could land a deal like that," Drift went on as they moved across the branchroad to a nearby late-night cabriolet. She would let the cab driver take Drift home first. At the moment, he needed the sleep more.

"I know," she replied. "Thank you for cheering me on." She kissed him on the cheek. "You know what this means now, though," she said, giddy. "I'll finally be able to put more money aside. Perhaps enough to make a … sizeable donation?" She held her hands up and shrugged.

She knew Drift understood. All couples who wanted to marry in Aobia had to first make a donation to child education, a custom that supported the next generation. She feared it was yet another thing that he could claim as a reason to never step over the precipice of what they had now, because, between the two of them, they hadn't the funds.

"Maybe I'll catch up to you one day," Drift suggested. "And then we can make that donation." He kissed her head and even though she was huddled into him and he couldn't see her face, she stiffened, unable to relax. She just wanted him forever, but all he seemed to want was to understand why he couldn't give that to her.

DRIFT

DRIFT'S HANDS EXPLORED THE *coioa* fish that swam amongst the Luminous algae blooms. The spectral blanket of blue, purple, and yellow glows created an aura that made the water seem otherworldly, like everything else down here in the forest below Aobia, the Great Tree.

His workday should've been coming to a close, though he hadn't done it justice—that much he knew. He sighed, throwing the last handful of ground chipbean into the water, a natural food source for the algae blooms. Last night replayed in his head. First, the argument with Vex at the bar. Then, Flow's news of the King of Adira. And after that … yet another failed attempt to allow himself to be happy. To do the right thing.

He'd seen the disappointment across Tarri's face when he'd suggested creating a schedule to see each other. He was just being practical. But he was also being protective of himself and he scowled just thinking about it. He'd stood at the precipice with her, looking out on infinite potentiality, and instead, he'd turned back the other way, towards the forest of self-doubt. Vex's last words on the matter rang out in his mind. *She wants to settle with you, you idiot! That is not a prison sentence.*

"Drift, are you finished?" a distant voice asked. Drift didn't bother looking over his shoulder to see who it belonged to. Any one of the engineers he worked with would have been finishing their workday and leaving, but not Layward. Often, Drift would go with the others, Eamil and Nida and Sophryn. They would take the lift back up into the Great Tree and drink away the day at The Minister's Secret. But never Layward. Layward was not Drift's superior, but he was an intermediary between Drift and Sedulus, who was in charge of operations here at the Water Management Facility, a role granted to him by the Magisterium itself.

"Nearly done!" Drift shouted back.

The reply took a moment. "Fine! But don't forget to collect the next batch. Meet us downstream in ten minutes!" The sound of Layward's footsteps trudging through the soft dirt of the riverbank faded as Drift shook his head. So much for drinks tonight. Not only were they down one engineer, but now they had to work late. This was no routine maintenance. Something odd had been spotted further upstream by Eamil earlier in the day and Layward was scrambling to put all contingencies in place before anyone on the engineer team could go home. Now, they were all in the process of oversupplying the algae blooms with additional nutrients to curb whatever it was Eamil had noticed. Drift wouldn't dare say anything to Layward about it, but the fact that the engineer kept Eamil's discovery secret from the rest of the team annoyed him, to say the least.

They were all in a scattered state now, Sedulus included. But here, in this section of river that Drift worked, he was at peace. Or some semblance of it, at least.

He was sitting out on a small raft that was tied to a nearby pole jutting from the surface of the catchment. This was one of his favourite places to be during his work hours. As an engineer, he wasn't just scheduled to feed the algae blooms in the river catchments. There was extensive irrigation being built to support life on the forest floor as well as basic harvesting of Luminous flora for various purposes back in the Tree. But despite how beautiful the forest was under the Great Tree, Drift got the most enjoyment working in the River Tomei. He saw the impacts of his role and the roles of his people as water was cleansed, filtered, and passed downstream for Adira to use freely.

As long as he completed his tasks, he could clean the catchments, feed the algae their nutrients according to schedule, and then relax on the still section of the River Tomei he and the other engineers tended, a collection of catchments that were separated by large rows of rock, moulding the landscape and the river to move downwards, like a series of stairs towards the viaduct and the land of the humans below.

Several more poles dotted the catchment's surface: ways to raft out onto the water without disturbing the algae. He could go around the catchment as he pleased, though he found himself using a regular pattern of travel these days.

When he'd first started working at the Water Management Facility, he'd relished every moment he'd had to himself and had chosen the most spontaneous routes for his algae control. He would raft around the catchments at his whim, randomising his paths as he'd fed the Luminous blooms and encouraged their growth. Now, he felt comfort knowing that maybe there was a chance he could stick to a plan, a habit he'd never had the ability to learn before. Maybe sticking to small plans like these were what he needed to stick to the bigger ones, like proposing to Tarri and building a home with her, if not a life.

A spurt of bubbles distracted him, sending a spout of water up and out of the surface of the catchment. Though the catchments were segmented parts of the natural river, there were no rapids and no rocks for water to blitz across, so it was an unusual sight.

It was even more unusual, then, when suddenly the water stirred, swelling unnaturally, like it was being filled with air from beneath. The current pulled harder than usual. He glanced around his raft, curious but not yet concerned. He'd followed the feeding schedule precisely. Even if he hadn't, surely nothing would happen to the water so quickly?

The water settled and he started to haul the raft in towards the mooring pole before untying it and throwing the lasso rope over the next one, metres away. The sun was setting, its orange hue mixing with the radiant complexion of Luminous life down here below the Great Tree, a blessing from the Tree itself, much like the powers granted to the Sleepers, who governed them all. Drift had never seen the places that existed outside of the shade of Aobia's canopies, but he'd heard the human lands to the north of Q'ara were bland and soulless by comparison.

Drift caught his breath as he pulled on the line, hauling the raft back to the shore. Further ahead was the final catchment, which led to a huge waterfall that bridged Aobia and the start of human territory.

A metre or less from the shore, he came to a halt when he noticed something out of the corner of his eye. He peered down into the shallow edges of the riverbed.

There was no algae here. Everything he had been feeding moments before was gone, in the blink of an eye. An unreal deep black transformed the once-lit ripples. River water without Luminous blooms to purify it.

"No," he breathed, his voice barely above a whisper. "It cannot be." He gulped, shaking his head in disbelief. He searched around his raft, frantic, finding the sack he'd just emptied of chipbean powder. Thrusting his hand into the hessian, he quickly ran the remains of the dust through his fingers, trying to look at it closely in the diminishing daylight. It seemed fine, like any regular chipbean dust. His team of engineers had even fed the blooms whole chipbeans when they'd needed to, usually at the first turn of spring into summer. Though the temperatures now were double the winter's average, these blooms had remained stable for weeks. But when his eyes darted around the raft, trying to take in the water again, his jaw dropped, aghast.

This was not possible. The algae, which was always glowing blue, purple, and green, was disappearing faster than it could grow, faster than he could do anything about. It was disappearing as quickly as his lungs expanded and contracted, as quickly as the sun was setting behind the viaduct wall. Had he killed the algae?

Years of propagating Luminous algae blooms as a way of filtering the River Tomei's poisonous water wasted. Over a century ago, something had happened in the south of Q'ara, at a place that had not been explored in many years. A Sickness had appeared in the water, like the personification of Death Himself. The river had grown wild and tumultuous like an ocean and thrashed about as though it had a mind of its own. Worse, anyone who had drunk the water died quickly, their skin melting from their bones. That's what had happened to the last Aobians of the South and the human Kathani tribes. Life erased in the space of a few days.

When the Sickness reached the part of the river that went by the forest below the Great Tree towards the human kingdom of Adira, the Magisterium of Aobia quickly developed a plan to filter the water using a combination of natural algae and Luminosity.

If the algae died, so did everyone else.

"Drift! Quickly, come back to shore!" The shout of a panicked Layward jostled him, his heart thumping.

The raft rocked as the water began to swell once more, frothing around him. "Quickly, to the station!" Layward said. "I'm going to get the others and I'll meet you there. We need harnesses and the emergency elements. Tell Sedulus straight away. Something is wrong—the river, it shouldn't be like th—"

Water raged, alive with the fury of a thousand breaking ocean waves. The river threw Drift to shore. He soared, raft still beneath him, directly towards the forest floor. The impact sent shards of the exploding raft everywhere and he closed his eyes, anticipating injury. It took the air from his lungs when he skidded a great distance from where he'd touched down. The water continued to rise violently in the background as Layward ran to pick him up.

"Roots below!" Layward swore. "Are you okay?"

Drift's shoulder burned like it wasn't properly attached, but he swore a muffled curse and groaned, "There's no time. Go find the others!"

As Drift ran towards the central station, the towering water of the river reached an all-time high and was no longer recognisable as the clean body of water that had run beneath Aobia before. Drift felt fear trickle down him like the water droplets moving across his back and legs. He had to find Sedulus, the overseer and superior of the entire facility.

Drift looked back as he ran from the catchment towards the large building that had been constructed in the most ancient roots of the Tree, the kind of roots that had gone hard and ceased to provide life to anything above them. This was the central station, where engineers, calibration officers, and forest-keepers reported for duty each day.

Workers crammed themselves into the building, watching the water with a mixture of fear and anticipation that it might inundate them. It seemed to crawl from the river up the side of the forest, like a high tide. Drift rushed in behind the crowd, searching around for the stairs that would take him to Sedulus' top-floor office. The superior had a personal lift, too, that could send him via a long stretch of twisted cereal ropes straight to the lower limbs of the Heart, where the enclosed headquarters was set up for the executive board of administrative Sleepers to meet with him. If Drift couldn't find him in the station building, he might be able to reach him back up in the Tree, but the time it would take for him to get there and back was risky.

"Please, move!" Drift shouted, shoving people aside. An array of silver-haired folk only showed how tightly packed the Aobians in the building were. Drift made his way to the stairs, racing past people as quickly as he could. When he got to Sedulus' door, he was pleasantly relieved to have it thrown open in his face as Sedulus stalked back in. The superior was already aware of the calamity occurring outside.

"Su-superior!" Drift stammered, following Sedulus into the room.

"We need to find out what this is, and quickly," Sedulus replied, an uneasy edge to his voice. He stood stiffly, his hands pressed firmly on the balcony rail. His eyes were as cold as the silver of his hair. He was somehow composed, but he was also unsure. Drift had never seen him unsure.

"Sir, there's no time! The algae began dying so suddenly, and the water, it's washing everything aw—"

"I know!" the superior barked, watching in some kind of frozen horror from the balcony as people scrambled about, trying to stand on their feet and run towards the station. The river was so great in size now that it seemed to have swallowed a whole section of the forest. Workers were practically swimming from what had been forest moments ago to the building, chaining together, hand in hand. Dozens upon dozens of them desperately flailing or holding on to one another, battling against a force so great, they might drown.

These people were going to die. The realisation was so visceral, it took all of Drift's self-control not to vault over the balcony and seize whoever he could from the wretched waves.

"How is the Sickness here, this far downstream?" Drift asked, but Sedulus didn't respond.

"Viaduct …" the superior muttered before turning to him. "The viaduct, Drift. We need to deploy the emergency elementals now!"

Of course. Elements from the earth were kept securely underground in the event that the Sickness breached the Aobian stretch of the River Tomei. He went through the list one by one. Calcium nitrate, sodium bicarbonate, phosphorous. Crushed limestone, Piatic natron, and a rigidly contained portion of stardust.

Layward burst in, accompanied—thank the gods—by Eamil and Sophryn. "Sir, elementals!" Layward cried. "We need to get them into the catchments *now!*"

The team ran back down the stairs, circling around the expansive, clay-walled laboratories and conference rooms until they came to the huge basement doors that stood at the top of a long stairwell. At the bottom were all kinds of supplies, but what they sought was a collection of elementals: piles of compounds and raw elements stored in tied-off sacks. Mineral and chemical adjustments were normally necessary for filter maintenance, but never at the scale they needed to deliver them now. Emergency elementals did only one thing in this situation: assault the Sickness with whatever chemical reaction they could, hopefully calming the water enough to get things under control.

One by one, Drift, Sedulus, and the engineering crew moved the sacks back up the stairs, racing to the front door of the station, where water had nearly reached the step into the building. Layward threw them all a harness to put about their waists. Usually, they were reserved for maintenance on the viaduct. This time, however, they would be the only chance of survival if something was to go wrong. A sure and quick lasso throw of the rope attached to the harness about a tree might just be enough to slow their run along the berserk rapids. "Go! Two to a raft, now!"

Layward pulled down three rafts from the large iron brackets that held them against the outside of the building, passing one to Eamil and Sophryn to share. Layward took another one alone, glancing at Drift. "Go with Sedulus!" he yelled as a massive wave began to swell.

"Hold your breath!" Sedulus roared as the almighty wave closed in around them. Drift felt himself go under, felt the stream of water fill his nostrils. He closed his eyes. The water had grown hot now, hot enough to feel unpleasant to be immersed in. Was this also a mark of the Sickness? When he finally broke the surface,

Sedulus was beside him, one firm hand clasped onto the raft. "Get on!" Sedulus cried. Once Drift was up, it was easy enough for his superior to get on it too.

The raft moved of its own accord, but where they could, Drift and Sedulus alternated using their hands as oars, trying to guide the raft around stones and undulations on the forest floor. The water was so swollen now, it had grown like a tumour, so high that it nearly spilled over the viaduct, which lay ahead of them, only a few hundred metres away. It was already a colossal drop from the forest floor beneath the Great Tree to the border of Adira; the violent waves risked them going over the waterfall.

It was truly dark now, night having set in already. With the hot water flooding the forest floor, steam clouds reduced the visibility significantly, Luminous plants and fungi unable to share their light. Against all odds, however, Drift and Sedulus were able to get close enough to a sack of elementals that drifted by them in the water.

Drift's hands were wet and shaking with a mixture of fear and cold when he and Sedulus finally got the sack onto the raft. He couldn't untie the end.

"Roots below!" Sedulus shouted. "Undo the bag, Drift. Do you want an exile order on your head? On all our heads?"

Exile. That would be the punishment if they did not fix this. The Sickness in the river needed to be stopped before it reached the Adiran people. Clean river water was the promise that had kept their alliance for a century.

Through a crazed effort to tear the hessian holding the elementals in, Drift and Sedulus got the sack open and began to pour its powdery contents into the water. Drift could only hope Layward, Eamil, and Sophryn were doing the same on their rafts, though they were nowhere to be seen.

He looked up as the bag ran its course, staring at what was coming.

The water was going to carry them over the viaduct wall.

"Sir! Sir!"

Sedulus whipped his head around, his eyes filled with horror. An exile order either way then. That would be their fate. In Aobia, crime alone did not necessitate an exile. Leaving also did. And any Aobian who was cut off from the Heart, Mind, and Soul of the Great Tree was nothing to them anymore. They would never be permitted to return.

"Row! Use whatever energy you have left and row, gods be damned!"

It was to no avail, and the raft swept against the viaduct wall. For a moment, they sat there, beaten mercilessly by the waves and smacking into the structure. Sedulus began uncoiling the rope attached to his harness, fitting it around one of the Greatwood posts that held the viaduct up in the ominous waterfall. Drift began to do the same when the raft suddenly gave way and the water dropped, letting the raft slip under the viaduct entirely. He and Sedulus fell, and he felt a tremendous burst of pain near his spine as he landed on a rock. He flailed about, teetering on the edge of the rushing waterfall.

A firm hand seized his wrist, dragging him off the rock. Sedulus was swinging from the viaduct's frame, harness secured. Drift took his superior's wrist in return and watched as Sedulus concentrated on trying to lift him back up. But the water kept rushing, consuming … It was nearly smouldering like a fire with heat, with *life*. The river seemed to be crying out in pain from that which infected it and frothy water churned past Drift's legs. He slipped again as he made it up to Sedulus' height and his feet came away from the rocks below. Dangling in the air, his weight pulled Sedulus forwards, the tension of his harness rope close to breaking.

Twang! Drift felt the line drop them a metre or more, causing him to scrape his arm along a sharp rock. He growled in pain and watched as water washed the grazed blood away. He panicked, trying to swing away from it, but stopped in his tracks. Whatever he did, he'd be taking Sedulus with him. But if this water already carried the Sickness, he wouldn't want it in a wound on his body.

Maybe Sedulus had to let off some slack before he could pull Drift back up. Surely, he hadn't unravelled all the rope?

Twang! Drift could see past the waterfall now. The world below loomed like a hungry mouth ready to swallow. One fall was all it would take, and life as he knew it would end forever. If he didn't die, he'd still be cut off from Aobia. He looked into Sedulus' eyes, and neither of them spoke. Both of them were thinking the same thing.

Twang! Another drop. Sedulus' face was wrinkling with the pain of holding onto him, the exertion. His line was about to snap.

His twisted face said it all as Drift opened his mouth in shocked horror.

"I'm … sorry!" Sedulus cried. And then it came all at once, without so much as a snap. Sedulus let go. Drift fell, screaming, hitting rock after rock, trying to keep his arms by his head so he did not strike it.

The night fell quiet but for the tiny splash Drift made at the bottom of the waterfall, a hundred metre fall where he could have easily been mistaken as a rock tipping over the edge, a blur in the rest of the chaos that the waterfall presented. The current spun him around and he couldn't see where the water was bending in the dark. Then something smacked his head and everything went dark.

NISCHIA

"THE fIRST EXILE SINCE the Queen's rebellion all those years ago." Nischia stood at the edge of one of the Mind's farthest branches, looking out over the Adiran landscape. The pain of seeing Queen Feldra's long dynasty collapse still echoed in her mind one hundred years later. At least Feldra had died in Aobia, though the body might not have been buried here, out of respect for the Tree and its people.

"I told you it would hurt," Koln, her superior and direct report at the Magisterium, said. "After a while, it stops hurting. Before your time, exiles were more common. It killed some of us, you know. To live each day knowing your own people would be cut off from the Heart, Mind, and Soul of this Great Tree."

"Do you think this exile is innocent?" she asked. Her eyes were watery, but she would not cry. That particular emotion had died years ago.

"I think we need to determine what happened." Koln turned to her. "The ambassadors fled the Kingdom of Adira, Nischia. Word was sent yesterday via *cism*."

Nischia raised her eyebrows, her eyes wide. "Fled?"

"I know nothing of the reasons for it, so don't ask. But I feel unsettled by the coincidence of these events. Something went horribly wrong with the river last night. Sedulus … swore the Sickness had taken over. Killed the algae blooms. Elementals did nothing. Every reserve of Luminous power in the generators was used. Staril has already elected upwards of thirty to Sleep for the next week and restore supplies. If lights went out in the streets or water stopped circulating, the people would react. We aren't in a position to advise the public about any of this. The idea of mass-contained Luminosity powering the river filtration would cause the people to question everything we do."

"If the Sickness made it past our filtration, then something must've gone wrong upstream," Nischia said.

"The reports suggested as much." Koln sighed. "This will take some thorough investigation, Nischia. You understand that, don't you?"

"Yes, but you mustn't chide me. I haven't been a child for many years, Koln. I've stood with you on the precipice of much worse." Ripped from her family at a young age. Forced to live as a Sleeper, exhausted by the appearance of her Orb and the connection she shared with it, and witnessing the end of her nation's greatest leader… All these events did things to a person's mind and she became frustrated whenever she needed to remind him of that.

Koln said nothing to her defensiveness, instead remaining sternly on topic. "We'll need to work closely with some others, Nischia. Sedulus will be involved, though I'll keep him at arm's length. I can't treat him without suspicion. After all, he was supposedly the one who saw our young exile fall. I'll work on Sedulus for now. My suggestion for you lies with the girl."

"The girl?" Nischia asked.

"That tailor you've sought out in the Soul," Koln replied.

"What does she have to do with this?" Nischia frowned, confused. She'd signed a contract with a dressmaker in the Soul in an attempt to diversify her wardrobe and encourage other young Sleepers to do the same and put value back into smaller artists.

"She happens to be the exile's betrothed."

Ah. Nischia scratched her forehead. "That is a curious link, Koln. I wouldn't usually involve a commoner in these matters."

Koln pursed his lips but nodded. "I understand. But she may have information that we could use. Get close to her through the work you're doing and perhaps she can join us as the case continues."

"You're asking me to use this tailor to help understand our exile's demise. Have you no heart?"

"Don't speak to me about matters of the heart!" Koln said through gritted teeth. "It never seems to matter how many years pass nor how many stories I tell you about my life. Will you always see a heartless person in me?"

"She will expect to get something out of this, Koln," Nischia fought back, rising in her place. "She will think that we will bring him home. But we cannot, and you and I both know it!" Exile was an irredeemable title to bear. It didn't matter whether this young Aobian engineer intended to leave Aobia or not. The fact was, he did, and so he was cut off. Nischia didn't agree with the rules—roots below, she would be the first to break many of the Sleepers' outdated customs and rebuild them—but she *did* know one thing. That Aobian, wherever he was now, was gone. In any case, the chances of survival after falling from the waterfall were slim to none.

"Look," Koln said. "Let's just find some answers, and if we do, I promise I'll talk to Staril. If these coincidences are related, perhaps we can make arrangements for the exile, give him a good life outside the Tree."

Staril was the prime minister of Aobia and the head of the Magisterium. She was Koln's direct report and would never abide conduct outside of the law. In her eyes, the law and its sanctions had been revised too much already since the monarchy had collapsed.

"She told you that we needed to get to work on this case, didn't she?"

"Quiet, child!" Koln seethed. "I am not shielding us." He opened his robes, the internal pockets empty. *Cism* were small glass spheres that could be imbued with Luminosity for several purposes, but they were especially relied upon for shielding Sleeper minds from conversation.

"You didn't bring a *cism* to tell me these things? Well, fine. I don't care whether she can hear or not, Koln." Nischia swept her loose hair back behind her ear. "If Staril can see connections we cannot, then she isn't telling us everything we need to know. Why have the ambassadors returned from Adira so suddenly?" she pressed.

"We go years without an ounce of childishness from you, Nischia, but still you manage to radiate the most juvenile attitude when you don't get what you want. I don't know anything about the ambassadors and I don't plan on knowing more until I am told. All we can do is use the information given to us. The rest is for—"

"The gods," Nischia said, finishing his words.

Koln scowled, flicking up his robes and striding away.

"Don't turn your back on me!" Nischia snapped, harshly enough to cause her mentor to crane his neck and glance back at her. "I need to know specifics, Koln. Ambiguity is not enough. Will the girl be harmed?"

Koln snorted. "Hearts can heal, Nischia."

"I will not hurt her, Koln. I will give her every truth I can." Nischia crossed her arms.

"I admire your sense of justice, Nischia. But this is the real world and this investigation will only harm her in the end. This exile cannot come home."

Nischia tsked, annoyed. "What's this exile have to do with the ambassadors? And Adira?"

Koln let out a long, deep sigh. He knew something that he didn't want to tell her. That much was clear. "I have no reason to believe this, Nischia, but for our ambassadors to flee the kingdom, something *very* bad must be afoot. Flow and Stag have been exceptionally close to King Terrens and his family. Why would they need to run away from them?"

"What if something happened to them? Or to the king?"

Koln grunted. "Something is not right. Staril is … reserved. I cannot help but feel we are on the brink of something tremendous."

Nischia cleared her throat. "Well… Where do I start with the girl?"

"Just ask her about the exile for now. All we know is that his name is Drift and that he has been a junior engineer for some time at the facility."

"Okay." Nischia nodded. "I'll start there. And I'll have to make it clear that she will need to agree to be a part of the ongoing investigation."

"Do that," Koln said, waving her words away.

"A final question, then." Nischia stepped forward to whisper. She never knew who was listening in the Mind. "Is this exile, Drift, a person of interest to the Magisterium?"

Koln stiffened. "Why would you assume that, child?" This was what he did. Made her feel small when she got close to truths he wasn't prepared to share.

"It's a very specific name for an Aobian."

"It is." Koln grimaced and then turned to go. "But that, I suspect, has nothing to do with the unfortunate turns his life has taken. Find out what you can about him and the tailor."

She watched her mentor go, thoughts racing through her mind. She had a lot to discuss with this tailor. A mere coincidence? She thought not. She'd sought this girl out, chosen Tarri's designs for her wardrobe. How much had chance a part to play in the fact that the tailor was related to the exile?

She digested Koln's words as she plodded home to her apartment in the residential quarters of the Mind, where all the Sleepers lived. *"I cannot help but feel we are on the brink of something tremendous."*

The need came to her thereafter, to Sleep in the Orb. To regenerate lost Luminosity. She'd need the power of the Tree more than ever, she suspected, over the coming days. Luminosity was used for everything, from filling *cism* and lighting streetlamps to heating water and stovetops and cleaning the river water below the Tree. It was also used in cases like this: crime investigations. She would recharge soon, she decided. But now was not the time. She would resist the Orb's call for some days yet, if she could.

TARRI

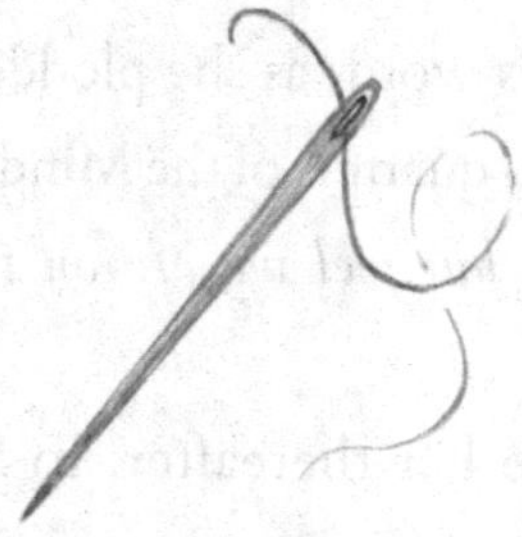

TARRI WOKE FROM HER sleep like she'd been shaken. Gulping for air, she sat up so quickly she felt her head rush. It was just a bad dream, the kind where she'd already forgotten what it was about. She got out of bed and changed from her nightclothes. Today was an important day. For the first time since she'd received the completed contract in the mail, a Sleeper would be visiting the Tailory, her beloved clothing store, in person.

Though they hadn't met in person yet, Tarri guessed what the Lady Nischia would be like, because she knew Sleepers. The Aobians, 'blessed' by the Great Tree with the mysterious power of Luminosity, leveraged their status to no end. Despite the monarchy's collapse half a century ago, the Sleepers hadn't changed the way they distilled the rules and mechanics of Aobian society. There was no queen anymore, but there was a prime minister, a Sleeper called Staril, who had been involved in the dismantling of the establishment in the first place. For all intents and purposes, the Sleepers were a kind of nobility. And nobility meant snobbery.

The Lady Nischia, therefore, was the kind of person who would create a problem if anything was to go wrong. However, the Sleeper *was* paying for an ongoing contract on top of the raw cost of materials and labour, and that made it worth Tarri's while to keep her as a top priority customer. She would also be the conduit between Tarri's current business and her dream as a dressmaker for the nobility in the Mind. If that became her life, then she knew she would have redeemed her past and done her mother proud. As a result, today was going to be a day of ensuring that best first impressions were made.

She put around her neck the slim, obsidian ring that Drift had given her. A ring of promise, but not proposal. She sighed. He would probably be at work by now, so there was no chance of a breakfast together. Perhaps she could surprise him for dinner.

She combed her near-white hair before tying it up into a bun and heading out the door, letting her nose lead her through the Soul's winding branchroads. She was hungry.

Eventually she came to the market square where her Tailory was. In the morning, the walkways smelled of baked goods, fresh fruit, and cinnamon-spiced black tea. It might have been her favourite thing about the district where she worked. She had heard that the businesses that were lucky enough to open a shop in the Mind enjoyed more privileged clientele. She had kept that dream alive, cautiously optimistic for years. Hopefully, her professional relationship with Lady Nischia would be the start of such a dream.

She walked past Passion's Bakery before the scent overtook her and she ran through the door. Hot rhubarb and basil galettes straight from the oven. Passion's oven was another Luminous object, leveraging Sleeper powers to generate heat for cooking. Though everyone had access to such things, Passion's was a gloriously industrious oven with several burners and a chamber for storing Sleeper power in the top. Sleepers contained their power in two places—themselves or the more portable globes that people could buy, refilled for purposes such as this.

Realising her eyes were glued to the galettes, Passion seized one with his tongs and shovelled it into a sleeve of wax paper for her. She brought out tokens to pay with but was silenced by Passion putting his hands up. "Could you take a look at some frayed edges on my aprons? We're going through them faster than the running river at the moment."

She nodded, smiling. "You're a darling. Of course I will. But you'll let me pay for a mug of tea?"

Passion stroked his chin like he was still deciding whether he had any more clothes to get fixed. "Ah, fine. Three tokens then, Miss Tarri."

He was a quiet man and once he took her coin and gestured at an empty table for her to sit at, he retreated behind his counter to check on whatever was cooking in the back. Alone at her table, Tarri pulled out her notebook, a beautiful leatherbound book that Drift had bought for her from a tannery that made goods from cured Greatleaf. She kept it on her so she could make lists and then check those lists off. She had always been a list person.

She took a bite of her galette and couldn't help but close her eyes to enjoy the experience. The base was so flaky, with buttery layers that complemented the acidity of the rhubarb. But best of all was its lightness. She recalled what her friend, Stag, one of two Aobian ambassadors to the Adiran Kingdom, had once told her about how human pastries tasted. "Flat and crumbly. Not worth what you pay. It's because their flour comes from wheat, you see. A pitiful grain to make flour from, if you ask me." Aobia, on the other hand, farmed rice all the way up on the highest branches of the canopies on enormous farms with their own contained rain catchments.

She licked her lips and took a sip of the sweet black tea that was a customary addition to her breakfast. The first thing on the list for the day was a quick check on her team before Nischia arrived. This wasn't micro-management, just an attempt to boost the girls' morale, she assured herself. Then, a meeting with the Sleeper upon arrival. Once she got through today, she would make her way to the Heart and wait for Drift to come home.

It sounded perfect.

Tarri walked through the door of the Tailory, telling herself she wouldn't comment on whatever state it was in when her team saw her. She didn't usually work on this day. She brushed through a wooden rack of drapery that hadn't been cut or shaped, a faux entrance to the back room where everyone worked. Two sets of eyes were locked on to what looked like a sketch of a dress. "How is the planning going?" she asked as nicely as she could.

Apris and Rela, Tarri's designers and confidants in the business, looked up. Both were younger than Tarri, barely out of adolescence, and had finished styling their craft at the Academy of the Arts in the Soul. They were two of the most skilled designers Tarri had ever seen.

"The drafting has gone well, Miss Tarri," Apris said. Tarri studied her: same clothes as yesterday, black bags hanging under her eyes.

"I must say, these sketches look fantastic," Tarri commented before switching topics. "You've been up all night, haven't you?"

Apris said nothing and Rela jumped in.

"We're very happy with them," Rela said. "So happy, in fact, that we're confident we'll please her."

"I am thankful to you both. Of course, today could be the most important day the Tailory has ever had. We could be setting ourselves up for a prosperous future. And just imagine," this was Tarri's favourite part, "one day we could be dressmaking for all the Sleepers, or at least a majority of them. We'd be able to keep this building open for industry work and then open up shop in—"

"The Mind," Apris replied. "We know. And we'll get there one day. But you *must* try to at least relax today. First impressions, Miss Tarri."

"Agreed!" Tarri threw her hands in the air. "I promise to not get more frazzled than I already am. Now, what time can we expect our Lady Sleeper?"

At that moment, the door behind her burst open, admitting a male Aobian in a pinstripe suit and tied-up white hair. A fancy cab driver for passengers that came from the Mind, where the Sleepers lived.

Behind him stood the Lady Nischia. Larger than life with her Luminous hair and glowing skin—the mark of all Sleepers—Nischia was simply dazzling. She wore a stunning daily dress to suit, an ornate cut of sage-green that reflected the springtime colours of the forest around her.

"M-my lady," Tarri bowed, and Apris and Rela followed her lead.

Isn't that just a prime example of Sleeper entitlement—Tarri stopped herself from allowing the thought to go any further. Being a Sleeper, Nischia could read minds using her Luminosity, the power derived from the blessing the Tree had bestowed upon her. In addition, Nischia's ability to Sleep in one of the Tree's magical Orbs provided all kinds of resources to Aobia, like the small globes of light that helped power her sewing machines, making her work ten times as fast. Maybe she deserved a bit of entitlement.

"Indeed, I do, Miss Tarri," Lady Nischia said and Tarri froze.

"I'm sorry, my Lady, but what are—"

"You know what I'm talking about," the lady said as she swept past Tarri and further into the room.

She had read her like a book, and while that was frightening, it was also amazing. Many Aobians didn't understand how Sleepers were able to tell what people were thinking. It was presumed to have something to do with proximity, which Tarri could attest to after *that* experience. But it could also be about how much Luminosity a Sleeper absorbed during Sleep. That was what frightened her most of all about the Sleepers: they ruled the nation as a collective government and yet the people didn't know all that much about how they worked.

As Lady Nischia moved past Tarri, she called out to Apris and Rela. "How *is* my summer dress looking? I would be honoured to see your drafting."

Apris fetched the sketches and showed them, thrusting the document into the lady's hands with perhaps a bit too much eagerness. Both she and Rela looked hapless, and Tarri felt a nervous giggle slip from her mouth.

"Miss Tarri," Lady Nischia said, waving her over.

"My lady?" Tarri gulped.

The lady didn't speak for a moment, giving Tarri too much room for doubt. Would her craft be tarnished amongst other Sleepers forevermore just from one compilation of sketches?

"This," Lady Nischia continued, "is a magical beginning to what I think will be a fruitful relationship."

Tarri let out a sigh of relief loud enough to prompt a raised eyebrow from Nischia. "I am impressed with the quality of your work and you have worked at it for only a few days! I may be hard-pressed to choose which of these I like best."

"I am so thrilled to hear that, my lady." She gestured at her designers. "Without Apris and Rela, I could not have presented to you such visions." She beamed at them.

"You have done yourselves and your mistress proud, ladies," Nischia said, nodding to Apris and Rela. "Miss Tarri, might I meet with you alone to discuss payment arrangements?"

Tarri put up a friendly hand. "My lady, I'm honoured, but it may be too early to determine—"

"No," Lady Nischia retorted. "I insist we have a discussion."

Tarri felt like a child and bowed her head. "Yes, if we must, my lady. Apris, Rela, could you make yourselves busy until we return?" They nodded and left the room.

Lady Nischia filled the room, a presence to be reckoned with. She stood over Tarri and her hair gleamed as if it knew what special qualities it indicated about her. The glow about her figure was more obvious now, like a warm, yellow outline that caused her to stand out against every backdrop.

"Do you know what I do as a Sleeper, Tarri?" Nischia said.

"I do not, my lady." Tarri swallowed.

"Sit next to me, child." The way Sleepers called other Aobians children always upset her, but she suppressed her annoyance. She took her place next to Nischia and looked her in the eye.

"I am one of a team of Sleepers who provide sponsorship as well as nutrient replication for the catchments our people built centuries ago at the point where the River Tomei meets human lands. I am responsible, in part, for the system that gives us the purest water straight from the river, free of the Sickness."

Drift. His name echoed around in her mind. Nischia had something she wanted to tell Tarri about Drift? Dread threatened to drop her to the ground and yet she kept her focus on Nischia.

"You are betrothed to a male who works there, are you not?" She paused.

Tarri nodded slowly, unsure.

Nischia sighed. "Your beloved, Drift, was reported exiled from Aobia this morning, just before dawn."

"Exiled?" Tarri looked in horror at the Sleeper. "He couldn't have left Aobia! He wouldn't do that, wouldn't risk it! He, he—"

Nischia stared at her with intensely blue eyes. "Understand something, Miss Tarri. Drift has not been exiled of his own doing. He has been involved in an accident."

Tarri looked up at her, her eyes wet. "What?" she exclaimed.

"Some time last night, he was working near the viaduct that overlooks the river, at the point where it cascades into Adiran land. He was accompanied by the rest of his engineering team and his superior, a male named Sedulus. They were dealing with a dire and unexpected issue with the filtration systems we have in place down there. From the reports I've received, two things seemed to have happened: the algae blooms that filter the water as it exits the Great Forest died and the water swelled like an ocean, seemingly possessed and acting of its own accord. The incident was reported directly to me and my team this morning."

Nischia went on without letting Tarri cut in. "It's important that I share some details with you and leave them with you to make your own opinion. Sedulus, the one who oversees operations at the facility, reported the incident. He said that Drift fell from a faulty harness after they were washed beneath the viaduct and managed to tether Sedulus to the structural beams underneath it. Where he would have been conducting the urgent repair was at the edge of the Great Forest. He dropped into the water and, as is Aobian law, was exiled immediately."

"For falling from a faulty harness?" Tarri cried. "How could you say that? Exiled? You Sleepers, all the same. Seeking to punish any of us who stray from the smallest—"

"I ask you *do not* continue with such thoughts in my presence, Miss Tarri!" Lady Nischia yelled. "This is *sensitive* information and I urge you to not share it, for the sake of all Aobia. I am offering you more truth than any other Sleeper would. In fact, I would go as far as to say that I had to practically beg my superior to discuss the incident with you directly. If it had been their choice, they would have sent an officer of the law to tell you he was dead and that would have been that."

Tarri took a deep breath, which Lady Nischia echoed in turn. Why was this noble lady helping her? What did she get from telling Tarri the details of Drift's exile, falling to … what, his death? To irreparable injury? To a shortened life, cut off from the reach of the Great Tree?

"Miss Tarri," said Lady Nischia. "I have investigations to conduct about this incident. I do not believe Drift's exile is entirely just. Through some poking around, I have discovered some holes in Sedulus' report. The chaos that the entire engineering team was subjected to was of course traumatic and disturbing. However, the case is … curious, to say the least."

She looked at Tarri with a dark gaze and her eyes seemed to take on the colour of lightning, as pure as when it struck the ground. "I think the report of your beloved's disappearance was sabotaged and I want to know why."

"I'm not sure I understand," Tarri said, her frown increasing. "Sabotage?"

"I think something, or someone, has decided it is time that we end our long-standing alliance with Adira. The river's Sickness fought its way through our prevention systems last night. The Sickness has not reached the people of Adira in over a century. Somebody wants Aobia to return to how it was before the Four-Front War, a middle ground of political tensions and a corrupt monarchy."

Tarri cleared her throat to interject. "Excuse me, my lady, if I do not seem to understand you. The human kingdom, Adira, is involved how, exactly?"

"There is more to the story, but nothing I am in a position to share." Nischia stiffened and Tarri saw the conversation for what it was: one-sided. The Sleeper got to keep her secrets, but she would gladly milk every last drop of knowledge Tarri could share with her about Drift.

"You wish to tell me about some sabotage that led to my betrothed falling down a waterfall and out of his home forever. I only wish to know how to find Drift and bring him back."

"We both may stand to gain something from this dreadful turn of events, Tarri. I have an investigation to lead to preserve peace between our people and the humans. You have a loved one to find. If you can remain … discreet on the matter, perhaps we might work together. After all, we cannot have our people knowing about any of this, but if they find out, I'll know where to look." A thin smile crept over her lips; there was something cunning about it.

"And I am expected to believe that you, a Sleeper, want to work with me, a lowly dressmaker from the Heart, to save Aobia from the end of years of peace and *un-exile* Drift?" It sounded like a joke. Exile was irreversible. Lady Nischia knew that—in fact, as a Sleeper, she was a proponent of the Magisterium's laws. Did she somehow think she could change that ever-binding rule?

"I have told you everything I know," Lady Nischia said, standing. "And it is time I left you. I will be back in three days. When I return, I want to know if you will help me discover the truth. Find the connections, as I suspect there may be, between Drift and the Sickness of the River Tomei. Oh, and do not forget: I have begun an account with your Tailory and expect you to fulfil my business needs as required, regardless of what you decide. I would like the first cuts of my new dress presented to me when I return. I suppose, if anything, you can take solace in the fact that I am as committed to being your customer as your ally." She swept her dress around her, turning to leave.

Tarri called out one last time. "Excuse me, my lady!"

Nischia turned to look back at her. "What is it, child?"

"You mentioned Sedulus made the report afterwards. Could he have had anything to do with Drift's exile?"

Nischia took a moment to reply. "I'm not sure what to make of some aspects of his recount, but I find it hard to reasonably doubt it. When I went to investigate, there was, in fact, a harness still attached to the viaduct. It appeared to be untampered with. I do not suspect him and I should think if you want to take our discussion further, you can start by leaving Sedulus out of it. It's easy to allow your mind room to craft a narrative that fills the gaps between the things we know. Tell me your final decision in three days, Miss Tarri. Until then, I bid you farewell. Trust, Compassion, and Wisdom."

"Trust, Compassion, and Wisdom," Tarri repeated the Three Pillars of Aobia, watching as Nischia swept her gown out the door.

That night, after a hard day spent between design work and serving customers alongside Apris and Rela, Tarri found herself agitated, a nauseating feeling pummelling her stomach. No matter what she did or where she tried to focus her energy, she thought only of what the Sleeper had told her.

"You can start by leaving him out of it." Nischia's voice rang in Tarri's head as she exited the Tailory. She was mad. She knew she was mad. Going against the suggestion of a Sleeper. One that

wanted to support her business, too. But something tugged at her and so she walked through the dark, lamp-lit streets of the Soul, propelled by grief and shock at the turn of events that had taken her beloved away. She called on the first cabriolet she saw in the streets and got in it wordlessly. Prompted by the driver to say where she wanted to go, she murmured, "The end of the Heart." That was where she needed to go. In some ways, she'd already reached the end of the heart. Her own. But her mind continued to repeat only one name.

Sedulus.

The only witness to Drift's exile sounded innocent enough when Nischia explained what happened at the viaduct, but to be sure, Tarri had to speak with him herself. As she drove through the empty streets of the Soul, the full moon illuminating a path between buildings, she hugged herself to escape the wind winding through the Great Canopies above. She hadn't been able to sleep and although it was past midnight, she had decided that she could not let this go. She could not sleep, knowing Drift was somewhere outside Aobia, alone, hurt maybe. Dead, possibly, although she kept that word shut up in a box, somewhere in the deeper parts of her mind.

Initially, she'd had the grand yet ridiculous plan to wake Sedulus and question him, but on second thought, it didn't seem like the best option. So here she was, taking herself instead to the furthest limbs in the Heart, where she could hopefully find a way to break into the Water Management Facility.

She got out of the cab a short walking distance from the narrow-ending branchroads of the Heart, which led to the high-clearance level entrance to the Water Management Facility. She hadn't yet thought this through and cursed aloud on the night air. "Roots below!"

Before her was a gate carved out of polished wooden beams, signifying the end of the residential district and the beginning of the facility, which was accessible by a lift she could see beyond the gates.

A stroke of blind luck presented itself, however, as the glow of lantern light cast a dim aura onto the end of the branchroad, where a worker was exiting. This was her moment.

Holding her breath, she scampered up to the gates, waiting for the worker to leave through them. She slid like a shadow between the gap they left as they strode through, leaving the gates to swing closed behind them. She was through. Before her was the lift, lit with Luminous light globes. She ducked inside and tugged the wall-mounted lever, letting the lift down to the forest floor.

She'd seen the forest from above, in the limbs of the Tree. But she'd never beheld it so closely before. Every corner was aglow with Luminous light coming from different ferns, bushes, and fungi. It was as though the world was soaked in a soft pastel glow. Beside her ran the River Tomei, which was calm despite what Nischia had told her. However, it lacked the vibrant blue it usually bore when it was spattered with brilliant reflections of the Luminous algae beneath its surface and was instead a drab grey, a sign that something had certainly gone wrong. Tarri would need to be mindful of these observations. After Nischia's warning to keep her knowledge of Drift's exile quiet, she was acutely aware of the gravity of this situation.

Following the river north led her eyes to a distant landmark, the Greatwood-made viaduct that stood as a marker between Aobia's border and Adira. The viaduct peered over a huge waterfall. She let her ears guide her to the sound of crashing water.

At the viaduct, Tarri looked out over the expanse of water, which was continuously being cleaned with Sleeper Luminosity and algae to make it safe for people to clean with, cook with, and drink. Moonlight shimmered on its surface, making it more transparent and glass-like than she'd ever seen it.

Up ahead, the outline of two figures stood at the top of the steps that connected the riverbank to the viaduct over the flowing river. She couldn't make them out, but they had not noticed her. She clambered behind the side wall of the stone steps, barely a metre or two behind them, concealed by the noise of the waterfall, and ducked into the reeds.

Though she could not make out their words, Tarri quickly realised that one of the people was Lady Nischia. She put a hand to her mouth. Nischia was here? At this time of night?

If Nischia wanted to search for Tarri, she knew she'd be undone. There would not be enough loudness around them to hide Tarri's thoughts. Most folk were asleep. Surely, Nischia already knew somebody was here; perhaps she even knew who it was.

The other person was a male Sleeper with a radiant yellow glow around the face and soft, straight white hair kept neatly tucked into the back of his cloak. His voice was low and stern.

The conversation went on and Tarri watched as Nischia gestured wildly in the direction of Adira. Was Lady Nischia involved in Drift's disappearance? *No. Shut up, Tarri. Don't think it.*

She was so close to them. They would hear her and then she'd never find Drift. She'd never work with a Sleeper to make their clothes again.

She bent her head around the corner, glancing at Nischia. The Sleeper had one arm inside her shawl and there was a faint glow coming from it. The glow began as a dull throb of light but slowly travelled down Nischia's arm, illuminating her more fully. It seemed to swirl off her fingers now, and she outstretched her other arm, opening her hand.

Suddenly, the ground around the three of them lit up in an array of colours, which changed as Nischia continued to move her hand. Her shawl fell back and Tarri could see in her other hand a round glass ball, which shone with the same radiance as the Sleeper's hair. It pulsed with more and more light the more Nischia moved her hand, shining new colours across the floor and wall of the viaduct. As she shrugged and stopped what she was doing, however, her hand flicked up, only to cast a red light on the body of the Sleeper next to her.

Heat. That's what she was looking for. Somehow, Nischia could channel Luminosity to detect heat.

It made sense. If Drift had only gone missing the night prior, then Nischia was using Luminosity to find any evidence of Drift's fall. If he'd been up on the viaduct at all, the heat map would show his tracks. Tarri knew about some of the domestic benefits of Luminosity—replacing the need for fire with concentrated heat, healing or relieving pain through a Sleeper's touch, and providing running water from the river up through a channel in the Tree's trunk. The histories spoke of Luminosity as a weapon that could be used in war. Sleepers could command magnanimous amounts of concentrated heat from their selves, blasting enemies in multitudes and levelling the land around them to fight through walls of opposition. But the risks of that were unsettling, like what had happened to the last queen of Aobia, Feldra, who'd died fifty years before Tarri's birth, burnt up like a dying star. It was said that she had been found in a state of ashes on the floor after a superior Sleeper and two of their students had obliterated her.

She went back behind the stone wall and bobbed down into the reeds as she saw another person approaching the bridge from the direction she'd come. *Canopies!* she thought, fear sending a prickle down her spine. Her heart pounded louder than the rushing water.

She ducked low at the same time that the figure turned in her direction, looking quizzically into the reeds. They stood there for a moment before continuing to the stairs. Like a tightly wound spring being carefully undone, she puffed out a sigh of relief.

She caught the back of the figure as they ascended the staircase and her skin crawled instantly. Broad shoulders and a confident gait. Long hair. Then the person turned again, somehow knowing they were being watched, and she saw their face caught briefly under the moonlight.

It was Sedulus, Drift's superior and the only one who'd seen him fall the night he'd been exiled.

"You can start by leaving him out of it," Nischia had said.

Tarri's breath caught, and she couldn't feel the air enter her lungs normally until she was safely back in the Heart, where she unlocked her door, clambered into bed, and lay sleepless, interrupted by tears for Drift and fear that the Sleepers had caught her.

Even if they hadn't, Sedulus certainly had.

DRIFT

Drift woke to cawing birds. Parrots, most likely; large rainbow-coloured birds that flew in the lower parts of the rainforest. He'd been unconscious and his head was as heavy as a rock. His legs felt like ice and when he looked down, he saw them dangling loosely in shallow, slow-moving water that was barely rising up the sides of the grassy riverbank.

He'd fallen from the viaduct, down the waterfall, and ended up here. He wasn't sure how far down the river he'd drifted before stopping or how long it would take to retrace his steps.

Then an uneasy feeling spread through him. He was exiled.

He was an outcast to the rest of Aobia. Aobia no longer was his home. Of course, he knew the waterfall was the boundary between human lands and Aobia, but he didn't mean to fall down. Surely, they would understand. Surely, the Sleepers would—

But no. Rules were rules and he had stepped out of Aobia without permission. If he tried to argue the point as an outsider, they might kill him or lock him up for life. The Sleepers were convinced that the potency of Aobian society was perfect for the individual. After centuries of nomadic survival and then monarchy, Aobia had taken the time to perfect itself. Now, there weren't many folk who would ever leave the Tree. It was away from the conflict and tyranny of the humans who had taken Q'ara from them all. The rule, therefore, was simple: if you left, you were simultaneously accepting that you were not ever coming back.

He stood and felt his body tip, dizzy. He fell over but caught himself with a splash in the river. The water here was so calm and if he hadn't been exiled, he might have been able to enjoy it more. There was no swell in the water in these parts, unlike the beast the engineers had struggled to contain the night before.

He thought of Sedulus. Would he be relieved of his duty at the facility? For the first time in over fifty years, someone had been exiled, and he had been the single overseer of the event.

The fact was this wasn't anybody's fault. Nobody could have known the Sickness would breach the filtration systems further upstream. They still didn't know *how* that had happened. All they'd done had been to try to manage the situation as quickly as possible, before people would start to consume the water and die.

Nobody knew where the Sickness had originated, but whatever it was, it caused the water to act as though it was alive. That had been what wiped out the humans of the south, the Kathani. It had been what drove the Aobians so far north, from their first Great Tree on the border of the Southern Sands and the vast rainforestry. The tree the Aobians lived in now was the only one left.

Drift wondered about the water here. He was so thirsty. He knew there had been a time when people had drunk from the river regularly, always boiling the water first. It had been the way things worked until Aobia had managed to filter it as it passed through. Filtering it put less stress on the Sleepers too, their Luminosity no longer needed to create heat. Maybe all this filtering did people less good than they thought. Maybe their bodies weren't designed to take in such pure stuff. Maybe he could drink it and be all right…

I'm an exile, he thought as he stared at the water. *Nothing to lose if I get sick.* He scooped up a handful of water. It was soily and grey rather than the illuminated look it carried in the catchments beneath the Tree, where the algae blooms glowed.

He swallowed before exiting onto the riverbank. The tree line was thinner and less dense than the forest beneath Aobia, allowing him to see longer distances. He could see the hills that went back up towards the waterfall, but the waterfall was not in sight. He checked his leg straps, which he always kept attached to his pants for work, and found both of his long utility knives.

Engineers used them to cut through brush and underwater root systems and for other menial tasks. His mind amplified what his stomach was telling him. They never used those knives for hunting. Aobians did not hunt. They barely ate meat beside the occasional Greatbird that dropped from the highest part of the canopies and was preserved for momentous occasions, such as weddings or births, treated as a gift from the gods.

Now, he would need to kill another creature with his bare hands to survive.

He kept quiet as he walked through the lush grass, squelching morning dew underfoot. Hopefully an opportunity for a catch would come soon. He stayed close to the banks of the river, walking upstream and noticing the environment grow more rocky, more jagged. Low hanging ferns filled the scene, evergreen and encapsulating something so different to the rainforest he knew grew under the Great Canopies.

This rainforest seemed wilder and unrestrained. It wasn't subservient to something bigger than it, like the forest that thrived beneath Aobia, which was more orderly, dense, and pure. Ferns reigned supreme, overtaking mossy clefts and stoney slipstreams. Smaller trees seemed to bow to the ferns. Bushes were thorny and covered with thick and dank green leaves. Mushrooms dotted the damp soil. He wished he knew how to tell a good one from a bad one. But then, none of these mushrooms were Luminous like the ones beneath the Great Canopies. It seemed the reach of the Great Tree ended long before this part of the forest. The Tree didn't just bless the Sleepers with Luminosity; it also blessed every other living thing beneath it.

As he mounted an embankment of rocks, half dry from the morning sun and half wet from the running river, he saw his chance for food: a small deer, white-spotted and moving through the scrub. It was no adult stag or doe and he thought it being unaccompanied would make it all the easier for him to get. But deer were fast.

Drift held his breath and set his foot upon a rock. The fawn still hadn't seen him. He had one chance from where he stood with not a single obstruction between him and the fawn. He gripped the handle of his knife, pointing its tip in the direction of the creature.

His aim was lined up, but his heart tugged at him. He didn't want to kill it, wasn't *supposed* to kill it. But he had no choice. He flicked his wrist, counting from three to one. The knife spun through the air and caught the beast in its side. Despite its cry however, the fawn found its escape through the ferns behind it.

"No!" He hissed. Now he'd lost a knife—a good knife at that—and a chance at a morning meal. He dove around the embankment, trying to follow the fading sound of hooves. The fawn surely couldn't last long with a knife wedged into its side.

Thin branches whipped past his face as he chased after it, catching a quick glimpse of its rear legs darting onwards. He was close enough to hear its panting.

Thud! The creature ran headfirst into a tree, hit the ground, and scrambled to get on its feet. Drift pulled out the second knife and pounced on the fawn. He pushed it into its neck, trying to cut its breathing short as quickly as he could. He wouldn't let it bleed out with a knife jutting from its ribs. It was more humane this way. He was Aobian, a patron of the land. *Not anymore, you aren't.*

The guilt of felling the young beast only added to his stomach pangs, but he had to keep himself nourished. He had no food wraps, no ways to preserve the meat he would get from the fawn. He might be able to tear off some cloth from his sleeve and then wrap the meat in that, but it wouldn't keep for more than a couple days in this early summer heat. Humidity here felt like a stiff wall, unctuous when inhaled.

Drift resigned himself to building a small fire near the river, hoping he would be able to get his food cooked before the sun became too bright. He settled down to skin the fawn and tried to suspend it on broken sticks like a spit roast, but to no avail. The creature was too heavy for any fallen branches, so he resorted to heating stones amongst a pile of sticks and resting the meat upon them.

Time dragged on as he waited for the venison to cook. He thought about Tarri and the people he'd left behind. The place he called home, the endless embrace of the Tree. Was this what it meant to drift? To move along the water's current without control, without say? Was that his namesake?

He turned from the thought, gathering his things and moving further from the water. He would find somewhere he could organise thin sticks and vines into a netting he could put overhead for the night. The Great Tree was always so temperate, even in the winter, and he was unprepared for what he might face without proper shelter. He thought of the humans in the mountains of Therador, surviving in the snow year after year, generation after generation. Maybe they were built of sterner stuff, like his ancestors, nomads who had come across the desert, forming a bond with the first Great Tree.

Eventually, Drift found a patch of crushed bushes under a dead stump. He gathered what he could, shook the dirt and dust (and spiders) from it, and settled beneath his weak assembly of sticks and leaves to sleep. Maybe it helped that he'd grown up within the canopy of a Great Tree, leaves overhead as though they stretched for miles towards the sun, because here under the cover of forest scraps, he felt okay. He wasn't as empty as he thought he might be. He nibbled on some overcooked meat that he couldn't get much more blood out of from cooking if he tried. It was chewy and it was foreign, but it was something. He let his thoughts depart his mind and gazed at the clouds through the gaps above his head.

Somehow, he fell asleep.

It was in the darkest hours, where the mind is most uneasy, that Drift awoke to shadows around him that stopped the light of the moon from reaching his place in the bushes. Groggily, he stirred, opening his eyes to assess his surroundings.

In the distance, a crow called, a beacon for the shadows that had begun to close in. A twig snapped somewhere ahead of him.

"Who's there?" he called, but no response came. A jolt of fear ran through him. It was probably nothing.

Whispers, softer than the running river, sounded around him. "Who comes here? What do you want from me?" He stood shakily, before tripping on a bush and falling onto his backside and scarpering back up against a tree trunk.

One of the whispering voices began to sing, a dirge-like droning thick with melancholy and foreboding. Layers of harmony rose above it as other voices joined in. His heartbeat raced faster than the music that was being projected at him, out of rhythm.

"Leave me alone!" he cried, a whimper cutting off his words.

Blade tips poked out from the darkness, their outline glimmering in the moonlight. Connected to them were black-cloaked limbs, the arms of those singing the song. The singing rose to a crescendo as the droning voices changed their tune to a more rhythmic pulse, like drumbeats.

"Night—ing—gales.   Night—ing—gales! NIGHT—ING—GALES!" the dark figures cried out in unison as the flurry of blades pressed towards him.

Only one of them stepped ahead of the others through the thorn-like enshrouding of blade tips. "A tree-dweller away from his Tree?" they asked. Their voice was as sweet and pure as honey trickling down the back of Drift's mind.

"What do you want from me?" he panted in reply.

"How," whispered the voice, "did a husk like you end up here?"

Husk. Drift gritted his teeth. So these were humans, then, and they were none too happy to encounter an Aobian. The leader of the Nightingale gang had called him by the lowest of insults. Husk. And yet, all throughout history, nobody could disprove that Aobians were on this land of Q'ara first. "Scum!" he snapped as a pair of strong hands, like clamps, seized him from behind.

"Hush now, little husk," crowed the leader, the moon casting a hint of a glow across her ghostly white cheeks. It was a woman, though she had no hair, no red to her lips, no colour to her eyes. Dark wells stared at him and he felt himself grow tired suddenly.

"I want to go home," he whispered.

"You cannot," she replied. "You are an exile now."

His chest throbbed. All his life he'd felt the need to run, to flee from stability. To see the world. Now, all he wanted was to go back, fall into Tarri's arms, and begin a normal life.

"Let me go," he begged, tears welling up behind his eyes, burning the edges of them.

"No," the woman whispered into his ear and he felt her cold breath on his face. His assailant pulled him back with force. His legs were grabbed next and he was lifted up, unable to break from their grip.

A howl filled the night air, yet the Nightingales took no heed of it as they walked away from the bushes with Drift above them.

Then the dog came.

A fierce, fur-matted dog, white as snow, bared its teeth at them from the edges of the trees nearest to the riverbank. Its guttural growl caused the Nightingales to step back, alert to the creature's hostility. They dropped Drift on the ground as the dog leapt at them, snapping its jaws around the ankle of one person and knocking them over. Drift got to his feet, seizing the blade from the fallen Nightingale's hand. He winced at the weight of it and the slip of the grip in his massive hand. He thrust it out before him as menacingly as he could so that the Nightingales who weren't distracted by the saviour dog might reconsider their attack.

The dog continued to rear up at them, leaping on the leader of the gang and pinning her to the forest floor. She wailed as the dog bit into her shoulder, thick blood oozing from the wound. "Stay back!" Drift cried as the dog turned around to face him. He held the sword out, unsure of the dog's next move. It was no wolf, but it was nearly as large as the smallest of the Nightingales and he had no reason to believe it was tame, given the intensity of its attack so far.

The dog barked at him threateningly, walking slowly forward. Its eyes reflected nothing but the night sky at him and he stumbled backwards as his foot hit a rock.

"Nightingales, begone! Death is on the air!" the leader of the gang cried, and the group quickly dissipated into the trees. Drift felt water on his hair. The river. He got up quickly, out of breath.

The dog crossed the river and scarpered up the embankment on the other side, crashing through a layer of scrub with its tail wagging. Something had called its attention away from Drift.

Drift turned to face the river and decided this would be the best crossing for a time to come as the river seemed to widen up ahead. He took a running leap onto the first of the large, flat rocks that jutted from the water's surface and continued across to the same embankment that the dog had exited from. On the other side, he caught a glimpse of the dog walking away into the trees alongside a person in a beige poncho. The stranger didn't notice him, but Drift suspected they were not of the same calibre as the Nightingales, who had hung his doom above his face.

He walked towards the stranger, water dripping from his long hair.

Maybe this would be the beginning of a new life.

TARRI

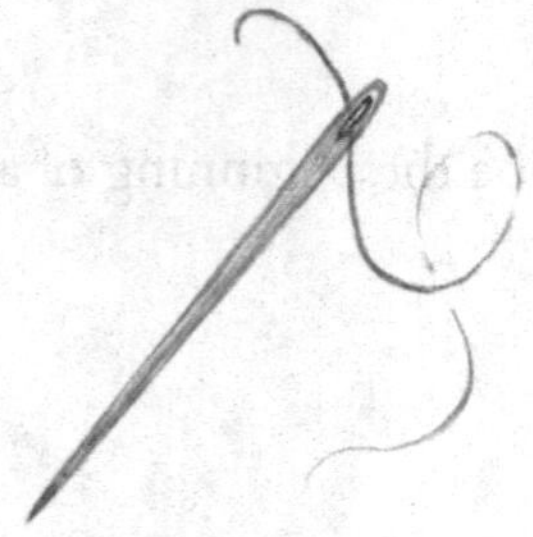

I T WAS MORNING AND time for work. Tarri rushed to get out the door, dressed less smartly than she liked, a light summer shawl trailing behind her to protect against the morning breeze. She skidded past Passion's Bakery, not stopping for her regular order of a rhubarb gallette and black cinnamon tea. Running through the streets, she stopped only to scrub the gritty remains of sleep and tears from her eyes. Drift was an exile.

An exile.

And yet, despite her grief, sleeplessness, and lack of care, today was the day she had to prepare a final presentation of dresses for Lady Nischia as well as let her know whether or not she would be working with the Sleeper on the investigation.

She would also discover how much Nischia knew about her whereabouts the night she went to the viaduct. This reason alone provided the jitters that spurred her to get the day over with as fast as possible.

As she raced through the market square, her heart beating wildly, her thoughts swirled. Would she be held accountable for her actions last night? Had she been seen by one, two, or all three of the people she had come across at the viaduct? And the involvement of Sedulus... There was nothing convincing her of his innocence at this point in time.

Then there was Drift, her beloved. Maybe he had been right all this time. Maybe there was something to a name after all. He claimed he never felt comfortable settling for anything and now he was ... gone? An exile in Aobia did not need to be convicted by the Magisterium before being sent away. Simply setting foot outside of the Tree's reach was enough to be considered an outcast, never permitted to return again. To leave Aobia was to reject the greatest gift the gods had given the Aobian people: new life in the Tree and the power of Luminosity.

She stopped outside her shop and rounded the corner to the front door, where she found Apris, Rela, and—

Lady Nischia with the same pinstripe-suited driver from the day prior. "Good morning, m–my lady," she stammered.

Lady Nischia glared before responding. "I want to have a private discussion with you. Immediately, if you please."

Her breath caught. Nischia swept past her with the presence of a goddess and Tarri felt so small. Did the Sleeper know what she'd done the night before?

"None of those things could be further from the truth." Nischia could read her mind and Tarri cupped her face with one hand.

Apris and Rela were waved on through to the main showroom, while Tarri moved into the workroom. The driver remaining outside the door didn't even blink. Tarri had no doubt he was getting paid a pretty penny to drive Sleepers around Aobia's three districts.

"I enjoy working with brilliant people, Miss Tarri," Nischia began. "But brilliance and intelligence are not the same things. I mean, look at the beautiful artistic creations all around you. They are a mark of brilliance." She tightened her gaze and did not mince her next words. "But you were not especially smart in your actions recently."

"My lady—"

"Let me finish," Nischia said. "Of all the things you could have done, spying on two Sleepers and a person who you believe conspired to exile your beloved is crossing the line. What did you think? That we wouldn't notice? You're lucky it was me who felt you nearby rather than my superior. It is *my* job to investigate extraordinary crimes such as murder and, in this case, exile… Of course, we had to include Sedulus in our inquest as he was the primary witness in the event. He simply showed us where Drift fell and explained what happened. Nothing at the site seemed out of order."

"I didn't know you'd be there, my lady," Tarri replied. "I am sick to the stomach whenever I think of Drift. I never intended to spy on you and your superior, and I promise I—" Tears sprang from her eyes and she tried to stifle a sob. She couldn't cry in front of this Sleeper.

"I know." Nischia put a hand up to silence her. "I am aware of the discussion we had not one day ago. I am committed to finding some kind of explanation as to what happened. That being said, your involvement shall be limited. This is to protect you, Miss Tarri. You are a successful artist and I do not want the Magisterium to frown on you because you were discovered watching us at the scene of the exile."

Tarri nodded.

"Thank you." Nischis nodded. "I have a question for you. Do you know that you can block a Sleeper from reading your mind?"

She could block a Sleeper from reading her mind? "I'm sorry, my lady," she replied. "I've never known about such ... behaviour." She chose the word carefully.

"You wanted to call it a skill, did you not?" A wry smile bent one side of Nischia's mouth.

Tarri blushed and hid her grin. She was not being condemned but merely put in her place. "My lady," she started. "I want to help. I went to the viaduct last night because I must know the truth. Drift would not want to be out there alone. I know he wouldn't. And something tells me his exile wasn't an accident, despite what you may say."

"If you only you knew how little power I bear. I do not necessarily agree on Aobian legislature regarding exile, Miss Tarri, but I do not have the capability to alter it. If your betrothed set a foot outside of Aobia, he exiled himself. Whether he did so willingly or not is another matter, however, and one that I believe the Magisterium could be reasonable about if we were to bring him home."

Tarri sighed. It was ridiculous to think that a person could be considered an exile just for leaving their home. It was times like this that she felt closer to understanding what Drift had thought: that Aobia was more of a prison than a home. Nobody questioned the Magisterium or its laws. It simply … wasn't done. And why would they if their life was so good in the Great Tree, uninterrupted by the politics of the humans that fought constantly for power over Q'ara? She glanced at Nischia, wondering if the Sleeper was reading her mind, before trying to change the subject. "If you can prove Sedulus innocent, fine. However, I will do what it takes and follow your lead to find the truth."

Nischia raised an eyebrow. "Tell me this, child: why would your beloved's superior at the facility want him gone? He has worked directly with the Magisterium for years, operating that facility without a single reported fault. Unless we can discover why the Sickness suddenly emerged across our part of the river, we can't begin to bring Sedulus into it. Even then, it was likely an accident that Drift fell from the waterfall. Do you understand?" She stood and pulled her glowing hair off her shoulders so it draped fashionably. "Now, at least *show* me the dresses I've contracted you for before I must leave you and return to my own devices."

"Of course," Tarri said glumly. She led her to the other side of the room, where a series of tables sat evenly spaced along the wall. Each one was fitted with a huge, mahogany lid to protect the felt surface where Tarri, Apris and Rela worked. She removed the lid of the table closest to the back of the room and waited as Nischia looked at her work. Upon the felt surface lay a dazzling, blue-dyed silk dress with a high-clasped collar and gold embroidery along the button line and around the cuffs of the elbow-length sleeves. This was the main one of the commissioned pieces for Nischia.

"It's beautiful, Tarri," Nischia breathed. "This is silk from our forest?"

"Yes," Tarri confirmed. "I have a contract with the only local source of silk, a male from the Soul, who sells all kinds of fabrics."

"I am … short for words," Nischia said. "It's a masterpiece."

"It isn't done, my lady," Tarri said. "I still need to complete the pocket on the waist and then, of course, we'll need to adjust it to your figure—"

"Nonsense!" Nischia chuckled. "Child, you are an incredible artist." She looked at Tarri, her steely blue eyes forcing Tarri to conform to the compliment.

Tarri felt her cheeks grow hot and hid her face from the Sleeper as she pulled the lid back over the table. "Thank you, my lady."

"Do not thank me for that which I did not give. Now, I fear I have taken too much of your time and I must be going. I will be in contact. Keep your eyes and ears open. Trust, Compassion, and Wisdom."

With that, Nischia swept up her trailing velvet outfit and left the Tailory without so much as a goodbye. Tarri followed her back into the showroom, watching through the front window as Nischia hopped into the cabriolet. The Sleepers never spent much time entertaining the common people. Against all better judgement, Tarri found herself admiring Nischia for doing so. The Sleepers were the ones who governed Aobia under the leadership of Prime Minister Staril. They were a stuffy bunch. Nischia, however, was astounding, confident, and beautiful.

"Miss Tarri?" Apris walked over to her, still finding her staring out the front windows of the store, distant.

"I'm sorry, Apris. What is it?"

"A customer asked for you while you were meeting with Lady Nischia. I asked whether he needed a suit or any kind of fabric work done for a beloved or family member and he said he only came to speak with you. He was insistent that I did not ask what he wanted with you."

Tarri felt her eyebrows shoot up in alarm. "Where is he?"

Apris looked guilt stricken. "I sent him on his way, Miss Tarri. I'm sorry. I did not think—"

"No, no!" Tarri put her hand up. "You're not in trouble. I'm curious, that's all. Did he leave his name?"

"His name was Sedulus, Miss Tarri. He said he came from the Heart."

Sedulus had come here? She frowned. Maybe he was doing his duty and passing on yesterday's tragedy to her in person.

"Miss Tarri? You're staring again. Are you feeling okay?" Apris grabbed her hands.

"I'm okay." Tarri shook herself out of the thought. "If you see him again, please let me know. I'll speak to him."

Apris nodded and slipped away to welcome another customer while Tarri headed back to the workroom. Her mind was fraught with worry about Drift's whereabouts. It didn't matter where he was, though. He was dead now, whether she liked it or not. He would be considered dead by the Magisterium and their ridiculous exile laws. She would be expected to mourn him and carry on.

She sighed. She had mounds of repairs ahead of her and needed to finalise the clothes for Lady Nischia. She needed to rest, but she couldn't. She needed to see Drift, breathe him in, hold him tight.

But she couldn't. He was gone.

Tarri took herself back to the workroom, locking the door from within. Then she cried. Because he was exiled. Because he was most likely dead. Because nothing would bring him back.

All she could do was find the answers to what had happened. Explain it to herself so she could have some closure. She would do what it took. She would find out how this had happened and she would never let it happen again. She might be a tailor from the Soul, but she knew a Sleeper now. She didn't know how, but she would find a way to change things in Aobia.

Tarri arrived at the tiny branch-home tucked deep into the twisted limbs of the Soul. Branch-homes were rare these days. They were special places, signs of the first settlers in the Tree, who'd shaped the limbs of the Tree itself into a dwelling. Branchrenders existed today, ancestors of original families in the same business, but they primarily restored old heritage buildings.

She unlocked the door. Its creak cut through the silence that came with the end of a warm summer's day. What she came for was no light task. It had taken a lot of work to convince herself to come here. It took more from her every time she visited this place, so much so that she was not sure she could do it again.

The inside of the home was equally as quiet as the outside world, inviting slumber. Though for Tarri, it was another grim day without Drift. Sheer curtains swung in the breeze from open windows and the cream painted walls seemed to echo the mood of the setting sun.

The house was an odd place, though Tarri knew it all too well. She'd grown up here, after all. Though it was beautiful, it was also a product of its time and nestled so far into the depths of the branches of the Soul that nobody would come across it by accident. Inside, there was only one dilapidated room. Under the spectacular windows that ran one whole length of it was a tidy, and nearly unused, kitchenette comprised of a basin and a Luminosity-powered stovetop. On the other side of the room was a tiny wall that segmented off a bathchamber, beside which stood a modest wooden wardrobe. In the middle was an ornate woven rug, perhaps of an old Sethi design, an arabesque pattern of flowers and branches.

Upon it, a fully formed Luminous Orb hummed, within which was the cross-legged figure of her mother, Leavening.

"I'm here," Tarri whispered, letting the door close behind her as she approached the Orb to rest a palm on its outside. It felt like glass, though she knew it was not, just like the small orb Nischia had carried under her arm last night at the viaduct had not been either. She'd known this since she'd been a child, since the first day she'd felt her fingers touch the Orb's surface, unable to enter it, unable to cling onto the person concealed within. A Sleeper could enter and exit their Orb with careful control. But her mother was too deep within its mystical places and could not be recalled.

Leavening did not look up, nor did her breath catch or a hand move. She simply continued to sit, her chin slightly raised, her mouth only open enough to process air. This was the same position she'd been in, every muscle unmoved, when she had left Tarri all those years ago. The only person that knew about her mother, from what she could work out, was Drift. Anyone else who might have known would've died long ago, besides the Sleepers, who had never bothered Tarri about her mother. She wasn't sure they knew she was related to Leavening at all. Not since she'd ended up stuck deep in the Orb. Two hundred years was the normal lifespan for an Aobian; four hundred for a Sleeper. The life her mother had lived had ended a long time ago.

Tarri had been held in a state of grief for years now while her mother fought off the nova event that had nearly stolen her life away. Too much concentrated light imbued in a Sleeper could burn them out, like a dying star. Now, Leavening was fixed in a state of mental and spiritual warfare, holding off the inevitable. Tarri would never forget the day it'd happened. The day her mother had assumed her place in the Orb, never to leave its depths again.

Tarri had told Leavening everything that had happened in her life since and telling her that Drift had gone missing was just as important to share, even if her mother could not respond. Though Leavening had never spoken back to her since she had given in to the Orb's call, she felt guilty for not sharing the news sooner.

"Drift is gone," she whispered, the lack of reply only adding to her sense of grief. The two she loved most in the world, forgotten by the world. "You remember him? He's visited before. Many times. You would be so happy to know he was who I shared my heart with." She felt tears prick at the edges of her eyes. "He was exiled. You know the laws. He did not break them with intention. I know that with certainty." She paused, like she did every time, hoping that she might open her eyes and see Leavening move or say something, *anything.*

"Something's *wrong,* Mama," she said, her voice squeaking as she tried to keep it together. Her thoughts were everywhere, darting between the current situation and years with Drift's idiosyncrasies and doubts. "He always thought… Well, it doesn't matter what he thought, does it? Now that he's gone."

She rested her chin on her hand, staring at Leavening through the Orb. "If only we could speak, you'd tell me… Well, it doesn't matter."

She choked on her tears. "What if I was the one to send him reeling away from us all? He always toyed with the idea of leaving, seeing the world. He's so cynical. He's never seen this Tree like we all do. What if there is no investigation to be had and all along he was just trying to tell me that he felt suffocated?" She covered her mouth, the worry within her spilling over like a dam.

Silence. Leavening's eyes were closed, as always, her shoulders slouched, her legs crossed, as though she was in a perpetual state of peace. Tarri looked long and hard at the one who had sacrificed everything for her. The one who knew more about the Tree and its people than the Magisterium ever would. If Tarri could just get her mother to wake once more, maybe she could help her find the answers to Drift's exile. Tarri's world was changing too fast and she wanted so badly for her mother to help her step through it.

"I know you can't speak anymore," she managed through sniffs. "I don't really know if you're alive. But if you can hear me, please pray to the gods that Drift is okay and that, maybe, with some miracle, he can come home."

She turned to leave, the hum of the Orb the only thing that disrupted the quiet. "And pray for me too."

DRIFT

SHIVERING IN THE COLD, dark mist, Drift reflected on how poor his tracking skills were. He'd lost the dog and the human it was with. He hugged himself fiercely. It was cold in the forest and there was a substantial breeze to accompany it. He would not use fire. Fire destroyed the earth, a perversion of nature's evolutions. His dinner was a small assortment of herbs and blackberries he'd foraged on the banks of the river earlier in the afternoon. He still felt sick when he recalled the attempt made to capture him the previous night. Who were the Nightingales and what had they wanted with him?

Goosebumps crawled down his arms the more he pondered it. They knew he was there, in the forest. It was nearly as if his fall from the waterfall had been planned from the beginning.

Had he been sent under the viaduct on purpose? Was his exile something that had been set in motion from the start? Sedulus' face flashed before him and he relived the moment before he'd gone over the waterfall. Sedulus had tried to haul him up. He'd been holding his hand. It couldn't have been his fault. He'd just lost the strength to keep hold of Drift.

The place was a maze, especially in the dark, which was why he'd failed to track the dog. He'd gotten so far into the woods that he'd been lucky to retrace his own steps to get back to the river. It gave him something to navigate by, the occasional bit of food, and, most of all, hope.

In the vast network of trees behind him, strange sounds cautioned him to stay near the river, just like they had the night before. He knew that it was just a mix of crickets chirping, the call of an owl, the patter of light-footed rodents and squirrels.

He sat up, leaning on a strong root that was exposed from the base of a suar tree, which had a flat-shaped canopy that mimicked that of Aobia.

He lay back and groaned. He tried to keep his eyes closed and listened to the sounds of the forest around him: cawing and scratching and the gnashing of teeth. He wanted to ignore them, but he couldn't, so he stood and slipped out from under his roughshod stick roof.

He kept his cloak tight around his chest as he marched in the direction of the sound. All hopes that the sound would dissipate were dashed instantly as snarls and squeals became louder. When the snarling broke into a gruff series of barks, he knew. It had to be that dog.

Drift walked into a low-hanging mist that connected the trees as though it were webs. Here, the trees were further apart and the mist consumed all.

The dog also struggled to see in the mist as it darted past, crashing into the side of Drift's leg before shaking itself and going on. Drift took up the charge and followed. The fog cleared slightly as he heard a voice call, "Morgan! Morgan, where are ye, girl?"

A broad-shouldered man appeared only a few metres ahead of Drift, but with his back turned. "Morgan!" The man called again with a voice that sounded like the rubbing of timber on steel.

Drift could no longer see the dog and the man was swallowed up into mist as everything fell quiet once more.

Then, in a blur of sound and motion, a twig snapped and Drift felt his ankle yank behind him. He fell over and his face slammed into wet leaf litter. He felt a tooth puncture his lip as he landed. Groaning, he tried to stand, spitting out dirt. He took a metallic swallow as his lip leaked blood.

He couldn't stand. Propping himself up on his elbows, he rolled over to see something had snagged his left ankle.

Whoosh! A hiss of cold wind brushed the back of his neck, like he'd been swooped by a bird. *Whoosh!* It happened again. Drift craned his neck, hoping to catch whatever was causing the sensation. The third time, his eyes widened in horror and he screamed. A blade swept across the top of his head. It disappeared into the trees before swinging back into view again, barely missing once more. The clamp on his ankle bit in harder as he moved. He stayed as low as he could. The blade that had been set up to swing down across its catch was persistent. A trap large enough to rival the greatest of beasts.

"Wha—Help!" He gasped, slamming his face into the ground. There was no glory to be had in this moment as he used his nose to dig himself a little deeper. "Help!" he screamed again when the blade was falling once more like a pendulum.

The barking started up again, this time closer as the hunting dog ran over to him, snapping its jaws. "No, please!" Drift cried. "Help me, somebody!"

The dog considered him. "Nice dog," Drift wheezed, planting his head again as the blade breezed past. Suddenly, he felt the awful snap of teeth around his arm. He tried to press his skull to the ground as the dog rotated his body, dragging him like he was a ragdoll. "I said nice dog!" He strained against the dog's strength.

"Morgan!" The broad-shouldered man appeared, running towards Drift. "My God! What have ye done, girl? Get off him!" He grabbed the dog by the jaw, opening its snout, then moved to Drift's leg. "Sit still."

The man put a key into the metal clamp around Drift's ankle. Relief flooded him as it came loose, the metal teeth leaving a zigzag of dents in his skin. Drift spun around, lying back on his arms and keeping his head low.

The man ran over to a nearby tree and, after a pulling motion, the blade stopped swinging, pausing directly over his head.

"Are ye okay?" The stranger grabbed Drift under the armpits and dragged him out of the way before hauling him to his feet.

The dog, Morgan, yapped at him, causing him to dance in his place.

"That's it with ye!" The man pulled a leash out of his poncho and hooked it over the dog's neck in a single action. He pulled the dog back, calming it.

"Thank you," Drift said. He'd never spoken to a human, never even seen one this close. They were … short. Incredibly so. And this man was rougher, covered with hair and leathery, weathered skin.

"'S okay, friend." The stranger nodded. "Don't mind my Morgan. She's a smart one and what her job is, is what she did. Though I'm sorry she charged you."

"That's okay," Drift replied, rubbing his hands together. Breath left his mouth and blended with the mist around them.

"Come with me, friend." His eyes were sincere, but Drift was unsure. Come away with a human? Under any other circumstance, he'd reject the thought, taught that Aobia was all his people needed. But here, in the cold, with no food… He could do with a softer bed and a full belly, whether it was in the company of a human or not.

"I've got some spare blankets and food on my farm and ye look ragged. No offense," he added.

The man outstretched a hand to Drift. "The name's Raegan," he offered. "And you?"

Drift hesitated before accepting the hand. "Drift." He paused before adding, "Er… Was that a deer trap I was in, by chance?"

Raegan chuckled. "A deer trap? You'd wish. You know there are King Elk around these parts, don't ye? Big enough, one o' them is, to take out a whole swathe of armed villagers. You're lucky you didn't end up dead in that trap!"

Drift looked away, the sick feeling of shock returning to his belly.

"Well, Drift," Raegan continued, "let's get you warm, fed, and maybe willing to tell me how the hell you ended up here."

It was not a short walk to Raegan's home, a lofty cabin made of logs and mud brick, somewhere close to the river but far from Aobia. It was certainly after midnight when they arrived outside the cabin, which was nestled in darkness.

"Come in and make yerself at home," Raegan announced as he tethered Morgan by the door and stepped inside. "Mola! We've a guest."

Drift kept his hood over his head as they both entered. The cabin was two storeys, something Drift had not made out from outside. A fireplace illuminated the top floor, which was a loft with a short stairwell that was nearly steep enough to be a ladder, from which descended an elegant young woman with neatly tied hair. Hand-stitched clothes aside, she looked nothing like a farmer's wife. Her skin, unlike Raegan's, was clean. Her hair was kept back in an ornate bun.

"This is Mola, me sister," Raegan said.

"Oh," Drift said, shaking her hand.

"You thought he was going to say 'wife,' correct?"

Drift nodded.

Mola shrugged. "Well, it's just Raegan, his three children, and myself here." She put a finger across her lips, whispering, "Oh, and they're asleep upstairs."

Raegan seemed more interested in his own story. "Me wife passed suddenly after the littlest one was born. Mola agreed to stay with me and get things under control." He gave his sister a squeeze around the shoulders.

"Let me set you up a bed… Sorry, what's your name?" Mola asked.

"It's Drift."

"Drift," Mola nodded. "A fitting name for a traveller." As she said this, Drift noticed how high she needed to tilt her head to see his face. Maybe Raegan was considered tall for a human.

"You're … quite tall, Drift," Mola frowned.

Raegan eyed Drift. "He is a big 'un, sister. Best make sure we set up a bigger bed. I'll haul some extra hay across from the barn to stuff a sack. You can sleep on hay, I presume?" He craned his head at Drift.

"Of course," he nodded. Drift realised that these humans did not yet know he was Aobian. But the intensity in Raegan's gaze seemed to suggest he'd worked it out. Were Aobians even welcome in human territories? They probably hadn't been seen in these parts since the armistice fifty years ago.

"Drift." Raegan waved him to the door as Mola threw her brother a sack to make up a mattress. "Could ye give me a hand making up a bed sack for ye? There's fresh hay in the barn."

Drift nodded and left the building with him, the light of the fire disappearing as the hefty wooden door closed behind him. He followed Raegan in silence to a modestly sized barn. Tools hung from or rested against the walls. A coop for chickens hid in the corner, handmade from timber. Hay was stacked in bales down one side of the barn and Raegan grabbed the closest one to the ground that was not going to cause them all to fall.

"Drift," he said. "Hold the sack open for me, will ye?"

Drift complied, watching the man work as he scooped and tore masses of clumped hay from the bale.

"I wanted to let you know," Raegan continued talking, "that as long as you need some solace, you can stay. That is, if you say you're a safe fellow. I have my children and my sister, ye see, and I would protect them with my life."

The cautionary welcome was not unexpected and Drift knew that he would do the same for his loved one. The thought of Tarri chipped away at his heart. "You can trust me."

Raegan nodded as he stuffed the sack with hay. "That's well and good then." He paused and looked up at Drift. "But I won't say I'm not curious about why you were out in the forest, tracking my dog, and I also won't say I don't think about why you're such a tall, silver-haired fellow."

Their eyes locked.

"You can pull the hood down, Drift," Raegan said. "Can't be wearing it all the time, can ye?"

Drift sighed and looked down. "Raegan—"

Raegan put his hands up. "My house, my rules, Drift. No hats inside." He smiled.

"Well, you see," Drift began with some cheek. "It's more of a hood than a—fine." He pulled down the hood, exposing his frosted blue eyes and Aobian features: the silver hair and the lack of facial hair.

"Knew it from the start," Raegan said.

"Please," Drift began, "let me go in peace. I don't mean any harm, Raegan."

Raegan shook his head. "Nah. You're at no risk, friend. Folk in this area help your kind more often than you think. Living at the base of the Great Canopies like this. How could we not be friends of Aobia? This isn't my first time meeting one of your kind."

Drift was speechless. Friends of Aobia? How many of his people came through these parts?

"Anyway," Raegan continued, "long as you don't cause trouble, we will share our hospitality. Only catch is that I need help 'round here, more than I can usually find. Do some errands for us, work around the property, and this is your home as much as ours. When you need to go, I'll arrange that for you too. Now what do you say to a decent night's rest on a soft bed rather than dense forest floor?" He tied a knot in the sack of hay and walked out of the barn, waiting for Drift to follow. When they re-entered the house, all was quiet. Raegan nodded goodnight to him and rose to the loft to an empty bed that overlooked the rest of the cabin.

Drift pressed his sack down in a corner of the floor and lay on it. This would do.

These were good people, simple people. Maybe he could find solace here for a while. At least while he figured out what it was he wanted to do next. For now, he was just grateful to have a roof over his head.

The stillness of the night was inviting and he was comfortable for the first time in days.

NISCHIA

Nischia sipped her jasmine tea with a reverence that only this tea, the saviour of her soul, deserved. She sipped it ritualistically at the same time every afternoon, both as an aperitif and a tonic. The only quietude she dared enjoy was always linked to this moment.

She was sitting in her tidy apartment in the Mind. In the corner was a rectangular arrangement of dark green curtains that blocked out all light. Behind them resided her Orb, the source of the Blessing bestowed upon her by the gods, or the Tree, or both—she could never settle on an answer. The reason her life had gone the way it had gone, despite all her better wishes. Thank goodness for the heavy drapery that kept it tucked away in the corner, for its constant thrumming was somewhat hushed because of it. But she knew that on her weaker days, she would succumb to it whether she wanted to or not. Years of learning to only listen to the Orb when Sleep was truly needed and the body was prepared did nothing. Koln would call her weak-willed. Maybe that was true.

She worked at her desk, which was carved out of the wall directly and adjacent to the tremendous glass panes that ran from floor to ceiling, allowing her to take in the warmth of the sun. Those windows were the greatest additions ever made to the Sleeper residential apartments. The entire apartment block was an exceptional feat of branchrending, the process of shaping parts of the Tree into dwellings. Fitting windows into them was no easy task.

Nischia moved out from her desk, agitated. She wanted to read. A book would distract her for the few moments she had before, inevitably, her duty would come knocking once more. She could not get the exile, Drift, out of her head.

She went to another corner of the room, where the walls were lined with tomes, old and new, a combination of smells. This place was the closest thing she'd ever had to a home, but never was it separate from her civic duty. She lived with the constant reminder that her only purpose was to serve her people.

As she eyed the spines of the books, wondering what to read, she took another sip of tea, accidentally tipping the cup too far and spilling some onto her dress.

"Roots below!" she swore under her breath.

The smallest of things were frustrating her. Tarri and Drift; she didn't know what to make of them. The situation was ridiculous, but she feared it pointed at an underlying rot in Aobia that she couldn't put a finger on. She swallowed a lump of guilt as she dabbed her dress with a tea towel. Oh well. What had started as a business relationship with Tarri was destined to end tragically, with the investigation into Drift's exile well underway now.

Of course, she knew Tarri would stop at no end of the continent to find justice for Drift, even if she couldn't bring him home. Though Nischia couldn't say her own motive was the same, however. It was Nischia's job to find the connection between Drift and whatever news would come of the returned ambassadors.

And she had to find out more about Drift. His name was curious, for example. It was not traditional. After the collapse of the monarchy a century ago, the unethical practice of Naming Rituals was outlawed. Children forced to comply with the meanings of their names somehow influencing their whole destinies with Luminosity. The idea was sick, but thank the gods, it was gone. She'd been there when it had happened. But what if Drift's existence threatened to protest against that truth? She hoped whatever digging Koln had done on Drift's background would reveal that he was one of the last Named children. That might explain his exile, whether it really was an accident or not.

But with answers came more questions. Why would his disappearance have been intentional? Was there truly a connection at the heart of that event and the death of King Terrens? And with questions came the stirring of war. Aobia had promised every other power on Q'ara that Naming would be made illegal. The ramifications of that being a lie would be great, particularly if the alliance they had with Adira was already being tested.

The knock came as she worked her way down to the bottom of the teacup. "Who is it?" she asked, though the lack of response told her exactly who it was. The door opened from the other side to reveal Koln looking at her with his typically blank expression. Koln had been around nearly as long as Staril, which was a long time; four hundred years, give or take.

"The Magisterium has called for a sitting. The ambassadors are going to speak," he said in the same flat manner as ever.

Nischia cleared her throat. "Okay." She brushed her hair behind her ears. The regular schedule meant a parliamentary sitting wouldn't be happening for at least a week. "When?"

"Now." He turned, his silk shawl swirling behind him.

The Magisterium was barely a walk out their door, as all Sleepers lived within apartments on a long branch of the Mind. At the end was the grandiose building that sat opposite the elegantly manicured botanic gardens and incorporated many natural elements of the Great Canopies into its design: millennia old vines intertwined and were moulded into the shape of a roof, covered with natural greenery and Luminous plants that showed only at night. There was a dome-shaped wood building twice the size of the Sleepers' apartments under the natural roof and along the front were extraordinary stained-glass windows that nearly spanned from the floor to the ceiling.

Inside, deep green leather covered an array of seats that faced a central stage, where the panel of twelve Senior Sleepers and their scribes would sit. All other Sleepers had an allocated chair next to their superiors and so Nischia sat behind Koln's seat, in the middle of the room. Quickly, the space filled with Sleepers; hundreds of them. The clambering of voices told Nischia what she'd expected to hear: the rumour-mongering had begun. Nothing was sacred in this sacred place.

Afternoon light hailed down and shone directly onto the centre stage through a window that sat right at the peak of the domed roof.

The voice of the Speaker, Cailin, controlled the political order and etiquette of every sitting in the Parliament. "All rise for the Senior Sleepers, those that Sleep by day and night for their people."

Immediately all the Sleepers, dozens of them, stood with right hands to their chests, drumming them repeatedly over their hearts in time with the steps of the twelve that approached. Old rites of passage, remnants of the monarchy that had been reworked into this new age.

Including Koln, the twelve Sleepers that walked down to the centre stage were some of the most ancient and wise people of Aobia, and Staril, the one leading the congregation, was the prime minister of the Aobian Magisterium. Nischia always soured at the sight of her. The old Sleeper had been Aobia's rescuing hand when the monarchy had fallen, and yet here she stood with much the same power as a queen, titles aside. Staril had seen significant changes happen both beneath the Great Canopies as well as the human lands. Staril had been an advisor of the last queen's; she'd been here for the Four-Front War against Therador and the Civil War, when the tyrant queen had fallen.

She knew better than how she led the Magisterium these days. As though she was its sole leader.

"First to speak, Ambassador to the Throne of the Sea King, Stag of the Soul."

As everyone sat to begin the proceedings, a young Aobian male with a hard face stepped up behind a walnut-stained lectern to the right of the stage where all members could see it. "Good afternoon, Senior Sleepers and all Sleepers of Aobia," he began. "For those of you who do not know me, my name is Stag of the Soul and I have been an ambassador to the Adiran Throne for two decades. I am here to give an account of my recent visit and subsequent leave-taking of the Sea Kingdom. I was accompanied by fellow ambassador for Aobia, Flow of the Soul. We were there for approximately a week, which is much shorter, as you know, than previous visits…"

Nischia leaned over to Koln. "Why did they flee back, Koln?"

Koln sighed. "I've been told it's serious news. Grave, in fact." His eyes remained firmly on Stag and Nischia redirected her flat stare to the stage.

"I have travelled as fast as possible to provide you with the devastating news that the King of Adira, Terrens, has been as-sassinated."

A gasp echoed about the room.

Stag continued as the noise dissipated. "It is unknown who committed the crime, but officials reported that the king had received multiple ambassadors that day. Each was, according to Adiran law, in the public forum of the throne room, where officials and guards could be in full view." Stag paused and took a breath. "My colleague and I were a visiting party on the day that the king died. However, it was disclosed to us and one ambassador from the Northern Fjords that there had been a visit from a representative of Therador that day, which, as we all may suspect, was the first from Therador in many years."

Of course. Nischia frowned and shook her head while watching the room. Tension with Therador never faded. Those barbarians from the West were always going to be trouble. The tyrant Emperor Jurin had tried to extend his son Rainol as a marriage partner to King Terrens' daughter and heir, Esme. Terrens had rejected Jurin's advances for years now due to Therador's reputation after the Four-Front War as a dirty, warring empire that stopped at nothing short of continental domination. As the crowd's cacophony rose, Staril stood, lightly pushing Stag to the side to silence the room.

"Fellow tree-dwellers," she began with such a steady breath, Nischia couldn't help but be drawn to her voice. "Please allow our ambassador the dignity to be heard, respected, and able to exit the stage." It was all she needed to say for the room to go quiet once more. She nodded at the young Aobian, who beat his chest three times before departing.

"There is always more to news like this than meets the eye," she continued. "A great leader and king, Terrens of Adira, has left our community of peace after a successful reign of forty years; a tragedy in itself, even by human standards of lifespan.

"It is not known how Adira will proceed, but it is presumed that his daughter, Esme, will take the throne in official proceedings within the week."

Nischia had seen Esme once. A scruffy young girl, blonde hair nearly brighter than sunlight on Adiran sand. She was impossibly young for the role of queen. There was also her younger brother, Sefil, though he was not owed the throne.

"Esme is a capable and caring pastoral worker of her land. She devotes her time now, and as always, to her people and retains the aspects of thankfulness and humility that her father always exhibited. When she is announced as queen, Aobia will defend her right to the Throne and continue to work with Adira as part of the peaceful community we have upheld for over fifty years." Several nods and mutters of agreement went around the room before quietening to hear Staril speak once more. "However, the news of a Theradoran visitor, while unsettling, must be treated without presumption. The fact is, Therador has tried to bind itself with Adira through marriage for years. There is nothing concrete as of yet that would suggest Therador was visiting Adira for any other reason than that. It is necessary for the peace of our home and for the valley that extends under us that we do not assume reasons and spread rumours. We will trade with the humans in the same way we always have and treat any contact with the people of Therador with graciousness."

That seemed to be the end to it as Staril lowered her head. Right as Nischia thought the Senior Sleeper would stand down and end the meeting, Staril looked up from the lectern and continued. "The final piece of information I have will not lighten the mood. You may have received the awful news of an exile this week. A worker from the Heart known as Drift has departed his homeland. This male has been of particular interest to me and the twelve Seniors since his birth fifty years ago.

"Earlier this week, a malfunction occurred in the filtration system on the River Tomei far south of the Tree. The Sickness made its way through our catchments but was expertly deflected by the Lead Operator at the facility, Sedulus of the Heart, and a team of engineers whose work includes aligning the algae cleaning with the Luminosity that we provide. Although we don't have any reason to believe this exile happened because of any foul play, we do have to determine the cause of the Sickness infiltrating the river at the point where we begin cleaning it. If there is even a minuscule breach, the repercussions could be significant. Of course, we understand that an entire race of humans was eradicated because of this foul water once before. We do not want this to happen again.

"If this exile attempts to return, the investigation—with more evidence of what happened—will be handed over to the Supreme Court to adjudicate on the matter. We place our trust in the gods of the Tree."

"We place our trust in the gods of the Tree!" the room called back, pounding chests in respect.

"Trust, Compassion, and Wisdom!" She shouted the Three Pillars of Aobia.

Nischia shifted in her chair. That couldn't be all. A person of interest to the Seniors since his *birth*? Koln had never mentioned that. She needed to see Staril, have Koln make an appointment, get an explanation as to how—

"Do not make a scene, Nischia," Koln advised as the Speaker announced the exit of the Seniors. Everyone stood.

"Koln, I must insist—"

"You will lose every privilege owed to you and risk losing everything for me too. We will speak about this afterwards, in private. And we will conduct ourselves with the utmost civility." He beat his chest as he followed the Seniors ahead of him out of the room before looking back at Nischia. "Do not go against me. I will find you later and we will discuss this."

With his gaze like iron, Nischia felt she could only back down. "Of course, Koln, I—" she stammered. "I will wait for you to call."

He moved to leave the auditorium and Nischia followed until he split from her and she was back at her front door. She let herself in and tried to digest all that she had heard. Had Koln withheld information from her?

Seniors. A sick feeling slid down her throat. She shuddered as she recalled the day Queen Feldra had torn Aobia apart, the day Staril had announced her as a traitor to the people. The feeling in the auditorium today was not so dissimilar.

She sighed. She was too tired to Sleep in the Orb. She needed tea and her bed. And *then,* she could address this.

DRIFT

SUNLIGHT STREAMED THROUGH THE window, waking Drift. His head hurt from the too little sleep he had gotten. It was ironic that a comfortable bed could've worsened his rest. Raegan was climbing down the loft ladder as his eyes peeled open. "Good morning," Drift said.

"Morning, Drift. Tea?"

Drift nodded and got out of bed, still drowsy. He hadn't slept as well as he'd have liked. Tarri stuck to his thoughts like tree sap and the deep sadness of being apart from the Tree was pervasive. He rolled his shoulders and stretched his arms.

Here he was, safe and comfortable, yet faced with the uncertainty of the unknown. What was to come of him? Would he farm out here in the human lands? Fear crept through him that he lacked purpose. In Aobia, everyone worked for the common goal of making the Tree the most bountiful place to live. But now, he felt affronted by how uncomfortable the idea of instability made him feel.

This was unlike him, who had always been seeking new things, always been trying to find fresh experiences away from people or places he'd known.

He was truly an exile, whether he liked it or not.

Raegan noticed his dark expression as he moved through the kitchen, grabbing a cast iron pot from above a roughshod basin and moving to the fireplace to light it anew. "What do ye drink? I have a black tea with dried orange peel, or I have wild jasmine leaf, or lavender flowers—"

Drift paused him with a raised hand. "Black. Black tea sounds just fine, Raegan, thank you."

"All well and good. Could ye do me a favour and fetch some eggs from the coop in the barn?"

"Of course," Drift replied. That was something he could do. Something he had often done for his father as a child when they'd kept a small number of chickens beside their home in the Heart.

He went outside and studied the sky. A bright, inviting blue with not a cloud in it. A welcoming summer's day lay before him. Maybe it was a sign that he could leave this human dwelling and forge a new path. He could ask Raegan for some food for the road and directions to the nearest town. Then he could figure out what might come next.

When he brought the eggs back inside, Raegan handed him a steaming mug of tea. "Drift," he started, "want ye to know that whatever time you need, you can take it here. No need to rush off."

It was like the man could read his mind.

"I just don't want you to feel a burden, is all," the man went on.

"Of course," Drift murmured.

"I'll have you know that occasionally we are a stop for a travellin' tree-dweller."

At this, Drift's ears pricked up. "What do you mean? Nobody travels from Aobia except—"

"Except for ambassadors and the like, right?" Raegan passed him a plate of hot eggs and took a gulp of tea.

"Right," Drift said, though his voice lacked confidence.

"You're not an ambassador though, are ye?"

Drift shook his head.

"You're not gonna get us in trouble if one comes along, then?"

Drift eyed the man. "I don't know," he replied. "I can't control what they might think of me." It was a harsh retort considering Raegan knew nothing of Aobian customs or protocol, but Drift couldn't help it. He didn't want the man making assumptions and formulating opinions of him. Especially not if he was going to be stuck here for longer than he thought.

"How about we keep things under wraps?" Raegan suggested. "You stay here as long as you need, maybe take some time away from the world so as to not cause a splash when you re-enter. Next of your folk comes a'knockin', we'll tell 'em you're here, as long as that's what ye want."

Drift looked away, sipping his tea. *A splash.* He couldn't help but snicker.

"Don't feel like you owe me any explanation, Drift. I understand something's the matter, but I know when not to press a point." He took a breath. "I'm expecting visitors to maybe come through here in a week, as it was previously arranged. Now, you can get out of here if you feel like you should or you can stay and see where a meeting might take ye. It's your fate, Drift. You make the choice. But for today, let's focus on something simpler. Let me show you the ropes here on the farm and keep you busy. God above knows I need the help and you look like the kinda fellow that needs things to do."

Drift shook the man's hand and accepted. One week. That wasn't such a long time to wrap his head around where he could go, what was around him, and what was out there for his pursuit. But Raegan's idea didn't hurt. If any Aobians were passing the farm, they could only be his friend Flow or Stag, Flow's pompous colleague.

Maybe he could travel through the human lands with them, see what he had always wanted to see and find a new life along the way. Flow would be the perfect guide. He suppressed a heartache as he considered what a new life would look like. *Tarri. I can't leave her like that.* But what else could he do? How could he ever get back to her?

The day began with Raegan's animals. Raegan milked the cows while Drift held the buckets in place. The creatures were enormous and Drift had no compass for their stature or their milk; they were not kept in the Tree.

Next, pigfeed was scattered and soil was toiled in preparation for planting wheat. Raegan showed Drift the rice fields, which required a brief horse ride to the edges of the Great Forest. Drift wondered how close he was to land he was now excluded from. Silty loam beds, drenched with constant moisture, sparked new growth in rice seeds, just like the rice fields under the Tree near the river. But all around the edges of the fields were plants that reminded Drift of home: ferns, spire-reeds, and a scattering of Luminous mosses and fungi on the outer edges of Raegan's crop.

In the afternoon, Raegan brought Drift back to the house and two inquisitive sets of young eyes peered at him from the doorway.

"This is Braddegh and Suan." Raegan indicated his son and daughter. The boy considered Drift with a hard stare, but Suan looked at him with excitement and he felt his heart melt at the sight of her. The girl had her fire-red hair tied into two pigtails and bore a combination of rosy cheeks and a nose that Drift thought was much too close to a cuddly toy. He recalled the kinds of caricature dolls Tarri had around her house and the Tailory, remnants from when she'd been a child.

Both children shook his hand and helped him to get settled around the place, playing children's games of hide and seek and teaching him the proper way to light the fireplace.

"Go ahead, Drift!" Suan giggled, handing him the stoker for the newly lit flame. Drift shuddered as he backed away from her and the girl look at him, confused.

"I'm sorry, Suan," he said. "Where I come from, we don't light fires."

"Where *do* you come from?" Braddegh asked.

"From up the river," Drift whispered. "A place you wouldn't know."

Braddegh glanced at Drift. Suan might not have known any different, but the boy knew that Drift was not human. When the time came to be seated for dinner, Braddegh marked his spot at the table right beside Drift.

After a long day, Drift found comfort around the family table, playing a betting game before and after dinner, one the humans called 'Demon's Dice'.

When the day ended and everyone was curled up by the fireplace, Drift watched the family from his bed with curiosity. He thought of Tarri and, again, something thrummed in him like a violin bow running across his heartstrings. He could have had this: a quiet life with children about, a warm fireplace, and a dog. Tarri had made her feelings known and he'd been too afraid to ask the question. Now, he was here, forever lost to her.

The family's nighttime routine seemed to happen before him in slow motion and he found himself lost in thought with his eyes buried deep in the hot swell of the embers cooking on the fire. When it was late enough and the others were asleep, Drift realised the kind of cold had come that bit at the back of your throat when you breathed in. He pulled the covers up around him, close. Sleep took him faster than a knife, so that he barely had a moment to register just how tired he was.

The next morning, Drift decided he'd begin repaying Raegan for his kindness. At dawn, he was hauling himself out of bed and tending to the cows outside. He fed the chickens and pigs and gathered eggs to cook as Raegan had the day before.

Before the family rose, Drift laid the table with breakfast food and a pot of hot black tea. He found a cinnamon stick in a canister on the countertop and dropped it into the pot too, and the scent rose up to immediately remind him of Tarri. *She loves cinnamon tea,* he thought. *And she's probably drinking some right now.*

"Drift!" Raegan exclaimed. "What have ye done? This is far too kind."

Mola gave him a peck on the cheek and the children added to the affection with quick hugs of thanks. He felt like a part of their world already.

"Please," he started, gesturing to the table. "I couldn't help but begin repaying my debt to you, Raegan. Thank you for your kindness and for sharing your family with me."

When the meal was over and the children had moved out of the room to play outside, Drift cleaned the kitchen with Mola.

Raegan had gone out to attend to some other errand. "Mola, can I ask you something?"

"Of course," she replied, wiping the countertop with a damp rag.

"It's just that … I can't help noticing that you are such an important part of the family. The children depend on you, Raegan too." She blushed at the comment. Her humility was not lost on him. "Do you ever feel like you might want a family yourself?"

She turned her head away from him to answer and he regretted his question.

"I have a fantastic brother, Drift," she said. "And … he needed me after his wife passed away. Our parents were long gone at that time and I was all he had left. I was living in Adira when I got the news and I left everything there behind to come and help."

When she looked up, her eyes were wet, and Drift felt ashamed. "Oh, don't pity me, please," she insisted. "I had never planned to stay so long. But the children needed me. They needed something like a mother around. Raegan will not remarry. And the place would be a wreck if he was the only adult around." She wiped the corner of her eyes. "I left behind pieces of my heart that I'll never get back. I was betrothed to a chancellor's son in the city. It was probably for the best though. Raegan and I are common folk. I should never have ended up with Symon. In fact, his family detested me. They would have been glad to hear I was never coming back."

"And Symon?" Drift asked.

Mola sighed. "I never had the heart to tell him and he doesn't know where the farm is located. So the words were never said, the goodbyes … never exchanged. It was probably the best ending we could have gotten, looking back on it." She looked at him in a way that suggested she didn't always act so full of goodwill. "You're a stranger in our home. I wouldn't have told just anyone such a thing, but you have a way about you. I can trust you with my story, right? Raegan never knew the full of it. He just knew I came when he needed me. Promise me you won't say anything." Her voice changed from defensive to pleading in a matter of seconds.

"Of course, Mola. I won't say a word. I'm sorry I asked. I'd just wondered. You see, I have a…" The words left him and he looked down. "A someone, I suppose, back home. I nearly lost her and for a time I didn't think I'd care if I did. But being around your family, the children… It's given me a reason to find my way back eventually."

"Eventually?" Mola asked. "Drift, I can keep secrets just as well as I can ask someone to keep them for me. Why eventually? What is it you're doing out here?"

"Well," he began. "I'm an Aobian—"

Mola interrupted him with a giggle. "I know that! Men always behave as though women are oblivious. You may have shared this with my brother, but you haven't maintained an act around the rest of us. The hair, your height…" She looked up at him. "It doesn't matter whether you wear a cowl or not. Besides, who does that in the summer? You're not like any other human I've met."

Well, that was his cover blown. She knew what he was. He supposed it made sense. He *hadn't* particularly tried to hide his appearance, because he felt so comfortable with these people. And Raegan had mentioned they looked after the occasional Aobian as they travelled to Adira.

"You might not know this about Aobians, Mola," he continued. "Those of us who leave Aobia without permission to go are not treated kindly." His expression darkened. "Even if one's leaving is not their fault."

Mola raised an eyebrow. "How can that be?"

"I thought I'd made a mistake, had an accident that left me outside the Great Canopies." He had half a mind to share the story of the Nightingales springing an attack on him on his first night in the forest, but he swiftly moved on.

"But on second thoughts, walking through the forest helped me decide that I was removed from my home intentionally." He put away the remaining cutlery. "I have been worried over the past few days that I would be doomed to a life without purpose. But I have resolved what my purpose is now. I will not stop until I find out what happened to me the night I was exiled from my home. And I *will* make it back to Tarri." He said this with a steely edge.

Through this conversation, he'd somehow made conclusions about his cascading thoughts, the ones that had been pouring through him these past three days like the river. He'd pieced together suspicions about what had happened at the viaduct but hadn't wanted to acknowledge them aloud. He'd realised Tarri might have a larger role to play in his life than he'd given her credit for. He now knew what to do.

He just had to find a way to do it.

TARRI

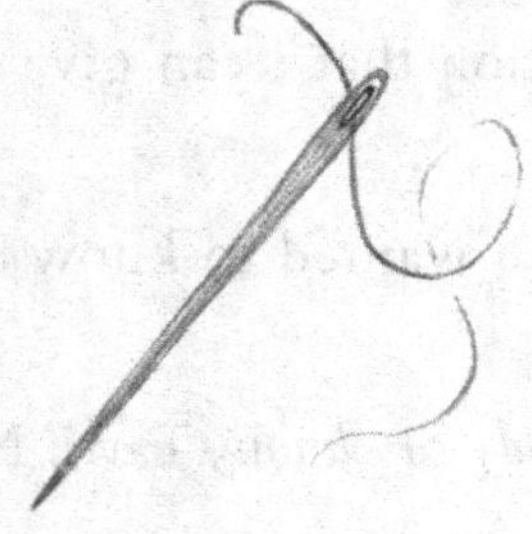

TARRI HAD STILL NOT heard from Lady Nischia and wondered if she ever would. It had only been a couple of days, but she was impatient. April and Rela had noticed too, catching her smoothing dresses when they had already been smoothed countless times. Once, Rela had to insist that Tarri stop tapping her foot as fast as a woodpecker every time she sat.

It was just her luck then that the door swung open to reveal Nischia. "My lady, I—" Tarri started.

"Silence, child," Nischia hissed. "Out of sight, out of mind."

When they were both safely hidden in the workroom and Apris and Rela were preoccupied with customers, Nischia flipped the lock.

"What are you doing?" Tarri exclaimed.

"We need to talk. They can't come in while we are doing so."

Tarri shook her head. "Then we should find some other place to talk! What if there are customers waiting to pick something up?"

"A customer waiting on a piece of fabric can wait a little longer!" Nischia retorted. "We need to talk about Drift. I have some new information that I can give you in exchange for your confidence."

Tarri nodded. She wanted to know *anything* about Drift. "Of course!"

"That means *nobody can know,* Tarri. Not a single person."

"I understand."

Nischia closed her eyes. When she opened them again, she spoke. "There was a meeting. A sitting of the Magisterium concerning some news from the humans of the Sea Kingdom. The Adiran king, Terrens, was assassinated and two Aobian ambassadors who had been visiting the kingdom were considered suspects." She paused.

"I believe there is indeed foul play involved with Drift's disappearance, Tarri," Nischia said. "The prime minister suggested that Drift has been a person of interest to the Senior Sleepers for years. All of this … cannot be a mere coincidence.

"I need you to keep a low profile for now," Nischia went on. "But I still want you involved with my investigation."

"Are you saying that the death of this … human king is related to Drift's exile?" Tarri asked. "How can that be?"

Suddenly, Nischia looked scared, a fear so deep in her eyes they seemed too dark to look at. She swallowed loudly and looked away. "My lady, what is it?" Tarri asked, frowning.

Nischia sighed. "Sleepers can use Luminosity to read minds. That is no surprise to either of us. However, we also have the means to shield our minds. But now I worry there is counterplay at hand. Two can play a game of shielding and the one with the weakest will shall crumble first."

"You're saying…" Tarri trailed off, her mind racing. "You're saying there are Sleepers who are trying to read your mind? Why would they do that?"

Nischia nodded. "I fear being exposed if I talk about this for too long, Tarri. I have not been imbued with Luminosity recently. I've been far too tired to Sleep. But I suspect there are connections between the king's death and Drift's disappearance. If the wrong Sleepers realise that I am pursuing that possibility, we might find ourselves in a precarious position with the law. I need evidence, and quickly, before anyone notices the ideas I'm entertaining. You already know that I expect nothing but your absolute silence on these matters, so see to it you keep your promise. Any moment another person learns about the river, or Drift, or Adira, we both risk imprisonment. Or worse."

Tarri was speechless. The peace that existed within Aobia was in part due to the power of the Sleepers. They regulated the law, industry, and so much more. They were the government. The people who had transformed a broken monarchy into a thriving republic. Yet over the past couple of days, she had learned people could block their abilities, and now she had learned that Nischia, a Sleeper in the Magisterium, had reason to believe other Sleepers could be using their powers for some kind of nefarious voyeurism?

Nischia moved towards the door. "I must go. Please, take this." She handed a small card to Tarri. "Read it. I will await you in my personal quarters for our next meeting—not here. For now, I need to Sleep. I risk everything without Luminosity within my reach."

Nischia rested her hand on the door handle. "Wait!" cried Tarri. "I need to tell you…" She had to tell her about Sedulus entering the store to see her.

"What?" Nischia questioned. "You need to tell me what?"

"Uh, n-nothing, my lady." Tarri bowed. If she told Nischia and anybody else was listening… "Please, enjoy your day." She turned around, hoping Nischia would go before she gave more away.

Nischia looked at her but turned and left. Tarri took a deep breath and recounted what she'd learned. Nischia was spooked by the Sleepers' ability to read her mind. The king of Adira had been killed … and, somehow, this was linked to Drift's exile. After the desperation Tarri had felt waiting for Nischia to visit, she now just had more questions.

Through the window, Tarri spied the sun beginning to hide behind the Canopies, a warm glow infiltrating the Heart. It was time to close up shop. Peeking around the door and into the storefront, she saw Apris and Rela waiting to enter, customers forming a queue behind the counter where they took enquiries. They'd have to clear this line of people, and fast. Then, she needed a drink.

Tarri was slouched over, occupying a chair in The Minister's Secret, her favourite tavern in the Heart. She had a glass of wine in one hand and the paper from Nischia in the other. She'd read it at least twenty times and usually after five or so reads, she'd get another drink from the bar.

Pay attention to those around you.

Apartment 57 at the Sleepers' Quarters in the Mind. Three days from now.

Tell nobody. If I am not there, do not try to find me. I will come to you.

Do not speak to Sedulus.

That was it.

"Ohh," she groaned, her head beginning to hurt. She never drank this much. Never. Not even around Drift and his friends during a night out in the tavern.

"Boom!" A loud voice interrupted her thoughts as a mug of beer smacked down on the table before her, foam spilling over the sides. She looked up, startled to see her friend Flow, the young male who'd connected her to Drift in the first place all those years ago.

"Hi, Flow," she said brightly. Too brightly. Did she stutter?

"I haven't seen you in an age, Tar!" He hugged her. "May I sit?"

Tarri nodded. "Of course, but forgive me… I've drunk some wine." She giggled.

Flow raised his mug in response. "Well, cheers to that, then. Too much wine's not like you, sweet Tarri." He leaned in closer to her, catching her eyes. "Everything all right?"

"I don't know, is everything all right with you?" The smartness in her reply made her laugh even harder and Flow dropped his cheerful demeanour in exchange for a more serious tone.

"I'll say it again, Tarri. Is everything alright?" He gripped her shoulder.

She sucked in air. "Drift's gone." The sentence came out as a mumble and she looked down at her emptying glass.

"What did you say?" Flow moved his seat around to be right next to her and lifted her chin. "Tarri? Is this true?"

She laughed, but she couldn't exactly tell why she did so. "Why would I say it if it wasn't true?" Her emotions changed so quickly, like a summer storm, and she could feel hot tears sting her eyes.

"Canopies above! Are you all right?" Flow wrapped her in an awkward embrace before sliding her wine glass away. "Come, let's get you home. I think a hot cup of tea and a conversation are in order, don't you?"

Tarri nodded and scrambled out of her chair, letting Flow lead her out the door.

They got about halfway to her home before she realised she did not have Nischia's letter. Panic wracked her and she pushed away from Flow. "I left something behind!" She darted off, leaving Flow watching on, puzzled.

She burst back through the doors of The Minister's Secret and over to the table she and Flow had just abandoned. The dirty wine glass and Flow's half full mug of beer were both still on the table, but the letter was nowhere to be seen. "No, no, no!" she whispered.

"Tarri?" Vex appeared behind her, a rag over his shoulder. He was coming to collect the drinkware. "Are you okay?"

She sniffed hopelessly. "No, Vex, I don't think I am," she said, catching her head in her hands.

"Did you leave something behind?"

"A piece of paper from a client," Tarri nodded. "It was so important and in the space of a few minutes, it's disappeared!" She got down on her knees, frantic, and ran her hands over the drink-stained sticky floorboards, catching foreign hairs and bits of crusty who-knew-what, but there was no paper. "What have I done?" She cried, her breath catching.

The door swung open, and she got up to see Flow coming in. "Tarri! What is it?"

"She said she left a letter from a client behind," Vex said to Flow, shrugging. "The Tailory does so well, I doubt it'd hurt her margins to lose one client."

"He's right, Tarri," Flow said. He reached a hand into his coat, retrieving a small, folded square of paper. "I took it with me when we left, you wine-drenched goose."

"Oh, Flow!" She reached her arms around his neck and planted a kiss on his cheek. "What could I possibly have done without you?" She smoothed her skirt. "Now, would you get this wine-drenched goose out of here and home to a cup of tea?"

"Of course," Flow obliged, holding out an arm for her to take.

In the middle of Tarri's small kitchen was a fading, purple lamp. It was powered with a Luminous core that had needed changing for weeks, but she hadn't had the time. Now, she and Flow sat at her table as the light dimmed. It was just past midnight, but the conversation had barely begun.

"So … that's it?" Flow asked, exasperated. "He's exiled because he fell? He could've died for all we know!"

Tarri shook her head. "I don't think he died. Nischia said somebody was bound to come across the body, especially if they were working around that part of the river."

"Do people work around that part of the river?" Flow pressed. "Anything past the viaduct is technically not our land."

"Any land that lies under the shadow of the Great Canopies is ours, though. That's why nobody else lives here until you get into human territory."

Flow nodded. "You are correct. There are a few small towns on the way to the Mountain Gate, but none of them feel enclosed in this." He gestured above his head as though pointing at the branches and leaves that led to the sky. "Tarri, I hate to be the bearer of bad news, but what if the Sleepers…"

He didn't complete the thought aloud and Tarri knew why. If there was a better time to spread secrets, it was while the Sleepers were actually Sleeping, regenerating in their Orbs. But the chance of being caught saying the wrong thing wasn't worth the risk. Especially for somebody like him, a trusted member of the community who was allowed to leave Aobia and bridge the gap between the humans and the Sleepers.

"He isn't dead unless someone says it to my face and has proof." Tarri's eyes dropped. "Besides, Lady Nischia has suggested that she knows something treacherous happened. I think if she wanted to find out, the reason behind that is too great to ignore."

"Fine." Flow put up his hands. "But don't go putting all your eggs in one basket. Is there anything I can do?" He looked sincere, and she realised how much he must be hurting without showing it. He had practically grown up with Drift.

Tarri was uncomfortable as the next words fell out of her mouth. "I don't think he fell, Flow. I think he was pushed." There. She'd said it. She was sobering up as she sipped her tea. She'd been terrified of saying that for days now, but a weight had lifted off her as she had done so.

"That's a serious allegation, Tarri," Flow replied. "What makes you think that?"

She took a sketching pencil and a piece of paper from her desk, the usual tools for planning and designing new clothes. She wrote: *His superior at the viaduct is a male named Sedulus. He was the only witness.*

Flow snatched the pen from her. *Doesn't mean he knew it would happen. Why would somebody want Drift gone?* He added aloud, "Just remember how easy it is to be overly suspicious, Tarri."

She shook her head and took the pencil back. *He wanted Drift gone for the same reason the Magisterium has been interested in him for so long. Read the letter from Nischia.* She handed the paper to Flow and watched as his expression moved from intrigue through surprise, to shock…

"'Do not speak to Sedu—'"

"Flow!" She cupped her hand over his mouth. "Quiet!"

He mouthed a *sorry* at her and gestured for the pencil back. *So, she suspects him too. It is interesting.* He underlined the word 'is' in the last sentence.

"That's all I have to work with," Tarri replied.

"What part does Lady Nischia have to play in this?" Flow asked. "Why's she so determined to help you?"

"I don't know, Flow. Maybe she's just a decent person."

No, he wrote. *Sleepers always have an agenda. Be careful.*

"Well, she told me a thing or two about your recent journey, I'll have you know. And it seems to be of great concern to all of … them."

Flow knew she meant the Sleepers. "I've half a mind to not go back, Tarri," he said. "Stag and I could have been killed."

He looked down before going on. "I can't stop thinking about that king though. It was so sad, Tarri. Seeing his daughter. I've known that girl her whole life." He sighed. "I can't help but feel worried that what happened to the king was the first ripple in an even greater current."

"I'm sorry you had to go through that," Tarri said, reaching for his hand. "What do *you* think the king's death has to do with Drift?"

"I'm not sure," Flow said, stretching. "But I don't like the connection between the two events." He leaned in and looked at her. "I can't promise I'll go back, Tarri, not without sufficient protection. And I'm sorry for that."

The words stung, even though she understood. She looked away while he finished what he was saying.

"But *if* I go back, I'll do whatever it takes to find out more. I can help you. Maybe your Sleeper friend as well. I know a lot more about the humans than most people in Aobia." He studied her. "Let me help. Even if it's only while I'm here. I can't live my life knowing Drift is out there, unable to get back."

"I'd love for you to help, but how would I include you? Isn't it significant enough that I've been included in Nischia's plans? Me, a commoner with a clothing shop?"

"Couldn't you … I don't know, talk to her?" He threw his hands up.

"I … suppose I could," Tarri replied. She considered Flow in the dim candlelight for a moment, his shadow a monstrous mimic of his every move on the wall behind him. She brought her voice to just above a whisper but couldn't hold his gaze. "Flow… You really want to help Drift? You're not just doing this, I don't know…" She shrugged. "For me?" She could feel herself stiffen as the words left her mouth.

Flow looked away and coughed, breaking the tension. "I'm a good friend, Tarri, and the best one Drift ever had. But I can't lie to you and say I don't wish you'd see me for who I really am, too."

This again. Tarri sighed. She had known Flow for so many years, ever since she had been an adolescent, really. For that long, Flow had tried to become closer to her, but she had never let it happen, especially not once she and Drift had become close. It wasn't out of distaste; it was organic, a natural development that had written itself alongside the story she shared with Drift. And the story she shared with Drift was by no means over yet. She couldn't let it be. She felt a sour taste in her mouth.

"Flow, I need to get some sleep." She stood from the table and offered him a hand. "Thank you for walking me home. You're a gentlemale through and through."

"Of course, Tarri. I'll let you rest." Flow said the words with his face turned away from her.

She led him out the door and barely made it to bed before she crashed upon the pillows, still in her clothes.

DRIFT

"**R**aegan," Drift called to the farmer as he was walking to the fields to work. "I'll come with you."

"Why, thank ye, Drift," Raegan said, handing him a steel rake.

"We need to turn the soil in the back half of this field," he continued. "It's up against the road that leads into town."

Drift's ears pricked up. "Town?"

Raegan nodded, an eyebrow raised at the way Drift had responded. "Yeah." He shrugged and kept walking.

"Raegan, you never mentioned there was a town," Drift pushed, following after him.

"Sorry," the farmer replied without turning around. "If you're worried about bein' seen, might be best if ye don't stay too close to the fence."

"I can't stay here forever, Raegan." Drift shook his head. "Though you're right. I just didn't realise we were close to a town, is all."

"Providence," Raegan said. Drift didn't know what that meant in context of the conversation, but a moment later, Raegan added, "Funny name for a dirt-heap town like that. We're closer to Aobia than any other human village. Maybe it's the feel of the forest that gave the town that name." He stopped walking. "If you aren't too worried about it, maybe you can come into town with me at the end of the week. I need to get some supplies and a lending hand will help."

A human town. A *real* human town, this close to his own home. He'd have to ask Flow about it when he got back—

That reminded him of the real reason he'd followed Raegan out here. "Raegan," Drift insisted. "I need to tell you something."

Raegan staked his fork in the ground. They were still not close to the field they were meant to be working, and Drift could tell he was getting testy. "Okay," he harrumphed.

Drift cleared his throat. "I've made my decision, Raegan. I need to keep moving."

"Ahh," Raegan replied, crestfallen. "I see."

"Please don't take it the wrong way… I'm not going yet, I—" he stammered. "I just wanted to make my intentions clear, is all."

Raegan's expression seemed to lighten. "Well, it'll be good to have your help while you're here."

Drift nodded. "You have such fine control over your life, Raegan. It's helped me see that I need to take control of mine."

Raegan laughed.

"What?" Drift asked.

"I don't have nothin', Drift. I've been handed this life and I found my purpose in it. What more are we made for than that?"

Drift chuckled. "I've always wanted to see more of the world and was never allowed to as an Aobian." His face tightened. "The ambassadors who will stay here, Raegan… I will leave with them, if they'll have me."

Raegan pulled his fork out of the ground. "Well, for now, I've got work for ye, and you're not leaving at this minute. Let's go."

They took off through the fields, past the cows, and into the dirty paddocks that Raegan was preparing for wheat. Drift had helped turn soil here earlier in the week after he'd arrived, but the field sprawled before him and provided an illusion of size. It was as though the rainforest he'd just left was smaller than this field, and he wondered how one man achieved something of this grandeur. But Raegan had grown wheat before, despite the conditions and manpower. The man was a marvel, in more ways than one.

"So tell me," Raegan called over his shoulder as they walked. "If it's about seizing control of your life, whose blood was on my dog's teeth that night I sent her over the river?"

Drift stopped.

"Don't lie to me, Drift. We both know you were tracking Morgan and I for a full day before you found us again. But that first night I sent her out, she found herself a hunt. And that was no animal blood. She always brings back her kill for safekeeping."

Time ticked past, the skin on Drift's neck crawling.

"I—"

"I'm not daft, Drift. Heard ye tell Mola you were exiled. I don't care what you did, 'long as you didn't kill anybody."

"Kill?" Drift sputtered. "All I did was fall. I didn't do anything to anyone. But that's not how exile works for us. It was an accident. I worked on river maintenance and fell from the waterfall." He squeezed his hands into tight fists. "However, I'm no longer sure that I *did* fall. In fact, I think I was forced into the circumstance."

"So, what are you saying? Somebody wanted ye gone?" Raegan spat onto the ground, scratching his neck.

Drift held the farmer's gaze. "Have you heard of Nightingales?"

Raegan frowned. "The birds, ye mean? Don't have 'em much round these parts. More of a woodland bird, like the forests that line the mountain ranges to the north, Sethiliquin and the like."

"I'm not talking about the birds, Raegan. Men and women, humans dressed in cloaks blacker than night, looking for me."

Raegan's eyes grew narrow, and he looked out into the distance, pondering Drift's words. "I can't say I've heard of them. But one comes knockin', they won't know what hit 'em. You're safe here, Drift, understand? Like the ambassadors that stop overnight." He sighed. "And as for your 'exile'… You find proof that someone meant for you to be down here and not up there, and I think they'll let you go home."

Drift bowed his head. "I fully intend it."

Drift was working up and down the roadside the next day when the first sign of new hope blossomed: a rusty cabriolet with dark wooden panels on all sides was coming down the road from the way of the forest. The front of the cab had on it a bronze badge, an eye inside a stylised sun. This came from Aobia. A grin broke his dirt-smeared face.

The two black horses that pulled the carriage slowed to a stop, giving Drift time to walk to the fence. There were only two ambassadors allowed to leave Aobia at any given time, and for the last twenty or so years, they had been the same people. That meant Flow and Stag were here. Drift acknowledged the odd blend of nerves and excitement in his belly. Flow was his best friend and he'd never been so excited to see him until now. Even Stag with his smug, arrogant face would be welcome.

The door opened with a squeak. "Flow!"

But no. Stag had come unaccompanied. Drift shivered. He'd spoken to Flow the other night in The Minister's Secret. Had something happened to him that kept him detained? "Stag," he said, his jaw dropping in disbelief. "But Raegan said…"

"Drift?" Stag said, pulling down the hood that was covering his head. "My friend, you're alive! You know the farmer?" Drift clenched his teeth. He and Stag weren't friends. But Stag was a necessary part of his circle. Tarri thought Stag was wonderful, Vex laughed at his jokes, and Flow loved him like a brother. And yet every time he met this stuck-up, snide piece of—

"It's good to see you, Drift. I can't lie. I never thought I'd say that," Stag chuckled.

"Well, if only it were under better circumstances," Drift replied coolly.

The gentle breeze rustling the grass was the only sound that disrupted the awkward silence.

"Drift, I was told about what happened," Stag said.

"I don't know what you were told," Drift replied. "Whatever happened it wasn't by choice."

"I tend to agree," Stag nodded. "Look, I have my own thoughts on the matter. And I know you're wondering why I'm travelling alone. Let's go to the farmer's house and we can speak properly. I need a cup of coffee, anyway. I'm awfully listless."

"Coffee?" Drift asked. "You drink that human stuff?"

"It's bitter, but I've grown to like it," Stag said. "Like many things in the human lands."

Drift considered Stag from a new angle. He had never seen him display enthusiasm for anything. But here, he was … natural. And Drift didn't find him half as annoying as he usually did.

"Let's go, then. Catch up in the house."

"Right!" Stag jumped back into the driver's seat of the cab. "Hop in and I'll detach the horses by the barn."

"Farmer Raegan tells me you've been an adequate worker, Drift," Stag commented while they ate at the dining table, a long hardwood affair that Drift knew Raegan had to have made.

"I try," he muttered.

Raegan coughed. "So, Ambassador, what brings you here so soon after your last trip?"

"Something happened during my last visit to Adira," Stag replied, chewing. "Have you heard the news? Surely, it's made its way here."

Drift watched Raegan and Mola raise their eyebrows. Of course they didn't know. He recalled Flow telling him about the dead king nearly a week ago when they had met at The Minister's Secret.

"Haven't heard any news." Raegan shrugged with a dark expression.

Stag hesitated and took a mouthful of food to cover it up.

"Ambassador, what is it?" Mola asked.

"Nothing's come from Providence?" Stag ignored her question, looking puzzled. "I hate to be the one telling you this, but King Terrens has been assassinated."

Mola cupped her mouth while Raegan put his fork down, shocked.

Stag waited a moment before continuing. "He was killed during my last visit to Adira. I was hunted as a suspect along with my colleague. But I'm certain of who killed him: an ambassador from Therador who arrived and visited the king that same day."

"Therador?" Raegan scratched his head, clearly perturbed. "This is no tale, Ambassador? Ye talk the truth?"

Stag nodded, not daring to say another word.

"Then we have to go to Providence. What if Gaudin doesn't know?"

"Who is Gaudin?" asked Drift.

"The town elder in Providence." Raegan looked to Mola. "Tomorrow at dawn, we leave with the children and these two." He gestured to the Aobians. "You'll be on your way from there and we'll have no further correspondence with ye after that. Never thought it would come to this in my lifetime."

Mola seemed to be choking back tears and Drift's frown deepened to a crater-sized line. "You'll not speak with us again? What is the meaning of this, Raegan?"

"Please take no personal insult, Drift," Raegan responded. "But there's about to be a turbulent world at our doorstep and we need to stick with our own. You've got Stag now and with him is the best place for ye. You said it yerself: you need to keep moving." He stood from the table, taking his plate to the kitchen. "Now, it's time to rest. Let's clean up and turn in for the night."

No words were uttered for the rest of the evening, as the fire burnt down, leaving behind the crackling of embers and the faint sobs of Mola upstairs in her bed by the window. On the other side of the loft, Raegan was snoring. Drift was lonely again, a feeling he was usually okay with, but recent events weighed heavily on him. He didn't want to lose any of what he had, from his old life with Tarri to this newfound appreciation for the human lands. He felt he was standing on the edge of a great cliff and would fall at any moment.

Stag was lying down on his own stuffed mattress, eyes open to the dancing shadows of the firelight on the ceiling. "What really happened to you, Drift? How did you end up here?"

Drift considered how he would recount his story. Stag wouldn't believe him. "There was a breach of the Sickness in the river, somewhere far upstream. In the chaos of trying to treat the water, Sedulus and I were caught on the edge of the waterfall. I've never seen water so … alive, Stag. It was terrifying, climbing up in waves I've only ever heard about in stories of the oceans. I slipped, and Sedulus tried to haul me up." He sighed. "I don't know whether he let go because he wasn't strong enough to hold me or because he had planned it all along. But I remember his eyes, Stag. There was something there."

Stag sighed. "If you really think something more … sinister caused your exile, then you need to find the answers."

"Have you heard of Nightingales?" Drift asked.

Something flashed across Stag's face, a faint recognition. "Mercenaries of a kind, but more dangerous. They were the intermediary between Queen Feldra and Therador all those years ago. An organisation aimed at exposing and containing the secrets of others. They sell the information when people offer enough money. They have no true loyalties."

"The night after I fell," Drift explained, "they found me in the forest. I thought it was poor luck. Now, I'm beginning to think they were waiting for me all along. But I don't know why."

"Why would your superior at the facility care about getting rid of you?" Stag asked, wary. "Be careful of being needlessly suspicious, Drift."

"I've asked myself the same thing, Stag. But my counter-question is this: why did those Nightingales want me in their grasp so badly? If not for Raegan and his dog, they would have seized me for sure. And they were a *long* way from home."

Stag nodded. "True enough, I suppose… But Drift, the Sleepers keep a tight watch on organisations such as the Water Management Facility. They would never let anyone communicate with humans on the outside of the Tree."

"I don't think the Sleepers are all they're made up to be, Stag. People like you and Tarri never gave me the chance to explain myself." Drift closed his eyes, turning over on his mattress to face the wall. "I don't like you much. I dealt with your stubbornness, your arrogance, because Flow was my best friend and he asked to include you when we were out together at the tavern and things. I hope I make myself clear in that regard.

"But I will do what I can to help you if you'll help me. Help me find the answers and figure out what really happened. Maybe you'll be proven right and it all will turn out to be an unfortunate series of coincidences. But I need to know. And I need you to bring me home with you, too. I can't leave my life behind like this. I can't leave Tarri or Flow." Stag had begun to snooze when Drift spoke the last words. "I can't have nobody at all."

That was when Drift began to understand a part of himself too foreign to yet touch and hold but close enough to see. This was his biggest fear.

To be alone.

The night was much colder and the patter of rain began with such serene taps on the roof that they slowly rocked Drift to sleep. The next day would bring with it a whole new world to explore. Whatever optimism he had left for that, he had to conserve.

His last thoughts let go into the deep night.

NISCHIA

NISCHIA LISTENED TO THE thrum of the Orb from behind the curtains in the corner of her small apartment, biting her lip.

She focused on its call, readying herself for Sleep. The dangerous journey into the heart of the Orb always carried a risk that she might not emerge again. But she needed to do this. She couldn't keep relying on pre-filled *cism* to shield with, and she felt so … empty without Luminosity rushing through her. A full cycle of Sleep would give her enough to protect herself and Tarri for the week to come. Something was amiss in the Magisterium, something Nischia couldn't quite put her finger on. Koln had still not come to speak with her since they had left the auditorium, and she wondered how deeply the investigation with Drift went.

A cup of hot tea quivered in her unsteady hand. The same nervous butterflies that she usually felt before Sleep fluttered about, stirring an uneasy aggression in her stomach. Sleep took everything from her, so much so that when she returned, she was more tired than if she'd gone a full night without bedrest. But she needed the Luminosity to be able to help shield Tarri and herself when they were in conversation, especially after Staril had announced that the twelve Senior Sleepers had been keeping Drift under their watchful gaze since he'd been born. These secrets should not have existed. Hadn't that been the primary reason they'd had for doing away with the monarchy all those years ago?

Her mind flashed back to the night after Drift had fallen from the viaduct at the Water Management Facility. She'd used *cism* then to heat map the area and analyse it for any evidence of tampering. There'd been nothing, not even the faintest outline of footsteps along the bridge. Sedulus had seemed honest, too, recounting the events without so much as a stutter. The algae had died upstream and the river had raged like a sea and washed any evidence of what had happened away. Then, Drift had been on a raft, set loose towards its inevitable end over the waterfall, and Sedulus had managed to grab his harness cable from the viaduct. He'd let go when he'd realised he couldn't hold on because of the water pressure.

Their conversation replayed in her mind.

"No sign of footsteps," she said after mapping the area. *"If you were here at all, there should be some sign of something."*

Koln pursed his lips but said nothing, waiting for Sedulus to reply.

"My lady, there is no simpler explanation than what I have already told you. I managed to leave the raft and climb onto the viaduct, but the water must have washed any signs of me away."

"It very well may be that simple, Nischia," Koln replied, his eyes like stone. *"The other workers were all witnesses to the river's sudden swelling. The Sickness must have been so highly concentrated that the river practically boiled on its way through."*

"If it had boiled, you would have been hurt, surely," Nischia said, turning back to Sedulus.

"No, Lady Nischia," Sedulus replied, shaking his head. *"I managed to escape the viaduct before the river rushed past. There were seconds between Drift's harness breaking and me fleeing to the end of the bridge. The water was hot, but it was not boiling. Clouds of steam enshrouded me and I could not find my way back to the station."*

She studied his face, looking for a hint of a lie. His eyes were as blue as the coldest winter day, as though they carried a touch of frost.

"And the algae?" she asked. *"Tell me with certainty, operator. Has the algae been restored?"*

Sedulus gulped. "Almost instantaneously. It seems that the cism *store was depleted on one of the backup generators."*

There wasn't much to support that happening unaided. *Cism* delivery was high priority to the facility due to the pertinent nature of fresh water needing to flow through to the northern lands. If a *cism* generator had gone down, there would have been plenty of backups to supplement it until it was serviced with new *cism*. Someone *had* to have tampered with a generator for the algae to have died. And for them to be revived instantly. Then again, Nischia still couldn't say with certainty that she'd seen deceit in Sedulus' eyes that night.

She did, however, see deceit elsewhere. Tarri had been there that night too and she hadn't shielded herself very well, although Nischia suspected the girl didn't have a clue she was already capable of doing so. But there was something in that little tailor. Nischia recalled her mother's words when she'd first exited their lives as a newly blessed Sleeper. "An insidious curse…" Her mother's own words to describe her. She wondered if it hadn't just been her that felt that way sometimes.

She shook her head as though she was trying to shake the thoughts out when a loud rap of knuckles sounded on her door. She walked over, unlatching the door and opening it to Koln. "Superior," she said.

"Don't toy with me, child," Koln seethed. "I saved both our necks today. The amount of times I need to stop you from saying the wrong thing at the wrong time… After all these years, you are still as impetuous as ever!"

"And you!" Nischia hissed, shoving a stubborn finger into his chest. "You still treat me as your lesser. I will never be good enough for you!"

Koln said nothing for a moment, but was cool as ever when he did speak. "Make it easier for me, Nischia, and you may get what you want one day."

Nischia huffed as she stalked back down the entrance hall and fell into her green armchair, crossing her arms. "Something is amiss, Koln. Do not try to tell me differently."

"After all we've been through," Koln started, "you think I would keep things from you?"

"You didn't tell me about the king, did you?"

"I DIDN'T KNOW ABOUT THE KING!" Koln roared, hurling an arm out and knocking a light green vase to the ground with a smash. Red-faced, he panted like a dog that had run its course.

Nischia recoiled. "I—"

"Enough." Koln rubbed his forehead, agitated. "I'm sorry."

"Of course," Nischia said, barely above a whisper. "I'm sorry, Koln. I just assumed that—"

"Well, you assumed wrong!" he retorted. "I was telling you the full and complete truth when I said that we had to go to the parliamentary sitting. I didn't know the extent of the announcement."

"You think Therador did it?" she pressed. The tyrant emperor, Jurin, was the next in a long line of bloodthirsty leaders, all of which had been responsible for much of the conflict on Q'ara since Settlement over two millennia prior. Nischia did not doubt Jurin's power, nor did she doubt how incredibly well he could toy with the world around him, like it was really in the palm of his hands already.

"I don't know what to think." He turned to face the window, standing parallel to her armchair and gazing out at the clean-cut botanical gardens across the branchroad. "But I'm afraid that the exile is not an unrelated incident."

"*The exile* namely being a boy called Drift." Nischia rolled her eyes. "Fitting name for an exile, isn't it?"

Koln caught her gaze with a dark expression. "What are you insinuating?"

"Nothing in particular."

"Naming Rituals have been outlawed for nearly a century, Nischia. That boy, Drift, is no Named child."

Nischia looked away from him, somewhere into the pits of the green armchair. "Mother was Named," she whispered.

"I never should have told you that." Koln's tone was self-critical, but equally gentle. "It was not my place."

"Eanif. In the Old Tongue: *tempestuous. Self-defeating. Inescapable.*" Nischia felt a tear well and wiped at it with an aggressive hand. "Look where she ended up. In bed, crazy, until she finally gave in to death's call."

"The Naming was not designed to doom people, Nischia."

She stood, surprised at her sudden anger as she shoved him backward, his shoulder colliding with the window frame. "Then what *did* it do, Superior? What did it do for any of us?"

She went to shove him again, but Koln quickly and easily took her hand. "It gave us what we thought was a perfect world. Until Feldra."

"Until Feldra." The last Queen of Aobia was the greatest heartache of Nischia's life. Not only had she been the first to welcome her into her vocation as a Sleeper, but she'd been the first of Nischia's kind to have betrayed them, sharing secrets of Luminosity with Therador in exchange for money. She'd started an uprising and died at Nischia's own hand. Her role model turned to char before her eyes. Years later, Koln had revealed that

Feldra had not been an ordinary citizen after all. She had, in fact, been Named after her birth and subsequent Blessing.

"Fe'l meant *good omen*."

"Indeed?" Nischia retorted. "A fat lot of *good* that omen was! She was doomed from the beginning, Koln, living a life driven by existential pressure and the inability to fulfil the purpose that had been imposed on her. What if she thought, in those last days, that she was right? Who should've been put in a cell for that, Koln? Staril and her Seniors?"

"I think this conversation has taken a turn for the worse, child. I expect you to meet me, accompanied by your tailor, in a few days' time. Until then, let us not pick at the scraps we have dropped."

"Fine." She strode to the curtained-off area that contained her Orb. "I will see you then, and not a moment sooner, thank the Canopies."

"You're Sleeping tonight?" Koln raised an eyebrow. "I thought you'd had enough for a few weeks. You'd said as much."

Nischia stopped, her thoughts whirling. She couldn't tell him she needed the Luminosity to shield both her and Tarri's minds. She couldn't tell him that her age-old mistrust of the Magisterium had worked its way back into her life. Preposterous, he would say. An outrage to be holding on to that history.

But she had not forgotten her pain. That of letting the final burst of concentrated Luminosity incinerate her queen years ago had never left her. Neither had the pain of her abandonment when she'd fallen to the Fever and awoken blessed by the Tree, cut off from her family and hurled into a new world, a new life.

Her mind crossed to other things, like the snow of the Mountain Pass, where she had seen so many good people die in the war. Her mother's death. Her sister's death. Her other sister, the one whom she'd depended on as a new Sleeper, disappearing suddenly.

It might have been history. But it was not dead.

"I … used too much. When we were scanning the Water Management Facility and trying to pick at the tailor's thoughts," she explained, though Koln's eyebrows remained unchanged.

"The girl has worn away at your probing?"

Nischia was prepared to save face. She didn't need to lie about this next part. "It seems she can block my probing, though she is unaware that she is doing so. Some careful control of her emotions and she'll be shielding like a Sleeper soon enough."

"A genetic trait?" Koln looked startled. "There aren't many, Nischia. You're sure about this? That would mean that she is the child of—"

"I know. One of us." She let air pass through her nostrils, heavy and thick. "I'm as puzzled as you."

"You must not teach her the control she lacks." This was no request, but a command.

"Of course not. Again, you take me as a fool, though I have been a good student for a century."

"You are still young, child. Being a good student is not enough to convince me that you are not, at times, fool-headed." With that, Koln turned sharply, paced towards the front of the apartment, and left, the door slamming behind him.

The silence that should have settled in after his departure was interrupted by the thrum of the Orb once more. Fear gripped her, as it always did. Fear of a nova event, of burning out and becoming not someone, but *something* else. Fear of never returning. But still, the Orb sang its song. It did not sing a song of repose but a song of life, of chaos and order, imbalance and harmony. It sang as she opened the curtains, submissive to its opulent, warm glow. It sang as she pressed her hand to its surface, feeling herself cross over into a place that defied the natural order, though it was given to her by the Great Tree. It sang. It roared.

It swallowed.

TARRI

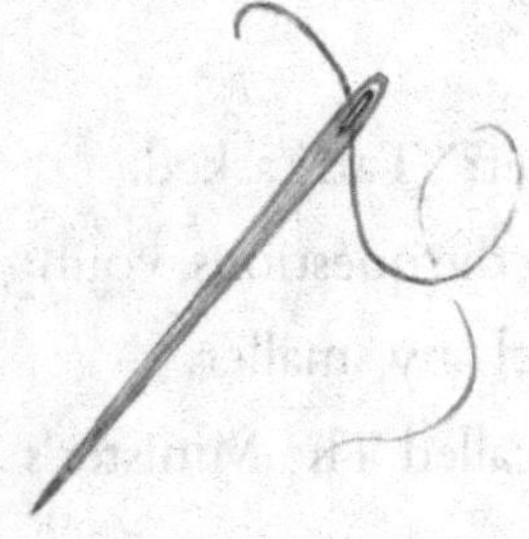

N ISCHIA STOOD AT THE door of the Tailory, wearing her flat and weary expression that suggested she was not in a good mood. *A new challenge for a new day,* Tarri thought. Her head ached from the wine the night before, and she didn't have it in her to face off with the Sleeper within minutes of unlocking the door to the Tailory.

"You look … ragged," Nischia said.

"I'd rather not talk about it," Tarri responded as she led Nischia inside.

"I recommend not over-indulging on wine until your emotions have smoothed out, Tarri dear."

It might have been the lack of morning tea or the headache that remained from the night before that caused Tarri to snap. "Excuse me?"

Nischia recoiled. "How dare you speak to me like that! What in the world happened to you last night?"

"I'm sorry," Tarri apologised. "You're right. I did let myself go last night."

Nischia stepped forward and grabbed Tarri's wrist. "Alone? In public?"

"Why does it matter?" Tarri asked.

"I'm the one asking the questions, young lady." That one stung. She didn't need to feel any smaller.

"I was at a tavern called The Minister's Secret," Tarri gave in, her eyes downcast.

Nischia shifted slightly, as though there was something significant about the old stomping ground.

"What is it, my lady?"

"Nothing." Nischia shook her head. "I succumb to superstition on occasion, that's all." She looked into Tarri's eyes. "Mind your manners, Tarri. And keep your head about you. Right now is no time for frivolity."

"It wasn't frivolity as much as anxiety, my lady," Tarri said, rubbing the back of her neck.

"It doesn't matter what it was. It was not appropriate and remains to be that way for the foreseeable future. I thought I made myself clear the last time we spoke. Putting yourself in a vulnerable position like that meant risking telling others about what's been going on. We both understand the importance of staying quiet. Be diligent. And grow up. Now is not the time for complacency. Am I clear?"

Tarri nodded. "Of course, my lady." She couldn't help but wonder: why the sense of urgency?

She felt like Nischia was trustworthy, for the most part, but the gap between the two of them was stark. They were worlds apart, two completely different people united by only one common thread in each other's storylines. Today, that difference felt especially vast, and Tarri was acutely aware of testing the Sleeper. She was playing with fire, and fire was the antithesis of life.

Then, there was the question of the letter Nischia had given her the day before.

Pay attention to those around you.

Apartment 15 at the Sleepers' Quarters in the Mind. Three days from now.

Tell nobody. If I am not there, do not try to find me. I will come to you.

Yet here she was, before Tarri at her place of work. And then, the most haunting part. The part that meant that Nischia could read her mind.

Do not speak to Sedulus.

"We must move on," Nischia declared. "You'll need to ask your girls to look after the shop today, I'm afraid. I'm stealing you away."

Tarri felt her mood lift. "I'm captivated. Where are we going?"

"The Mind," Nischia replied.

Tarri was going to the Mind. The home of the Sleepers. The centre of politics and leadership for all of Aobia. It was rare that an ordinary Aobian would need to travel there, but if the occasion arose, it was always a highlight. Many, as it turned out, had never visited the Mind, as their respect, mixed with wariness for the Sleepers, usually made them feel as though they should remain in the Heart and Soul.

Tarri had complicated feelings about the Sleepers, overall. On one hand, they created clear elitism between the people of Aobia, even though any Sleeper would present their societal position differently and accentuate the myth of a hierarchy. They still listened to the people without permission, and if they did that, what else did they do? On the other hand, they managed the judicial system well and protected the freedom of Aobians, which was something she could not say for the Sleepers of times past, when they'd used their Luminosity for the wrong reasons, like the outlawed Naming Rituals.

Drift used to always say—or more truthfully *insist*—that some people were still being born fixed to their destiny by their names. He had been superstitious about this for as long as she'd known him, uncomfortable in his own skin and unable to hold down aspects of stability that infiltrated his life. Was Lady Nischia's superstition of a similar nature?

"I thought you'd react more, in all honesty." Nischia shrugged after interrupting Tarri's racing thoughts.

"Oh!" Tarri covered her mouth, suddenly aware of her rudeness. "No. I'm sorry, my lady, I got lost in thought for a moment. I understand what a privilege it is to—"

"Pfft." Nischia waved a hand past Tarri's face to shut her up. "Privilege. There shouldn't be such a thing. But you are, of course, correct. Now, please go and tell the girls that you're leaving the shop up to them and come along. We've got places to be and deadlines to meet."

"Of course." Tarri whirled in the other direction and went into the shop to tell Apris and Rela. It was both tickling and sobering to see Nischia react to Tarri's mention of privilege. Either the Mind wasn't as interesting as it seemed to the common Aobian or Nischia was highly aware of the shortcomings of the social ladder in Aobia.

"Ah, there you both are!" Tarri said as she went from the shopfront to the storeroom. Apris and Rela were both in cheery conversation and had clearly just shown up for work. "I've got some bad news for you both, I'm afraid."

"Miss Tarri, is everything okay?" Rela asked.

"I have some business to attend to in the Mind today, so I'll need you two to do the best you can and hold down the fortress."

Apris cupped her mouth. "Miss Tarri, the Mind? Is Lady Nischia helping you to expand already?" She squealed with delight.

"No! No, sadly you've got it wrong. I am going with Lady Nischia, but I do not yet know how it relates to the business. I will have to report back to you tomorrow."

That shut the mood down and both girls looked sombre. *Go easy,* Tarri thought. *They have no idea what's going on, nor should they.*

"Is everything all right, Miss Tarri?"

Tarri turned back to the door as she replied. "Of course, Rela. Just business to attend to, as usual."

The streets were raucous as Nischia and Tarri practically fled the Soul in a horse-pulled cabriolet.

"Are we in a particular rush, my lady?" Tarri called over the rushing wind. She'd ridden a cab dozens of times, but never this fast. People darted and dodged around them as they travelled down the packed branchroads.

"Of course, my dear," Nischia replied without looking at her. "A rush to leave the Soul at Endweek!" She pulled on the reigns. The Endweek crowds amongst the markets, taverns, and shops were tremendous every time, but Tarri loved the energy of the Aobian people out and about after working for days on end. She thrived off the buzz. At the same time, being a shopkeeper meant she could take her rest days when most others worked, leaving her with quiet time to herself, a relished occasion.

"You're not a fan of the crowds then?"

"No," Nischia replied. "And I don't think I'll ever be. Thankfully, being a Sleeper keeps me in the Mind most of the time."

Tarri felt uncomfortable hearing that. They were taught that the Sleepers looked over people and watched after them through their Sleep, which powered every part of the Great Tree. Tarri tended to believe what she was taught, but she couldn't help but feel that Nischia enjoyed, maybe even revelled, in the separation between her and the 'common people'.

The drive connecting the Soul to the Mind was no short travel, taking a few hours and laden mostly with silence. They hadn't spoken to each other since they'd left the market district. Finally approaching the Supreme Court, which bridged the two Great Canopies, Tarri wondered why Nischia pressed on with such intensity. Her shoulders were tight and her head was down, as though she could not be moved off her path. Maybe she was nervous. That thought made Tarri nervous. What were they to truly face in the Mind?

Tarri tried to let these worries go as they sped past the Supreme Court and into the Mind, the road laced with manicured botanical gardens. Hedgerows edged the paths, and beyond were vast arrays of different plants, most in bloom and drenched with natural perfume. "It's beautiful," Tarri found herself saying. She'd been here before, as a young child. But the sight of the place was always something to behold.

"It is," Nischia agreed. "It's like this all year."

All year? How could these plants be green or colourfully blooming all year? Nischia seemed to read her mind.

"Luminosity, Tarri," she said.

Tarri nodded. "Oh." She couldn't tell whether she could ask more questions about that or not. She knew little of how Luminosity could be wielded, but she also knew with certainty how powerful it was. What could Luminosity *not* do? It lit the streets, worked machines, healed the sick, and could even be used as a weapon.

"You don't want to ask about it," Nischia replied. It wasn't a question but a statement.

Tarri looked away as Nischia eyed her. "Well, my la—"

Nischia put up a hand. "It's because we listen, isn't it?"

How can I possibly answer that? She felt heat rushing to her cheeks. An inexplicable anger washed over her. She felt like Drift. Conspiratorial and never trusting the Sleepers. But why would Nischia prompt this discussion from her?

Nischia was stiff, but her voice was softer than usual when she responded. "My dear, may I excuse myself with ignorance, just for a moment?"

Tarri nodded slowly, cautiously.

"Tell me if this is what people really think. Be honest, Tarri."

Tarri swallowed as her mind raced, trying to put a sentence together. "Um … in my experience…" She hesitated. "Yes."

"The truth is what you deserve," Nischia said quietly, as if to herself.

"And what is that?" Tarri asked.

Nischia took a long sniff of the clean air as they turned a bend in the street. "Come," she said. "We have much to do and never the appropriate amount of time in which to do it."

Around the bend, the world of the Great Tree opened to an array of spectacular architecture. This was the Mind, the home of the Sleepers.

Grand buildings stretched as far as the eye could see, still fronted on the opposite side of the road by carefully arranged and maintained gardens. The buildings were several storeys high and yet they were somehow still carved *into* the Greatbranch of this section of the Tree, the mark of the most skilled branchrenders. Vinous and floral carvings decorated supporting wooden pillars along the expanse of buildings, painted beautifully and shimmering in the daylight.

One of the furthermost buildings she could see, but equally the most breathtaking, was the dome-topped Magisterium. It had been described to her many times, but never had she seen it with her own eyes. Perhaps the most striking thing about it, though, were the windows. The Great Tree sat above dense rainforest, thus making it relatively temperate all year. But between the costs involved and the chill in the middle of winter, most Aobians relied on window cavities that could open and close, never a glass panel through which you could look out. Windows along the Magisterium, conversely, spanned ceiling to floor, allowing the greatest views to those who worked within. Even odder, Tarri noted, was the fact that she couldn't see into them.

"It's stunning, isn't it?" Nischia asked.

"The windows," Tarri murmured.

"The windows?" Nischia stifled a snort. "Oh, child, they're just windows!"

Tarri felt her anger from earlier return. They were not the same. She bit her tongue and said nothing.

"We're nearly there," Nischia said as they turned down a street that forked off into the gardened area. "And this is home." Nischia gestured to a long building that extended all the way down the street, once again walled with the same all-encompassing windows Tarri had seen at the Magisterium, though not as large.

Tarri couldn't take it all in at once as they stepped out of the cabriolet, the horses stopping by a neat water bath on the side of the road. "Which one is yours, my lady?"

"I'll show you around, of course," was Nischia's reply as she beckoned Tarri to step past the ornate, open iron gate that bordered the property and its gardens from the street.

The first thing Tarri noticed once they'd walked through a carefully upkept garden and into the foyer of the branchren-dered building was the oppressive silence. The inside of the building was neat, yet overall plainer than she would have presumed. Green hall runners reminiscent of the colour of the foliage within which they lived covered the floors and windy staircases between levels. Grand banisters marked the stairs, decorated with embossed patterns of vines that caught in the sunlight streaming through the windows. But besides that, the building was a simple, mahogany thing with tightly sculpted and painted walls and nearly perfect floorboards that mimicked the branchground outside.

"Come, child," Nischia whispered before climbing the stairs. Tarri followed, sensing the sound of her feet padding gently into the green rug and trying to quieten them even further. Nischia must have sensed her anxiety as she whirled around and said, "I would have you relax when you visit my home."

Well, Tarri thought. *An order's an order.* "Thank you, my lady."

They wandered down the hall, which forked in different directions along the windowed backdrop of an expansive garden. On the opposite wall from the windows, however, was a repeating pattern of green panel doors decorated with beautiful carvings that mimicked the design language of everything else in the building. Each one had a brass number plate upon it and Tarri realised they were the homes of the Sleepers. Given the spaces between the doors and what she'd seen of the front of the building, she could only assume they were no small apartments.

Eventually they stopped in front of one of the green doors, the carving on it depicting an eye in a large circle that looked like the sun. Nischia removed a key from under her dress and Tarri noted that she must've had it strapped to her thigh as some kind of precaution. Was she a typical, classist Sleeper? Or was she practical? Tarri couldn't decide which side of the female she'd seen more of.

"Don't stand there, child," chided Nischia. "The door is open for a reason."

Tarri took a step, crossing a threshold that felt too significant for her, a common tailor. Inside were Nischia's personal quarters, and Tarri was shocked at how humble a home it appeared to be. The entryway was a long hall, giving Tarri not much of a glimpse of what lay beyond it. But what she did see was a simple coat stand, a small dresser beside it for things like jewellery or a pair of shoes.

Tarri stood by the door, not daring to move as Nischia returned from another part of the apartment. "Well, it's not going to bite, dear," Nischia said, mystified at Tarri's stillness. "However, we don't have time for more than a glance anyway. We need to go now. We have a meeting." Under her arm, Nischia clutched a leather roll designed to keep a longer piece of parchment paper protected.

"A meeting, my lady?"

"My superior," Nischia replied. "His name is Koln. He's a good person, albeit firm."

Nischia swept her back out the door, closing it behind her, although Tarri noticed she did not lock it. Nischia caught Tarri's eye in a moment so quick, she wasn't sure whether she saw mistrust or concentration there.

Nischia went on. "Koln is among the highest-ranked Sleepers. He's a Senior in the Magisterium, though he still works a hard job, unlike some others, who exist only for Sleep and the occasional meeting." Her words carried with them a tinge of spite.

This was true. Many of the Senior Sleepers, the ones that powered The Great Tree, Slept in their Orbs for much of the year, as they were elderly and less involved in the political machinations of Aobia.

Turning the corner down the hall, Nischia pointed out the window to a neatly managed square hedge that closed in around a smaller tree, affronted by a square of beautiful benches for private sitting. On one sat a male Aobian with the specific marking of a Sleeper: shining, silver hair glowing around him despite the bright sun that shone down from above. "There he is," Nischia said. "Let's not keep him waiting."

With her back to Tarri, Nischia explained, "Once we've met with Koln, we'll be conducting an interview."

"An interview? With who?"

"The male, Sedulus, with whom your beloved worked."

Tarri felt her face go warm with rage. Nischia and her superior might not have had the proof they needed to verify Sedulus' place in Drift's exile, but Tarri needed nothing more than a feeling. Nischia still hadn't explained the meaning of her letter or why Tarri had been collected by her in person, despite the clear warning in her message.

"Your silence does not inspire confidence in me, dear," Nischia said, her voice low as she turned to face Tarri, stopping them.

"With respect, my lady," Tarri started, "I do not know what you expect me to say or how you expect me to react. You write a vague message, telling me that—"

"Do *not* speak and watch your emotions around Koln!" Nischia hissed, pushing an assertive hand in front of Tarri's mouth. "Can you not *read,* child?"

"What can I possibly respond with, then?" Tarri retorted, frustrated. Watch her emotions? What an outrage! "You leave things unexplained and then you shut me up! Why must we meet with Sedulus? You would have me believe he is innocent!" Exasperation revealed something in her voice that she didn't want Nischia to hear. Weakness, perhaps, subject to the wiles of love. "I saw you that night, my lady. Speaking to him with your superior."

Nischia raised an eyebrow but remained silent.

"Yes, that's right," Tarri pressed. "I've seen him before, too. And I can't say I trust you or your actions entirely."

"You wish to be involved? You go out at night. You're irresponsible and with an unequivocally untrustworthy friend. And you pretend so much. Our secrets will get out, Tarri, if you continue down this path. Well, if that's how this will be, then perhaps this relationship will not work at all!"

"How do you know about that?" Tarri could only think to ask about the night before, the drunkenness, and Flow, because she was humiliated about it.

"I know less than I would like of when that *pest* involves himself in higher business."

"Flow?" Tarri urged. "He is a friend of Drift's and mine, incidentally."

"A friend?" A nasty curl turned Nischia's lips upward as she said this and Tarri felt a seed of doubt that she had not felt before, as though the Sleeper knew things about someone in her life that she didn't. "My dear, that sorry excuse for an ambassador is no friend of yours. And I'd expressly ask that you stay away from him. Do not offer him any information you would not otherwise offer a person off the street."

"How dare you say such things! Flow is a good person and a loyal friend!"

"Well," Nischia said, "that loyal friend is, and has been, of particular interest to the Magisterium. I would wager he did not tell you that he has been retired from his position, did he?"

Tarri said nothing and Nischia went on.

"Many have reason to believe his intentions are more malevolent than most would presume. Perhaps if you trusted me more than you just explained, you would see that for yourself." She continued down the hall. "Maybe I've made a mistake in bringing you along. Your passion outweighs your rational sense, though you are no idiot. Your maturity, however, leaves something to be desired."

Tarri's cheeks burned. So Flow had something to do with Drift's exile, too? Or was it a different matter that had led to Nischia's hatred of him?

"This is your chance, Tarri," Nischia murmured as she headed down a set of stairs leading to the garden where Koln waited. "What you do is up to you. But if you go back, I hope for your sake that we never cross paths again."

The Sleeper's ice-blue eyes seemed to stop time.

"Do not test me, girl, for I could crush you like a bug."

DRIFT

"**A** TRIP INTO PROVIDENCE is no small venture, though it is our closest town," Raegan said as they prepared the horses. Morgan gazed up from the doorstep of Raegan's homestead.

"Be good, girl," Raegan said, fluffing up her white mane. She had ample food and water out for the two days it would take the farmer and his family to return.

They packed into Stag's carriage like sardines. It was lucky they could all fit and Drift had thanked him for bringing a 'comfortable' ride with him.

"How long, roughly?" Drift asked. It was just after dawn as they departed the farm.

Mola took the turn to answer, glancing up at the low sun. "We'll get there in three hours, maybe a little longer. It's no short haul to go there and back in a day. But it can be done."

"And what an occasion like no other," Raegan agreed with his sister, though Drift could tell by the hard lines on his face that he was hesitant to proceed down this road with two Aobians, one an exile and the other an official who seemed slightly unhinged. Drift couldn't blame him, really. The outburst from the previous night still echoed in his mind.

"When we arrive," Raegan said, "we'll need to follow the same storyline and keep up with it. I believe the mayor, Gaudin, will be in for a hard word with ye both once the news flies—if he doesn't already know. Don't say I haven't warned ye."

"So what's the plan?" Drift pressed.

"We will need to be quick about it. I don't want my family to be involved in the truth-telling."

"I understand," Drift nodded. "I wouldn't think anything less of you, Raegan. The care in your heart is great."

"Thank ye," Raegan conceded. "The children will go with you, Mola." He nodded to his sister. "I'll go to the town hall and ask to speak with Gaudin."

"Is this Gaudin a … sensible leader?" Stag asked.

"He can be," Raegan huffed. "Though only if his temper stays in check. Man's got the kind of fury you don't want to be on the wrong side of. However, with a reasonable explanation and you two by my side, I believe he'll come around. With two Aobians coming from the direction of the Tree, he'll know ye don't have anything to do with the matter. Gaudin won't shoot the messengers, I can guarantee that.

"But if something goes wrong, my first duty is to Mola and the children. We do not leave without making sure they are safe. That clear?"

Drift nodded. "Of course."

"Now that that's out of the way, we'll need to detour you. I'll put us up in a tavern that belongs to some close friends. Ye'll stay with us and leave on the morrow."

"Sounds like we don't have much of a choice," Drift commented.

"Ye don't," Raegan replied.

The party did not exchange many more words on the road to Providence. Drift did not want to speak to Stag. Stag did not want to speak at all. And the humans kept to themselves.

Drift watched as the scenery changed over the next three hours. Sunlight was coming and going through low-lying trees and dew-laden greatferns. Scrublands morphed into rolling hills and grasslands, leaving the sense of a forest well and truly behind. Eventually, the road met the banks of the river one could follow to Aobia in one direction or Adira in the other. Here, the water seemed so … foreign. It was less rapid, for a start, with no rocks jutting from the surface. Water moved slowly. It was nearly still, and high up the embankment.

Finally, small homes started hugging the riverbank, growing in number until they became a town. Dusty, pebble-laden roads ran like gridwork through rows of clumsy buildings and homes and taverns blended seamlessly into a messy conglomeration that, on the whole, lacked any real identity.

"The name Providence may be more fitting than I once thought," he murmured to Stag, who merely grunted in return.

The town seemed to be alive with a hopeful spirit. There was not much hope to be found, though. Drunks sprawled in the same streets the children danced down. People sold food in front of their homes rather than in a cluster of markets like what the Soul contained in Aobia. Somewhere deep down, the place's disrepair made Drift uneasy. He'd always wanted to see a human town, but this one made him long for home.

Stag patted Drift on the shoulder. "Don't worry, it's not all like this. I'll tell you about Adira someday."

Stag would 'tell' him about Adira. He didn't expect Drift would ever see the whitestone city on the sea. He just assumed he would have to 'tell' him. Drift grimaced.

Raegan glanced outside. "We should stop here. Mola, take the children to Margam and Noel. The rest of us can walk to the town hall."

Raegan, Drift, and Stag slowed the horses, wedging the wheels to stop the carriage from moving. The horses were quickly detached and Stag tied them to a nearby tree.

Raegan hugged his children. "Now you two run along with your aunt and stay safe," Drift heard him whisper after kissing their heads.

A twinge in Drift's chest caught him off guard. Seeing Raegan say farewell to his children so seriously made him think that maybe it would be better if he and Stag found their own way from here. What if something *did* go wrong in this melancholy place?

Then panic raced through Drift's mind. He'd only known the farmer and his family for a few days, and until now, they were the only humans he'd met. What could he do in Providence to blend in? To maintain conversation or conduct himself civilly?

At least he would have Stag.

Drift considered the town hall as they approached, feeling well and truly alien to the world around him. In Aobia, the Parliament was a grandiose building made of preserved silver birch and carved or embossed with great panels and decorative patterns of brass. The town hall of Providence, instead, was a large enough building in the context of the town but scruffy in comparison to what he was used to. It was made from logs with peeling and flaking bark and had a thatched roof that seemed like it had not been maintained for many human generations.

Inside the double doorway, small bowls of wax lit the gnarled, wooden walls and the crumbling clay cladding. People flitted around, carrying rolls of official documents, or stood in corners, exchanging conversations about things like land rights or the approved width of roads. A long hall stretched the length of the building with gaps for doorways every two metres or so, opening to a new collection of rooms and open meeting spaces. At the end burned a crude fire in a chimney pit that puffed smoke up and out of the roof in a poor way. By the fire sat an old man with frightfully bushy eyebrows that draped down his face like a rain shelter and a short-cut white beard. The seat he sat in was adorned with the skin of an elk and was situated behind a deep walnut-stained desk. The man had skin the colour and texture of tan leather, a weathered leader if ever there was one.

"Raegan, our farmer, our reaper of grain, our provisioner of beasts felled," the old man said as he stood, his maroon cloak flapping around him. He gripped Raegan's hand and held on to it, perhaps for too long. "And who have you invited into our humble town?"

"Gaudin, this is Stag and Drift." Raegan indicated each of them. "They visit us from the Great Tree."

Gaudin eyed the two Aobians cautiously but eventually offered a hand. "Welcome to Providence, tree-dwellers. What brings two travellers from the land of Aobia to this place?"

Stag cleared his throat and stepped forward. "We are ambassadors, Your Excellency, travelling to the Throne of the Sea King."

Gaudin's expression darkened at Stag's words and he instantly looked away. "What throne will you visit? Our king is dead. We received word from travellers who came from Relond a week ago." He looked at Raegan. "I am sorry, farmer. This news does not spread easily and I wish you didn't learn of it upon your arrival in town."

The bitter-tasting humility of the old leader spoke to the hall in which he resided and the town from which it sprawled. Perhaps Providence was not such a desolate, dirty place but rather the worthy home of an unassuming working class.

"So," Gaudin continued, "I am sorry to burden you all with this news. But now you know. Although I assume your Sleepers would not have sent you on your way without already telling you of Terrens' death?"

"I was there, actually," Stag said, sticking his chin up.

Roots below, Drift cursed in his mind. This wasn't a necessary detail to add. Gaudin's emotions seemed temperamental enough for someone they hadn't met until a few moments before. Of course, Stag's arrogance would stand tall before the wary town leader.

"You were there?" Gaudin asked. "Forgive me if I presume incorrectly, but you just said you have come from the Great Tree. If that is the case, that means you've been through Providence on your return home and didn't disclose the tragic news."

"You dare accuse me of such a depraved crime as this?" Stag retorted. Drift noticed Raegan receding into the walls. "I saw visitors from Therador there the same day. Yet you, in your tiny, dying town, claim that Aobia is the cause. We've had an alliance with Adira far longer than either of us have been alive, town leader."

The room seemed to go dark, though sunlight was flowing freely through the window.

"They speak poison, farmer." Gaudin's voice was hard enough that Drift practically felt it stabbing him in the back. "There are only two possible explanations for the king's death, and one of them involves Aobia. Raegan, you are smarter than this. You must understand these people have toyed with us. We're done here. I will decide by tomorrow morning what is to happen to you all. If my king's death can be vindicated by your capture, then so be it. Put them in the pillory."

In the split second that Drift wondered who Gaudin was speaking to, a set of strong hands had his arms yanked behind him and hot breath warmed the back of his neck. Stag fussed about as he too was held, but Drift was most concerned to see another person with a tan leather bodice over their shirt reaching around to pull on Raegan's arms too.

"Not Raegan!" Drift cried. "He has done nothing but bring us here. Isn't it us you want, Your Excellency?"

Raegan hung his head.

Gaudin let out a snort. "You come so far to spit such lies?" The old man was practically quivering with rage.

"I speak only the truth that I have lived with my own eyes, old man," Stag answered.

"You will remain in custody until morning. Whatever humiliation is beset upon you is what you deserve. At dawn, I will order a public meeting, and there we will settle your fate, tree-dwellers. If you are judged as guilty by the town of Providence, you will know your end soon enough." Gaudin reared up at them, spitting his next words in Stag's face. "I will call on the townsfolk. I will send every dog, stray or otherwise, for your guts. I will turn every sword on you until you lie in pieces beneath the river."

"Gaudin, please hear them out," Raegan pleaded in a quiet voice. "They bear us no ill will. They came to deliver the news to you, in case you were not aware. And I made them do it."

Stag spoke up, panicked. "I reported the incident myself to our Magisterium upon returning home. I needed to travel back from Adira as quickly as possible, and I regret not making the necessary stops to alert the towns along the way."

"You dare side with these runaways, Raegan? These defectors? They are not ambassadors, Raegan. Do you not see? They are not travelling to Adira for work. They are fleeing their own!" The old man's voice was filled with rich venom and Drift swore he could hear the turbulent waves of saliva swish around every word he spat.

"Ambassador Stag has stayed with me many a time, Gaudin," Raegan said. "What crime has he committed by coming here with important news? He could have travelled through without stopping yet again and you would never have noticed."

"I hear nothing but falsehood in your words, farmer. You live so far from our town, why have I ever considered you a part of it? Perhaps you fraternise with these creatures regularly, but you will not bring their filth into my town without punishment. You have until morning to choose your story. Then Providence will decide."

At first, the pillory did not bring with it the humiliation Drift had thought it would. But by the darkest heart of the night, his wrists were bleeding and his neck felt about ready to snap, all fixed in their places upon the stand. They were publicly displayed to any passerby who wanted to spit on them, insult them, or merely consider them from an angle, as though the three of them made up some kind of art piece.

Drift, Stag, and Raegan had remained quiet since they'd first been placed in the cuffs of the pillory and though the need to speak seemed pressing, Drift was thankful the other two hadn't once uttered a word. He felt his stomach clawing at itself, hungered beyond belief. His skin burned against the splintered, tight wooden holes his arms and neck were kept in and his mouth was parched from spending the summer afternoon in the sun without water. What made everything worse though was the fact that Raegan was with them. He'd never wanted to involve the farmer in his issues. He'd only received hospitality from Raegan and Mola, but now, he and Stag were to blame for taking the man from his family.

Soft footsteps interrupted his thoughts as his weary eyes blinked, half-open, in the dark street where they stood outside the town hall. He gasped upon seeing the two smaller humans stepping trepidatiously towards them. Braddegh and Suan had come here, alone.

"Children!" Raegan spluttered out a cry, his dry voice breaking as they rushed to their father, gripping his bound hands. Suan pressed her face into Raegan's cheek and Drift sniffed back tears. How could Gaudin have done this to one of his own citizens so suddenly?

"It's okay," Raegan said, trying to sound reassuring. "I'll get outta this one and all will be okay. Shh, little one."

Suan sobbed as Raegan continued to soothe her. Braddegh turned around to Drift and Stag, his voice rich with anger. "You did this!" he cried. "You've made my father a criminal!"

"Braddegh!" Raegan snapped. "'Tis enough, boy. I won't have ye speak like that. Drift and Stag are friends and this is through no fault of their own." He eyed the two Aobians from his end of the pillory. Stag looked down at the dirt road.

"I'm sorry," Drift croaked. "I never meant to hurt you or your family, Raegan."

The farmer sighed. "Nonsense. In the morning, we'll be outta this. Ye'll see. Gaudin'll come 'round." Then, as though noticing the children were alone for the first time, his eyes widened as he snapped at Braddegh. "Where's your aunty, boy?"

Braddegh shifted uncomfortably, looking away, but Suan didn't hesitate to respond. "She's asleep, father."

"No, little one," Raegan said, an edge of warning to his voice. "Ye can't be out here without her knowing about it. Did ye do this alone?"

Suan began to sob, shaking her head. Braddegh's bottom lip started to quiver, but to Drift's amazement, he brought himself forward, a repentant son. "It was me, father," he said, head bowed. "I did it. I convinced Suan to leave with me so we could see you. We saw you from the other side of the street earlier, and—" He began to weep. "I'm sorry!"

"Sorry?" Raegan whispered. "Don't be a fool, son. I understand. But yer aunty did the right thing by keeping ye both away. Now go before she sees that ye're gone and raises even more alarm."

The two children kissed their father on the head and disappeared into the dark from whence they'd come. This was love like no other. And yet, Drift worried, as the night went slowly by, that it would be frayed, cut off too soon.

Because of him.

TARRI

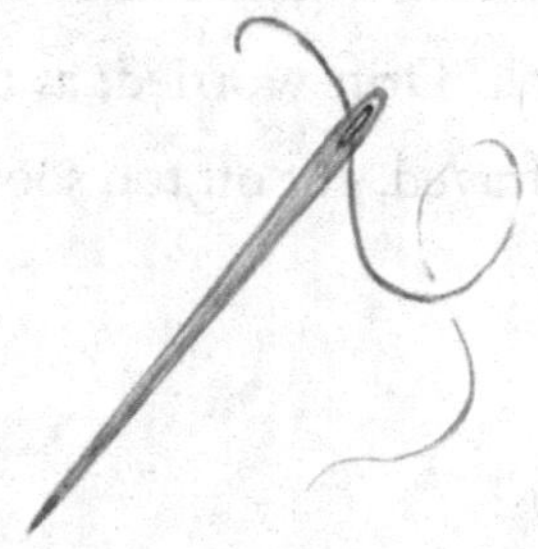

"AND *THIS* IS YOUR tailor?" The tall male practically spat the words at Tarri.

"Tarri, sir." She bowed her head, hoping that Koln would return her greeting.

Nischia's superior, Koln, batted her away with a hand. He had hard eyes. His silver hair was shorter than most other Aobians' and the lines of his face were somehow indicative of an egotism that made Tarri feel smaller than any other beast in the world.

"Does she speak this formally all the time, Nischia?" Koln asked.

"No, Koln. She is just trying to be respectful." Nischia sighed.

It was the perfect barrage of insults. Tarri couldn't tell whether being formal was less impressive than 'trying to be respectful,' as Nischia had put it. She'd had enough of these people and their stuffy ways. Maybe they *were* like Drift had always said. Conceited, power-hungry figures of corruption.

"We are not as vain as you might like to think," Koln said. "And not all of us are corrupt."

Roots below, he'd heard her thoughts. She needed to be less emotional, more guarded. "I-I'm sorry," she stammered.

Nischia looked from Tarri to Koln as though asking him to excuse her.

"My name is Koln, child, and I'd appreciate it if you understood what a bother it is to meet you later than I was told to expect you."

Tarri gulped and nodded. He was a terrifying figure compared to the approachable Lady Nischia. There was not a hint of intimidation to his movements or his cool and collected body language, but his words, his tone, cut like a knife.

"There are a few things I'm here to tell you and I'd ask that you listen and not forget. I do not appreciate saying something twice."

Tarri held eye contact, because if she broke it, it would most likely be to her and Nischia's detriment. "Of course, sir."

Nischia looked away, crossing her arms as Koln continued. She must've known what was coming.

"The first rule you will follow," Koln started, "is that you will not allow yourself to be seen with Lady Nischia within your regular working hours as part of this investigation."

Investigation? As in, the particular investigation that Nischia had only touched on for the last week? The investigation that

Tarri would *maybe* be allowed to participate in? The investigation that, ridiculously, had no defined objective, just something to do with Drift and the dead Adiran king. "Pardon me," she interrupted. Nischia glared at her with a brow raised. "I've met with Lady Nischia a few times now, as you may well be aware."

"Of course. I am not oblivious, child." Did the Sleeper's expression never change from flat and egotistical?

"Every time we have met has been during my work hours, because it appears as though she is simply a client of the Tailory."

Koln nodded. "Interactions such as these will continue, I daresay, for the specific purpose of business. You are here to convince me that you can be part of an upper-Magisterium investigation involving politics that are potentially outside the reach of the Great Tree. Being an active participant of such an investigation requires that you retain any interactions regarding it for times outside of your work as a tailor. Is that understood?"

The only thing Tarri took from this was the idea that she was there to convince him of allowing her to help Nischia. Why hadn't she explained this to her ahead of this meeting? She flickered her gaze to Nischia, who had returned to looking down at her lap. "I understand, sir."

"The second rule"—Koln held up two fingers—"is that you will not be privy to knowledge shared with us by other Sleepers. I will not have a regular Aobian disturb the relationships that I work tirelessly to maintain in the Magisterium. The scale of conflict within our government if they were to know we were working with the likes of you is indescribable." He spat the words at her, a fierce reminder of her class. This wasn't just about politics or the mysteries that Nischia was trying to find answers to. This was about preserving Koln and Nischia's social standing.

Koln was not finished. "This rule, I'll have it known, does not just apply to you." He eyed his mentee, and even she, the unflappable Lady Nischia, seemed to bend to his will in expression alone. "It also applies to the Lady Nischia, who will uphold the confidentiality of the Magisterium or suffer the consequences."

"Of course, Koln." Nischia inclined her head towards him. "I understand."

Koln stared at Tarri, waiting for verbal confirmation. "Of course."

It seemed as though this part of the meeting was done, as Koln stood. *Thank goodness,* she thought. *That was like being chided by your elders for speaking out of turn at the dinner table.*

Koln's face remained serious as he spoke again. "It's time for the interview now. I've had the male, Sedulus, occupy a seat in an inquiry chamber at a private room in the Courts. We shall walk quickly."

The Courts were located within the Supreme Court of Aobia, the first building that Tarri had seen when they'd entered the Mind earlier that day. Tarri had always found the Courts a methodical approach to the justice system.

If you did something wrong, you were sent there and tried at the court appropriate for your deed. Rarely was there an instance where one would fight the authorities and if they did, they were collected by Sleepers who administered a tribunal. And nobody would dare stand up to a Sleeper. Besides, wrongdoings in Aobia were so rare.

They had exited the apartment complex and were halfway down the road before anybody spoke. "I understand Nischia has spoken to you about a particular … skill you seem to have acquired." Tarri looked up from the road as though she hadn't realised the comment had been directed at her.

"My lady has not gone into details, sir," she replied. This was the truth. Nischia had simply told her that some people have the ability to block Sleepers from listening to their thoughts. A true autonomy, Drift would have called it, and the thought made her chuckle.

"Miss Tarri?" Koln prompted with a frown, arms folded behind his back.

"I'm sorry, sir," she replied. "My beloved used to comment on things like … this." It wasn't the best choice of words and Koln confirmed this as he eyed her. "I suppose he had ideas about the relationship between Aobians and the government. He thought a lot about freedom. We usually saw eye to eye, but ideologically, I guess you might say he was somewhat more … cautious than I was."

"Ideologically cautious?" Koln asked. "Go on."

Nischia waved at her to be quiet. Tarri gulped. "He didn't think anything too outlandish and he respected the Sleepers. He just wondered about the meaning of freedom a lot, that's all."

Koln took a breath. "Would you say that he was … inclined to think about the outside world?"

Tarri frowned at the Sleeper. "I don't know. He never said as much. Why?"

Koln stopped on the road. The Courts were up ahead. He held her gaze for a long moment. "*You* cannot ask 'why,' Miss Tarri. *You* have not earned the privilege. Do not make me reconsider my offer to have you a part of this investigation." With that, he swirled around, the sides of his coat flapping around with him. Nischia widened her eyes and Tarri felt her jaw snap shut in response.

The Courts were much the same in design language as the rest of the buildings Tarri had seen in the Mind. Behind the huge front of the Supreme Court was nestled a collection of buildings that sat in a circle, a striking fountain in the middle. This was something that, all her life, Tarri had not been able to explain. How could a moving water display operate this far above ground? Even Drift, who'd worked at the viaduct, had not been able to understand it. *Luminosity, Tarri,* she thought to herself, quoting Nischia's words. *Isn't that the answer to everything in this place?*

The fountain depicted three nondescript Sleepers standing back to back, spears held menacingly. The spears bore large, rounded blades at the top, like teardrops, and a long shaft that appeared like vines, intertwined almost like a braid. These were the Three Pillars of Aobia, holding the Three Spears of Life.

Trust, who held their spear with two hands, one gold and one green, as though to depict the trust that existed between Aobia and the outside world, though many interpreted it as the shared trust between the Aobian people and the Sleepers. Wisdom, who touched two fingers to their forehead as they looked to the sky. In their other hand, they raised their spear skyward too. And finally, Compassion. Drift hated the statue of Compassion, and thinking of it made something stir in Tarri. Compassion held the spear with two hands, like Trust. But unlike Trust, Compassion held it in such a way that they were *pushing* the spear into their *own heart*, its tip poking out the back of the figure, which stood in a painless pose.

Don't you see? Drift had written at the top of a note that he'd given to Tarri in the garden one night. He hadn't been willing to say his thoughts aloud. It'd already been bad enough to think them. *They use compassion—love for their people—as a cloak for what it really is. They think they know what's best for us. They Sleep to power our home and so we should be infinitely grateful. But we're all thinking the same way within the confines of their worldview.*

She shuddered as she remembered the night. She'd slapped the paper out of his hands after she'd read it. She recalled gripping his face as she'd pressed hers up against him, tears flowing down her cheeks. She'd shaken her head at him, wanting him to take it back. The world hadn't been against him, she remembered thinking at the time. But looking at Compassion here and now, as she was embroiled in something she suspected was much larger than she... She no longer knew what she thought.

Nischia patted her shoulder. "I would have thought you'd been here before. As a child?" All children visited the Courts. It was an essential part of their education of Aobian Civics.

"Yes," Tarri murmured. "But truthfully, I had not thought of it in some time, my lady."

Nischia nodded. "We must always strive to live by them." She sighed. "It is time, Tarri. Koln is waiting for us in the foyer of the head office."

The head office of the Courts was a grand sight in the fading daylight. Long, wooden pillars supported an overhanging roof, which had etchings of the Three Pillars on the rafters. A wall of glass from ceiling to ground made the building fit right into the world around it, where it both reflected the nature of Aobia but also told different stories within. Inside, they were greeted by two staircases, this time winding to the top floor from both ends of the foyer. Koln was already at the top, a silhouette against the sunset, gesturing to them to come up.

"The male in question today. You know him?" he asked Tarri.

"Only by extension," she replied. "He worked with Drift at the viaduct."

"He is one of the only people who work around the river who has access to all worksites, at any hour of the day." Koln let out a sigh and Tarri noted that this made him more affable.

Tarri clenched her teeth. "Given what rules you had me agree to before, I suppose I'll need to do some sleuthing myself to learn about all this myself. But please answer one thing: do you suspect this male of exiling my beloved intentionally?"

It took a moment before Koln nodded. "I do. I suspect that Drift was not exiled fairly. And … I have reason to believe that this is the lesser of Sedulus' crimes." He turned to face a door and reached for the brass handle. "Miss Tarri, I politely ask that during the interview, you do not speak. It is important that my questioning follows a process. Do you understand?"

Tarri nodded.

"Good. Then it is time."

DRIFT

SQUEAKY, BARELY ATTACHED WHEELS scraped across the dirt road, upon which sat a large timpani in a brass frame. Drift tried to blink away the sleep that had built up in his tired eyes, feeling the sharp grit get caught in the edges. Cocks crowed from several places at once, alerting the town to the rising sun. It was just before dawn, and a sombre mix of darkness and light toyed with the colour of the sky. He hoped their judgement would be swift and that Gaudin had sought after their innocence first and foremost.

A man with a long, orange beard used a mallet to strike the timpani, which swelled to a boom before the town hall, the mark of a public announcement.

"Start prayin'," said Raegan in a gravelly voice. "If things go poorly, I'm sorry."

Next to the timpani appeared Gaudin, a mad look in his eye, with a small group of councillors around him. Residents scurried out of homes and holes like vermin, forming a crowd that ebbed and flowed like wild water, the same kind that had put Drift in this very position.

"People of Providence," he began. "It is with regret that I inform you of some difficult news," Gaudin continued. "Before you stand a man of our own and two Aobians of the Great Tree who claim to be ambassadors to the royal throne. Yesterday, they were arrested. These three criminals are recognised in Providence as suspects on the count of the murder of King Terrens of Adira!" A gasp ricocheted through the crowd.

"Suspects?" Raegan spat. "Provide us with your evidence, Gaudin, or set us free. I've been tending my farm a lot longer than some of these townsfolk have been alive. Had I the time to go to Adira and kill my own king, I'm sure someone would've noticed the simple fact that I *wasn't home*."

"Briar, step forward," Gaudin said, ignoring Raegan's words. "As is customary in Providence, our law is not bound by the throne. I ask you all, my people, to make your fair judgement of these criminals once you have been given the pertinent details."

A man with thinning red hair stepped forward into the ring the town had made around the pillory. He had a cropped beard and eyes as cold as ice. Drift shivered at the sight of him. The man returned his gaze, staring long and hard at him in a way that felt both uncomfortable and oddly familiar. He was cloaked in thick, dark robes uncharacteristic of the rest of the town, and wore sturdy black boots.

"I am Briar Sevardson," he announced to the crowd. "I am here today as a representative of the Relondian Assembly of Criers. It was I who announced the king's death to your leader Gaudin one week ago. I came from Relond as soon as the news reached us and crossed the Mountain Gate in record time. I was to return to Relond last night, but my stay was extended because of the arrival of these two Aobians."

The crowd's muttering rose in volume and Drift gulped. Stag was looking forlorn at the man called Briar, and Raegan had his eyes closed as though he already knew what was to come.

"The official news from the throne is that the king was assassinated. There is no easy way to summarise this further: visitors from all nations across Q'ara were present, as is common. But we know guests from Therador had departed prior to the king's death."

The crowd's gossiping grew to a roar and Gaudin grinned, allowing Briar to step back out of the ring. "Providence, my people, Briar Sevardson the crier has proclaimed what he knows to be the truth. Now it is your turn to determine the fate of these criminals. Do you accept that the farmer, Raegan, is an accomplice to murder, hiding the Aobians for a week before bringing them to town?"

Raegan shook his head and snorted as the crowd proclaimed, "Aye!"

Gaudin nodded. "And the Aobians. May we make the best choices we can with all the information given to us. Providence, what will you have me do with these tree-dwellers?"

At that moment, the crowd erupted, swinging fists and spitting fierce remarks. Drift caught, from the corner of his eye, the sweeping robes that belonged to Briar as he disappeared through the mass of people. One man surged forward, screaming, "Murderers! Filthy, murdering husks!" but a particularly tall and menacing councillor sprung at him, shoving him back into the crowd.

Gaudin smirked, waltzing up to Drift and Stag. "And there it is. The truth comes out in our guts, tree-dwellers. Never doubt your instinct, unless you wish to live a lie."

He turned to the councillors. "Release them from the pillory and throw them in a cell. Their lives will come to a just end tomorrow, for all to see. And make sure you find that farmer's family. They will undoubtedly know something about this, wherever they are."

Raegan roared as he was released from the pillory, one arm chained to the other before his head was freed. Drift looked away. They'd done this. *He'd* done this. He'd condemned innocent people to death, because he knew not the behaviours of humans. It was too late now to correct that mistake. This was the same arrogance the first settlers had carried when they'd arrived on Q'ara and taken the continent from the Aobians and the Hidden Ones. This human 'justice' would be his ultimate end.

He felt the bars over his hands unlatch as they too were bound in chains, before his head came loose from the stand. Raegan was thrashing around, screaming. Stag stood up from the pillory, motionless, eyes lost somewhere far away from Providence.

Then, the ambassador threw his head backwards, straight into the chin of his captor. He came undone from the councillor and ran towards Gaudin, barrelling into him with his full weight. They rolled around in the dirt as the crowd began to descend upon the pillory. Stag forced a knee into Gaudin's crotch and the old man shrivelled up on the ground, howling in pain.

Stag got to his feet with a forward roll and Drift wasted no time. He shoved himself backwards into his own detainer too, the force of which sent them both to the ground. He rolled lengthways as a random person in the crowd staggered over him, their nose bleeding. The townspeople were growing divided and anxious in the chaos.

Stag kicked at Drift to get up, crying, "Raegan. Run at him. Now!"

The two of them ran for the councillor that was trying to drag a thrashing, kicking Raegan away, crashing into them both. Drift's hands came loose and he realised his chains hadn't even been locked together. Free-handed, he gripped Raegan by the collar and hauled the man to his feet. "Raegan, listen, we need to go! Raegan!"

Gaudin staggered to his feet, dry dust from the ground en-shrouding him like a cloud. "If these men do not wish to die with dignity, we will force them into the ground ourselves!" he seethed. A number of townsfolk cried in affirmation of his words. The crowd's eyes settled on Drift, Stag, and Raegan.

Raegan breathed loudly through his nose. "Damn it," he said. "Let's go while we still can. Run with every inch of mass you have. Run like a battering ram. Run together. Go!"

They'd been warned and given their chance. But nevertheless, Drift could not believe how things had escalated. It was as though the whole town was unhinged.

"He's always been quick to judge," Raegan said as they blitzed through the streets.

"Raegan," Drift called.

"What?" The reply was gruff through Raegan's panted breaths.

"What's the plan?"

"Huh?"

"The plan. Now, I mean."

Raegan whirled on the two Aobians, grabbing Drift by the scruff of his cloak. He dragged him down a side street, which was quiet, save for an investigative cat that straddled the half-rotten timber fencing behind a building.

"Raegan?" Drift exclaimed. "What are you doing?"

"Telling ye the plan, Drift," Raegan exerted. "Ye wanna know the plan? Here's the plan: I leave my family, my only sister and my kids, to their own devices for a *day out* in Providence," he spat. "'What a treat!' they'll think when I return. If I return. Damn ye, damn ye both. Every person in this town knows Gaudin's senses left him five years or more ago, when he should've stepped down as he promised. Tired minds break. If I get to be that old, I hope my boy knocks me down with a shovel."

He dropped Drift, shoving him away. "This was my promise, to get ye back on the road. I'll honour that. But if anything happens to me, you go back for my family. Ye make sure they're safe, whatever it takes. These people will turn on a man in an instant, whether he lived here his whole life or not. I've seen it happen before."

The side street that Raegan had taken them to was half the width of a normal road in Providence, but it stretched down the length of several blocks. "We will stop at Margam and Noel's, the only people I could call family after Mola, though they aren't blood. Margam will protect the children and Mola, and Noel will help distract the town from us. We don't step a foot inside, just get our distraction and go. Then we'll go for the carriage, take Mola and the children, and head back towards the farm. Somewhere along the road I'll drop ye off and ye can find the long way 'round Providence."

Drift nodded and Stag looked a shade of white Drift had never seen. The pace at which things were changing came as a shock to Drift, particularly because change had never bothered him. And Raegan's treatment hurt. He'd been the first human to treat Drift well, let alone the first human Drift had ever met. He'd shown him deep care and hospitality, only for the entire relationship to be ruined.

Raegan paused at the back of a building. A wooden door was ajar, and from the gap flowed the scents of beer and rich meat braising slowly. He waved them over to the door. Meeting them at the step, along with the rich aromas and the mahogany-toned walls, was a man smaller, thinner, and kindlier than Raegan. He reached out with a hand to both Drift and Stag and introduced himself with only a name. "Noel."

"Glad to make your acquaintance," Drift replied.

Stag added on, "Sorry to, uh, sorry for—" but Drift silenced him with a gesture.

"We're going, then?" Noel asked.

Raegan puffed out a breath. "We're going." He nodded.

"Well then," Noel called back into the room. "If we're gonna go, it's gotta be now or never."

Raegan nodded. "Enough said. What's the plan?"

A woman, much larger and shorter than Noel, popped her head up from behind him. This must've been his wife, Margam. "You bring him back here in one piece, Raegan, or I swear you'll find yourself in more than one when I'm done with ye."

For such a short woman, Margam seemed intimidating enough, and Drift winced at her threat. "Raegan," he whispered, "why is this man coming with us? I'd risk no more lives."

"Quiet, Drift." Raegan flexed his knuckles. "You want a chance at getting the carriage back? Let's just be done with this."

Stag gave him a look that suggested he agreed with Raegan that they be silent, and Drift conceded.

"I'll be in the street right here," Noel clarified. "I won't be going any further. I'm just a distraction to lure the townsfolk away from your direction. Isn't that right, Raegan?" The glare he gave the farmer was enough to stop Margam from adding more to the conversation.

"Not a step," the farmer grunted in reply. "Noel gets us this carriage, we leave town together back towards the farm. I'll put ye Aobians on a single diversion track that goes around Providence. It's the only one I know of." Raegan's frown was deep. "Nobody has any reason to use it though. But it's maintained as a fire trail for residents. You'll have to find your way through dense bush, I'm afraid. Once you're past Providence, it's on to the Mountain Gate. You might be able to get a decent horse there."

"Mountainers," Stag said, teeth clenched like the word itself was bitter. "Brain-addled Theradorans who have been let out to dry on the mountain's pass."

Drift raised an eyebrow. "Go on?"

"They say it's the altitude," Stag replied. "Must get to their heads or something." He twisted a finger around his ear.

"I'm yet to discover what ye really think of us then, ambassador," Raegan retorted. "There isn't much else to plan. Whatever happens on the other side of these walls is indeterminable."

As they started moving back down the street, led by Noel, the wind blew through at a blistering rate, and though the air was warm, Drift swung between too hot and too cold constantly as they made their way back to the carriage.

Cobblestoned road extended beyond them, walled in by wooden fencing that shaped properties and buildings. Beyond the small amounts of sunrise light that illuminated the polished surface of the stones, Drift couldn't see a thing.

"Summer sunrise," Raegan said. "Taking it's damn time."

The sun finally rose just enough over the horizon that they could see the stables, outlined in orange.

"This street runs through to the entry into town, coming from Raegan's farm," Noel commented as they walked. The wind cut the volume from his voice. "While you can, take your carriage and go. I'll go further into town now and do what I can to draw attention elsewhere."

"Godspeed be with you, friend." Raegan grimaced as he took Noel's hand. The thin man saluted the Aobians.

The trio got to the stable as the first instance of a threat made itself known. The carriage lay in hundreds of pieces of snapped, sawed, or collapsed wood. The horses' reins had been cut and the beasts were nowhere to be seen.

"I'll be damned," Noel whispered.

Raegan responded with a quick snort and then a deep, angry grunt. "I'll kill him," he said to the wasted carriage before him.

"I guess we know what comes when you make an enemy of Gaudin," Stag said, trying to keep the air light, but failing.

"With any luck, ambassador," Raegan said, "ye won't have to find out what comes when ye make an enemy of me."

Drift caught Stag roll his eyes in response and shot him a stiff glare, though he wasn't certain the other Aobian could see all that well in the low light.

Raegan looked around the stable walls and down the main street of Providence. "Damn it." He looked at Noel. "Noel, go home. Now!"

Noel ran down the lane that he had led the group through and Drift could see him yank off a shoe as he did so, trying to soften the pads of his feet on the ground. As Noel was enveloped in the black, a shiver ran down Drift's spine and his hands felt oddly detached from his body. He was light yet heavy at the same time, rattled by nerves.

"Raegan," he started. "How far did you say the fire trail was?"

Raegan shook his head, his back to the stable wall. Drift stepped closer to him and noticed he was shaking. The farmer was fearful for his life. Or his sister's and his children's.

Drift reached out and tried to grab Raegan's wrist. "Hey—"

No words escaped Raegan's mouth but for the twisted sounds of panic and exasperation as he leapt forward, trying to knock Drift to the ground. Drift leapt backwards, putting his hands up.

"Drift," Stag whispered. "They're coming. They're nearly here! The whole godsdamned town!"

"How far, Raegan?" Drift snarled at the farmer. "You want to live? You want to see your children again?" Drift gripped Raegan and hauled him onto his feet by the collar, feeling the man wheeze from the tightness around his throat. "We need to move if that's what you want, farmer. Get us out of here, alive. Then you'll never have to deal with us again. Move!"

It felt impulsive, Drift's sudden aggression. But he couldn't risk their lives because the man wouldn't pull himself together. Faced with the threat of death, Drift felt adrenaline run through his body, telling him how to react, keeping his decision making as quick and tight as possible. But for the farmer, the prospect of a death sentence would make him freeze with anxiety.

Gaudin was lighting the way down the street with a metre-long torch, a gang of townsfolk around him with whatever home-sourced weapons they could use, no matter how blunt or crude. Drift couldn't make out much past those details as the rising sun behind them painted the crowd under a dull kind of silhouette. He just knew they would have their choice of death by cast-iron pan or smithing tools or horseshoes if they did not make haste.

"Which way?"

Raegan gestured to the right and darted off towards the trees. Drift and Stag followed as the townsfolk appeared like a cloud of mites or locusts, erupting from the town gates. A hive mind whose only consideration was the death of three treasonous liars.

Amidst the tangle of low branches, dense shrubbery, and long grass, the trio ran down the roadside for what felt like an hour before Raegan finally made the call to divert.

"It's just up ahead." He breathed in a way that suggested he hadn't run a long distance in some time. For Aobians, their leaner, taller builds tended to mean they leant themselves toward any kind of running or endurance-based activity.

Drift, who was barely out of breath, nodded. "They haven't caught up to us yet."

Raegan bent over, putting his hands on his knees for support as he wheezed. "No, but … they'll keep tryin'. Never known

… man like Gaudin to stop… Gotta get back in case they find … the children."

Pain tugged at Drift's chest. He felt as though both he and Stag were going to abandon this man who had given them so much: reprieve from the endless forest, shelter, hospitality, and, most importantly, he'd risked his own safety. He thought of Mola looking after the children in a hostile place, trying to get back to the farm unharmed.

"Drift, no," Stag began. "We … we can't."

Drift rubbed his chin, but Raegan put a hand on his shoulder. "Ye may be indebted to me from now on, friend," he began. "But tonight is not that night. Go now, while there's time."

Drift couldn't help but feel the farmer was a saint. "Raegan…" His stomach dropped. "Thank you, for everything. If you need to find us, come to Adira if you can. Even if he's not there"—he gestured to Stag, who was standing behind him—"I will be."

Raegan reached out and Drift took his hand with a firm squeeze. After a beat, the farmer reached for Stag's hand too. "Ambassador," he said.

"Farmer," Stag said, letting go of his hand as he looked away. "Thank you."

"Ye'd best move. This sun's lit up the whole damn forest. Head to that tree over there," Raegan gestured. "Ye see the one that sticks up some past the rest?"

Drift and Stag nodded.

"The trail starts there. Don't ye dare get off it until it leads back to the main road. It'll take ye out of Providence by a distance of fifteen kilometres or so. That should be enough of a lead for ye and hopefully by then, Gaudin will have given up his charade."

The tree to which Raegan indicated stood in its dizzying height, some kind of odd addendum to the Aobian forestry that had found itself all the way out here. It signalled the start of something indescribable in Drift, an oncoming sense of adventure mixed with a obscene and insurmountable sense of fear.

Stag had begun walking through the undergrowth in long, nimble strides, clearly moved by fear of Providence appearing behind them at any moment. Drift knew it was time to leave, but for the first time in his life, he lingered, holding Raegan's eyes. He couldn't leave this man.

He had to leave this man.

"There they are! In the trees!" a voice cried.

Drift's eyes widened and everything seemed to happen all at once. Raegan began to open his mouth to say something, but a crude shaft whipped its way through the trees, appearing as a stiff protrusion in the back of his calf. He yelped in agony as he fell to the ground and tried to haul himself under a dense, tiny-leafed bush.

"Raegan!" Drift cried, staggering towards him.

"No!" Raegan yelled between bursts of painful cries. "Get ye'self on that trail, Drift! Or it was all for nought."

Stag appeared out of nowhere as a confusing dance of sun and torchlight began to envelope the forest around them. Drift felt his arm get grasped behind him, and Stag dragged him away. "No! I came back for you, Drift. I'm not letting us die here. Not to these lunatics!"

A group of townsfolk appeared, sweaty and dirty-faced alike, looking around the area. Stag pulled Drift down behind the trunk of the grand tree that marked the beginning of the trail.

"There!" came a woman's charged voice. "They just went behind that tree!"

"Roots below," Drift breathed.

"We got one, Gaudin!" came a voice.

Drift held his eyes shut tight as he heard the town leader speak. "Well, well. Farmer Raegan. We should get him patched up, don't you think?"

The response was a chorus of "Yes!" followed by laughter. Drift heard a set of footsteps coming closer through the undergrowth.

"No!" growled Gaudin. "Let them go. We have enough to deal with as it is. They're dead when they get to the Mountain Gate anyway. And if they dare crawl back to our town again, we'll gut them then. I want posters around the town; see if that doesn't catch them the next time they need to come home to their damn tree."

"Drift!" Stag hissed and patted him on the arm until he opened his eyes. "We must go now while we can!"

The chaos behind them sounded catastrophic, a cacophony of voices mixed with Raegan's howls of pain. But Stag was right. This was their only chance. Drift felt sick about leaving Raegan behind, but as the two Aobians crept through the bush to the beginning of the trail and the sounds faded, he couldn't help but feel relieved that they were on their way out of this mess and toward the sea.

This was no longer about Drift embracing a new life. This was no chance to restart. He had a duty, he realised as he walked alongside Stag in silence, and that was to get his fellow Aobian to Adira, the only place they might find answers to what seemed to be hundreds of mounting questions.

TARRI

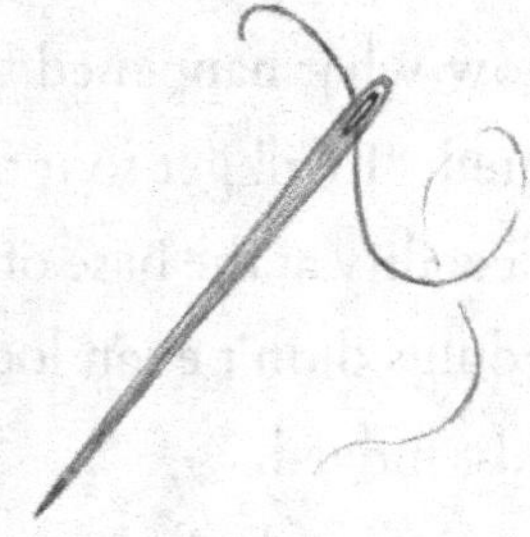

KOLN OPENED THE DOOR into the meeting room. A long table filled the room, three prominent lamps powered by Luminous crystals upon it. Koln gestured for Tarri to sit at the end closest to the door. A small iron loop had been fixed to the surface at the other end of the table, clamped over the hand that belonged to Sedulus. It was a powerplay—he wasn't going to be arrested. Anger rushed through Tarri like a wave. Nischia sat next to Koln, who was adjacent to the taciturn Aobian.

"Sedulus of the Soul," Koln began. He lived in the Soul? Well, that was probably more sensible than living in the Heart, for a male with none whatsoever.

"Trust, Compassion, and Wisdom." Sedulus nodded at Nischia and Koln.

"You are being interviewed as a suspect for a crime committed on Aobian land. Anything you say can be retained for use in the

Courts if it's decided that further inquest must be made. Is this understood?"

"Yes," Sedulus responded. This was all formality since Sedulus couldn't lie before two Sleepers. Maybe the answer Tarri wanted would be given quicker than she'd expected. Maybe she would finally know what happened to Drift.

"Well," Koln grunted. "I will get to it then. You work at the Water Management Facility at the base of the Heart of Aobia?"

"Yes, my lord." Sedulus didn't even look Koln in the eye. A meeting of two minds, indeed.

"You have the highest level of clearance, allowing you to obtain access to any part of the facility. Is this correct?"

"Of course, my lord," Sedulus responded. "I am a superior at the facility. A promotion offered to me after years of service."

"Yes," Koln nodded. "I have heard from your superior at the Magisterium that your efforts have been tireless."

"Twenty years, my lord."

Nischia leaned forward so Sedulus could see her clearly. "And in those twenty years, Master Sedulus, did you ever come across a fault in the facility?"

Sedulus raised an eyebrow. "Faults are increasingly common. We attend to frequent upkeep and maintenance of all aspects of the facility, as the infrastructure there is old, in human terms."

"Old in human terms?" Nischia questioned. "Why is that relevant? Our infrastructure is fifty years young in Aobian terms and created, in coordination with the Sleepers, to be a hundred times the quality of common human engineering. Luminosity-imbued materials fortify everything, both within the Tree and below it."

"I apologise, my lady," Sedulus replied. "Any metalwork that is subjected to a constant flow of water is susceptible to being worn down at an accelerated rate. I meant no disrespect."

Nischia cut him off with a wave of her hand. "It is not just a simple matter of rust in the catchment filters that caused the events of last week, Sedulus. Can you explain why, five nights ago, there was an incident where the algae in the water was killed? Why the Sickness returned?"

Sedulus looked at Koln. "My lord, can I ask why—"

"I would suggest you answer the question," Koln said.

Sedulus looked away before staring at Tarri. Tarri felt her bones go cold as he spoke. "The outright collapse of our algae population was unprecedented, my lady. I understand there was a tragic event that occurred that night, however—"

"*We* will be making the inferences, thank you," Nischia said with pursed lips. "What about the *cism* supply? Did you not think to resort to backup generators?"

"It seemed the backup generators fixed the problem temporarily," Sedulus replied. "But it was too late. The viaduct took damage, the mesh filter on the final catchment broke, and one of my workers died. I checked the generators after the tragedy and all was in working order. We were able to restore the algae early the next day. I do not foresee the Sickness affecting the human lands."

"And you did not think to check the failed *cism* before dragging another worker into this mess?" Nischia hissed, standing up. "What were you thinking?"

Sedulus said nothing.

"The tragedy that you describe," Koln said. "Can you tell us more?"

Sedulus sniffed as Nischia sat down with a huff. "An employee unfortunately fell from the viaduct as I assisted him with distributing elementals. It seems his harness was not … of decent construction. I offered him my hand, but with the force of the waterfall upon him, he couldn't maintain his grip and neither could I. I did all that I could to not let go." He looked down, as if embarrassed.

"Do you believe he could have survived such a fall?" Koln asked.

"I do not believe so, my lord." Sedulus shook his head. "A fall like that, through an Aobian-made waterfall of hundreds of feet… It would have to be a miracle."

Koln nodded, satisfied so far with Sedulus' responses. Then he changed the topic. "Tell me, Sedulus. Are you aware that the King of Adira, Terrens, died last week?"

Wariness flashed in Sedulus' eyes. "A human king, my lord? Why would I preoccupy myself with news of that kind?" He looked squarely at Koln with a steady gaze.

Koln studied his face for a moment, while Nischia's frown seemed to only grow deeper. "I will repeat the question one final time, Sedulus. Were you aware of the death of King Terrens of Adira?"

"I am now," Sedulus replied, an edge to his voice.

The gall of this male! Tarri couldn't believe what she was watching. She had to know what prompted Koln to ask Sedulus the question, too. Nischia had hinted at it already. What was the connection between the Sea King's death and Drift?

Koln rapped his knuckles on the tabletop once before standing. "Thank you for your time, Sedulus. You are excused but not exonerated. Any further consideration of the case in question may mean Court involvement and we will let you know as early as possible if that eventuates. Please return to your residence and workplace as per usual."

That was it. Sedulus nodded before leaving the room.

As the footsteps grew distant, Koln resumed his place at the table and gestured that Tarri move closer. "Miss Tarri," he began, "what did you observe about that male?"

"Let me ask you a counter-question, my lord," Tarri said. "What is being covered up in regard to the death of the human king?"

Koln snorted. "This is a distraction from your real problem, tailor."

"No," Tarri retorted. "It isn't a distraction. I suspect there are more connections between Drift's disappearance and this king. And you didn't seem to be hiding that with Sedulus, so I don't expect you should feel the need to hide it from me."

"Tarri, dear," Nischia interrupted. "It's more complicated than a direct connection. We are dealing with two seemingly unrelated coincidences, both of which are rather serious in regard to the workings of the world that we have created. We're simply trying to leave no stone unturned."

"I might ask you then, my lady, if you think there is a connection?" Tarri left the question dangling in the air while Nischia patted down her dress.

"I think there are reasons to ask about both events in the same conversation, Tarri. That is all I can say right now."

Tarri nodded. She could accept that, but she couldn't accept the extent of Koln's knowledge because he was *certainly* holding some details back. "To answer your question, my lord, I don't know what to make of Sedulus. I don't want my anger cross-contaminated with my tendency to be suspicious of him given the circumstances. It would not be fruitful."

Koln looked surprised. "What an astute comment, Miss Tarri. I think that is both a wise and strategic point of view."

"Strategic, my lord?"

Koln waved a hand. "Investigations only benefit when you can detach yourself from them. Now that you've learned that, we can all proceed much more comfortably."

Tarri gritted her teeth. "All I want is to find justice for Drift and bring him home."

"Justice we can work towards, of course. Bringing him home is another point entirely, one that is sadly outside my control within the Magisterium. It's not a guarantee that either of us can make." He gestured to himself and Nischia as she crossed her arms.

She'd had enough. No holding back. "And who is to say that ridiculous rule can't be changed?"

Nischia bit her lip as Koln took a deep breath. "Miss Tarri. I'll have you know that I am a traditionalist. I know my blessing has been bestowed upon me by the gods. I also know you to be a well-educated citizen. Our souls and our bodies are connected to this tree. It is spiritual as much as it is biological. If an Aobian severs that connection, their decision is irrecoverable."

Tarri bit her lip before replying. "I love my home, my lord. I love Aobia, its people, and our culture. But I won't deny that I am a realist." She paused. "Of course, you know this already."

Koln coughed. "Ahem. Unfortunately, it isn't as simple as reading people's minds at the drop of a hat, Miss Tarri. Every ounce of Luminosity used takes away from us and, to be entirely honest, I have better things to do with it than read mundane thoughts." He stood and moved to the door. "I will not lie to you. It goes against every fibre of my being to criticise the Magisterium; however, I have found some cause for concern in Sedulus' response to discovering the death of the human king. There is more to uncover. I will speak further with those in the Magisterium who oversee operations at the water facility. If I have anything else to share with you, Nischia will let you know."

Outside, the night had set in and the streetlights lit the road that Koln had already continued down, walking back in the direction of the Sleepers' homes without so much as a goodbye. Nischia stood facing Tarri, having called a cabriolet to collect her. A sympathetic lilt showed on the Sleeper's mouth. "My child," she said. "All will be well. One way or another. Please, understand that we both have the same interests at heart. And we know you do too. I know Koln can be hard, but…" She took a moment to formulate her words. "You did wonderfully today. I know that if I had lost the love of my life in such a tragic turn of events, I would react *much* more strongly than you—and that is, by no means, a good thing."

"Thank you, my lady," Tarri replied. "When can I expect we will meet next?"

Nischia let out a breath. "Let me focus on the next few days, Tarri. I'll call on you when it's time to work on this case. With so many things happening, we must take a careful approach, you understand." She turned to go before looking back, displaying a sly smile. "But bad news is always accompanied by good news and I may soon call on you for a different matter, too. There's been a selection of fitting real estate along these roads deeper into the Mind." She winked and followed Koln.

Real estate? Tarri covered a grin, suppressing excitement because she couldn't feel justified to be excited given what had happened and, added to that, she didn't want to get her hopes up. But the opportunities for her business, for Apris and Rela… Yes, it was exciting.

She got in the cab, mind still racing. It was as though she was fighting for two feelings at once. One gnawed at her like she was food and took more of her every day that Drift did not return home. Then there was the second feeling, the one that begged her to do as she was asked without question. Because she was on to a good thing, as Drift would say. She was making a success of her business and that was a dream come true.

Where it stung the most, of course, was that deep down, in her heart of hearts, she knew: if anything was to happen to her relationship with the Sleepers, her world would come crashing down.

Now she faced a new frontier, a world where the death of a human king was possibly linked to the disappearance of her betrothed. The Magisterium was being tested with suspected internal corruption. And she still felt as though she was grasping at straws for more understanding. It was like watching the beginnings of a disease affect a person.

It was like a rot growing in the branches of Aobia.

DRIFT

T HE SUN HAD RISEN nearly an hour before Drift and Stag hit the road, bleary eyed and muscles burning with exhaustion. Drift walked with a brisk pace ahead of Stag, letting the morning chill spur him on. He wanted anything, even the rush of the breeze past him, to take his mind off of the previous night's events. He couldn't stop replaying them if he tried. Raegan, trapped by Gaudin's townsfolk... A shiver radiated down his spine.

Raegan was probably rotting in a cell in Providence and the thought made Drift feel sick. After all the farmer had done for them, this is what he got in return: his children to never hold him again with Mola left to care for them and his farm.

Gaudin was not as concerned with Stag and Drift's escape as he had pretended to be. *"They're dead when they get to the Mountain Gate anyway."* Those had been his words. Drift didn't know what to expect of the land before them, the expanse of the Adiran and Theradoran nations that split the land in two. All of Q'ara was spoken about as being in an endless tug of war between them. It was not until the uprising of the Adiran people centuries ago, when they'd fought for freedom from the tyranny of the emperor at the time, Crolm the Thirsty, that Therador had lost the vigour they'd had when they'd first invaded Q'ara thousands of years before.

The Theradoran people and the lands out to the West belonging to the Sethi people were therefore always considered barbaric. But Drift knew better. Aobians were, after all, the original custodians of the land, along with the weasel-like race known as the Hidden Ones in the south-west, who lived their lives largely unseen, unless they were called to be present because of some dire circumstance.

Though the two Aobians were headed to the Sea Kingdom of Adira, which was also the strongest human alliance the Sleepers maintained, Drift knew they'd have to brush with the Theradorans as they crossed the mountain pass into the Adiran town of Relond.

"Stag," Drift called.

"Hmm?" Stag's voice was distracted and Drift caught him shoving something quickly away into his pack.

"What were you doing?" Drift asked.

"That was not your original question," Stag said stiffly.

"It's my question now." Drift eyed the ambassador.

"Roots below," Stag swore. "Fine. I was about to make a report to the Magisterium, let them know we were—*I* was—run out of Providence."

"A report?" Drift questioned. "But how?"

"Linked *cism,*" Stag said. "Please, don't ever tell anyone that I shared this with you. It would be the end of my career." He retrieved an object from his pack once more, a piece of fabric separating it from his fingertips: a glass sphere filled with yellow and white light, swirling around like it was liquid. A Sleeper's portable container for Luminosity.

Drift had heard of these devices before, but he'd never seen one. "Don't Sleepers store Luminosity in these?"

"Yes," Stag replied. "But I can use it to communicate with them. My direct report in the Magisterium fills two *cism* in a single Sleep cycle and connects them. I can simply hold the object and send an audible message to them when I want. But if I use it too much too often, I'll waste the light within."

"Stag," Drift started, "you wouldn't tell them about me, would you?"

Stag shook his head immediately. "No. It would damage me as much as it would you. But will I need to explain how I lost my caravan and had to make my way from Providence on foot? Undoubtedly, because it significantly slows my journey."

Drift nodded. "Okay. I trust you then. My original question was about Relond… Is this place another Providence?"

Stag snorted. "Nothing like it. In fact, it's somewhat of a nice place. A small city, rather than a town. It's a lot like Adira, which

I suppose is obvious given it's part of the kingdom, but of course it isn't set near the sea. Lots more infrastructure and less social collapse than Providence, I daresay." He paused before going on. "Relond is halfway between Aobia and Adira. If we can use my reputation in the city to secure us a horse and cart, then we'll be well on the way to Adira."

It sounded like a decent enough plan. Drift had to admit that having Stag along made some things easier. He got to travel with someone familiar, who was also well-travelled. And he could leverage Stag's credibility amongst the human communities as an ambassador.

"The only small encumbrance we may encounter," Stag went on, "is the Mountain Gate."

Drift sucked in a breath. "Gaudin was more than happy to let us go in its direction."

"A small settlement," Stag qualified. "Theradoran, actually. Militia mostly. They're a border check in the mountain pass through to the east or west. It's not technically Theradoran land. In fact, it hasn't belonged to any nation. The armistice was called on the top of the mountain and as part of the armistice agreements, Filens of Adira gave Therador free reign to control the Mountain Gate as a border between north and south."

Drift frowned. "So you've passed through this area many times before?"

"Of course," Stag proffered. "But don't say I didn't warn you. Those people don't always play by the rules and, depending on which officers man the gates, they might demand near-ransom levels of currency to pass through. After all, it's the only way to the north, unless you want to fight your way over the uncrossed ranges on either side."

Dread fell to the pit of Drift's stomach. The guard at the mountain pass could be on the lookout for any Aobian after what had happened in Providence. If Gaudin had sent men ahead to the Mountain Gate, there would be trouble when Drift and Stag finally arrived. The face of the Relondian crier, Briar Sevardson, flashed in Drift's mind. That man had wanted them vilified to the townsfolk of Providence as much as Gaudin had. Maybe he would be the one to report their whereabouts to the Theradoran guards at the pass.

Drift had heard stories of Therador, of course: the original empire that ruled the continent, the bloodthirsty reign of the emperors, a long line in a dynasty that refused to die, even after the Four-Front War. At the moment, a man named Jurin sat on the golden throne, who would be followed by his son Rainol. Drift could only guess at what the two of them were like, given the stories he'd heard. An emperor who promoted the Ethos of Dirt to his people: that any man, woman, or child who did not work for the land, and the empire, would be thrust back into the earth that had first birthed them. Drift had heard that Jurin had sacrificed his own children because they'd been girls, and thus, not suitable heirs. The son who had survived had apparently been a part of the decision-making that had led to his own siblings' demise. Sickening.

The silence broke when Stag prompted Drift with a new question. "So… Let's say we get to Adira, hopefully with all our limbs still attached and without an angry crowd of humans hot on our heels. What will you do there?"

Nothing Stag ever said came unaccompanied by an agenda and Drift couldn't help but feel a jab of anger at the question. He wanted the freedom to go home if he wished. That feeling, as though something had been torn from his soul when he'd left Aobia, was still present. "I … don't know. Maybe I could find a way to return home. If not, then I could start a new life. Maybe I could work with you? When you're on the outside, of course."

Stag cleared his throat.

Drift didn't even give him the time to reply. "You know what? I'm sure I'll work it out."

"It's not that…" Stag sighed. "I suppose we're beyond the reach of the Magisterium now. It's about Flow, you see."

"What's Flow got to do with it?" Drift shot back.

"Flow … is being watched, Drift. By the Magisterium. For something so serious, even I know none of the specifics. We got back from Adira and he was dismissed immediately, relieved of all duties. Then I was told to return to Adira and give them the news immediately, so that they would not think our people capable of breaking century-long oaths."

"What did he do?"

"I don't know, Drift. I swear it. Even if I did, I wouldn't share it. Those who are implicated in this sort of knowledge risk…" He trailed off, looking away.

"What?" Drift pressed.

"Exile," Stag muttered back. "I'm sorry, Drift. I understand it's touchy."

Touchy was a word, all right. "It's the worst punishment, Stag," Drift said. "And I *feel* different, Stag. We are taught all our lives that we are like extensions of the branches of Aobia. If I think on it too much, I feel … cut off. Mixed up. Incorrect, somehow." None of these explanations really made sense. Drift himself couldn't understand the way he felt. "I wouldn't wish it on my worst enemy."

Stag nodded, taking a moment before responding. "You're right, Drift. I can't imagine it. I don't understand why what happened to you happened. But I do wonder whether there is something more to it."

They walked on in silence, the landscape unchanging. Finally, Stag sighed. "This is all I'll say and you will not ask me about it again. Agreed?"

Drift nodded. "Very well."

"Flow would meet with someone in a tavern near Relond whenever we were there. I feigned ignorance and let him go about it. I thought it was a whore, if I'm being honest. The last time he met with them, however, they sat in the tavern, tucked into a corner. I was at the bar and saw them for the first time. I couldn't make out the person's features, but I began to wonder if it was an Aobian. They were far too tall to be human."

Drift raised an eyebrow. "Are you suggesting that Flow was meeting with someone else from home? Outside the Tree without permission? The last exile was the Queen and she died before she could be cast out."

Stag shook his head. "I'll say no more. Whatever Flow did must've been serious. He always seemed like the kind of fellow who would end up in a mess. More like you and less like me."

That comment set something alive in Drift. "And what? He and I don't have what it takes to do what you do?" he asked, incredulous.

Stag pursed his lips as if considering Drift's words. Then, he simply said, "No."

Drift chose not to fight back. It would get them nowhere and Stag was all he had.

Sunset came and they gathered and prepared a roadside meal of berries and fragrant, wild rosemary leaves.

It was the first night Drift thought about lighting a fire, but his fear of it kept him from sharing the idea. When he saw Stag shivering, however, he knew he was not the only one who could use some heat.

Together, Drift and Stag sat with a silence that was both uneasy and unappealing, resting against twin tree trunks. Drift looked at the tiny canopy above him, considering how oddly small trees were in this part of the world, before the silence broke with Stag's careful next words.

"The dam back home, Drift. What happened?"

"You tell me. You know things, Stag. You told Raegan as much. That I was pushed from the viaduct."

Stag shook his head. "I never said that. I was debriefed by some Sleepers before being sent on this job and they gave me three potential storylines. The truth is, they're investigating Sedulus too, Drift."

Sedulus. The name swelled an anger in him, like the beginnings of a river rapid. He still couldn't believe Sedulus could have done such a thing to him. "He couldn't have, Stag."

Stag looked down. "I'm not so sure. And after hearing about Flow's dismissal… Nobody leaves Aobia. Not without the proper permissions, as you know." He kicked in frustration at a long stick in front of him, sending it bouncing across the ground. "I'm being paranoid. Told myself it was a ridiculous idea in the first place."

Drift felt himself connecting the dots. "You think Flow met with him outside Aobia when you were on a job," he breathed.

"I don't know." Stag practically spat the words. "I don't know what to think, Drift. And it's dangerous to make assumptions. Did I see Sedulus that night in the tavern? No. But I saw an outline of someone who became him in my mind the moment I found out Flow was being removed from his position. I nearly reported the incident via *cism* that night but I…" He sighed. "It's ridiculous. Forget I said that."

Drift was inclined to agree with Stag that these assumptions were nonsensical. How was it possible that Sedulus could've met with Flow in a human town? He pictured Sedulus' ice-blue eyes piercing his own at the very moment he slipped over the waterfall.

"This is the stuff you knew about, isn't it?" Drift asked rhetorically. "You really *are* scared they will read your thoughts."

Stag would not return his eyes to Drift's level. "Would you blame me? Would I ever truly know if they have?"

"No," Drift said. "Stag. It's okay. We're here now, on the way to the Sea Kingdom. We need to communicate. We need to work together, which means we have to be transparent. From now on."

Stag met his gaze. "Okay." He nodded.

Drift swirled nondescript patterns in the dirt with a stick. "The Sickness bypassed our filtration systems further south of Aobia. I was there when it happened. Then the river rose with waves as tall as buildings. The water was hot and it foamed up. Just imagine what would happen to our relationship with the humans if we ruined the river. What if we could only keep enough of it clean for our people? Imagine how many people would die and how much of that would be our fault. Skin melting from bones, like the eradication of the Kathani."

It was an old but assumed piece of knowledge from Q'ara's history: unless the Aobians used the powers of the Sleepers to filter the water of the river, it was toxic. Nobody knew what caused it, but it had wiped out an entire civilisation, human settlers to the south known as Kathani, as well as the last of the Aobian settlements that had remained close to the Janub desert. The water looked and smelled the same but tasted like blood and would kill any who drank from it within a day. The stories told of bodies turning to mush, skin homogenising on the ground in thick, soupy pools. For centuries after, the water needed to be boiled before consumption, a process that drained resources.

At that time, only Aobia benefited from the treatment the Sleepers could provide. The Sleepers would power the filtered catchments at the highest point of the river to the south, a collection of thousands of species of algae and fungi that destroyed whatever was spoiling the water. Studies had been conducted by the best scientists, and even theologians, but there had never been a conclusion reached: the Sleepers' Luminosity somehow cleaned the water and the organisms responsible for filtering it as it coursed its way under Aobia were able to keep the water clean. Both processes had come to work in tandem.

Originally, the water had been redirected into old waterways carved into the branches of the Great Tree itself, where Aobians had gathered and used it. When Aobia had made treaties with Adira, they'd agreed to build a viaduct that could pool water from the river, clean it, and continue the flow over the top of a dam that sent the water all the way to the coast.

Therador had never gotten access to this, not even after the armistice had been signed at the end of the Four-Front War. Another thought struck Drift. "The king who died," he began. "Are there tensions with the humans of Therador?"

"I suspect there's something there," Stag confirmed. "Water is a vital resource. It always has been. But what is the most vital resource of all? The same thing that started the Four-Front War, that divided our people and demolished the monarchy. Luminosity and its secrets have been the greatest motivation for every inch of control Therador has tried to exercise in the past. Now, think about Q'ara today. Right now. A dead king disrupts continental peace. The Sleepers are concerned. Parliament has been held more often than ever. There are other machinations afoot both in Aobia and beyond the Tree. I fear we've sheltered ourselves too much and it's helped me realise something."

"What's that?" Drift asked, curious.

"We are our own worst enemy."

TARRI

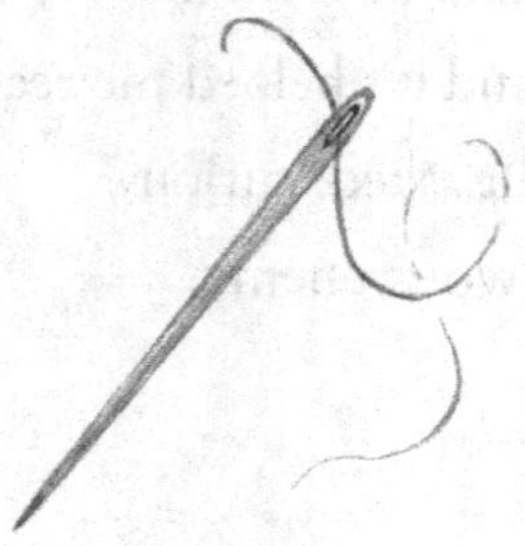

T ARRI SAT AT HER dining table, the afternoon light leaking in through the windows like a final offering from the sun.

After she'd gotten back home and prepared a hot cup of green-mint tea, she'd sat with a large piece of parchment paper sprawled on the table before her, a paperweight in one corner and an inkwell and quill in the other. Something she always did when her thoughts were too spread out, like a sky-stretching cloud, was to map them out on paper and consider each one individually, as well as part of the bigger picture.

In the middle of her page, she wrote: *Drift*. With an arrow extending down from that, she wrote the next name that came to mind.

Sedulus.

Drift was her whole world, so he needed to be at the centre of the page. But despite the conversation Koln and Nischia had had with Sedulus earlier that day, she knew—just *knew*—that there was more to Sedulus' story.

She extended another arrow from Drift's name to a corner of the page, writing Nischia's and Koln's names.

Tarri still had no idea how to fit the Sleepers into the picture. She knew Nischia and Koln would not tell her everything they knew. Thinking about Drift, she recalled his lifelong mistrust of the Sleepers and the Magisterium in general. It had come from his father. She'd known him well and wished he was still here today. Despite the illness that had taken him far too early, he'd loved her like a daughter.

There was a particular memory she had of him though that found its way to the front of her mind as she considered the page before her. He'd been lying in his bed with wet rags on his wrists and forehead. He'd told her that the Magisterium had known he'd been sick and that they could have chosen to heal him, but they had not. The same fate Drift's mother had met, too.

Beneath the two Sleepers' names, she wrote *Luminosity* and then a shorter arrow was drawn from all three to the words *Water Facility*. She's seen them that night: Nischia and Koln meeting with Sedulus the night after Drift had gone missing. And Nischia had seen her, although they'd never returned to that conversation since bringing it up briefly in the back room of the Tailory. When they'd met with Sedulus, Nischia had mentioned as much: that Luminosity helped to power the facility in some way.

She went through her thoughts again, writing *Adiran King* in the top left corner of the page and connecting it to *Nischia* and

Koln. The lack of a line between *Adiran King* and *Luminosity* struck her, but she left it blank.

She moved back down to Sedulus. There were lines of connection here, far too many to fully understand. Then she considered one last name, which, as of her findings today, definitely connected Drift, the Sleepers, and Sedulus.

Fl—

As she started to write the next name, the door flew open. Flow stood there, straight backed with that ever-endearing smile. "I thought you'd be here," he said. "I went to the Tailory this afternoon and you weren't there!"

"Oh," Tarri said, surprised, as she stood from the table and straightened her skirt. "Flow! Is everything all right?"

"I wanted to talk with you," he said with an insistent edge to his voice. "We haven't spoken since the other night."

Of course. *That* particular drunken endeavour. Tarri had gotten home and gotten partially sober, because of Flow, after her meeting with Nischia. But the thanks she'd had for Flow had been eroded. He had tried to make an impression upon her, knowing her heart was with Drift, and she didn't feel good about it.

"Flow, I-I don't think—" Tarri stammered the words, cutting herself off and putting her hands up while stepping back as he invited himself over the threshold of the front door.

"It's okay!" Flow put his own hands up in a defensive stance. "I just … haven't been able to stop thinking about Drift."

Relief blew through Tarri. "Oh," she said, dropping her arms. "Of course. I feel the same way."

She caught his eyes, unsure if she saw sincerity deep within them or some other thing, like a gem buried at the bottom of an ice-cold stream. Her thoughts flickered to Nischia. *Do not offer him any information you would not otherwise offer a person off the street.* She broke eye contact and sat back down. Flow followed her to the dining table, the afternoon light leaking in through the front door behind him as he left it ajar.

She glanced down and saw the paper. What was Flow going to think if he read it? Thank the Sleepers she hadn't written his whole name out yet. She quickly moved her paper weight as discreetly as possible across the letter 'F' that she had written before he'd walked in.

"What's this?" Flow asked about the parchment.

"It's nothing," Tarri said. She took a breath. "I … like to get my ideas out on paper, is all."

"Of course," Flow replied, considerate. "I'm much the same, truth be told. So, what have you arrived at so far?"

Tarri sucked some air in. If she chose to engage Flow in this conversation, she would be choosing to manage him as well as everything else for the time being. Then a thought crossed her mind. If Flow was being held at arm's length by the Magisterium, perhaps she could bend him a little and twist this conversation in her favour. "I am meeting with the Lady Nischia more often now. And today, I met her superior, a Sleeper named Koln."

"I know of Koln." Flow nodded. "He's stern, but a good person. Stag and I would sometimes report to him, though we haven't done that in years now."

"And what do you know about Nischia?" Tarri asked. She would take what she could get from him. She couldn't trust Flow and she couldn't trust Nischia, not totally. If she had to make these choices alone, then so be it.

Flow seemed caught on her words for a brief moment but moved smoothly on. "Not much. She was taken in by Koln at a young age when she first became a Sleeper. I'm no god, Tarri. What could I possibly know about either of them that you need me to share?"

"I—nothing," she stammered. "Just curious, is all." She had to play this game carefully, like knowing when to step with a dance partner. Flow was a person of interest to the Sleepers. She had to know why. Maybe that would give her a clue about any connections between Drift and the dead king of Adira.

"I wanted to talk to you about the Sleepers though. They don't hear everything. They need to be actively listening for your thoughts specifically. It takes a lot of Luminosity to read minds."

Tarri nodded. "I always thought that was the case."

"The other thing," Flow responded, "is that you can block them. The Sleepers."

"You're telling me nothing new," she replied coolly. "Nischia mentioned as much."

"Really?" Flow seemed annoyed. He wasn't getting the response he'd wanted from her. Why was he here? "And she told you about the specifics of that?"

"Well, no, but—"

"Did she tell you that *you* could do it?"

"Me?" Tarri put a hand to her chest, woefully exaggerating her movements. She knew this from Nischia, but she had to feign ignorance until Flow explained where this was going.

"It's a learned skill." Flow held her gaze. "But *you* already know it innately, somehow."

Nischia had told her the same thing. "How do you know that?"

"Because I have this."

Flow pulled something out from the inside pocket of his cloak and the warm glow was immediately recognisable. A *cism*. The very same tiny sphere of Luminosity that Nischia had used to shield them when they had been conversing in the Tailory. Only this one carried a lacklustre glow within it.

"How did you get that?" Tarri gasped.

"Let's just say there are certain … benefits to being a government official. This one is nearly empty, anyhow," Flow said, allowing Tarri to behold the small globe for a moment. "Tarri, we could learn the bounds of Luminosity."

She watched speechlessly as he picked up her hand and placed it on the *cism*. Immediately, light flowed from the sphere and into her arm. It felt oddly warm and looked just as it had when she'd seen Nischia do the same thing. The room went dark around them, as though there was no light in the world besides the glass *cism*.

"I knew it," Flow breathed. "You can access Luminosity. But how?"

She backed away from him, and all the ambient light rushed back into the room. She wouldn't be toyed with like this. Nischia had warned her about Flow, and rightly so. "What do you know?"

Flow placed the *cism* back in his cloak, putting his hands up. "Now, Tarri, I—"

"You want anything to do with me? You want to speak to me ever again? Tell me what you know." She felt his resolve breaking under her stare. *Bend him. Break him.*

Flow sighed. "Fine. I acquired this *cism* from someone I've been meeting with in Relond, an Adiran town on the other side of the Mountain Gate."

"A human? And how did they get it?" Humans had fought for access to Luminosity for years. On the brink of discovering how it worked with help from Aobia's traitor queen, Feldra, they'd lost it again, and Aobia had overturned its own monarchy as a result. If a human had given Flow that *cism,* that could mean Aobia's greatest gift might already have been made someone else's. The continental ramifications of it would be extreme.

The dead king. Therador.

She gulped.

"Not a human," Flow said. "One of our own. But I refuse—I *refuse*—to say any more about them. That's not what this is about, Tarri. Look." He leant over the parchment she had laid out on the table and took up her quill in his hands.

He drew a line from *Sedulus* to *Luminosity*. "Do what I need and I'll tell you more. I'm close, Tarri. Close to finding out more about Luminosity than some Sleepers would know."

She scoffed in disbelief. What did that connection to Sedulus mean? "Does Drift relate to any of this?"

Flow looked away. "Roots below," he swore under his breath.

"I need honesty, Flow. You don't get to make demands of me."

Flow nodded. "Understood. That parchment… Talk me through what you have so far and I'll share what I can."

They both sat around the paper as Tarri explained the links she was trying to form between the Sleepers, Drift, Sedulus, and the dead Adiran King. She kept one hand firmly planted on the paperweight that covered the beginning of Flow's written name.

When they came back to Sedulus' name, Tarri looked up from the paper with pleading eyes. "Tell me what you know of him, Flow. Everything."

"He's been in the business of shielding for years, Tarri," Flow said.

"It's a business?" Tarri didn't understand. Were people selling something that gave others this ability?

"It's not just an expression," Flow affirmed. "The secret to learning such a thing is coveted by all. You can buy secrets if you have the right connections, Tarri. That's what Sedulus did. But he went straight to the top."

"What?"

"The Sleepers. He bribed his way into the knowledge he needed to be able to shield himself. Not permanently but … nearly that. The thing is, a Sleeper wouldn't notice this unless they had reason to target a particular person. And he was always the law-abiding, quiet type. Besides, he can turn it off when he wants. The Magisterium would be none the wiser."

"Do many others know these ... secrets?" Tarri asked, aghast.

"I don't know," Flow replied. "That's the truth."

Tarri felt the need to be direct now. "Do *you* know these secrets from Sedulus, Flow?"

Flow shuffled in his seat. "I do."

"Then I will not have you tell me another thing on the matter." She held her head high. "I'll discover it myself if what you say is true."

"Don't be so petulant," Flow retorted.

"Petulant?" Tarri repeated the word, laughing. "I can't trust you. I can't fully trust Lady Nischia. I'm not being petulant. Can *you* bring Drift home?" She waited for the silence that told her Flow knew he could not answer. "I thought not."

"I'll be on my way then," Flow said finally. "I've said all I'm willing to say and you aren't willing to help me. That's not how friendship works, Tarri."

Friendship. That's what she'd thought she'd had with Flow all these years. But now, when it came down to it, there was nothing in it besides his own self-interest. She wouldn't help Flow discover more secrets of Luminosity. She would find them herself and use them to bring Drift back.

He wasn't leaving. Flow stood, facing her with a menacing look. "Some Sleepers have found that they can use Luminosity to move themselves."

She wanted to tell him to stop talking, to leave. But her curiosity got the better of her. "Move themselves? How?"

"That's what I'm trying to find out."

The silence that came was slow and creeping, like the crawl of a quiet night's breeze, though it was still sunny outside. Tarri felt her skin tingle in response. "I'm not sure I understand what you mean."

"I think Sedulus was involved with Drift's exile, Tarri. Because I know he can bi-locate. You see, while he was dealing with Drift, he was also attending a meeting with a human from Therador."

It couldn't be true. Being able to be in two places at once was old folk-story magic. It came up in children's stories, like *Esmeralda and the Rescue of the Earthchild*, a story about a Sleeper who helped save her people during the death of a Great Tree. Esmeralda Slept in the Great Tree whilst also moving around the forest floor. But even in stories like that, the Sleeper was never able to exist in two locations at once *without* Sleep. The Orb within which Sleepers generated their powers was in itself a place.

Tarri could only form one feasible solution. "Sedulus is ... a Sleeper?"

"What?" Flow suppressed a chuckle, then continued with wide eyes as if realising where Tarri's thoughts had gone, "Not at all. Oh, you don't mean the stories, do you? No, this is more useable than what's in those. Without a doubt, Sedulus can be in two places at once."

Trying to take it all in, Tarri squinted, waving a hand for Flow to slow down. "Wait. How do you know where he was, Flow?"

Flow levelled a look at her. "I've seen it."

Tarri stood from her seat and began to pace. "Explain!" she hissed. He had protected something as important as this information. And to what end? To save himself from the Sleepers?

Flow winced. "I met with Sedulus in Relond. He gave me the *cism* and taught me how it worked. All the things it could do: heal the sick, channel Luminosity into pure, concentrated heat… The first few times, I would return the *cism* to him and he'd give me a new one. I don't know how he got them. But then he refused to give me more, because I was getting too close to accessing the Luminosity without leaking it all away. But, Tarri, what if anyone could use Luminosity?"

And there it was. "You want me to get you another one? A *cism*?"

"Listen," he said. "I know I made a mistake. But this world could be made so much better if we could all use the Tree's power. Imagine it. Continental peace at last. Adira is in the throes of grief right now. Could Terrens' death have been avoided if Luminosity was freely accessible to all? If monarchic power didn't really matter?"

"If I get this *cism*, you'll teach me what you know? About how to draw from it?"

Flow nodded. "You're close to Nischia, Tarri. She'll never see it coming." Flow shrugged. "Look, I have access to knowledge I shouldn't have. But I don't have the means of acquiring the *cism* itself. This"—he pulled out the globe of dwindling light once more—"is no Luminous core, like the ones in the streetlights or in your oven. Those are like one-way faucets designed for a purpose. The *cism,* on the other hand, is contained Sleep."

The Sleep that Sleepers entered into within their Orbs was a very taxing and arduous task. Tarri knew that from what had happened to her mother. *Cism* alleviated their need to Sleep so often to help avoid the risk of burning themselves out on raw Luminosity. She could get a *cism.* Whether she'd give it to Flow or not, however, was for her to decide later. There was still one other thing left unanswered though.

"You still haven't explained how you knew I was able to access Luminosity, Flow."

Flow hesitated. "When I first learned to use the *cism* to shield, I thought I could use it to read. I couldn't quite figure it out. But I *did* find out you were shielding yourself, unbeknownst to you at the time."

Tarri recoiled. She felt exposed, watched. And he'd dared to call himself her friend not five minutes earlier. "I don't know when you tried to do that or how you tried to do it. Just get out. Get out and stay away from me! Go!"

Flow hung his head with shame and the sincerity of the action stung her briefly. But then, he turned and left her home. He closed the door behind him and was gone.

She sighed in relief. There was too much to recall, too much to make sense of. But Flow had planted one seed in her mind that she couldn't let go of. Hesitation met her immediately. Everything hinged on this decision. Nischia's trust. Her business' success. Her life as an Aobian. Drift's life as an exile. But if she pulled this off, maybe it would equip her with the upper hand she needed as long as she continued on her mission to bring Drift home.

She would steal the *cism*. She would try to uncover its secrets alone. And if she couldn't, well, only then would she go to Flow.

It was worth both everything and nothing at all.

DRIFT

THE AIR SEEMED TOO thin with the higher elevation. The river had already veered off, no longer a guide for their travels. He felt oddly attached to it, an umbilical cord keeping him connected to his motherland. When it disappeared, he became intensely aware of his only chance to find his way through the Mountain Gate: Stag.

The land here was epitomised by the lack of flowing water. The ground was shale, dusty debris that caused the foot to slip if proper attention was not paid on steeper inclines. Though there was still a path cut here, it wound about the trees and got lost in the ever-changing flora, which only got drier and shorter as their walking progressed. And as they escalated, the scenery went from dry and arid, bound by the laws of the summer, to frigid and cold, a new world that seemed to pay no heed to anything beneath it.

The day had gone slowly, but Drift felt as though they'd made significant progress. Without any reference of a map or guide of some kind, he could only guess that they'd covered a good distance since running from the town mob at Providence. He was still unable to let go of thoughts of Raegan and his family. He'd stirred through his sleep the night before as a result and had found himself awake before dawn, looking skyward and feeling how high above everything else he finally was.

Aobia had always been his home, one he had taken for granted, but in times like this, Drift could reminisce about how special it really was. Nestled between the morning rays of light and the forest that fell away beneath the cliffs they walked, the skyline of the Great Tree could still be seen, like a gemstone in a moving river. The kind that Drift had fished out when he'd gotten the chance and had saved for Tarri, to give to her after a day of work.

His neck burned. Yet again, guilt choked him. In the time since his exile, the ache in his heart had only grown. He wanted to see her, to hold her. To smell her hair or dance with her or take her out to dine at her favourite spots in the Soul. There, they would bicker about the options, the endless choices to experience artisanal foods. Aobians who had had the chance to experience the human parts of the world through one means or another, whether retired public servants or veterans who had fought in the war, would set up outdoor tents, serving cuisine that was foreign and interesting. He would pull her in the direction of something new every time, but she would ground him, yet again, in what they knew. What they could rely upon.

He had none of that now and was no longer grounded in anything. Not here, hovering thousands of feet above the dense treeline of the distant forestry, careful not to slip down a cliff. In the world of the humans, Drift had realised that everything was a gamble. And perhaps he missed the stability of his home and his betrothed more than he had ever given them credit for.

He wondered what Tarri was doing now. She was filled with ambition for her business, and for life in general, but she was also deeply rooted in Aobian life, something that Drift had always looked at as monotonous. Perhaps she'd try to find out about what had happened to him. Where could she start? What if the Sleepers pretended as though nothing had happened? He hoped she'd have sense enough to go to Flow.

Then again, after what Stag had said of Flow, maybe Tarri wouldn't be safe with him. If it was true, Drift couldn't do a thing about it.

They rounded a corner, winding through the mountainside like a chiselled-out staircase, slippery masses of shale on shale, a sea of constantly dispersing shards of earth. He watched as Stag missed his footing, one leg sliding back nearly a metre before he got grip, anchoring himself with a large stick he'd found earlier that morning before the presence of trees had started to dwindle.

Forcing a breath through tight lips, Stag looked back at Drift, wincing. "That was too close for my liking. This is what I warned you about."

"I can see that," Drift replied. "And I don't envy you. It isn't going to get much easier from here, is it?"

Stag shook his head, visibly upset by the near miss. "Steeper, looser ground." He let out a few puffed breaths. "The worst combination of variables. Even in a carriage, being up this high doesn't inspire much confidence in the horses. Or me."

They continued on their way, Drift evaluating Stag's footing from behind, trying to both critique the bad steps and match the good ones. Not an hour had passed before the staggering heights of the mountain changed again, aided by the sheer drop of the cliff they followed, where the Mountain Gate was tucked in between two peaks. The sickness Drift felt from looking down was nearly dizzying, making him recalculate every move he made.

These heights were nothing like the heights of the Great Tree, yet the only thing Drift could pick that was different between the two was the path they walked, which was barely wide enough to fit a carriage. He glanced out at the expanse of Aobia's Great Canopies in the distance. In Aobia, nobody worked on the tips of the Great Tree's branches, though occasionally people did live on the edges where the streets thinned. And nestled in the denser twig-like streets of Aobia were branch-homes, dwellings built into the tree naturally rather than at the hands of branchrenders.

As the path twisted, Drift found himself clutching to toughened roots sprouting out of the ground, the kind that only grew in the arid conditions at the top of the mountain. Stag was opting instead for balancing himself with his walking stick, one arm extended where needed. Drift felt ill on the next clamber to a flat patch, as though suddenly aware of how high up he really was.

They made the next turn, when, everything he feared seemed to happen at once. His foot skidded so fast off the shale path that he felt a tear in his thigh muscles as his legs spread. His foot kept going, however, sailing over the edge of the path and causing his other leg to hit the ground knee first, then keep slipping back.

His balance lost, he scrambled for grip on anything but found no solace in the dizzying heights or the unsteady terrain. He tried to manage a cry for help, but Stag was up ahead; nothing came from his throat, as though even the words he wanted to scream had escaped him, all at the wrong time. In seconds, he was dangling from the edge, on the precipice of freefall, his feet searching for something—anything—to place themselves on.

The horror of the moment did not escape him as memories of the viaduct came rushing back. Tumultuous water threatening to lose his grip. Sedulus trying to grasp his hand and haul him up to safety but losing the strength to bring him up all the way. His arms tiring so quickly that letting go was his only choice. Would this have the same sad outcome? Would Stag turn around? Even if he did, would he have the strength to drag Drift back onto the path? Maybe he'd tested the universe and its plans for his fate too much, and he would fall to an abrupt, bone-crunching, neck-snapping, skin-tearing death with no water to save him.

His hands went numb from the pulling weight of his body and he began to panic that he would let go whether he wanted to or not. "Stag!" he puffed through dirt. "Help!"

Stag whipped his head around, his jaw dropping. He ran towards Drift, catching the slipstream of shale with some intention and sliding perfectly into position. He got onto his belly, the best way to plant his weight on the path, and seized both of Drift's wrists.

With grunting and heaving, he managed to get Drift back onto the path up to his elbows, at which point Drift was able to drag himself the rest of the way. Once safely planted, he spun his head away from the view, feeling nausea radiate through him as a shock response. He had nearly died then and Stag had saved him.

They lay disarrayed on the pebbled ground, wheezing in the cloud of dust that had formed around them as though announcing the close call that had just occurred.

Stag shot up, looking at him wildly. "You nearly died!"

Drift coughed. "I feel as though the gods are telling me something, Stag," he replied.

"What's that?"

"That one day, I'll die falling."

That night, they moved off the windy track that wound around the mountainside, heading uphill on somewhat grassy patches and into the denser collection of trees. They found a small enough patch clear of any close trees, setting up again for the evening to caress their bones against the unnerving whisper of the breeze. Drift could feel the cold really piercing him now and half-considered a fire once more. A fire could warm his inners before it did any damage, couldn't it? A sin against nature is what it was.

But in Aobia, this cold would never be as assertive, as brazen, because the higher parts of the Great Canopies would seal in the warmth. Even throughout the winter, snow would stick and fall from the crown of the Great Tree, occasionally hitting the branchground, but it would never be threatening enough for anyone to feel the need to dress the way the outside world appeared to require. However, here on this mountain, Drift felt every stab of the wind like a knife. It didn't matter that it was the start of summer.

"How do you adjust to this cold?" he asked, shuddering beneath his tightly pulled cloak.

Stag fingered another dried, nearly dead berry that they'd picked the day before. "Truth be told, the mountains make me the most bitter out of all the human lands."

Drift eyed him with a frown but said nothing. He enjoyed this more open and honest Stag. The one who wore his feelings on his sleeve instead of a false face of bravado and the air of arrogance that had always sent Drift in the other direction when he'd seen him.

"I'm happiest near the sea." Stag put his bowl down, pulling his cloak around his shoulders. "But this part of the world wasn't made for us, Drift. We're meant to be in a tree, working like bees in a hive. I know you probably think that's a disgusting idea or a perverse attack on free will. But I feel comforted by it. It's what gets me through trips like these, through these dismal parts, where everything's grey and dirty and cold. Maybe you'll see what I mean one day." He lay down, placing his head upon the soft bottom of his pack.

Against the dim light of the moon, Drift could see his fellow Aobian already closing his eyes. "I'm already seeing it that way," he admitted in a whisper that went below the hum of the mountain air. "I'm already feeling my heart's distance from what it truly loves."

In the bitter cold of the mountainside, there was no place he'd rather be than his home in the Tree with the love of his life. But here, just like everything else, the truth too was harsh, and he knew he may never experience that again.

NISCHIA

T HE DOOR OF NISCHIA'S apartment slammed open, colliding with the entryway wall. It caused her to jump, spilling hot tea from the pot she was pouring from. Koln strode in, clearly angered, and Nischia rushed over to the door to close it behind him.

"What is it?" she asked. They'd already met once today to talk about what they'd noticed when they'd met with Sedulus. It turned out the facility superior was able to shield Sleepers. After a full night of Sleep in the Orb, Nischia had had enough Luminosity to search his mind as they'd spoken. But during the conversation, not once had she been able to breach him. She needed to understand how it was that he could shield her.

"There's something more malevolent afoot than we've suspected, Nischia," Koln said as he looked out the window. "Do you know Maya and Fern, those two young Sleepers that work beneath Staril?"

"Yes, of course," Nischia said. "What about them?"

"Removed!" Koln snapped. "They're gone. Exiled? Jailed? Who knows?"

From her perspective, neither she nor Koln knew those two junior Sleepers well. They were still students. They'd probably broken their Fever only a year ago, the survival of which granted people with the Tree's blessing to Sleep and access an Orb. They'd been lucky enough to have been brought into Staril's fold of Magisterium leadership in clerical roles so soon into their new lives as Sleepers. But gone? It was strange, to say the least.

"You're not saying anything," Koln breathed.

"I'm merely waiting for you to finish all you have to say," Nischia replied.

"They were questioned," Koln went on, unwavering. "I heard it from Emdo, who was informed by the upper ministers that both of them had been brought in on suspicious charges of being embroiled in some kind of bribe."

Emdo was one of the twelve Seniors, the one ambassadors reported directly to, along with Staril herself. If the message had been passed on to him, it was because the ministers of the Upper Magisterium were being intentional about how they wanted the information to spread. This bribe, though… Perhaps it involved Sedulus or Flow, the ambassador who had been removed from his role upon returning to Aobia. Emdo was a trustworthy member of the Sleeper community who never embellished anything, so telling him was a controlled way of leaking the news to other Sleepers.

"The nature of the bribe…" Nischia left the question hanging in the air.

"An exchange between an Aobian and Therador."

"Therador?" Nischia was suddenly alert. Her palms were sticky with sweat and her thoughts went back, back to a time of trauma. A time when she'd seen her queen fall. She looked away into the distance, breathing deeply. The moment Feldra had died had never left her. The queen's betrayal was the greatest shortcoming in all of Aobia's history.

"Do not allow your heart power over your mind, child. I was there too. It will not happen again, I promise." Koln's gentle tone soothed her as he gripped her hand tightly, silently asking her to ground herself, to put her trust in him.

"I fear there is more at play than we've caught on to, Nischia," Koln continued. "The Adiran king, this matter with the exile… I feel tempted to say there is mass subterfuge afoot. Aobia is changing, Nischia. We both know it."

Nischia began carefully. "What evidence do we—"

"Have we not got enough?" Koln exclaimed before shaking his head. "I apologise. It's a gut feeling. There's something to be said for that." He let out a sigh.

"It's good enough for me, Koln. Truly," Nischia insisted. "But Staril, the Magisterium…"

"We're missing something, child." Koln drew the blinds and Nischia knew what was coming. Something Koln had only ever done a handful of times before.

He reached into his robes. Of course he had *cism* with him. He pressed his hand to the tiny orb, drawing on its Luminosity.

The light inside the room darkened. They were shielded now. "All these coincidental events are, as you say, an oddity. An extremity of collisions," Koln said. "I do not treat this lightly, so consider the severity of my next words, Nischia: someone from the Magisterium is involved."

Nischia breathed heavily, wordless. Koln was ever-devoted to the Magisterium and the culture of Sleepers in general. For him to suggest something this defiant… She couldn't fathom it.

"We need Tarri to do some things independently of us and report back," he said, moving on before Nischia could catch up. "She has an in with that ambassador friend. The one who's on indefinite probation."

"Flow," Nischia offered, swallowing. "I asked her to keep away from him, Koln. I can't go back on that."

"We can't risk having you out there, making inquiries. I need governmental support for these investigations, Nischia. I can't have them compromised because Staril grows unnerved by our movements. If we don't have the prime minister on our side, we'll end up like those two young Sleepers."

"What can the ambassador offer?" She looked at him, eyes searching.

"He and the tailor could speak with Sedulus."

"You'd send her into the lion's den?" Nischia asked. "We don't even understand the extent of the ambassador's suspension."

"I sent you to this tailor," Koln pressed, "to have a contact close to the exiled one that you could bring into the investigation. I did not expect you to strike up a friendship with her, let alone make a purchase—"

"Do *not* dare!" Nischia hissed. He wasn't talking about the commissioned dresses. How did he know about *that* purchase? "I am not letting anything get in the way of our work, Koln, and *you* of all people should know that!"

"Do I?" Koln laughed. "I didn't expect you to find feelings for this commoner, all because she lost her betrothed to—"

"Yes! She lost her betrothed!" Nischia yelled, chest heaving. She shoved away from him, storming over to the kitchen bench. "And I know what it feels like to lose people. I have holes in me, holes that will remain to the day I die!" Tears stung her eyes as she heard Koln exhale. Flashes of her family, the queen, and her time in the Four-Front War crossed her mind, vivid strokes of a paintbrush, coated with blood for one reason or another.

"I'm sorry, child. I misspoke." He hung his head.

Nischia sucked in a breath. "Have some compassion. What else does the child have but her business?"

Koln looked hurt, but he sank back. "You let your feelings rule your choices and it was me who pulled you out of every hole you ever dug for yourself. Do not get too close to Tarri. I warn you out of *compassion*."

The words were neither bitter nor cruel. Koln would discard Tarri without hesitation if he needed to; Nischia knew that. But she would not do the same. It wasn't just about Tarri's artistry. Nischia had come to see the child as she really was: someone who missed her beloved dearly and would stop at nothing to find him. Nischia saw that aspect in herself, except that when it came down to it, time and time again throughout her life, she had failed.

Her losses had outlasted the end of the Four-Front War. Part of her wanted Tarri to find all the answers she sought. Perhaps that want could atone for the sins of her past. It was a selfish sense of charity, an oxymoron. But to her, it made sense.

"What do you want her to do at the facility, Koln? What do you know?" She was calling his bluff, but behind her back, she kept her fingers crossed that her gut was right. Koln *always* knew something. He had always been a step ahead of her.

"The water filtration systems," he replied. "Tell her to survey them, report back on what she saw, how it was explained to her that they work. The algae, the use of Luminosity. We both know how the entire place is powered, but that's not the point. I suspect that ambassador has corroborations with Sedulus and I want to know why. Put them in the same room together and your little tailor will know whether something is odd about their interactions or not. She's smart."

"I've never heard you spill compliments like that. Some more of that talk would be nice on occasion." Nischia smiled. "You understand that we will have to reveal more than we usually would about Luminosity to a commoner?" Nobody but the Sleepers knew the intricacies of the Sleep. All the public knew was that the Blessing was given to certain individuals who survived the mysterious Fever, seemingly at random, and that it came from the Great Tree.

"I am willing to risk as much. If she finds out what is going on between Sedulus and that ambassador, I'll give her exactly what she wants. More knowledge, in exchange for her word."

"And how can you promise that?" Nischia sniggered. "You don't even know where Drift is."

"She doesn't need to know that." Koln crossed his knuckles together. "You tell me she's trustworthy and I trust you. Perhaps for now, we must play partly by the tailor's rules."

"I won't lie to her. *I* don't have the answers. How is Drift's story connected to the rest of this? All I can think is that it has to do with the Naming. Staril said as much. Naming is the one lost scion of our ways. A dead art."

"Naming is, as you say, a dead art. A world without it is a world better off. We agreed on that a century and a half ago." He was right about that. Naming used to be enforced on every other child born in Aobia. At birth, children would be 'Named' using a concentration of Sleeper Luminosity. Then, they would live out their life in accordance with many aspects of their Name. The theory at the time had been that if enough people were Named with intention, the monarchy could shape Aobia into a utopia. Instead, it had shaped society according to its own will.

"And you swear you know nothing of those practices since they were outlawed after Feldra's betrayal?"

Koln pursed his lips. "Swear? You would have me make an oath?"

"You're still shielding us. So tell me the truth. Were there any Naming Rituals after the ban?"

Koln hesitated, but he eventually gave in. "I … don't know with certainty. But I'm trying, slowly, to find out. I can't push at all my connections with the Seniors or Staril. It could come back to bite us."

"Or Logis?" One of the daughters of the All-Mother, who'd fled the Tree after Feldra and the All-Mother had both died. Surely Koln had thought to reach out to her via *cism*.

"Logis wouldn't know. She wasn't here." He said it with clenched teeth, an obvious mark of his resentment for his old friend.

Nischia decided to move swiftly on. "If you find evidence for Naming Rituals to have taken place after the monarchy collapsed, what will you do next?"

Koln said nothing. He looked at her and in his eyes, for once, she saw genuine fear. If Naming Rituals had gone on behind the backs of most of the magisterium, it would create the same division within the government that had first dismantled the monarchy.

Corruption. She wouldn't say it aloud. But she knew Koln was hiding something from her. Something that disappointed him to share. Government corruption, leaking secrets of Luminosity to the Theradoran Empire, an exile lost in the world, and the return of the Sickness in the river…

They were playing with fire, and she was willingly throwing Tarri into the flames.

DRIFT

Tʜᴇ ᴄᴀᴍᴘѕɪᴛᴇ ᴀᴛ ᴛʜᴇ Mountain Gate was in sight and despite the upcoming solace they might get from the cold and wind, Drift was not optimistic. Up here, the blustery wind was greater, the air was cold as a knife to the heart, and the frost and snow were eerily defiant of the warm earth below, which was held firmly in the clasp of Summer. Here, things were dead, the land devoid of even the chirp of a cricket, which Drift usually grounded himself with, a reassuring contribution to the noise of life. Here, the mountain sat tall and defiant in the face of nature itself.

The campsite atop the mountain pass seemed to fit the environment: a small patch of thick-walled tents, fire pits, and a menacing barrier of wooden, pike-shaped fencing, walled in by vast mountainsides. Luckily, there was no fire yet. Drift felt sick just to imagine it, the licking of flames, the essence of destruction.

Drift was astounded by the sheer number of travellers passing through the gates. He watched as the crowds were organised, stopped, and admitted by the guards. Because he and Stag had noticed a rapid concentration of traffic outside the Mountain Gate, they kept their heads covered as much as possible. They didn't want to meet anyone from Providence here. The Relondian crier, Briar Sevardson, was still occupying space in Drift's mind. There was something about that man that he couldn't put a finger on.

This was the only thoroughfare connecting the towns and villages in the south, as well as Aobia, to the northern territories. People here would be coming from Adira, Therador, and the distant places of Ghabbat, Piat, and Sethiliquin.

Ahead of them was the carriage they'd followed for much of the morning. In it were two strangers, guided by a pair of horses attached to the front of the cart. Drift couldn't help but wonder whether they had two horses in case one didn't make it through the harsh cold of the mountain.

The guards seemed to be working on a schedule and the travellers in the carriage ahead had not been allowed in. Finally, within an hour of noon, the strangers were admitted. Drift hoped he and Stag would have better luck.

Stepping up to the gate, Stag and Drift were greeted with silence. The wind up here was thick and there was no use calling out to any of those beyond the gates or trying to listen to what they said to each other.

Finally, an officer came to their aid, accompanied by a small group of three men. The officer had a long, unkempt moustache, peppered with grey, and was balding beneath the thick woollen skullcap he wore, which was so loose-fitting it was as though he was hiding a potato or two beneath it. It was embroidered with a golden battle-axe and other decorative symbols—a sign that this man was from Therador.

"State your business beyond the Mountain Gate," the man said with a thick accent.

"We seek to cross the Mountain Gate as political ambassadors for the Magisterium of Aobia." Stag's reply was just as flat and Drift predicted that this was the etiquette to follow with these kinds of men, the ones who stood rigidly by policy, mandates and the like.

"What is your destination?" The man whipped out a leather-bound book and a pencil carved from graphite, another sign of his heritage. The mountains in Therador were known to contain great quantities of the stuff and it was a worthy enough export for the nation, along with coal and marble, which were all found in the shale-ridden ranges that Therador encapsulated.

"Adira, sir." Would these soldiers have a problem with them going to Adira? He considered the dead king. Surely tensions were rising.

"Wait here. We'll check the grounds and see whether we have space for you here tonight. You'll have to move on at first light, though. As you can see, we are running out of space to accommodate people. Is that agreeable?"

"Of course," Stag replied. "Thank you."

The men headed back into the settlement via the gates, leaving Drift and Stag to the crowds.

"So nobody's reported us? From Providence?" Drift asked, goosebumps spreading across his arms.

"If they had," his companion replied, "we wouldn't have gotten that far. I'd say Gaudin and his band of townsfolk have proved to be less of a problem than we first thought. Everything these men are doing now is protocol. I was more worried they wouldn't let us in without a carriage."

Drift stood up straighter, inquisitive. "Why's that?"

"They know if they meet an Aobian, it'll only be some emissary on a political visit, and that means they'll bring a carriage, a horse, some stock of supplies… We have nothing but scrapes and scratches and empty satchels. Maybe that's what Gaudin was betting would give us away when we got here. I only have one change of clothes in my bag."

"Only one?" Drift replied, mocking. "I fell down a waterfall, Stag. Besides that one wash, I'm in the same clothes that I left in."

Now that he thought about it, his smell was pretty ripe. Perhaps the clean mountain breeze, mixed with the fire pits wafting smoke from beyond the gates of the settlement, were enough to keep his own stench from stirring the senses of others.

"Wait until you have to resort to human clothes," Stag snapped. "They don't fit right. I hate it."

"And how would you, an ambassador from Aobia with supplies and a carriage, find yourself in a situation where you would need to wear human clothes?"

Stag shot him a glare. "I'd prefer if you didn't—"

"No, no, humour me." Drift couldn't help himself.

"I had an … accident. Once! Only once. They gave me human clothes to change into. Some foods the humans eat don't agree with me. It's not unusual!" Stag cried as Drift stifled a snort. "In Therador, they eat so much beef and they curry it… You'd be in pain too, you know. Just wait and see!"

Drift couldn't help himself, and erupted into laughter.

"I'm glad you're pleased," Stag replied. "Maybe all that laughter will warm you enough to stop complaining about the cold. Everything's cold here. Even the people."

Eventually, the officer and his three guards emerged from the gates. "You have clearance for the night," he said. "There's an empty plot with no firepit, a pot of water, and additional rugs for warmth. 'Tis the best I can offer."

"Many thanks, officer," Stag replied. "We will be on our way at first light."

"Be sure that you are," the officer replied. "I'll have one of the lads take you to your tent."

The fires that were lit up that night were an aura of evil, but the humans who sat around them were warm, something that was not lost on Drift, who shivered underneath the rugs that had been given to them.

Music travelled through the nighttime air, originating from a few plots away. It came like a trail of sound from near the carriage that had been ahead of the two Aobians that morning. There was a foreign ambience to it as the two travellers' voices collided with each other, sometimes harmonious and sometimes discordant, above the battling melodies of the odd string instrument playing at the same time. Their voices danced around microtonal chants and the music sounded prayerful, perhaps, as though driven by an awareness of the transcendent. The songs seemed to put Drift both at ease and discomfort, yet he welcomed it. Some part of him was glad to have an unnatural cacophony of sound break the eerie breeze of the mountains.

Above them, sitting in the carcass of a dead tree, was a crow, peering over the campsite like an officiator of the night. As the music came to its natural crescendo, the crow matched its intensity with caws that sent chills down Drift's spine, reminding him of how cold he really was. The singers at the other campsite stopped abruptly, as though in response to the bird, and everything fell to a silence that showcased only the gentle crackle of low embers.

Drift continued to look towards the travellers' campsite, making out the silhouettes of the two people as one of them packed away their instrument and the other blew their fire back to life from a smoulder. Their small ground went suddenly dark against the surrounding campfires.

He heard the flap of the departing crow's wings, followed by a thick and sudden pat from a hand upon his shoulder. Immediately startled, Drift jumped up from his seat and Stag became alert.

"I am sorry!" came the thickly-accented voice of the person who'd touched Drift's arm. As the man came into the light, Drift could make out the familiar features he'd noted earlier that day. It was the travellers who had been singing, a man and woman.

"It's okay," Drift said, reassuring. He gestured for the travellers to take a seat on the log opposite him and Stag. However, they remained standing.

"We noticed you this afternoon," the man said. "You look cold. Do you want to warm yourself at our fire?"

Stag shook his head. "We are thankful, road partners. But we are emissaries from the Great Tree and using fire would be a great offence to our people."

"We understand," the man's female companion said.

Drift smiled at the travellers. "Fire is a great evil, but maybe you're right. It is so cold here, after all." He shrugged at Stag. "Shall we?"

"Fine," Stag responded begrudgingly before following the travellers to their site. "You were before us on the road this morning. You are Sethi?" he asked.

"We are," the woman confirmed. "This is my husband, Ibham, and I am Dayajin." They both had accents unlike any Drift had heard, distinct from the Theradoran soldiers. They also had dark olive skin. Drift beheld them both with wondrous eyes.

"I would like to see the West beyond Therador one day," Drift commented, trying to be conversational. Stag shot him a glare. *What?*

"The mountains of Sethiliquin are amazing compared to this cursed place," the man called Ibham replied.

"What brings you here?" Stag asked.

"Well," Ibham sighed. "What brings anyone here besides business?" He let out a wry chuckle. "I would not live anywhere near Therador, and I don't. But I like the sea and the people who live there, despite being a lakesider. The Adirans treat Sethi well, even though our political allegiances lie with the Empire. They had a good king and we can take our business anywhere in Adiran lands and be fruitful."

Stag lifted an eyebrow. "You've heard the news then?"

"Yes," the Sethi man said. "King Terrens was as good a king as his father before him. I wish it was he with whom we shared our table instead of that cutthroat tyrant, Jurin."

Stag frowned. "Dare I ask why you dislike Therador so much? You are political allies."

"They are barbarians," Ibham replied. "You would feel the same way, tree-dweller."

"Would I?" Stag asked bitterly. "The last time Adira or Aobia interacted with the East ended with a decades-long war of attrition with hundreds of thousands of lives lost and the collapse of several empires, including our own."

"Several empires?" Ibham said, his voice increasing in agitation, but Dayajin drew him back, smacking his hand.

"Ibham!" she whispered.

"The only collapse was yours, tree-dweller, and that is what started the war. Fifty years of tension following your traitor queen." Then he turned to his wife and barked at her in a different language. "La, muthir imra!" The woman shrunk back, humiliated, as her husband held up his hand threateningly.

Maybe Stag had a point. Drift would never even think of laying a hand on Tarri, but this looked commonplace for the two Sethi travellers.

Ibham smirked at his wife and returned his attention to the Aobians. "Theradorans are barbarians. We've all seen what they've done. Eating people in sadistic, cruel rituals. Burning children when they are not what the parents wanted. Burying folk alive for working poorly. The Sethi though, we are fierce."

Drift couldn't agree more, watching Dayajin quiver behind Ibham. He was no longer sure he wanted to be near these humans. So far, every one he'd met had been unpredictable in more ways than one.

"You should share a fire with us this night," Ibham said, extending a welcoming hand. "I respect someone who can put up a strong debate."

"My name is Drift, and this is my colleague Stag." Drift forced a smile. The woman, Dayajin, smiled back at him.

Ibham scowled slightly at her before going on. "My wife and I heard you were travelling through the Mountain Gate to the eastern seaboard from those guards," he said. "We have a small caravan, and there are two more seats going that same direction at dawn if you'd like to join us."

Dawn? They could get to Adira within a week via caravan. Then, he could find a way to get home. Maybe if he could prove himself in collaboration with Stag, the Magisterium would accept his exile was a mistake. "I think that would suit us just fine," Drift replied.

"This is joyous news," Dayajin said, a little too brightly. "The Huntress knows we need some company on this next stretch of road. Where will you be stopping?"

"Relond, and then Adira," Drift said. "Will you be heading that way?"

"Yes," Dayajin smiled. "We have a market in Relond this week, and then we head for the capital. The Huntress smiles upon us, my friends. Our fates align under this night's stars, the sky in which she finds her kill."

Above them, the crow from before had returned, perching on the branch of the dead tree. Perhaps it was a mark of what was to come. The coldness of the night reached him then, and he became aware of his closing eyes and the taut skin of his eyelids, a sign of exhaustion.

"Thank you both," Drift said, standing. "We've come a long way on foot and I cannot express our gratitude for your offer. However, my mind grows weary after the last few days on foot and I fear we must sleep."

"Of course," Dayajin said, standing. Ibham tried to reach for her hand, but she pulled away. Perhaps their tension was the reason for her excitement to have guests with them on the road. "We must be going anyway. It is late." She gave Stag an amicable grin and placed a soft hand on Drift's shoulder as the couple passed them, returning to their campsite.

"You weren't going to consult me?" Stag asked. "I can't travel with these Sethi. The man could be a problem, too. Did you see the way he handled her?"

"Consult you? You led yourself into that conversation with insults, Stag. Besides, if we go with them, maybe it'll ease their conflict a little."

"Forgive me, Drift, but that man abused his wife in front of us with no shame!" Stag retorted. "This human world is not as you think. I know how these people work, Drift. They will take advantage of us."

"Maybe I am naive, Stag," Drift replied. "But weariness is getting the better of me, and I sure could use a seat on a comfortable caravan. We could reach Relond so much faster with the help of those merchants."

"Perhaps, but what's in it for them?" Stag asked. "You don't understand. People do not extend generosity for free. There is always something we must give in return. You'll see." He shook his head, ducking into the tent and fluffing up his bedroll. "I just hope that what they want doesn't take more from us than we can bear."

TARRI

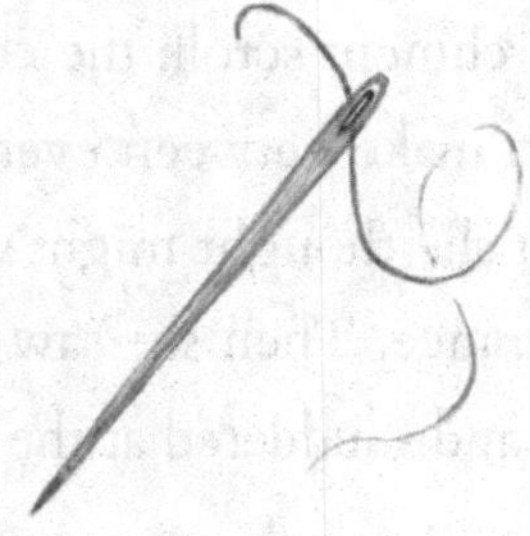

U PON LEAVING HER HOME for the day, Tarri came across a note on the doorstep. *Dearest Tarri, it read, I request your attendance at my apartment today so that we may discuss my summer dress requirements for the season ahead and recapitulate our progress thus far. It excites me to see how our business relationship may continue to grow. This begins with the expansion of your Tailory. Unfortunately, we must keep our meeting brief, as I have other matters to attend to this evening. Sincerely, Lady Nischia.*

Expansion? Tarri felt her heart leap into her throat. This was the business meeting Nischia had mentioned when they'd last met. Her dream of opening a second store in the Mind… Could it be that Nischia was going to help her arrange that? She darted back into her room, concealing a squeal despite nobody being in earshot. Tarri hunted through her drawers, where she kept much of the Tailory's paperwork—receipts, inventory lists, and more—and found a scroll that showed a continuum of the last yearly period of revenue. This included her staff wages as well as her stipends. Nischia was a precise and diligent lady and would no doubt want these details from her. Perfect.

On the way back out, she paused at the dining table where she'd laid out her parchment scroll: the connections she'd been ambitiously trying to make between every variable, idea, incident, and person that she thought might've had anything to do with Drift's disappearance. Then she saw Flow's name with an inky circle around it and shuddered at the thought of their most recent conversation.

She'd already decided what she would do. She looked guiltily down at the bundle of business documents she had under her arm. Nischia was likely to help her grow the Tailory and Tarri was going to betray her, breaking into her home and taking a *cism*.

She didn't need Flow to discover how Luminosity worked. She knew the basics from her mother and was sure Nischia would divulge smaller details as time went on. But Tarri *did* want to understand how it was that she had been able to channel the light within the *cism* the other day. And the best way to find out the answer was to practice. Then, if she managed to do that, she could bribe Flow with the knowledge and use him to get closer to Sedulus.

All she could do was her best.

And by the canopies above, she would *not* fail.

"This," Tarri said, "is our first completed work together, my lady." She watched as Nischia gushed over the dress Tarri had withdrawn from the bag. It was a royal blue with flared shoulders, a sash about the waist, and a pleated skirt. The back was partially open with strips of fabric connecting each side like a diagonal grid. In the afternoon light, it danced without being worn.

"I love it," Nischia breathed. Tarri could tell Nischia had no further words, but she respected her enough to let her have this moment. She wondered what she would do with such a fine article. People asked her all the time why she made nothing like this for herself if she had the skills. Truth be told, it took the work of Apris with her drafting, Rela with her perfectly proportioned garment cutting, and Tarri with her sense of assembly to put something like this dress together. She simply didn't have the time or expenses to dote on her own wardrobe collection. But Nischia would add this one to a collection more expansive than Tarri could possibly imagine and wear it only a handful of times in the summer. The idea of it not being worn all the time made her feel somewhat lowly, yet she knew this was the reality of being such a public figure.

"Tarri, dear, I... I don't know what to say," Nischia said, standing but keeping her eyes plastered to the dress. "It's perfect. It's more perfect than anything that's come before it."

"Out of all your dresses?" Tarri pushed.

"Out of all the dresses in the world." Nischia shook her head in disbelief as she looked up at Tarri with a broad smile. "The kind of dress that deserves all the praise I can possibly give and a celebration too."

"A celebration?"

Nischia nodded. "Let us not be late for our next meeting. It is only a few streets from here, but we should get going. And let's bring the dress with us. I sense it will help our cause."

Tarri packed the dress carefully into the sky-blue fabric sleeve she'd made for it, which had a neat handle on the top of it to make it easy to carry through the streets.

Nischia led the way down the long entrance hall in her apartment and held the door out for Tarri to pass through.

This was her chance. Without thinking, she wedged her free hand into the crack of the door as Nischia slammed it shut, howling in pain.

"Tarri?" Nischia cried. "I am so sor—oh no! Look what it's done!"

Tarri blinked the tears of pain out of her eyes, not daring to look at her fingers, two of which were bleeding profusely, the tops of the nails ripped off.

"Come child!" Nischia said, reopening the door. "We must keep the hand in water for a few moments."

Roots below! She'd practically sacrificed two of her fingertips for the door to be reopened. She would need to find another opportunity to jam the door again or find another way in.

Nischia led her to the kitchen and turned on the faucet. The Luminous Core, a tiny crystal filled with light, immediately glowed, a sign that it was powering the water system. Tarri held her hand under the cool water for a time before Nischia switched the faucet off and glanced across the room at her large, green velvet seats. "Do you need to sit, child?"

"Uh, no," Tarri managed. "It'll be fine. Thank you, my lady."

Nischia breathed a sigh of relief. "I'd really rather us not miss this meeting and that you keep both your fingers. Let's go, quickly now."

They raced back down the hall, Tarri wiping her wet hand on one side of her skirt and clenching it in the fabric, the pressure of doing so relieving the throbbing. She glanced down at the dress tucked under her other arm. *That won't do it,* she thought. *The dress will rip if it gets caught on the latch.*

"I might let you close it yourself this time," Nischia said. "I wouldn't want a repeat of that incident!"

"Of course, my lady," Tarri replied. She walked through the door, heart pounding, watching Nischia go on ahead, and stayed close enough that the door's latch clicked against the frame, feigning its closure.

She'd done it. The door was situated in such a way that made it seem that the lock was depressed, but with a closer look, it did not line up with the line of the wall at the top or bottom. Hopefully, this would be all she'd need to return later.

They walked in silence, Tarri clutching her hand and Nischia moving with purpose a few steps ahead. The mood was soured by the door jam and Tarri sensed that Nischia did not like being responsible for making errors like that.

"Before we arrive, I wanted to talk to you about your friend, the ambassador," Nischia called from ahead.

Tarri's ears perked up at this and she worried Nischia knew she was thinking about Flow. "My lady?"

"I spoke at length with my superior, Koln, after we last met. As it turns out, I need to send you on a … job of sorts."

Tarri's eyes sparkled. "A mission?" Her first chance to prove her worth to Nischia, to actually find real, reportable evidence of what had happened to Drift.

"I did not use that word with intention, dear," Nischia replied. "Don't put yourself ahead just yet. However, it is the kind of job I wish to have you complete with the assistance of your friend."

"Flow?" She couldn't believe it. Her heartbeat grew loud in her head. Should she alert Nischia to what she'd found out about Flow?

Nischia nodded. "He knows something about the water filtration processes that he shouldn't. *That's* why he was suspended indefinitely from his work. I need you and Flow to go to the facility and meet with Sedulus. See if you can get either of them to explain how the filtration system encountered a major failure and let the Sickness breach."

"My lady," Tarri began. "Forgive me. I don't want anything to do with Flow."

Nischia raised an eyebrow. "What is your reason for that? The last time we discussed him, you felt quite differently."

"I…" Tarri tried to find her words. "I sought your advice. I realised I couldn't risk letting someone in his position of knowledge know any more about Drift's exile."

"I am impressed, child," Nischia said, eyes wide. "Given that you've abided by my words, listen now when I say that Flow will be his own undoing. Unfortunately, you are in the best position as an old friend of his to facilitate that. So here it is: have Sedulus explain what he can about the way water is filtered. Watch Flow's behaviour carefully. If anything odd occurs in your interactions, report them to me afterwards. Do whatever you can, Tarri. Play the game."

Subterfuge. That was the game.

"When can you accomplish this by?" Nischia asked.

"I-I can't promise you a time, my lady." Tarri stumbled over her words. Nischia's demand was unwavering and Tarri was beginning to reconsider her choices. *Maybe I don't need to steal anything from her. If I can find out what's gone on between Flow and Sedulus in more detail, I can leverage that to get what I want.* Then again, maybe she could accomplish both things. After all, she needed to understand how Luminosity could be used more. Flow had mentioned that Sedulus had found a way to exist in two places at once. A secret that great would not be concealed for long, and she felt the urgent need to find it out for herself and keep the knowledge safe. If she was able to bring that knowledge to Nischia, maybe the Sleeper would trust her even more and they could start to understand how many secrets of the mysterious power were being shared around Q'ara. "I need time to think through my strategy for this meeting."

"You *do* tend to think things through, don't you?" Nischia said this as though she was speaking to herself, making an observation about the behaviours of an interesting animal. Tarri knew she was prone to overthinking and Drift used to tell her the same, but that did not change the fact that she needed to feel comfortable to act on Nischia's command.

Walking through the gardens that joined one end of the Mind to the other, the residential buildings and the parliament behind, and the storefronts ahead, Tarri considered the terrain. Blooming, purple flowers sprang out of bushes in dense, colourful pops across the ground. Fresh green willows hung with plumage above her, sheltering her from the heat of the sun. All along the ground, what looked like clover seemed to invade the grass, with small pink and blue flowers spitting up out of it in clumps. "What is that?" she asked.

"A weed," Nischia replied simply. "It looks like clover, but it grows these." She bent down and picked up one of the flower clumps, which tore out of the weed with ease, leaving behind a stringy collection of roots. "Its name is Heartcall, or *alquab* in the Old Tongue. The flowers are so pretty that nobody wants to kill the weed. Though you can take the flowers out with ease, they will drop spores, remnants of life, spreading the weed everywhere you go with them. It's mostly found in the forest below, a ground cover, but a botanist procured it when we came to this Tree centuries ago and grew it here, containing it in the gardens of the Mind. Pretty, isn't it?"

The sun seemed to sparkle on the edges of the tiny flowers, catching the light like dewdrops in the morning. "It is," agreed Tarri.

"It might be pretty, Tarri," Nischia continued, "but it's still invasive. A noxious liar hidden in plain sight."

Tarri frowned, wondering whether Nischia was directing the comment towards her. Was she the Heartcall weed, in amongst Nischia, Koln, and the others in the Magisterium? Or was it someone else, like Flow?

"Here we are," Nischia said as they exited the gardens, emerging on the other side by a road with a long strip of businesses, two-storey buildings much like the residential areas of the Mind, but made from uncoated timber.

Directly across the road from them stood a male with a thin, white moustache and a bundled but wiry head of hair. He was rounder than many other Aobians and Tarri guessed he was much older than she. "This is Cogens, a real estate manager here in the Mind. And behind him is your prospective new location for the Tailory. What do you think?"

Tarri's heart dropped through the ground beneath her. The generosity of the Sleeper might have been earned, but it tore at her that she was going to betray her later. The conversation with Flow had made Tarri wonder whether or not she could trust anyone and Nischia was a part of that. Now, she wasn't sure she had it right. The Sleeper was going to give her a building for her business. Then again, maybe this was the kind of appeasement Tarri should expect from the Magisterium, now that Drift was gone.

Tarri looked up at the bespoke building, a two-storey, quaint-looking place that had ornate windows with golden sills and awnings over each of them. The front door was, in fact, two doors that opened in and had frosted glass on the top of each one, arranged into a neat four-square pattern. In the building, she saw a stairwell that rose to the second level and a long, blue-patterned runner.

"Lady Nischia," the real-estate agent, Cogens, said. "It is such a fine day, only made finer by your presence."

"Of course, Cogens." Nischia inclined her head as the round male took her hand, kissing it lightly.

Ick. Tarri despised these kinds of people; in fact, she'd had to deal with an overly pompous, sickly sweet-talking real-estate agent before, back when she'd bought the Tailory. At that time, she'd have done anything to open her business, but her tolerance for these people was at an all-time low, especially now that she'd seen the kind of person Cogens was. Anyone in real estate for the Sleepers was there as a result of one thing only: greed.

"And this is?" Cogen looked at Tarri disparagingly. Of course, a Sleeper couldn't be seen spending time around a commoner. Tarri rolled her eyes.

"The Lady Tarri," Nischia introduced her, "and the prospective owner of this beautiful piece of history. Tarri, show Cogens the dress."

Cogen's stance changed once Tarri unveiled the blue dress. He practically swept Tarri up, leading her to the door. She was the reason he would be making a tidy sum from the sale of this building. "Well, it is a pleasure, my dear!" he said. "Of course, you are correct, Lady Nischia. This is one of the original buildings that occupied the Great Tree when we settled here over eight hundred years ago."

Tarri raised an eyebrow. "The people and the Sleepers resided here together?"

Cogens squinted, correcting himself. "Not exactly, my dear. All Aobians lived throughout this side of the Mind and in the Soul too. The Heart was used for what it is still used for today—industry and production. The history of the Soul as a cultural centre is a recent one and the current residential sector of the Mind for the Magisterium is no older than three hundred years. The way we live now is reflective of changes we started to make early into our resting in this Tree."

"I wonder why that is?" Tarri asked, half-intending her question to be taken rhetorically.

"Pardon me?" Cogens furrowed his brows, twisting one side of his snow-white moustache.

"Nothing," Tarri replied, deciding to drop the topic as Nischia eyed her. "I suppose I need to brush up on my history of our people in this Tree."

"Of course," Cogens said, gesturing for her and Nischia to come inside. "Our history is rich and, as you may know, we have resided in Great Trees for thousands of years! You might say we are merely a ripple in the grand lake that is Aobian history… But do not let that take away from the heritage of this building! Shall we?"

"Of course, Cogens," Nischia said, impatient. "Let us proceed. I will be, after all, occupied with other matters after this, and I cannot take long."

As they walked through, past the dining and living area with a beautiful ceiling rose the size of Tarri's bed, out into the still-maintained garden, and upstairs into the various bedrooms and chambers, Tarri blocked out much of what Cogens was saying. She could see the Tailory coming to life in a place like this: outdoor seating amongst the roses and champagne for waiting customers; three individual fitting rooms upstairs, along with an inventory space and a lavatory; and the grand floor of the living space downstairs, where customers could peruse Tarri's work and have conversations.

As the trio left the building, Cogens drew out a pad of parchment and a pencil, beginning to make notes as he spoke. "Lady Nischia, the costs for the property have, of course, already been settled. I just need confirmation from you both of what needs to be done for the final procurement. Of course, much of those costs will need to be covered by yourself or Miss Tarri, but if there is anything outstanding, it will be repaired prior to moving in."

Tarri balked, covering her mouth and turning away from the other two. She couldn't believe it. The building had already been acquired?

"Of course, Cogens," Nischia replied. "You have been so good to me, once again. I hope you get in commission what you deserve for this sale. Indeed, I'm not sure you've ever managed a finer estate. I don't think there are any outstanding repairs to be made, unless Tarri disagrees. Dear?" Nischia grabbed Tarri's wrist, spinning her around to face the conversation.

"I… um…" she stammered, trying to find the words. Surely there was a catch. Nothing was free, was it? "It is positively charming, Cogens, and I thank you for your time. However, I must decline the opportunity to purchase. I… Lady Nischia, might I have a word?"

Cogens frowned, but Nischia put a calming hand on his shoulder, whispering to him to give her just a moment with Tarri in private. They walked down the street, the gardens across the road lighting up the afternoon shadows upon the old buildings in colour. "Tarri, what is the matter?"

"My lady, I…" Tarri gulped. "I cannot afford this property, not right now, at least. I am so grateful for everything you have done and I know you have set in motion things for my business that I could not have done without you. This is all coming out wrong." She put a hand to her mouth, tears welling in the corners of her eyes.

"Might I be blunt, child?" Nischia asked. "Take your hand from your mouth and do away with those tears." She sniffed. "I have purchased this heritage property for you and your Tailory, so that you can expand your business and take on more well-paying clients from the Mind. It is the least I can offer, considering how obliging you've been as my dressmaker ahead of this season and how much I wish I could fix what's gone wrong in recent weeks. But the truth is, I cannot fix those things. Not right now. So instead, I've come to you now, using money that I am in no shortcoming of, to help you in the smallest way I possibly can. Is that agreeable?"

Filled with a smorgasbord of feelings, Tarri let out a whimper, which became a cry and then a flood of tears, each one filled with the pain of the loss of Drift, the joy of appreciation for this Sleeper and her untold kindness, and the confusion of everything else that was happening; Flow's conspiring with Sedulus, her ability to channel Luminosity, and what the Sleepers wanted from her. Tarri knew not what to do with all of it and by reflex, she seized the dress of the Sleeper to hug her close, sobbing.

"My child," Nischia cried, taken aback. "Please, control yourself! We are in public and this is not the decorum I've come to expect from such a well-kept lady as yourself! Now go back to that agent, sign his papers, and celebrate at home with some wine!"

With that, Nischia pushed Tarri off to hold her firmly by the shoulders and look straight into her eyes, letting through the hint of a smile. "I am glad if you are," she whispered to Tarri through the mess of sniffs, chokes, and sobs. "Now, I must go."

Tarri nodded, blinking back the flood surfacing on her eyes. "Of course, my lady," she breathed. "Thank you."

DRIFT

Drift looked beyond the mountain that morning, out onto the land that unfolded below. In one direction he could look toward home, Aobia. There, the greenery of the forest was alive. Here, the sun felt like it did nothing but provide light. Turning around to look the other way, he saw the land's expanse in several tones of mottled green, brown, and grey. The humans' lands.

He'd considered several times how disconcerting it was that adventuring into human lands no longer excited him like it had when he'd lived in Aobia. Admittedly, he'd felt jaded since abandoning Raegan to the townsfolk of Providence and here, stuck with a bunch of ragged, forgotten Theradoran soldiers and two Sethi travellers, he couldn't see this feeling changing any time soon.

"Spare hare?" Stag appeared next to him, chewing on something and holding out a particularly uninspiring piece of meat attached to a slither of skin.

"Rather not," Drift pushed back, feeling his stomach tighten at the thought of leftover hare from the Sethi couple's fire the night before.

"We're growing lads, aren't we?" Stag grinned. "Gotta eat."

"I'm fine." Drift shook his head. "Are the Sethi ready to go?"

"Seems it," Stag responded, dropping the long string of hare meat into his mouth from above. "I'm not happy about this, you know."

"You've made that quite clear," Drift said, rolling his eyes. "But if it's going to get us off this gods-forsaken mountain and into a warm tavern for a day or two, I will take it time and time again."

Stag chuckled. "And here I was, thinking you were well-fitted for travel away from the Great Tree."

Drift tried to laugh along with him, but a deeper longing reached for his heart once more. *Tarri.* It was yet another time that he'd put her name to the feeling of being away and now that he did, he felt an overwhelming emotion, as though he might suddenly weep. He stalked away from Stag, proceeding to roll his pack up. He would suppress his aching heart until the day he saw her again, held her in his arms, and felt her lips on his.

"Aobians!" Ibham called out, wandering over from his campsite. "We are ready to go."

"Is the travel long?" Drift inquired, slinging his pack over one shoulder.

"If we leave now and drive through the night, we could manage to get to Relond right as the cock crows," said Ibham.

"Of course," Drift said. He watched Dayajin with curiosity as she handfed grain to the two horses hooked up to the front of the enormous caravan. The woman seemed perfectly content, despite what had happened by the fire the previous night.

Drift and Stag placed their packs in a side compartment closer to the front of the caravan. This seemed to be where much of the couple's goods were kept, while the back was open seating for travellers. There was one long bench seat at the front with the horses, which Ibham occupied, with space for another person if need be.

"Have either of you ever driven a caravan?" he asked, clambering to his seat and picking up the reigns.

Drift shook his head, but Stag responded, "Just carriages. There are bigger types in Aobia, called cabriolets, but I've never driven one myself."

"Perfect!" Ibham exclaimed. "You can take over when I need a break!"

"You couldn't be better matched to the task!" Drift said, grinning. Stag rolled his eyes at him, walking around the other side to jump in the open door.

The inside of the caravan was lined with elaborate cloths covered with symmetrical shapes and patterns. "This pattern is called Naian," Dayajin said, noticing Drift's gaze. "It is named after the beautiful city of Nai, where our gods reside."

"Your gods?" Drift wondered, studying the cloth. Small flowers, each one linked by hand and divided between bigger clusters of them, all perfectly symmetrical, with borderlines running around the edges of the fabric, and tassels hanging on the ends.

"Each flower you see represents a life, one of us," Dayajin replied, waving a hand across the patterns. "The large flowers connect them all together. These are our gods." She gestured to a huge, flower-filled star, enclosed in a circle, all still perfectly symmetrical. "At the centre is our matron-goddess, Tabriz the Huntress, who birthed all others, from whom all life grows and all life is taken." She paused a moment, still considering the great pattern in the middle of the drapery. "What are your gods like?"

"Our gods?" Drift chuckled.

"Our gods are alive," Stag interjected dramatically, turning around from the driver's seat.

"Alive?" Dayajin said, looking puzzled.

"Forgive him," Drift replied, gritting his teeth. "Stag jests. He's talking about the Sleepers," he explained. "But they are not gods. Just people among the rest of us, chosen to bear the powers of the Great Tree."

"Ah," Dayajin breathed. "The Luminous ones. They are said to provide your home with … light?"

"Yes," Drift smiled. "They can provide light. But they are more often playing politics like it is a children's game. They oversee our laws."

"And you do not have access to the magic of the Tree within which you live?" Dayajin asked.

"That's right."

"Then why do you stand so far from the word 'god'?"

Drift frowned. "The Sleepers are not dissimilar from the rest of us. They are certainly ordinary Aobians. They simply shine with the magic of the Tree, and that somehow puts them both higher and separate from the rest of us. It's a random selection. Why should that justify the difference between gods and people?"

"It would seem to me," Dayajin replied, "that if that is the common view of your people, you reject the notion of the divine completely."

"I don't know if I would go that far," Drift said. "I believe in a divine earth, that nature itself is our god, and nature commands how we live and die. Nature gave us the Great Trees, within which we've dwelled for thousands of years. The Luminosity is less explainable. Some say there are gods who fill the tree with it, and that is why every inch of forest beneath its canopies is illuminated. I'm not sure if I believe that. So… I suppose you could call me a sceptic."

"How do your Sleepers gather their power?"

"Nobody knows how it works," Stag called from the front seat. "But many of us believe in it because we've seen the real effects of the Sleepers' work—filtering the water from the corrupt end of the River Tomei, for example. It is the only reason water in this part of the world is safe to drink."

"I have heard of the corrupt river," Dayajin remarked. "In Sethi, the name of it is 'the place where the snakes sing,' or Mohrho. Where we gather water, the river is clean all the way to the sea.

We learned not to drink from Mohrho when our people came to this land."

"It's not all magic, though," Drift protested. "I worked at the Water Management Facility, as do many of my people. We had to maintain the filtration system by hand through hard work. But there are things below the Great Tree that … grow. They seem to do something similar to the Sleepers."

"Things that grow?" Dayajin asked.

"We call it algae," Drift explained. "But it's not just that. There are all kinds of life, plants, even insects that I've seen under the tree that are influenced by Luminosity."

"Drift, leave the poor woman alone," Stag called. "You'll bore her with your science. Some things are better left explained by magic."

"I'm just—"

"Drift, stop!"

"Stag?" Drift asked, confused. "What's the—"

"I said *stop,* damn it!" There was some moving around, and Drift cursed under his breath as he heard Stag asking Ibham to halt the caravan. As quick as the breeze, he whipped around to the side door, hauling Drift out by the arm.

"Stag! Get your hands off me!" Drift pushed against him, but the Aobian's determination was unstoppable. Before long, Stag had pulled Drift by force to the wayside, ducking behind thick greenery that lined the road.

Shoving Drift into a tree trunk and covering his mouth with a hand, Stag seethed. "Don't divulge another thing about Aobia to these people!"

Drift tried to argue back, but he couldn't wrestle Stag's hand off his mouth. Eventually, he went limp with resignation and Stag warned him to keep his voice down with a gesture. "What do you see in these strangers?" Stag asked.

"What crime have I committed by being curious about their culture in exchange for sharing some of my own?" Drift answered. "Do you not wish for this world to change? For people everywhere to embrace each other and their beliefs and traditions to be respected, no matter where they are on the continent?"

"We are Aobians, not simple humans!" Stag hissed.

"Forgive me for making conversation with a woman who offered us succour, food, and transport alongside her husband."

"Do you not see?" The frenzied look in Stag's eyes grew the wider his stare became. "They are fishing for knowledge about our lives, our ways! They have no right!" Stag reinforced his words by shoving Drift harder against the tree.

"I can't believe you!" Drift said, his voice rising. "You're suspicious of everything! I don't know how you could have managed to be a decent ambassador for our people with an attitude like this. For all I know, it may have been your poor attempts at diplomacy and communication that led to the death of the king!"

Immediately, Stag released Drift, dropping him to the ground, and Drift knew he had gone too far. He hadn't meant them, but he had tried to make a point. "Stag," he pleaded. "I'm sorry. I misspoke and let my frustration control me."

"You fool," Stag said cuttingly. "Humans misunderstand us, disrespect us, on principle. Many of them would be happy if we were all dead, our Tree knocked down with us."

"You take your opinion of one group of people and apply it to them all," Drift cautioned.

"You are so naive! Don't you understand? Take us out of the picture and you have a continent that can be fairly fought over and won. Without the Tree, or Luminosity, Q'ara would be no different to the place the humans came from two thousand years ago. This world is not for us! Not since they took it."

"And the Sleepers?"

"What are Sleepers if everyone can Sleep?"

Drift narrowed his eyes. "What are you saying?"

Stag shook his head, moving away. "Let's go. We're wasting daylight." Turning, he stalked back through the bushes to the caravan. Drift moved with him.

When they returned, Ibham stood facing the trees where they emerged, but, upon seeing them, moved to the front of the vehicle, grasping the reigns without a word. Had he been watching them? The man made Drift feel uneasy.

Soon enough, the reigns pulled and the horses began to move. Dayajin sat in the back with Drift, quiet, her arms crossed, not daring to move. The silence that had grown was awkward and Drift knew that his argument with Stag must have been louder than he'd thought.

At nightfall, the group unpacked the caravan silently and Ibham set up the fire and fold-out wooden bench for preparing food, which seemed to be a hefty sack of rice and boiled water taken from a nearby brook. Between the staggering silence of the day's travel and the oncoming crackle of flames from the campfire, Dayajin filled the space with her voice, singing tunes once more of her forebears and her people's myths and gods. Drift did not know the words, but he listened, at first letting her sound carry his fears of the fire away, then feeling the intensity of the rising and falling notes, hit purely on the night air, sending his heart into vibrato.

Stag, with his nose to the air, found some quieter space in the cabin of the caravan and curled up behind the door, disinterested in being a part of the camp. Ibham cooked, his focus on the knives that struck the uprooted ginger and onion bulbs they had scavenged earlier.

Though there was music in the air, the silence and tension still remained, presiding over it all. As the night grew darker and the fire dimmed down, so did the hearts of the four people crowded around it.

TARRI

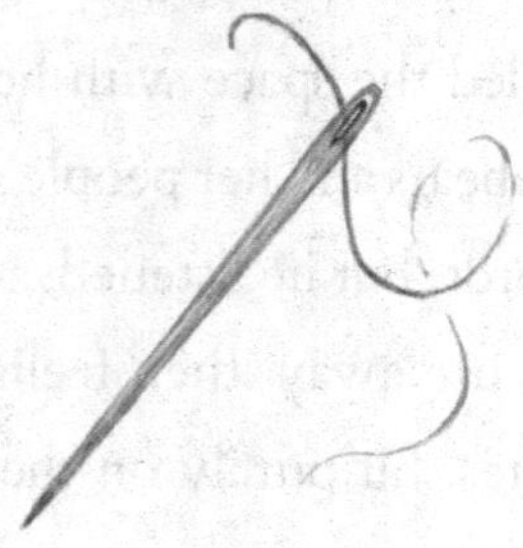

Nischia's apartment was understated, perhaps a little like her. It overlooked the botanical gardens with a luxurious oriel window that was affronted by a large wooden desk with a leather top. It only took Tarri a moment to realise how extraordinary the desk really was, as it was built right into the floor. It had been sculpted out of the Great Tree itself, a part of the branchrendered home.

A large armchair made from a rich green felt lay under a cascading shelf of books. It was a good library, overstuffed with all kinds of treasures, and it fitted with Tarri's image of Nischia. Of course, Nischia was a bookworm. Tarri wished she knew more about Nischia. Though a part of her ached for friendship, the sensible part took over and reminded her that this was a business relationship. Dresses in exchange for Drift. That was it. Sleepers couldn't be friends with common folk.

She stood, taking in her surroundings. How had she managed this? There was no going back now.

A ceiling-to-floor navy blue curtain, thick as a pile of linen, hung next to the library to separate Nischia's private space from the rest. She tugged at the curtain and peeked her head around. There it was.

Immediately, she knew it was something she was never meant to have seen. A bright, orange glow penetrated the room, accompanied by a deep, pulsing hum that came from a glasslike ball the height of one of the bookshelves behind her. This was Nischia's Orb.

Every Sleeper in Aobia Slept in one of these to regenerate their Luminosity for the rest of the population. Yet throughout their history living in Great Trees, the majority of Aobians lacked knowledge about how Luminosity worked. All they knew was that Sleepers took their fill of the mysterious power via the Orb.

The Orb was private and special, a sign of the unique connection a Sleeper had with the Tree. An Orb would be brought into existence, but only for those chosen for it. If a person survived a sickness known as the Fever, they were often given a Blessing from the Tree in the form of the Orb.

She felt sacrilegious letting her gaze rest on the beautiful Orb. Her mother's Orb had been a common enough sight for her. She shoved the memories away, deep into a place in her mind that was made for forgetting. A place for compartmentalising pain. She closed the curtains, cupping her forehead with a hand.

Somewhere around here would be some *cism*, the real reason she was here. But she wasn't sure that she could pluck it from Nischia's home, now that she was this close. What had she done? She had violated her trust with a Sleeper, an enforcer of the law. She could be exiled, imprisoned at the very least. Death would be a glad result in the context of them all.

A squeaky hinge alerted Tarri to the twisting of the front door handle and she looked around for a chance to escape. None came. She raced over to Nischia's desk as two figures entered the room, talking with a heavy air about them.

"… surprised less and less every day," came the first voice, but Tarri had been unable to make out the beginning of their sentence. Koln. *Canopies above, protect me!* she thought, though she knew her deception was no defensible action.

"I suppose that is true for the both of us." Nischia heaved a sigh. "All we can hope now is that Tarri finds something from Sedulus and Flow. We may just get to the crux of the suspicious activities he's all but admitted to." So far so good. They settled into the chairs by Nischia's bookshelf, clearly not having noticed her crouched behind the desk.

"We sent that young ambassador to his doom, Nischia," Koln replied.

"He seems to be awash with the same slime that covers Sedulus. Isn't that reason enough to condemn him?"

Koln grunted.

"What?" Nischia asked. "Do you not agree?"

"He is an odd variable in all of this. But you're right. The bribe Emdo told me about… It would make sense that Flow would know something about it, given he has the necessary permissions to travel."

"If that ambassador has had a part to play in giving something to Therador…" She sighed. "We haven't dealt with anything so serious in a great number of years."

"And what about King Terrens?" Koln went on. "Everyone knows Therador has been on the back foot since the war ended. And they signed the armistice out of necessity more than anything—Don't glare at me like that, it's true! They would've crumbled within weeks of the battle at the Mountain Pass."

"We're still grasping for the short straw, despite our suspicions. These are serious accusations that you throw about, despite having no evidence to support them! What if Tarri finds nothing and her presence there tips Sedulus off as to how much we know?"

"Is not my tenure in this world evidence enough?" Koln retorted. Tarri heard him stand up. "For the century you've been here, Nischia, I've been here thrice as long, and as such, I've seen thrice the number of atrocities strike at the heart of our people! To be embroiled yet again in the affairs of humans is infuriating enough. To suspect two of our own people being part of their schemes is not something I accept lightly. After Queen Feldra and the war, surely *you* could understand!"

A shudder went through Tarri and she struggled to contain her reflexes in her rigid kneeling position, causing her to crash to the ground. The thump clearly alerted the two Sleepers, who paused their conversation. Tarri held her breath, silencing herself so that the only thing she heard was her heartbeat. She'd come all this way, tried to play the balancing act between her friendship with Flow and her allegiance to Nischia. And she'd just left Nischia earlier in the afternoon, standing before the building in the Mind that she now owned—The evolution of her Tailory that she'd never dreamed possible. Whatever came next, she would deserve.

"Tarri," Nischia started. She stood at the edge of the kitchen beside her superior, who looked down at Tarri with a stern glare. She felt as though she would fall to pieces if she looked at Koln's face for longer than a second.

She was in trouble, and worse.

NISCHIA

Words caught in Nischia's throat as Tarri stood from behind the kitchen bench, quivering with nerves. The girl's teeth were practically chattering. Nischia wasn't sure what to say. How much had Tarri heard? What was she doing here in the first place? How had she gotten in?

How had she shielded herself so well all that time?

"What are you doing here?" Koln asked, his voice low and quiet.

Tarri hesitated. "I—"

"Roots below! Why are you here?" Koln snapped, loud enough to cause both Nischia and Tarri to jump. "This is not your home, child. Do you not understand the basic principle of breaking and entering?"

Tarri sniffed, choking back tears that welled in her eyes. *Oh child,* Nischia thought. Tarri didn't want to be here, Nischia could sense that much. But she could not hide the disappointment written upon her face. "Tarri," she said, her voice shaking. "Answer him."

"I didn't mean it—I mean, I did, but I knew I shouldn't have—No, I *know* now that I shouldn't have, and that's much too long to know right from wrong… I'm so sorry, please forgive me!" Tarri finished her words by sliding into a wail and Nischia, for the first time, recognised just how young Tarri was.

"Ridiculous," Koln spat, slamming a closed fist on the countertop. Then he turned on Nischia. "When will you learn? When will you grow up?" he roared.

Nischia felt her cheeks redden, but it was anger that carried her response, not humiliation. "There is a two-hundred-year difference between us, Koln, and a fifty-year difference between her and I," she said, pointing at Tarri. "How dare you speak to me like that. This is *not* my fault."

"Not your fault?" Koln scowled. "You insisted on involving her. *You* promised you would be careful. *You knew* the implications her involvement would have if we were not in control every step of the way!"

"That's all it ever is with you, isn't it?" Nischia seethed. "Control. You sought it for years. You crave it. You aren't happy, Koln, you're bitter. But as long as you have control over everything and everyone around you, at least you can have some damn peace!"

Nischia's chest heaved as Koln clamped his lips shut. He turned his back on her and left the apartment, the door slamming behind him.

The silence was devastating. Tarri dared not sniff and Nischia dared not move in the wake of Koln's abrupt departure. She looked at Tarri out of the corner of her eye before turning away, betrayed. "Why are you here, child? What games are you playing?"

"My lady, I…"

If Tarri had intended to explain herself, Nischia wasn't going to wait to find out. "No!" she bellowed. "They are simple questions with simple answers. Grovel and I will remove you from this place and from my life. From any chance of ever seeing your beloved again. Tell me—not with sincerity, not with sorrow, not with pity. Tell me the facts, Tarri. *That* is what I deserve."

"I cannot," Tarri said, shaking her head.

"You enter my home unannounced, uninvited, with nary a person here, and offer me no explanation? Do you realise the position that puts you in? We are struggling enough to find people around us we can trust!" Nischia held her stare before dropping her head, talking at the floor. "If you will not speak, then we have no trust in our relationship. You doom yourself to a plain life, in a plain job, invisible to me and my peers. Never to be told the truth about Drift, or your sick, lying friend Flow… What would you have me do? Disown your services? For goodness' sake, we both just came from a business meeting to set your career on its future path. I feel as though you are throwing it all back in my face by staying silent."

Even after saying all that she felt, and all that she meant and didn't mean, Tarri remained quivering, unable to speak. Nischia shook her head, letting out a long breath. "Well then. You must go." She marched away from the kitchen towards the front door, not looking back to see if Tarri followed. Nischia was suddenly very aware, as she stood with her back against the door, of her throat tightening, her skin becoming itchy. The manifestation of her sadness. She'd always been told she had a cold heart, because she was never very good at expressing her feelings. But she knew the symptoms her body threw at her, like a wave of anxiety crashing over her at the thought of losing somebody. Though it had been a century or longer, she recognised the feeling.

Tarri walked past her, her head down, before pausing in the hallway before the apartment. Her eyes were bleary with trapped tears. For a moment, it seemed that she stood on the precipice of saying something, of just spitting it out. But it never came, and before Nischia could waver, she spoke, rendering her words with an emotionless, clinical professionalism. "I trust you understand that our relationship cannot continue. I wish you all the best." And with that, she closed the door, not with a slam but a gentle push.

TARRI

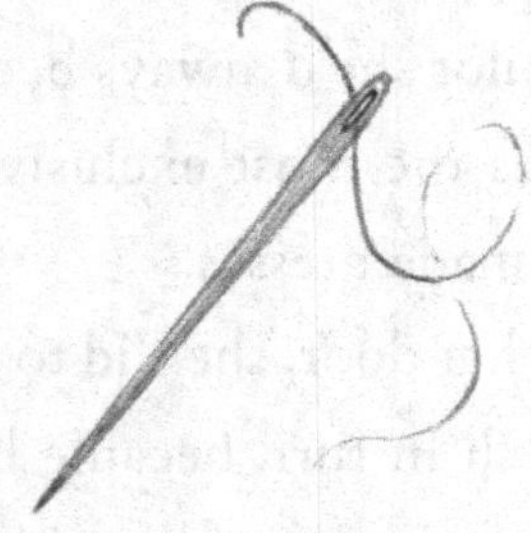

Tarri arrived home as the sun was setting, a mottling of purple-grey sky up above that mirrored the way she felt. Two colours colliding, both grim in their own ways, never meant to mix. Like a bruise. She was a bruise on Nischia's character. Worse still, she felt sick with betrayal, a feeling that seemed to set into her bones like the early winter cold, even though it was a balmy summer evening. The last few steps before she reached her front door were somehow more testing than the rest of the hours-long journey home, taking the cabriolet back through the Mind and Soul.

As she crossed the barrier of her door, she felt her fate closing in. She'd never hear from Nischia again. She'd never be allowed the chance to work with the Sleepers, find the truth about Drift and the changing world. Interestingly, both these things weighed on her more than the establishment of the new Tailory building.

Only now, with the power of hindsight, Tarri realised that she had been onto something great. She'd had a higher purpose, even if only for a week, and felt her place in the world more than ever before. Now, she'd sleep the devastation away, wake up in the morning suppressing the remainders of it all, and go to work, the same tailor she'd always been.

She no longer was the most exclusive dressmaker in the Soul. Now, she just made dresses.

Slouching against her door, she slid to the floor, her sorrow becoming sobs, which in turn became heaving bellows. She closed her eyes, letting the tears fill up inside her lids, stinging the skin around them. She hadn't had the chance to properly grieve Drift. But with this now punctuating her future, the sadness she displayed became a blur of lamentation and mourning. Between her crying and her closed eyes, she didn't even notice as the door was pushed open against her weight, and someone scooped her up off the floor, carrying her to a seat at the table.

"Flow," she choked, looking up at him. "Why are you here?" She sucked back the tears. She would not cry in front of him.

He handed her a glass of water. "I'm sorry," he said.

"Flow." Tarri breathed deeply. "They caught me. Trying to steal a *cism*. Now, it's all over. I'll never find Drift or bring him home." Her bottom lip quivered uncontrollably. "You planted the seed in my head. But I can't trust you. You've committed great crimes and they'll find out, Flow. No matter what you do or say, they'll find out. You can't run from them."

"No." Flow stepped back from her, holding up his hands. "I cannot. But you're the one that dooms me. You could've taken a *cism* and given it to me. I could've continued shielding myself."

After all the late nights sitting at her table and trying to find the connections, here was the real reason for Flow's request. He didn't want to be found out.

"I won't help you cover up what you've done," Tarri seethed. "I never would have given you any *cism* I found anyway."

"You lost everything because you didn't do as I asked," Flow responded. "I know you were siding with the Sleepers. Now I'll take the fall. I never even wanted to be involved in Sedulus' games. You could have rebuilt my reputation with the Sleepers, and we could have found the truth, accomplished everything that we wanted ourselves!"

"Everything we wanted?" Tarri squeaked. "All I want is Drift. What do you want? Nothing but power and secrets that don't belong to you. You want to see the entire continent buckle at its knees while nations fight over Luminosity. Where will that get you? What happiness will that bring?"

"I want nothing of the sort," Flow snapped. "I want a world where our resources are shared, not hoarded. Where we can live with humans in harmony. You go on thinking otherwise if it pleases you. I don't know why I came back here today."

"I don't know why you did either," she said. "I told you to stay away from me. You're dangerous."

"I'm dangerous?" Flow scoffed. "What about the Sleepers? We can't trust them either, Tarri." He struck out an arm aggressively, knocking over the clay vase Tarri kept on the table. Water and old flowers spilled everywhere, all over the map of connections she'd slaved over for the past few days. Tarri watched as it reached Sedulus' name, causing the ink to distort and the paper to ripple.

Suddenly, a thought struck her. Maybe she could still use Flow to get what she needed. If she could uncover the secrets he'd been keeping with Sedulus, she could expose him to the Sleepers and win their trust back. They would go to meet with Sedulus and report in detail on the inner workings of the river management. She didn't care if this worked against her. She'd either gain everything or lose nothing at all. And if it backfired on Flow, so be it. He'd tried to play her. She felt no remorse for whatever fate beheld him.

"You want to be free of all this?" Tarri looked up at Flow, a confident twinkle in her eye.

"Of course," Flow huffed.

"Well then, here's your chance. Do as I say, or I'll tell the Sleepers what you've done."

"You're blackmailing me?" cried Flow, smacking a hand to his chest. "How dare you!"

"You've done it to yourself, Flow," Tarri said. "I'm done with these mindgames. Help me and I'll help you. I need to report on the filtration processes at the Water Management Facility. You have been brought into the operation, whether you approve of it or not. And I doubt you'll get far if you flee Aobia, Flow. They'll have ample reason to want you dead if you try that. So you'll need to come with me."

Flow gulped, taken aback. "You can't be serious?"

"What's the matter?" Tarri asked. "Don't want to be a part of it? Too bad. Before I was caught in Nischia's apartment, they'd already asked me to interview Sedulus with your help. That means it's significant enough for the Magisterium to be aware of what we are to do. You don't have an option, Flow. Not if you want to be a free citizen once more."

"My help?" Flow scowled, stepping closer. "*They* suspended me from work. *They* took my livelihood from me. All they do is take!"

Flow whirled around, slamming a fist through a wall-hung mirror behind him and sending fine shards of glass everywhere. Tarri didn't flinch.

A moment of tense silence passed between them, the quiet of the empty late-afternoon streets disallowing Flow any comfort. "You win," he said, barely above a whisper. In the shards, she caught the fragmented outline of his defeated face, angry angles of broken glass reflecting his emotions right before her. "Name the time and I'll be there. But then, I'm out and you're on your own." He walked to the door and opened it. Tarri caught the silhouette of his head in the afternoon light as he turned back to glance at her, before he stalked out the door and slammed it behind him.

I don't need you anyway, she thought, gritting her teeth. *I just need your secrets.*

DRIFT

Tʜᴇ ᴄᴀᴍᴘsɪᴛᴇ Iʙʜᴀᴍ ᴀɴᴅ Dayajin had set up was nestled into a tiny clearing surrounded by trees. They'd been travelling hard all day and had found themselves a mere six hours away from Relond, on the final decline of the mountain.

A fire in the centre of the clearing, which had been roaring hours before, was now at a smoulder, charcoal lumps of wood hot enough to have roasted the duck Ibham had caught in the afternoon. Drift had seen it with his own eyes and envied the human's quick reflexes. The duck had paused with its family along the roadside and as it had taken off, Ibham had thrown one straight spear and caught it out of the air. Now, here it was, flightless and crispy and dripping with fatty juice as the Sethi couple carved it before the two hungry Aobians.

Before long, Drift and Stag were chatting with Ibham and Dayajin as though they were old friends and two different bottles of spirit were being passed around from one sticky hand to the next. The first drink was the colour of mud and was spiced heavily with cinnamon, while the second was a clear spirit that Ibham described as 'life-endingly good'.

"Watch yourself around that bottle, ambassador." Ibham grinned as Stag took his second swig of the darker stuff. Stag tried not to wince as he swallowed and Drift chuckled.

"Not much of a spirit drinker, Stag?" he teased before taking the bottle from him.

"I prefer wine," Stag sputtered, wiping his mouth. "But I'd just as soon take a drink of this again if it meant I'd rest easier in the night."

"These drinks are distilled from anise," Dayajin said. "They are called arik, meaning 'milk of the lioness'. In the summer, we dance for the Huntress and set fire to our bellies with these drinks. Then, we send the most prized possessions of those who died in winter off on a raft across Lake Sethiliquin, where they will be frozen in time below the surface next winter. A celebration of life and death, altogether."

Ibham frowned at her. "You need to tell them all that?"

She looked back at him, quizzical. "I—"

"You don't feel the pain of my loss like I do," he snapped, cutting her off. Then he got up and stalked away, taking both bottles with him.

Drift and Stag lowered their gazes and the sound around the fire quietened enough for the crackle of the logs to come forth. Eventually, Dayajin sighed and spoke again.

"His father went first," she said over the fire. "Something was wrong with his heart and right on the turn of seasons, he died. My husband is right. I won't ever feel that pain the same way he does. But I will feel the other pain the same way he does, if not more. One week after his father left us, our son was killed in a stampede. He had a farm at the bottom of the mountains. A landslide, miles away, scared the cows. They struck him down, and we found him there, pressed into the ground." She stifled a sob. "We danced, days before we left Sethiliquin, and we said our farewells. Never before have I danced in the summer with such a heavy heart."

Stag continued to look down, uncomfortable. Drift reached out and took the woman's hand. "I'm sorry," he said. What more was there to say?

Dayajin nodded and slipped from his grip before also walking away, back to the caravan. Drift watched her as she went and Ibham's shadow emerged behind her. The man was gulping down dark spirit, coughing as he swallowed. He swayed back and forth, stumbling forward to reach Dayajin before taking her into the carriage. Suddenly, Drift understood the darkness in Ibham. The aggression and the short temper made sense. But there was still a choice behind those actions. Drift had lost everything dear to him. As a younger person, he'd lost his mother and father; now he was exiled, cut off from Tarri and his home. If he thought about these things for too long, he felt miserable and hopeless. But what choice did he have? His life went on.

He watched the dark outline of the caravan, reflecting on the tragedy Dayajin had recounted to them. If Tarri was to die, would he feel the same as the Sethi couple?

If he was to die without ever seeing her again, would she feel the same?

His mind swirled as he cleared his throat to excuse himself. "I need some rest," he explained to Stag.

Stag merely grunted before getting up too and toddling off in the direction of his bedroll, tucked under a tree on the far side of the clearing. Drift walked to his own and lay down in it. It smelled like Raegan's farm.

He thought of the farmer and prayed quietly to whatever was listening that Raegan, Mola, and the children were okay. Then the red of the charcoal faded from his sight and sleep took him.

A cold blade against his neck woke Drift from his sleep. Lying flat on his back, his head had rolled back over the top of his bedroll, and thankfully he was able to stop himself from raising it when he realised what was pressing against him.

"Ibham," he breathed.

The hand that held the knife's handle was firm, the grip unwavering. "I have always wanted to see a husk bleed," the Sethi man growled.

"We can talk this through, Ibham," Drift whispered. "Just drop the knife and we'll talk it through."

"A body filled with the sap of a tree," Ibham breathed. "Filthy husk!"

Drift looked around, trying not to move his neck. Dayajin was nowhere to be seen. Stag was likely still asleep under the tree on the other side of the clearing. He was well and truly alone. Yes, he could scream, but that would only bring down the inevitable upon him before anyone else could come to his aid. The hate that permeated Ibham's voice was like a thick, choking cloud and Drift did not want to tempt the man's next course of action.

"Do what you need to do, Ibham," he said, resigned. "Just answer me this: what did we do?"

"You?" Ibham questioned, chuckling. "Not you. Her. Telling you our story. Telling you *what we lost.* And what have I gained? A full caravan of wares, a disrespectful wife, and two husks?"

Dayajin. "What have you done to her, Ibham?" Drift demanded. "I've seen the way you treat her. But it's not her fault. Nobody can bring back those you love. Nobody!" He felt frantic as he said the words, but he could not move a muscle without risking his neck.

"Don't speak to me about those I love! You know nothing of me!"

Drift felt the blade press into his taut neck, splitting the skin. A sharp sting followed. This was it. He'd come all this way just to die to the hands of a human, the kind of person he'd always wanted to meet and learn from. In the two millennia since the

Great Settlement, nothing had truly changed. Both races still detested one another. "Why are you doing this? You want to spill more blood? I'm sorry, Ibham, I am. I could never understand your grief, even if I tried. But you must realise this is not the way to handle it."

"Sorry?" Ibham retorted. His breath reeked of spirit. This man was drunk. An angry drunk. "I've slept with a thousand nightmares since that day—"

"Drift!" The cry of his name broke the altercation as a body came hurtling into Ibham from behind. Stag had the Sethi man pinned to the ground, but not for long. Ibham swung his knife maniacally at the Aobian, who slid off him in an instant, springing backwards.

Drift jumped to his feet, watching as Stag pushed Ibham into the fold-out table where they had prepared their food earlier that night, knocking over pots, pans and—

The small pitcher of crude oil fell from the table, shattering against the ground. Before Drift could do anything, it had trickled into the fire pit, where the coals had burnt down but were still warm.

"Drift!" Stag cried as Ibham managed to get a hand around his neck, a large ceramic water jug in his other. Drift leaped for them both, trying to break them up, but Ibham struck Stag on the head and knocked him out cold.

Drift and Ibham circled each other. Drift watched as Ibham retrieved a long, reed-like thing from behind him, flicking it through the air and causing a loud *crack!*

Suddenly, there was a quick flash of pain across his face as a whip struck his cheek and buried itself in his skin. It was barbed and Drift screamed out in agony as Ibham yanked on the other end, causing him to fly forward, led by the face. Drift grabbed the whip and ripped it out, seeing flecks of flesh shine in the moonlight with it.

He growled through the pain, tasting the river of blood that was pouring from his cheek. The whip returned, wrapping around his neck. "Ahh!" he yelled, panicking. The whip squeezed, cutting into him and sucking the air from his lungs all at once. He caught a grin across Ibham's face as his vision began to cloud over. Ibham charged forward, yelling and shoving him down into the ground.

He fell on top of the firepit, choking as he struck the coals, which somehow managed to kick up enough friction to spark some new embers. He prayed that the oil trickling into the bowels of the fire pit wouldn't have enough fuel. Ibham spun him around, ripping the barbed whip free and shoving his head towards the coals.

The fire surged around his face. He thrashed with all his might, but Ibham kept his grip firm, edging his face closer to the flames. Sweat beaded around his forehead from the heat. His cheek had stopped hurting, and he wondered whether the need to survive had taken over or whether the fire had already cauterised his wound.

On his right, he saw the glimmer of a cooking knife, the same one that Ibham had been holding, within reach on the ground.

He screamed, pushing through the flames, igniting them more. He seized the knife, swung his arm behind him, and connected with something that was soft enough to be skin.

Sure enough, Ibham cried out and fell over. Drift rolled out of the fire pit, shoving the Sethi man into it without thinking. The sound of the man burning was akin to the raging scream of a hungry wake of vultures. A collision of squeals and screams ripped free of his throat.

As the fire raced down Ibham's canvas shirt and the man realised his fate, he threw himself around as though in a fit, kicking coals in all directions. Instantly, the trail of oil along the ground lit like a piece of thread unfurling from a spindle, extending a thin wall of fire towards the caravan. Drift ran to Stag, hauled him up by his limp arms, and moved him away from the rising flames. Tossing Stag down beside a tree, he raced to the front of the caravan, where the horses were secured to a tree, alert.

A shriek sounded from the other side of the caravan and he ran back to see Dayajin watching her husband burn, tears pouring down her fire-lit face. "We must go!" he cried, taking her hand. "This forest will burn, Dayajin, and we'll burn with it!" He tugged, but she wouldn't move. It was only then that he saw her left eye, closed with a black bulge, liquid weeping from its corner. Her cheek was a mottled hue of blue and purple. Ibham had done this to her.

As the smoke began to thicken, obstructing their view of the place where Ibham had fallen, she returned her gaze to Drift.

"You will die, husk," she heaved. "You will burn with him. You will burn!" The shadow of the Dayajin who had smiled once, offered them hospitality, and told them stories was gone, illuminated in the flames.

Drift let go of her instantly, raising his hands in defence. "Dayajin, please… We didn't cause this! He attacked me, threatened me with a knife!"

"A life for a life!" she screamed as the fire bloomed around them, racing up dry tree trunks like rain moving from ground to sky. "If my son and my husband must be taken so soon, you will go with them. The Huntress permits it!"

She charged at him and together they fell into the dirt. Grit filled the gaps between Drift's teeth and he grunted. His thoughts spun. Did she not see the danger her own husband posed to her? Did she care? These people were brutish. Humans were brutish.

Dayajin screamed as she rolled on top of Drift, pinning his chest down with a knee. Behind her, red flickers danced, exposing the dirt on her face. Her eyes were wide and ferocious and her teeth were clenched. The hate she'd tried to hide.

Drift winced as the first blow landed, her hand heavier than he'd expected. The second came swiftly, knocking his head in the opposite direction and causing his neck to make a cracking noise. "Please, stop," he said, his mind growing weary. The brightness of the fire was starting to dim, and he felt himself slipping away from consciousness as the next fist struck his cheek. Blood spurted from it as it was mashed into his teeth.

"Please," he whispered, no strength left to even speak. He felt limp, his chest heavy. He coughed as black smoke shrouded what was left of his vision. *Please. Let this not be my end, gods above…*

Wind escaped his lungs in a burst as he was yanked by the collar to the edge of the line of fire that was dancing in the dregs of oil. The flames licked him passionately, raw heat burrowing into his skin. She'd thrown him in here, into the antithesis of life.

"Stop!" a loud voice boomed over the burning. Stag.

"I will avenge him, husk!" Dayajin cried.

Drift tried to focus on them, but all he could make out was the movement of blurry outlines in the smoke. He heaved, moving slowly to the side, away from the flames. "Stag!" he croaked.

"He made his choice, Sethi!" Stag cried. "You don't need to make the same one. Step away and we can all escape here before it's too late—"

Dayajin's chortled scream echoed across the air as a burst of fire blossomed, like a flower opening in spring. The smell of cooked meat poked at Drift's nose. The fire must've gotten through Ibham's skin.

Stag stumbled across Drift's body, hauling him up to his feet. "We need to go!"

"Where … is she?" Drift tried to look around, but his head spun.

"Can't see her!" Stag shouted. "But we need to go before this whole damned forest comes alight!"

With one arm haphazardly around Stag's shoulders, Drift limped away from the centre of the fire as it swallowed the entire clearing. He looked back only once to see burning fat where Ibham's body had once held form, causing the fire to splatter, and grow, and soar. Wherever Dayajin was, she was dead if she had not made it out by now.

Drift slumped into the caravan, his face stinging from the burns.

"Wait here," Stag said as he raced to the front of the caravan, where the horses stamped and neighed, wracked with panic. Drift braced himself as Stag detached one of the horses, immediately securing its reins to the caravan and jerking it forward. He moaned in pain. Every part of his body hurt and his lungs wouldn't let him take in enough air.

In moments, Stag had gotten the other horse attached and was driving the caravan through the dark forest, the fire behind them being the only source of illumination. Drift watched out the back from his seat, hugging himself and drawing long, slow breaths. Red flames reached for the sky, like the hands of the dying. And then, he saw her.

Dayajin was sprinting from the fire, holding an arm across her belly. Her tunic was torn, her hair ragged. "Wait! Please!"

"Stag!" Drift barked, feeling his throat choke on the word. "Go back!"

Stag continued driving, paying no heed to him. He was going to let Dayajin die. Maybe she had tried to doom them. But in Drift's mind, nobody deserved to die. Not even her. "Stag! GO BACK!"

The horses reared up, causing the caravan to shudder and stop in its place. Wordlessly, Stag began to guide the horses into a turn.

"Please!" Dayajin wailed.

Red was all Drift could see as the caravan made its full turn. His heartbeat pulsed as he tried to hold his breath, billows of smoke moving across them.

Then, a tremendous *crack* sounded from the right, the limb of a long-standing tree perishing to fire.

"No!" he screamed.

The massive bough slammed into Dayajin's comparatively small frame, pressing her into the dirt. It landed on the back of her head and Drift gasped as he saw her face crack and contort unnaturally. Her eyes bulged before her body became still.

"Move!" Stag exclaimed as the horses pulled back the other way. There was no life to recover here. All that was behind them was a wasteland.

DRIFT

DRIFT WIPED GRIT OUT of the corners of his eyes as he awoke to a rapidly changing terrain. The land had flattened out dramatically and alternated between forestry and pastures fitted out with houses or barns, or a mixture of them both. Before long, the distance between homes narrowed and the road became a wide, open street leading toward a large arbour on a hill that welcomed the swathes of people entering beneath it to the city of Relond.

Drift had been asleep for eight hours, perhaps a longer rest than he'd observed since the day he'd woken outside Aobia. His cheek stung with the singe of the previous night's fire, which had thankfully not burned through him. He still had a wheeze and coughed whenever he tried to speak.

He recalled Stag had taken the reins the night before. Etched into his memory was the final picture of death: Dayajin's shattered body beneath the tree branch. Now, he and Stag were commencing their entry into Relond, two Aobians in a stolen caravan with blood on their hands and obvious injuries. He'd been partly responsible for the fire that had burned Ibham alive. An anxiety arose in him and he matched the feeling to the same one that had occupied his mind when they'd been chased out of Providence or snuck up on in the night by Ibham. A fear of how unpredictable the humans were.

"We're already here?" he said between coughs.

Stag turned his head briefly, droopy eyed and pale as a ghost. "It took longer than it should have, for what it's worth. We should've been here two hours ago, but I had to keep stopping. Patrols from Relond heading up the mountain road. Look behind you and you'll see what I'm talking about."

Drift craned his stiff neck. The skyline was a haze, a long gradient between dark grey and the blue of the morning. For as far as the eye could see, smoke doused the view of the mountain. It was still on fire.

"What have we done, Stag?" he murmured.

"We've done nothing!" Stag shot back. "And you'll keep that opinion as long as you wish to stay alive. We're Aobians. Why would we light a fire?"

"Why would we come from the mountain in a Sethi trading caravan, looking like a couple of torn up rags?" Drift countered. "Besides, we have no way of knowing whether anyone from Providence made it this far already to report our impending entry."

"Well, we're arriving," Stag said. "So we don't have much of a choice but to stick to the truth if it comes down to it. Look."

Drift took it all in as they approached the city of Relond. The arch that welcomed people into Relond was just the start, and beyond, the densely packed buildings and grid-like roads reminded him of the sprawling cities of the Heart and Soul in Aobia, albeit a little more organised upon the flat ground on which it lay.

The buildings of Relond displayed an interesting architectural language, as they each sported domed roofs of thatchery or tile, causing the view of the city to look like a neat arrangement of bubbles from afar. Another thing, Drift noticed, were the doors on many of the buildings, which were round instead of square, a defining feature of Relond's design. The road into Relond was a marker for the kinds of people who lived or worked there; it was filled with a mixture of working-class citizens, travellers, merchants, and soldiers.

The soldiers caught Drift's eye as the caravan approached the arbour, but he knew they were different to the Theradorans at the Mountain Gate—these Adiran men and women sported pointed steel helmets and polished chestplates, as opposed to the rougher, ragged leatherwork and thick canvas tunics of the Theradoran men.

People moved beneath the arbour, in and out of Relond, and Drift noted they were rarely stopped. However, his breath caught as several soldiers gestured to Stag to pull the caravan over on the roadside rather than enter the city.

"Roots below," Stag swore as the soldiers approached.

"State your business, Sethi," one soldier practically spat. He was tall for a human with an angular jaw and a blue, circular wave adorning his chestplate.

"We're here to sell our wares," Stag said.

"What kind of wares?" The soldier scoured the caravan, gesturing for his men to do the same. They hadn't even taken a closer look at Drift or Stag. They proceeded to give the caravan's main compartments a once-over before reaching the back doors.

Finally, the first soldier leaned his head into the open cavity above the door where Drift sat. "Might I ask you to please step out, sirs?"

"Of course," Drift obliged, hearing Stag murmur something similar behind him.

The soldiers looked confused as Drift and Stag stepped out from the caravan, nearly two heads taller than the shortest of them, and realisation quickly dawned. "You're Aobians."

"We are," Stag said. "And we've important diplomatic duties to attend to in Adira, so if we could hurry this up…" He gestured towards the caravan, letting the guard fill in the gap of his words.

"You're in a Sethi caravan," the soldier replied, gesturing towards the Sethi inscription on the side of the door. Drift couldn't read the words, but he knew these soldiers were already asking the wrong kinds of questions.

Stag sighed, casting a quick glance at Drift. "Officer, truth be told, we were with two Sethi merchants prior to our arrival."

The guards exchanged looks, the one in charge smoothing his beard. "Tell me more," he replied.

"They perished in the fire up the mountain. We couldn't save them." Stag said the words flatly. Drift's gut dropped as he relived the moment Ibham began to scream, immersed in flame. Then, Dayajin, running desperately, pummelled by the tree.

"That fire burns out of control," another of the guards said. "My own brother is up there, trying to stop its course. They could be there for days."

"They'll run out of trees to fell in its wake if it's that big already and will have to flee home," the head guard responded before returning to Drift and Stag. "Do you two know how the fire started?"

Drift looked away. He couldn't hold their eye contact and lie at the same time. "It's just so dry," he explained. "The Sethi lit a campfire and it got out of control, fast."

"We wouldn't even warm ourselves by it, as you would understand," Stag added.

"Of course," the guard said. "But why were you travelling with them in the first place?" the guard asked. "I wouldn't expect two Aobians to be in the same caravan as Sethi."

True enough. Sethiliquin, its lake, and the mountains all encompassed the far northwest of Q'ara. Drift couldn't envision how long it would take to travel there. He swallowed, unprepared to answer.

With confidence, Stag replied, "We were unfortunate enough to lose a wheel on our carriage. Hence, our travel has been delayed by several days. We met the Sethi couple after traversing the Mountain Gate on foot."

The guard smirked. "I had no idea something of Aobian quality could suffer a fault like that."

"Don't you have a senior officer to report to?" Stag retorted. The guard huffed, walking off with his colleagues. "I need some damned breakfast."

Drift sighed. "So do I. But Stag, what are we going to do?" The impression of Relond before them was overwhelming in itself. They had nowhere to go.

As if answering his thoughts, Stag replied, "I have a contact in the city. Arjan. He runs a hotel called Al-Faqada and will book us without notice."

A hotel? Hotels were where the most important people stayed. Only Sleepers, for example, could afford hotels in Aobia. "And with what coin will you pay for us?"

"I've coin enough," Stag said defensively. "Besides, these Sethi will have kept their savings somewhere in the caravan. We just need to find it." He began to snoop around, going through the rear compartment where the Sethi products were: jewellery of all kinds, beautiful stones, and shawls encrusted with gemstones. This was what Dayajin had made by her own hands.

"Well," Stag said, stepping back. "Even if there's no money here, we can sell some of this."

"Completely plausible," Drift shrugged wryly. "Two Aobians selling Sethi artpieces in an Adiran city. Sounds like the start of a bad joke."

Stag scowled as the guards returned.

The senior officer nodded, writing something down. "Okay. You're headed to the capital for diplomatic purposes? You're both clear then." He put his pen down and displayed a rehearsed smile. "Be safe, tree-dwellers. The death of King Terrens has increased everyone's unease."

Drift let out a sigh of relief as the guards went on their way. Had nobody come from Providence yet? On horseback or via carriage, they would have beaten the two Aobians by several days. Maybe Gaudin had never sent anyone after them.

Stag hauled himself back onto the driver's bench. "Let's be on our way then, Drift. I've got an empty belly and five thousand layers of dirt on me." Giving Drift barely a moment to get inside, Stag clicked his tongue to start the horses, commencing the slow roll under the arbour into Relond.

The two Aobians were quiet as the caravan moved through the streets of Relond. Drift looked out at the city, taking it all in. Here, the streets were cobblestone and the buildings were a mixture of clay, thatch, and log. The city took on an antiquarian ambience, similar to Providence, though a lot cleaner and more refined.

Its appearance was upheld by the people who travelled through it. They wore colourful sashes and tunics rather than the leather-wear of the locals or the modern garb of Aobia, which was said to be similar to the sea people of Adira. It seemed that here, at the base of the Mountain Gate, the intersection between East and West was at its most obvious. Given the warning they had received from the guards upon entry, Drift didn't want to guess what the recent news from Adira had done to any easterners who had made a living here.

Eventually, the caravan rolled around a narrow slip lane, coming to a stop before an enormous building. Yes, it was clay and wood with a thatched roof, but it appeared to climb towards the sky itself, being over four storeys in height and painted with the most beautiful arrangement of warm colours, like a shining beacon in amongst the drab of the rest of Relond.

"Greetings!" A voice came from outside the caravan and Drift returned his gaze to eye level, only to see a human male in a soft yellow tunic waving at them.

Stag did not wait to make his presence known. "We are hoping to obtain two rooms. Arjan is aware of our stopping by."

The man peered into the doorway of the caravan, his eyebrows shooting up as he noticed the two Aobians. "Of course, tree-dweller. We can have two rooms ready in no time."

"Thank you."

"Shall I call a valet to move your caravan and have the horses stabled?"

"Please. We will wait here for you to show us to our rooms." Stag opened the door, stepping out onto the cobbled street and pulling his pack out with him. Drift followed shortly behind.

A young girl, not yet having left the fruits of childhood behind, appeared at the front of the caravan, jumping in quickly and taking the reins.

"The Tree knows we all need plenty of rest after the last few days," Drift said as they watched the caravan drive away. "What say we find our rooms, unpack, and unwind with a drink?" He eyed Stag.

"Of course," Stag replied. "Only the best food and drink are served here."

Drift's stomach groaned in response, but first, he just wanted a place to wash, himself *and* his clothes.

The inside of the building was styled with long, vibrant rugs on the floors and stitched tapestries upon the walls depicting bears, wolves, and other creatures. The floor was covered with long mahogany tables and benches, though it was not a busy time of day for patrons to frequent, judging by the lack of people drinking, eating, or making merry. At the front of the room was a counter, behind which stood a man, also dressed in a yellow tunic, with a long, shaggy beard of salt and pepper. "Good morning, I am Hijian. Welcome to Al-Faqada. How can I assist you?"

Drift was taken aback by the hotel. He'd never been in an inn this large, let alone a place with a valet and counter service upon arrival. Aobia certainly didn't expend any less than what was deserved of their messengers and seeing how little the Sleepers released people to travel, Drift could understand how that was the case.

"Two rooms, please," Stag said.

"Of course, sir," Hijian nodded. "That will be forty marks."

Drift sucked in a breath. Forty marks? Human marks were one and the same in Aobia, the global currency that had appeared shortly after the armistice that had ended the Four-Front War had been signed. He couldn't imagine spending forty marks on a room at a glorified inn. That was more than he'd earned in six weeks of work.

Stag sighed, tipping a hefty sack onto the desk and counting eight thick coins, five marks each. Drift shouldn't have been surprised that he had been equipped with serious money.

"One bedroom is a top floor suite," Hijian said, counting the coins himself. "It is the same suite that the former king's father, Filens of Adira, stayed in during his time conducting peace envoys in Relond after the war. Which one of you would like to take that room?"

Unsurprisingly, Drift watched as Stag raised a hand.

"Very good," Hijian replied. "Here is your key, sir." He nodded to Drift. "This is your key, tree-dweller." Hijian handed over a bronze key to Drift, unclipping a metal latch that kept the counter he stood behind shut. He stepped out and walked ahead of the party. "If you'll follow me, I will show you to your rooms." With a short bow, the man walked off.

Drift caught Stag's eyes and his companion simply nodded stiffly at him.

Now, he was in the other Aobian's world.

"Tea?" Drift inquired. The hot, steaming cup was placed down before him, a waft of some strongly brewed black leaf. He was lying in a steaming bath, soothing his muscles and holding a facecloth to his burned cheek. He'd eaten a full breakfast prior. He hadn't felt this relaxed in days.

"Yes, tea," Stag said. "First you make me fetch you a drink and then you complain about it."

"Well, not only is it *not* a mug of ale, but it's also poorly made tea." Though coming from an Aobian, this wasn't hard criticism to give; the high-grown jasmine and greenmint leaves of the mountains around Aobia harvested a much better product than this lowlander stuff. Stag said nothing, already edging towards the door of Drift's bathroom suite to leave.

"Arjan, the owner, is from Ghabbat. Ghabbatians do not drink, Drift."

"Ah…" Drift said. "It's fine, thank you. But there's somewhere we can go to drink, surely?"

Stag snorted. "Yes. We can go to a public house, with all manner of eyes on us wondering what we're doing and asking us questions."

"Fine," snapped Drift. Stag's sarcasm was not lost on him. "I'll drink the tea. But leave me in peace."

"Gladly," Stag shot back. "Don't take an age, though. I found money in the caravan. We need some clothes, Drift. I'll take you to the merchant's quarter right in the heart of the city." He took a sip of his own tea and spat it out, impulse taking over. "For once,

I agree with you," he coughed. "This stuff's nasty. I'd gladly take a pint of Blacksmith's Swarf if I had the choice."

With that, he whirled around to face the door and was gone.

Drift chuckled, settling himself lower into the steamy water. This respite would be short-lived, but it would live a strong life.

The merchant quarter reminded Drift of the way the hotel had appeared the first time he'd set eyes on it: drowned in colour, a stark contrast to Relond's thatched mud-brick homes. In addition to this, life flourished here, a mixing pot of culture and art. It was not dissimilar to the Soul of the Great Tree. He smiled and was reminded of Tarri's first stall in the market square. That small stall had worked wonders for her. Within a year, Tarri had put enough money aside to secure a lease on a more permanent building that had quickly taken on the persona and success of the Tailory as it was known today. There was no denying the power of handcrafted goods or simply the connection between people and the ways one can grow and learn from another. From small things big things grew. Just like the Tree itself. Just like the beloved that still had his heart. *I miss you.*

"Come!" Stag exclaimed. "All the wonders of the continent are here in this tiny quarter."

Drift followed in silence, taking it in. The ambience. The people rushing about, making interested comments, greeting new vendors. The sound of rustling bags, paper wrapping, hot soup being poured into mugs from a large ceramic pot at a nearby stand.

"Here we are," Stag said, interrupting his observations. They paused in front of a large stall decorated with garments for all purposes, with opulent furniture inside and a curtain for trying on clothes. "This is Rafa's stall." He indicated a short, stout fellow in a purple tunic with a cylindrical headdress, a black tassel hanging limply from its top. The man sported a thick, dark moustache peppered with the occasional grey hair and a braid swinging down from beneath the headdress. Upon spying Stag, his eyes lit up, a cheerful wrinkle appearing at their edges.

"My dear friend," the man said, pulling him into an all-engulfing embrace. Stag stood stiff as a board, forever made uncomfortable by any kind of touch. "Another stint in Relond and we cross paths."

"It's good to see you, Rafa." The Aobian grinned.

"And you," the man replied, his smile growing only wider. "Where is Flow? I must see him!"

"He is gone, Raf," he said. "Back to a normal life. It was time."

Rafa considered Stag's answer for a moment before shrugging. "I understand. It hurts to leave your home. This is his replacement then?"

Drift's cheeks felt hot, but Stag nodded. "This is Drift, a good friend of ours and Aobia's newest ambassador."

Drift smiled. "It is an honour."

Rafa bowed his head. "And to you, tree-dweller. What is it that brings you both here today?"

"Uh—"

"Clothes!" Stag said. "We need clothes, Rafa. We ran into some carriage trouble on the way here and had to leave our vehicle behind."

"Well!" Rafa exclaimed. "You'll need a set of gowns, a tunic for light travel, and a shirt with pants. Oh, and undergarments, of course!" Rafa shook a finger in the air. "I doubt you'd be seeing me if you didn't need well-fitting and well-presenting clothes. I trust you are … passing through to the capital?"

"Yes," Drift replied. "We've important work to continue in Adira."

"Hmm," Rafa began darkly, "now that the king is dead."

Stag merely nodded, keeping his words in. Before Drift knew it, Rafa was slinging garments over his and Stag's shoulders alike. By the end, Drift stood draped in fabric like a scarecrow. Rafa laughed.

"Come in, come in! There is a curtain drawn at the back. You may change there," Rafa said. "Inside is a mirror and you can decide what you like."

Momentarily, Drift emerged from the changing room with a new outfit. After his drab green-brown Aobian workclothes, he now wore a rich blue tunic with a belt to hold it close against his waist. The tunic was adorned with long decorative lines of velveteen piping in an even darker shade of blue and beige rope zigzagging down the middle, creating loops for the wooden buttons. His worn, ragged boots were held in one hand, a fresh pair of knee-length tan leather waders covering the maroon pantaloons underneath.

"Perfect!" Rafa said, clapping Drift on the back. "That will be three silvers."

Drift had to stop himself from scoffing at the price. "Of course. Stag has the money."

Stag exited the changing area at that very moment in a smart cream outfit with a rope-tied belt and black pants. "This is brilliant, Rafa. Three silvers?"

Rafa nodded. "Each."

"Of course. Clothes of this quality deserve a price tag no less." He handed the coins over to the Sethi man as though they were mere pebbles.

"My pleasure," Rafa nodded, turning around. "Allow me to pack your old clothes into a bag for you to carry."

Stag raised his eyebrows as though to show Drift how impressed he was by the Sethi merchant's treatment of them.

"Three silvers?" Drift murmured. "An exorbitant price to pay!"

"Not in this city," Stag replied. "The man makes good clothes that fit us Aobians well enough. I would not begrudge him a living for that. Now, where to next?" He gestured out to the chaos of the merchant quarter.

Drift felt his stomach rumble as though it was alerting him to something: lunch time. "Perhaps we should—"

A wisp of a woman moved through the crowds, her familiar homestead-style clothing and black bun of hair catching him off guard. It couldn't be. He darted away from Stag in an instant, following the woman in the blue farm clothes. He had to see her face, *know* it was who he thought it was with certainty.

"Wait!" Stag called. "Drift!"

He pushed through the crowd, shoving people to the side. The woman continued on her path. As he got closer, a line of children ran past him. "Excuse me, mister!" one cried, the others giggling. He recalibrated immediately, his eyes searching. "Roots below," he swore. He'd lost her. Then, in the distance, the faded blue cloth of her clothes shone in the afternoon sunlight. He pushed through the swarms of buyers, knocking a plum out of a man's hands by accident. "I'm sorry!" he exclaimed, keeping on.

The woman turned a corner and he followed, exiting the merchant quarter completely. The streets opened up to twice their width here, carts driving down their centres, people sticking to the sidepaths. She was heading down the cobbled road, two cane baskets in tow.

"Please," he whispered to himself. "Please turn around…" He reached out an arm, manic to see her face.

The woman, sensing her assailant, spun suddenly, a vicious swing of her shopping baskets sending the weighty object reeling into Drift's chest, knocking him back. He stumbled, catching himself as a passing carriage rang a bell of warning at him. Bystanders ignored what they saw, but Drift knew that his suspicions were confirmed. The woman stared at him and he back at her, a sense of recognition in her wide eyes.

Raegan's sister, Mola, was here in Relond.

DRIFT

"**M**Y BROTHER IS GONE." Without so much as a hello, Mola dropped her gaze, unable to conceal the falter in her voice. "He's gone. Shot full of arrows and dragged along the streets of Providence, a cowbell around his neck to let us all know."

Drift knew he could never say sorry and be forgiven. He and Stag were the reason Raegan was dead. And now Mola was the only relative his children had left.

"The children are here," she stated. "We arrived two days ago."

Drift's eyes widened. "Two days ago? You must have left Providence immediately."

Mola sighed. "The night they killed my brother, they sent people to the farm. What was I to do? A single guardian with two children under her wing and no property to her name? I couldn't face it, so the next day, Noel drove us here and I found work as a baker's assistant before I slept the first night. I… Anyway." Before Drift could respond, she shook her head. "I must go." She began to walk away, head down.

"Mola!" Drift called after her. "Wait!"

She stopped, but she did not turn her head. "Yes?"

"I know it can't bring him back," Drift said, shaking his head. "But for what it's worth, I'm sorry. I'm *so sorry*."

Mola's whole frame shook and yet Drift could do nothing but listen to her sob. Had he said the wrong thing? No. He'd said the worst thing of all. No amount of apology could reverse the tragedy that had befallen her.

He looked down at the road as Mola sucked in a breath and went on her way.

When he got back to the hotel, Drift was immediately stopped at the door by Stag. "You *left*. Without an explanation or a single word."

"I'm sorry, Stag," Drift replied. "I saw Mola."

"The farmer's sister? Here in Relond?" Stag asked, his eyes showing disbelief.

"One and the same," Drift replied as they went inside together, sitting at a table near the entry. "Raegan is dead."

"No," Stag breathed.

"I'm going to go and see her," Drift said. "We did this, Stag. We got him killed. Those bastards in Providence never even came after us, so what did he die for? Nothing." He spat the last word out.

"See her?" Stag scolded. "There is nothing to see of her or the children, Drift. They are not our problem." Stag's eyes flashed with irritation. "You form attachments far too quickly."

"Too quickly?" Ridiculous. He'd always struggled with attachment, with the idea of being obligated to another person, whether by blood or some other debt, it didn't matter. But the news of Raegan's death, and seeing Mola here in the city… Now he couldn't shake the feeling, let alone walk away from it. "I think I can help her."

"What are you going to do? Ask her and the children to tag along with us?" Stag hissed. "We're carrying enough baggage as it is, Drift. I've got enough important work to do on behalf of the Magisterium, let alone deal with your shenanigans. With the king dead and nobody owning up to the crime, what's coming could tear this continent apart."

On one hand, Drift knew that Stag wasn't exaggerating when he spoke of his worries. They were foreigners in a world that no longer belonged to them, pursuing an entirely new frontier of political interaction guided by tension instead of peace. Drift was the first exile in centuries, the first since the end of the monarchy, when Queen Feldra had escaped her own exile and encouraged a quick and villainous rebellion. The queen had been outcast for selling knowledge of Luminosity to Therador a century ago.

Now, Stag seemed to think that Flow was involved in something similar.

Shaking Drift from his thoughts, a man with a princely beard and a deep red tunic appeared at the side of their table, out of breath.

"Ambassador," the man puffed. "You need to pack and go."

"What is it?" Drift said, looking from the man to Stag. "Who's this?"

"This is the innkeeper, Arjan." Stag gestured to the man who was with them. "What's happened?"

"Pier never came, but his name is on the ledger to visit the hotel," the innkeeper said, his eyes wide.

"Who is Pier?" Drift asked, confused. "Stag, tell me what's going on!"

"Excuse me, sir," Arjan the innkeeper said. "Lord Stag meets regularly with Lord Pier, a representative of Relond to the Adiran Throne. He was supposed to be here for a meeting today. When I noticed his name was in the ledger, I asked my staff who had signed him in. It was a new worker, but when they described him to me, it did not sound like the same person."

"We've been found out. Someone's trying to get to us before we get to Adira," Stag said, covering his mouth with a hand.

"What did they look like, Arjan?" Drift asked.

"Red hair and an orange beard, sir," Arjan replied. "But Lord Pier is an older man with no hair at all."

Red hair. A vague memory begged to come forward in his mind, but he could not grasp it. "Were there any other details?" Drift pressed.

"Just his clothes," Arjan said. "Black boots and leathers. I don't know who this person is, but I do know they came here in person to see you while you were both out earlier. I am not confident they won't return."

"Wait!" Drift smacked the table with his hand. "There was a man with Gaudin outside the town hall that day in Providence. A crier from Relond!"

Stag's eyebrows pushed together. "That's right. What was his name?"

"Briar," Drift said. "Briar Sevardson." He would not forget the man's face. The crier had come, delivered his lies to the crowd, and left before they'd all known what had been happening.

"Forgive me, but have either of you seen a crier in Relond before?" Arjan asked. Both the Aobians shook their heads. "That man was no crier. They wear official uniforms with the mark of Adira on their chests. He was dressed in black from head to toe."

"There's no time to waste, Drift. Something is amiss and I'd rather not be here to find out what. Gather your things. Arjan, see to it that we exit the city with the littlest noise possible. We can take the Sethi carriage, concealed."

Drift shook his head. "I at least need to see Mola—"

"No!" Stag growled. "We have no time!"

"I must make my peace with her." Drift levelled his eyes with Stag.

"Your sense of honour would take you off the path to safety so quickly? Then be it on your own head." With that, Stag turned, his coattail sweeping past Drift as he left the table, heading for the stairs up to his room.

DRIFT

Drift wandered the streets, gazing up at the sunset-soaked rooftops of Relond. He walked with his hood over his head, concealing everything down to his nose in the fading afternoon sun. He would have an hour or two at best before he was expected to meet up with Stag.

Winding his way through the streets, Drift looked up at each busy shopfront he passed, hoping to find what he was looking for. How many bakeries would be in this city, anyway? But then, in a wide square intersection filled with people, he spotted a corner shop with a line of customers outside the window. As he got closer, the smell wafting out at him confirmed his guess.

As he made his way through the line, he noticed Mola working in the window. But when he got closer, she made no attempt to notice him in return. Maybe he'd made a mistake. Maybe he'd said all he could already and Stag had been right. Before he knew it, he was the only person in line and he froze before her. "Mola."

"What are you doing here?"

"I don't have long," Drift confessed.

"Of course you don't," she replied. "But clearly, you've come to say something. What is it?"

Drift inclined his head towards her. "Walk with me?"

Mola hesitated, biting her bottom lip. This was clearly a hard choice to make. "Fine. Just let me tell Scov." Mola turned and walked behind the counter, where a wall concealed the outside world from the heart of the bakery.

"Scov?" Drift called out. "Who's Scov?"

A minute or so went by before a small creature covered in light grey fur that nearly looked blue in the fading light walked out from behind the wall, sliding over a stool with a five-fingered paw so that it could reach the countertop to take orders. The creature had whiskers and a very pink nose and the deepest black wells of eyes Drift had ever seen, though a white baker's hat fell loosely over its head, covering half its gaze. "Scov is Scov," the creature announced in a heavily accented voice.

"A Hidden One," Drift breathed. The Hidden Ones were small creatures who had lived alongside Aobians on Q'ara as long as the histories stretched. They occupied a large area of the forest northwest of Aobia, known as the Hidden Forest. They didn't often leave their home.

"Scov might be a Hidden One, but Scov no longer hides. Instead, Scov bakes! And do not generalise, *tree-dweller*. I am a Nestler, not a disgusting Burrower." The creature shrugged lightly, leaping up onto the counter itself. "Scov will give you hot tea rolls if you bring Mola back in fifteen minutes. Is that agreeable?"

What an odd fellow, Drift thought. *A Nestler of the Hidden Ones in Relond?* "Of-of course," Drift said. Mola then walked out of the bakery, appearing at his side.

She smiled uncomfortably at Drift. "Where to?"

They began to walk away from the small creature as a new line of customers wanting to get their fill of hot bread for the evening suddenly formed behind Drift. "You better not be late!" Scov warned as they left. "Scov waits for nobody!"

"A Nestler?" Drift asked once they had gotten some distance from the bakery. "I've never seen one. They retreated back into the Hidden Forest years ago, after the war."

"Neither had I until Scov gave me a job at the counter. Noel recommended I seek him out upon arrival here. They were supposedly connected during the war. When I first met Scov, I couldn't believe it. I thought the Hidden Ones were most comfortable with your people."

"Since the war? No," he responded to Mola's question. "I've never seen one, though I'm still young."

"I see," Mola said, curt. "How young are you, exactly?"

"Fifty-three," Drift replied. "Can I ask you the same question without being impolite?"

"And yet you look younger than I. That's twenty-four, by the way," Mola said. "Too young."

Twenty-four. Drift had been in school at twenty-four. Drift hadn't known Tarri until he'd been twenty-five, but even then, they'd still been children. He looked at Mola, noticing the age in her eyes. She might've been younger than he, but in human years, she was an adult. And she had the experience of child-raising beneath her now. It did not hide itself from Drift: Mola was no child and nor did she look it. Though she appeared youthful, her experiences, her gait, and her manner showed to him the truth of a hard life.

The silence between them grew, nearly sealing out the blur of the city ambience. Drift let Mola break it first.

As he let out a long-drawn breath, she spoke. "The children would love to see you."

Worry flashed in his mind. He didn't have long until Stag left for Adira, with or without him. "Mola, I…"

"You're too guilty?" She shot the words at him like an arrow intended to wound. "Is that what it is?"

"No, that's not it," Drift protested. "But we're still being hunted, Stag and I. I don't know whether it's to do with what happened in Providence or if it's someone who hates the alliance between my people and Adira, hunting Stag because he's an ambassador." *Or both.* "I had to practically beg on both knees for Stag to give me some time to find you and talk." Glancing at her, he found a puzzling sense of comfort in her eyes, as though he could forget his worries and stay with her. But in the deep wells of her pupils, he also found something else. A darkness that only grew as the sun hid behind the rooftops. She'd come to this city out of desperation. Raegan's children relied on her. And, apart from the bakery, she had nothing. *Roots below,* he thought, realising what he needed to do.

"Five minutes with the children," he agreed. "But then I must go. I have no choice."

Mola shot him a hurt look but grabbed his arm despite it, leading him around the bend of the street.

The small home was wedged into what must've been an alleyway at some point. Drift could not believe how thin it was. Compared to the homes on either side of it, it was also an extra storey high, sticking up past the roofline. Like an Aobian in a world of men or a Great Tree in the forest. The thought struck him as Mola twisted the doorknob, stepping inside. "Braddegh! Suan!" she called. "We have a visitor."

The sound of rushing feet matched Drift's heartbeat as the children reached the bottom of the pencil-thin staircase. "Drift!" They both cried, tugging at his limbs and leaping into his arms. "Well, well!" Drift said, feigning cheerfulness. "Look at you both!" He gave Braddegh a high-five as he held Suan on the other arm. "Isn't it good to see you!" Tears welled in his eyes, but he sucked them back, Mola noticing the noise that escaped him as he did so, though the children were oblivious.

"Now, Drift doesn't have long," Mola said, killing the atmosphere.

"What do you mean, Aunty?" Braddegh said. "He's only just arrived!"

"Well—"

"Braddegh, I am still working with my colleague. You remember Stag?" He nearly laughed as the boy's face soured.

"Can't you let him go by himself?" Suan asked.

"No, child," Drift said, putting her down. "I need to see my duty through. It's an honourable thing to do in Aobia and I sense it is no different in the world of humans."

Disappointment crossed their faces as Mola ruffled Suan's hair lightly. "You both run along," she said. "Tomorrow we will go to the market square, so there's lots to be excited about. Now let me speak with Drift."

"Farewell to you both," Drift said, saluting them. Suan hugged his leg tight. Braddegh, however, simply held Drift's stare.

"Goodbye," he murmured, his low spirits apparent.

Before he could blink, Suan raced off, back up the stairs. Braddegh followed her, less energetic. He looked back at Drift only once and Drift knew from the boy's forlorn expression that he never should have come here. Braddegh was old enough to know Drift had had something to do with his father's death. He'd even led his sister out on a nighttime venture to visit them all in the pillory.

For the father you lost, I will make my amends, Drift promised silently as Mola gripped his shoulder, turning him to face her once more. *I have too much to answer for already.*

"Drift, I—"

The door of the house slammed open and Drift held Mola back instinctively. Outside was the little Nestler who ran the bakery, Scov, accompanied by another man who looked different to any other human Drift had seen before. The man had jet black hair cropped neatly around his head. His skin was darker than Mola's but not as olive as the Sethi's.

"Scov!" Mola exclaimed. "I'm sorry! I was about to come back!"

"Come back?" Scov asked. "No, you're not coming back. You must go now. Scov's friend, Jilo, alerted Scov to a dangerous group of people looking for this Aobian."

"Group?" Drift asked, swallowing.

Jilo nodded. "There is no time," he said. The timbre of his voice was soft but pressing. "I understand I am a stranger, but you must trust me. Do you know of an organisation known as the Nightingales?"

Mola frowned, but Drift covered his mouth with a hand. "Nightingales? How do you know of them?"

Jilo inhaled. "They have caused problems for me in the past. But I don't want to be dismissive of their threat. If they are after you, they will not stop until they get to you."

Drift raised an eyebrow, confused by Jilo's sudden appearance. "What do you know of them? And why are you here?"

Jilo sighed. "Please, tree-dweller, I implore you listen to me. I know nothing of your circumstances, but I presume you are affiliated with the Aobian Magisterium. You should take my advice. If the Nightingales get to you, who knows what international incident it could begin."

Drift looked away. He couldn't believe this. "Where are they?"

"Scov received one as a customer, tree-dweller," said the small Nestler. "Jilo came afterwards, letting me know he'd heard tavern talk of them in the city."

Jilo shook his head. "Not quite, Scov. There is a man involved with them with hair the colour of fire. He came looking for two Aobians in the tavern I frequent. I had just arrived and overheard him asking for their whereabouts. Thankfully, nobody could help him."

"Briar Sevardson," Drift replied at once.

"Sorry?" Jilo asked.

"At least, that's the name he goes by. He already tried to convince a town leader to condemn us to death in the town of Providence." Drift felt guilt creep up his throat as he finished his recount and spied Mola turning away from the corner of his eye.

"Well, if he finds you, I suspect your fate may not go in your favour," Jilo replied. "Are you the only Aobian, then, here in Relond?"

"No," said Drift, perhaps a little quickly. "My friend, erm, colleague is here too. Stag."

"Where is he staying?" Scov asked intently.

"A hotel named Al-Faqada."

"Home for the lost," Jilo murmured.

"Pardon?" Drift asked.

"That's what its name means in Ghabbatian, tree-dweller. Is your friend still there?"

Drift bit his lip. "Stag wanted to leave tonight. I … felt the need to come here."

"He would leave without you?" Jilo asked, perplexed.

Drift shook his head. "No … as long as I do not overstay my time here. He leaves at sunset."

Jilo crinkled his face up, stooping over. Reaching into a pocket, he took out a small sliver of steel with the engravings of many flowers on it. Drift's eyes widened. The piece of metal was *glowing.*

"That is…" he started, unable to get the words out.

"Yes," Jilo nodded. "A Luminous object. Or at least a piece of one. And it's telling me we need to leave *now.*"

"You and the children included, Mola," Scov said. "It is time to go."

Without a word, Mola sprung up the stairs. Jilo looked around worriedly. "They are nearly upon us," he said.

It was impeccable timing, then, as all the light in the house seemed to be sucked out and the door slammed shut, leaving Scov and Jilo on the outside. "No!" Scov cried, his voice muffled through the wooden door. "Open it, tree-dweller!"

Drift attempted to turn the handle, but it wouldn't shift under his grip. "I'm trying!" he cried. He looked around, but he couldn't see a thing. The children were crying out from the top floor and he heard Mola trying to dispel their anxieties, shushing them.

"Roots below!" he hissed under his breath. Then a strong hand took a fistful of his hair and slammed him down to the ground. He felt his nose crunch as it hit the floorboards, the stream of warmth that was his blood moving across his lips and chin. He tried to crane his neck as much as he could but felt the click of his nose as it ruptured, a wellspring of blood flowing to the corner of his mouth. The collision had caused him to bite down on the same cheek that had been burned by fire a day before and he howled in pain. Hands were at his neck next, pulling him up off the ground.

The sounds of Scov and Jilo taking turns to bust the door open from the other side fell away into the distance as he took in his assailant's image. A dark cloaked wrapped them entirely so that their face was hidden by the shadows in the room. Their hands and arms were painted black, the paint's sheen the only thing Drift could make out in the dark room.

"What ... do ... you want?" Drift gasped as the hands clamped his airway.

No answer.

"Who ... are ... you?" he managed to get out.

A multitude of black-clothed figures appeared around Drift and his assailant as light returned to the candles around the room. The one holding him was the same woman that had nearly taken him the first time they'd met at the base of the waterfall. They had been waiting for him, all this time.

As one, they chanted in response to his question, "We. Are. NIGHTINGALES!"

The woman pulled her hood down, exposing her thin lips, colourless white eyes, and hairless head. Those behind her did the same and Drift shuddered as the hood came down on the last one. Standing there with his fire-red hair and empty expression was Briar Sevardson. How much had he orchestrated everything since Drift's arrival in Providence? He was no town crier and Drift should've guessed as much when he'd first spied him.

At that moment, several more Nightingales descended the stairs, bringing with them Mola and the children, hands held behind their backs. Suan was sobbing, her cheeks flushed. Braddegh stood with the stoicism of his father, tormented, perhaps, but unyielding. "No!" cried Drift. "Leave them alone if all you want is me!" He thrashed enough that the woman released his neck from her grip, stepping back from him. The door rattled behind Drift, bursting open. Scov and Jilo charged into the room. The baker had two tiny knives gripped in his paws, while Jilo gripped with both hands the centre of a long hardwood stick.

The female cocked her head, curious. "What is this? A Hidden One?" She croaked a laugh. "And you…" she continued, gesturing to Jilo. "The last of your kind."

Drift furrowed his brows, mystified. *The last of his kind?*

Jilo lunged without warning, swiping the stick across her face and sending the Nightingale leader back into her companions. Scov darted into the gang, flashing his knives around as he thrusted them at each of the Nightingales that tried to fight him off. Drift blinked at the sheer speed of the Nestler, his animalistic movements untrackable to the ordinary eye as Scov leaped at the Nightingales who held the children.

Drift charged over the top of the Nightingale leader at the one holding Mola, tackling them to the ground. Mola shuffled free of the tangled bodies and raced for Suan. Limbs flew around the room, the chaos destroying the few pieces of furniture around them and sending splintered fragments of timber across the floor. Scov bounced off the Nightingale he'd knocked over on the stairs, swiping his blades across the throat of the one who had Braddegh fiercely tucked under their arm.

Drift rolled over, pinning the Nightingale he'd wrestled to the ground with an elbow to the neck. Blood came in waves down the stairs before him, and when he looked up, Scov had cut through the neck of Braddegh's captor, bits of throat, cartilage, and skin falling out their front. The Nestler snatched Braddegh by the collar, hauling the boy off the stairs.

The woman who led the group was staggering to her feet, snarling as she reached into her cloak and pulled out a small glass sphere filled with warm yellow *light*. She had a *cism*. The same object Sleepers in Aobia used to contain their Luminosity was in the hands of a *human*.

"Enough!" she boomed, holding the sphere up for all the room to see. Her clan of Nightingales was strewn across the room, some dead, others injured. Jilo stood with his wooden weapon over the chest of Briar Sevardson. Drift kept his elbow down on another. The rest watched their leader with intrigue. "I will take all the light in the world, and then I will get what we came for. Bag the tree-dweller and the woman. Kill the rest."

She clasped her other hand over the sphere and the light from the candles in the room seemed to be sucked into it, extinguishing all ability to see a thing. Drift felt the flat palm of the Nightingale under him strike his jaw, a sharp crack echoing within his skull. The room spun as a sack went down over his head.

"Aunty!" Suan's tiny voice screamed.

A calamity of scuffling happened around him as Drift felt a knee drive into his stomach. He was dragged off his knees and carried by several people at once, unable to move his arms or breathe properly from the pain. He felt the air grow colder and heard the thud of the door closing. They were being taken. Mola screamed, her cries stifled. She must've been bagged too.

Drift grunted as they moved through the streets, the pace at which they ran bumping his spine. Surely someone would see them carrying the two bodies. Surely someone would help.

But then, Drift heard the opening of a creaky door and felt his body hit a hard, splintered surface. They were in a caravan of some kind, all the ambience of Relond instantly silenced as the doors were closed, the sound of a key fidgeting to turn the lock. Nobody would hear them scream. Nobody would ever know they were there, travelling along some of the busiest city roads in Q'ara.

Nobody would save them.

STAG

Stag heaved his sack into the Sethi caravan as Arjan, the hotel owner, appeared from the rear of Al-Faqada. They were ready to go. Drift's pack was already in the caravan and so the only thing Stag was waiting for was Drift himself.

"Lord Stag," Arjan began, walking over to him. "You must get on the road. There is no time to spare."

Stag shook his head. "It isn't sunset. Have you seen Drift?" he asked. The idiot had gone against Stag's recommendations to visit the dead farmer's sister. What it mattered, Stag could not guess. Oh well. At least he had offered his advice. The matter at hand still remained: if Drift hadn't returned by the setting of the sun, Stag would leave without him. It was unfortunate, yes, but then again, he still didn't know what part of Drift wanted to remain a wanderer in this hostile world of humans, political tension, and a brooding war. Stag, on the other hand, would see his duty through.

He would meet with Esme and explain everything he'd been briefed on at home. The need for an alliance against Therador, the problem they posed, and the secrets they shared with the underbelly of Aobia. Then, he would have to sit back and hope Esme would chomp at the bit to remain close with Aobia. If not, it was each nation for itself in the largest three-way conflict the continent had seen since the Four-Front War. In a war like that, allegiance meant nothing and survival was paramount. No diplomacy, no alliance, no compassion.

Worry tickled at the back of his mind, reminding him of the ever-dimming light as Arjan shook his head. "Not a sign of him," he said.

"Hm." He closed the back door on the caravan, which contained the packs along with the Sethi jewellery. "Well, then. Best make tracks, regardless. I've given him all the warning and patience I can."

Arjan raised an eyebrow. "Are you sure?"

"What does it look like? You just told me there is no time to spare!" Stag hissed, climbing up onto the driver's bench. "Look. I'll wait for him until the moment the horses are prepared. But not a minute more. Have them watered and brought out." The hotel owner nodded before heading back towards the building. "He better be here," Stag muttered. "Canopies help me if he's not."

REMEMBRANCE I
DRIFT

FATHER ALWAYS LOCKED THE cabinet at the end of each day, no matter how much Drift wanted to get inside. The great mahogany thing loomed in the corner of their small branchrendered home, threatening to tempt him away from his bed again, night after night.

This night, Father was asleep first. A deep slumber prevented him from being disturbed. He kept the key to the cabinet about his neck on the same leather cord that contained the key to their home and Drift's mother's locket. There had not been a night since Mother's passing that Father had not held that locket close. It was as though it was embedded in his neck, a permanent reminder of her presence, but equally of her ghost. The remnant of a person who once had been.

The good thing, however, was that Drift's Mother's ghost was content and even encouraging when it came to reading from Father's cabinet. The last time Father had been in this deeply unshakeable sleep, Drift had gotten the locket and key free easily enough.

He inched towards his father's neck, listening for the regularity of deep cool breaths exiting Father's nostrils, knowing he would not stir. Drift carefully unlatched the leather cord, which was fastened with a small, magnetic clasp shaped like a Greatleaf. As he leaned back, the prize successfully in his palm, the old timber bed frame creaked enough to cause Father to stir. Drift fell immediately backwards, trying desperately to cushion his fall with his elbows as Father shot awake and looked around, disoriented.

"Drift!" he snapped. "What are you doing?"

"S-sorry, Father," Drift said, trembling. He kept his fist tightly closed around the necklace, hoping Father wouldn't notice its absence. "I just…" he fumbled, "wanted to give you a hug before bed."

Father's eyes softened and he stifled a smile. "Right. Well, on with you. We both have sleep to catch, son." He leant over the side of the bed as Drift got to his feet, keeping his hand behind him at all costs. Father planted a quick kiss on his forehead before lying back down. "Cloak the lamps when you leave, would you?"

"Of course," Drift said, picking up a cloth from behind the lamp stand with his free hand and tossing it over the Luminous bedside lamp to dampen its glow. "Goodnight, Father."

"Goodnight, Drift."

Moments after Father had returned to his familiar snore, Drift beheld the wide array of books, compendiums, and journals that were collected within the mahogany cabinet. They practically radiated with the glow that was missing from the home, which now slept beneath the overlay of night. Drift plucked at the first tome that caught his attention; it had been the last one he had read from when he had most recently been granted access to the cabinet.

"*The Allure of Trees,*" he breathed, reading the title aloud. He opened the book as gently as possible, but it still made an audible crack. *The All-Mother Tala had located the first of the Great Trees shy of the southernmost boundary between the northern aspect of Q'ara and the vast desert that encompassed the south. It was already suffering in the climate, though Tala's spiritual exchange with the Tree revived it over a number of years as Aobian settlement truly began. No longer were we a people of nomadic countenance; now we formed the collective heartbeat of our new home. It was here that Tala fell terribly ill, and succumbed to the Fever. Her people endured without her for a time. Her daughter helped to restore her, but when Tala awoke, it was said that she 'sang with the brightest melodies of the suns'.*

No person could hope to understand such events. The Trees saved her and in reciprocation, she was to use the powers associated with their blessing to restore the forests, save the other Great Trees, and show her people their new direction: pastoral carers of the gardens of the gods.

Drift felt his heart flutter at the words. Even in history classes, he had never been taught the origins of his people with any depth. The All-Mother was a disputed topic and was largely seen as a figure of metaphor for the first settlers in the Great Trees as a whole.

But nobody could explain Sleep. And yet, here they were today, governed by those who could do it. The ones who lived in the higher limbs, the Mind of the Tree.

The next essay in the book, however, drew Drift's attention and he skipped the last few paragraphs to move right onto it.

The Song of the Trees: A Network of Life and Light.

The next page was even more curious.

Line by line, the words had been ruined, covered with blotches of ink. Old stains covered possible new findings. "Roots below!" Drift swore, throwing the book back into the cabinet. He was sick of this place. Sick of the way the Magisterium selectively revised aspects of history to 'protect' the people. Nobody shed a tear over it, but he knew. Father knew, too, and it wore away at him, like living with dozens of chisels carving holes out of you to bury fake dreams in.

Father had had a brother once and he had fallen sick. When he'd recovered, he'd left his family forever. Whoever he was, Drift knew he glowed, somewhere high up in his majestic home, the ability to control his people placed into his hand like a sceptre.

Drift scowled, closing the lid of the cabinet and locking it. It was better for him to sleep and wake the next day to do as he was bid, blindly and mechanically, like everyone else who pretended the home they had was infinitely better than the world it stood in.

He threw Father's locket on the table beside him, knowing that in the morning, he would be in trouble. But it wouldn't matter; not once Drift showed Father the pages that had been smeared in black. Not once Father caught wind of another cover-up.

A network of life and light, indeed.

THE END *of*

PART I

PART II

An Exile of Gold

"O Zeus, why is it you have given men clear ways of testing whether gold is counterfeit but, when it comes to men, the body carries no stamp of nature for distinguishing bad from good?"

\- Euripides

ESME

NINE DAYS.

Esme leaned over the body of her father as it was lowered into the canal by four servants, the high priest on her right and her half-brother Sefil on her left. Though they stood solemnly, she bent over the body, peering at the details that told the story of her father's demise. Light grazing around the neck, like a carpet burn against a child's legs. Mottled in and over the grazes was a long, thick band of purple and near-black bruising. But the head was covered entirely, bandaged so nothing could be seen. The dip in the fabric showed the unusual contours of her father's face and was a sickening reminder of the way she had found him, head cored like an apple. Nine days of preservation, as was custom, hadn't hidden any of his wounds from her.

Poisoned? she thought. *Oh Father, dear. They send you to the sea with the veil of a lie given to the people. And me. They can't even tell me the truth. What kind of state will Adira be in after this day?* She thought back over the past nine days, when Sefil had sat beside her, in mourning for most of them. The more she'd looked at her father's broken body, encased in that glass dome, adorned with new swathes of fresh herbs by the hour, the more she was unable to let go of the truth. And without her interception, she was afraid the truth would never come out. Terrens hadn't been poisoned. But even her brother had been fed that narrative, and she couldn't bring herself to tell him what had really happened.

"O Deliverer, deliver me,

To the endless living sea."

The hymn, 'O Deliverer, Deliver Me,' ended abruptly, shaking Esme out of her unorthodox stance, and she returned to standing straight-backed and solemn, like the other members of the funeral party. Sefil shot her a quick, questioning glare and she shook her head in return, putting an end to his inquiry for the time being.

Poor Sefil had been a sobbing, wretched mess when their father, King Terrens, had been pronounced dead. Esme had had barely a moment to process the loss before she'd been required to provide comfort to the boy, who was going on twenty yet was absolutely naive about the world. To be a royal bastard and be unaware of it, despite the constant gossip about how he looked, was proof enough of that. Esme knew she would have to shatter his ignorance soon.

The man who had given them the 'official' news of Terrens' death, High Priest Soren, stood next to her, presiding over the congregation and giving his final Blessing of the Sea to the crowd. Then they would depart this wretched place, the Hall of the Dead, where Adiran kings and queens past had been placed in the single canal that had carried their bodies out to sea. The night would turn to drinking, stories of the great man who had fallen in such an awful way, and lots of song and dance.

But Esme knew her obsessiveness and she knew she'd find a spot, alone as usual, to ponder and draw conclusions about what had happened to her father and *why*. She'd reject three to five men who'd asked for her hand to dance, just like she had on every other night. Then she would go to bed, knowing that she would be up in the night, more than once, to comfort Sefil and his recent night terrors.

In the morning, she would be queen, and the week after that, she too would die, so that she could concentrate on what was truly important to the people of Adira, the Sea Kingdom. The Priests of the Deliverer, the royal council, the common people—none of them knew what they needed, but Esme did—the truth. That's why she had to disappear. Was it so evil that she had already planned how she was to do it?

Everybody on the continent knew that Adira's best export was its gold, mined from the dry lands to the city's north and the Outfields to the east. In the black sand of its beaches and deep down in the sea, below the reefs, gold was also found in vast quantities, and there wasn't a place Esme could think of that didn't seek gold for various purposes. From the golden throne in the Palace of Thorns in Therador to the mint in Piat, gold was rife.

If, on her watch, some of the gold stores in Adira were to go missing… Well, she'd be outlawed. An exile of gold. And if *all* the gold was to disappear, then she would surely die, and in her death, she could pursue her father's killer, the ultimate vengeance. She could finish her father's, the Overworker's, scientific inquiries, support Sefil in his kinghood from the background, and live life as a regular person. Her identity hidden behind a tragic turn of events. Everyone would be none the wiser and she would find the answers she wanted.

If only it didn't have to come to that. She sighed, causing Sefil to shoot her another look. She quietly slapped his wrist, returning her staunch gaze to the lowered casket, which was now fully upon the gentle current of the water. As the servants began to cut the ties that held the boat back from taking its leave, the people of the congregation, along with High Priest Soren, began to depart. Esme was caught off guard as she felt a tear roll down her cheek and she nearly audibly choked when trying to suspend her reaction. *Don't let them see a thing.*

"Don't let them see a piece of you that really, truly matters," her father had told her, time and time again. But it was the last time he'd said it that stuck with her. They had been sitting together at a sporting event and behind them, the violent scene of a pole vaulter who had made a fatal error jumping over the last pit of nails had been in the process of being cleaned up. Esme'd had her back to the crowd, throwing up into a bucket behind her Father's seat. "They're all yours, Esme, and the world with it. But you are

also theirs. Keep some of who you are for yourself and yourself alone."

Perhaps that had been why Terrens was so good at leading Adira, but why he'd been so bad at relationships. Her mother could never stand him. Yet she'd been gracious about his requests, like allowing Sefil to become a public-facing member of the royal family, though he was biologically half the work of Terrens and half the work of a whore he'd met on a drunken night out in Relond, supposedly. Maybe that was the way of the world: nobody truly let anyone see every piece of themselves, not even her parents to one another.

Esme became acutely aware of the change in the air, though summer was very nearly at its fullest, and shuddered, realising nobody was around but the guards at the door. The candles that were lit throughout the hall flickered like a symbol for all those who had died, yet even though they were numerous, they could not warm her. She left the room, trailing behind the rest of the funeral party, which would be headed back to the palace for the king's wake. She glanced back at the small image of the casket in the distance reaching the end of the canal that exited out a hole at the back of the room. She regretted it immediately.

The palace had been her home for many years, but not for her whole life. No, at the beginning, she had lived on a large estate in rural Relond with her mother and her father had made infrequent visits. She remembered how he'd been when she was a girl, like a shadow trailed him, threatening some kind of disaster. He'd walked around in a paranoid stupor, always cautious of the world changing from its recent state of peace. In context, she didn't blame him, because he'd been old enough to have seen as a boy the end of the Four-Front War, which had brought Q'ara to its politically divided knees. But as his child, Esme had still felt resentment towards him. And then one night, he'd brought back a bundle with him, a wrap of blankets, within which had lain a baby boy.

When they'd finally come to Adira to settle, she'd been maladjusted for many years, unaccustomed to the noise of the city, the demands of the people, and the rigorous lessons she'd needed to take as heir. She'd been the favourite to the people of Adira, but her introversion had kept her from accepting the honorary title, and she'd often found herself fleeing at the first sign of a thanks being given to her for some menial voluntary service. The heir to the throne *had* to be on the frontlines, offering up her time, did she not? Where was the need for praise in that?

"My queen-in-waiting," came the voice of her father's advisor, Pretch. The old, leathery-skinned man's wispy white chin beard swayed as he spoke. "It is time for the wake. And you need your rest before tomorrow. Good things come to those who sleep through a full night's darkness." He winked.

Esme nodded, following the old man. Then, she remembered something she had to do before she could be crowned. "A moment, Pretch." She took off at a sprint before Pretch could react, running up to her half-brother, who was at the back of the crowd, walking alone, as usual. No doubt others would have tried to comfort him, but Sefil was the kind of boy who found more comfort by himself than with others. Another reason her decision to break the law was further debated. "Sefil," she said.

"Don't, Esme," Sefil said, sniffing back tears, refusing to look her in the eye as they walked. "I'll do my duty and show up at the party, but please don't make me do any more of it than that."

"Of course I won't," she said before gripping his wrists. "Come with me."

"Where are we going?" Sefil asked, confused. "Don't we need to make an entrance?"

"They can wait," Esme said. "I need to talk to you. We'll go to the wharf."

"The wharf," Sefil murmured, clearly uncertain.

"Father's wharf as the sun sets. We can take a moment, like a brother and sister should, without all the false politeness and formality."

The comment sparked a light grin on Sefil's face. He nodded. "The wharf."

Their father's private wharf was a summertime comfort to the small royal family and they would often go out to fish for halibut in the balmy early mornings before retiring to cook it together and pretend, for a day every now and then, that they were merely a family with none of the 'royal' connotations. The wharf lay at the rear of the castle and was enclosed by a private beach that was walled off with stone, a centuries-old job that was said to have taken two generations to complete. At the other end of the beach, the cliff sides of Adira's northern aspect adorned it like a crown and the rocks grew closer, jutting out of the sea. At the top of those cliffs was the northernmost part of Adiran territory; beyond that was a small community of people at Port Town, descendants of those first to cross the seas from Na'ar to the continent.

Esme and Sefil found their way to the wharf with ease; after all, it had been a private escape, like an oasis in the desert, when they'd been children. They'd hidden here from schoolmasters, maids, and advisors. The only access point was from Terrens' study.

Esme and Sefil sat on the edge of the wharf, looking out into the vast, endless sea. Despite it being high tide, the waves were fairly even. They did not scarper or claw at one another to fight their way to shore; rather, they lay low like a collective flat bed of glassy water, reflecting the magnificent sky above, a cataclysm of yellow and deep violet.

"I brought you here to tell you something. Because I knew if I said it here, you'd have nowhere to go," Esme said, receiving a worried look from Sefil. "But now I'm doubting myself. Whatever you think about this next part, please don't lob yourself into the sea. I need you, Sef. And besides, I can't handle another tragedy."

"For the gods' sakes, Esme, you can't handle another nine days of mourning!" Sefil replied. "How could you have anything worse to tell me after today?"

Esme chuckled. "Father would like it, I think, that we are as light-hearted as possible today. I'm glad to laugh with you and watch the sunset, brother." She let that last word hang in the air and Sefil did not respond for a while. Whether he had recognised what she'd alluded to, or he was simply caught up in the beautiful array of colours the evening sky was producing, she could not tell.

Esme realised there was no easy way to say what came next, and they had a wake to get to. "You're a bastard, Sefil."

"So are you," Sefil said with a chuckle. He thought she was playing with him.

"No, Sef," Esme said, quietly this time. "It isn't a joke."

Sefil frowned, his gaze steely. "What?" he breathed.

"She was an Adiran noble from Relond," Esme said stiffly. "So maybe that relinquishes some of your pain."

"Wait, please." Sefil put a hand up, signalling for her to stop talking. "This is no game?" When Esme shook her head, Sefil grabbed his head in his hands. "This is no game," he whispered.

"You're still my brother," Esme said, reaching for his hand, which sat limply on the wharf beside him.

"I … need to process that," he said. "You said … she was Adiran?"

"Yes, but I don't know who exactly," she said. "Father never told me that."

"What exactly *did* he tell you?" A hint of resentment hung in Sefil's voice. "He clearly thought it was better to tell you about my origins than me."

"Sefil, it's not like that—"

"Not like that?" Sefil retorted. "What's it like then, Esme? What's it like to live a life that *isn't* a lie?"

"Well, about that." Esme widened her eyes, preparing her next words. "It seems you'll have a chance to swap places with me."

"What are you talking about?" Sefil stood. "No. No, Esme. I'm not going to deal with this any longer. On the night of our father's funeral." He began to walk away with brisk strides. "I never thought you would have it in you to unload something like this on me. Not tonight. Not in that way."

"Sefil, wait!" Esme hopped back onto her feet, running after him.

"No, Esme!" he barked.

Esme had nearly caught up to him at a full sprint before she caught her toe in one of the wooden slats on the ground of the wharf. As she went down, she gripped the back side of Sefil's leather belt, hoping it would hold her. Instead, he was pulled back with her and they tumbled from the wharf into the shallow water below.

"Ouch!" Sefil yelled, fighting his way out of the water. Esme choked and spluttered, being on the bottom as they'd landed, and inhaled a breath full of salty water. Sefil scooped her up and brought her to the sand, where he paddled her back with the flat of his hand. "Come on, cough it all up, Es."

When Esme felt she could speak without coughing, she parted her soaked blonde hair from her eyes and attempted with futility to brush the excess sand off her dress. The dress she was supposed to present in tonight at the wake. By this point, one thing had become apparent: the sky above was beginning to take on its nightly residents, a random collection of stars casting their thin light down onto the purple sand. "The wake!" she cried.

"Damn the wake," Sefil said, taking her hand. "I'm sorry I walked away. I just…" He shook his head. "Why didn't you ever tell me this? Why didn't he?"

"To keep you safe, Sef," Esme replied. She saw the look of hurt in his eyes trying to latch on to something, something he could understand. "If everyone knew, you'd probably not be here. Father probably would have lost the throne." She heaved a sigh. "The woman he… Well, let's just say Mother paid her an awful lot of gold to keep her mouth shut."

"So you *do* know who she is?" Sefil replied.

"No," Esme said. "I promise. That was never conveyed to me." It wasn't the full truth, but it was enough to settle Sefil into this new reality. She couldn't tell him that his mother was actually a whore.

"If you wanted to keep me safe," Sefil went on, "why tell me at all?"

Esme looked away. "Because I cannot take the crown. *You* must."

"What?" Sefil's voice rang below a whisper. "What do you mean, Esme?"

A dull thud drummed in her chest, like a mallet on a skin. "I'm going to be outlawed."

"You'll be the queen, though," Sefil said.

"I will," Esme replied. "Tomorrow I'll be queen and the week after, I'll empty the royal coffers of a large amount of Adiran gold. They'll need to outlaw me. They may kill me instead. I have work to do, Sefil, and I can't do it while I'm queen."

"B-but," Sefil stammered, "you've been preparing for this all your life. I've been taught nothing of leadership!" He threw his arms up at her. "Why would you do this?"

"Isn't it obvious, Sef?" She sighed. "I didn't want to tell you this—at least, not today. Father wasn't poisoned. He was murdered in cold blood."

"The doctors said the wounds were related to the poison, bruising his skin from the inside out," Sefil said, looking down, a hand under his chin.

"The doctors lied, Sefil. Worse injuries lay beneath the bandages. I saw them with my own eyes. Besides, what kind of poison does that?" She said it rather bluntly, but he needed to see her point of view for this to work. "You need to grow up, little brother. You need to start thinking like he did. Be less naive. For both our sakes."

The setting of the sun brought with it a cooling sea breeze, though after a dunk in the sea, it was a little *too* cooling. "Now, we must get to the party," Esme insisted, shuddering. "Get dressed and we'll do it together. And tomorrow, after the crown's been placed atop my head, we'll talk more. Make sure the plan is set in stone."

Sefil said nothing; he just stood there.

"Well, Sef?" Esme urged. "Are you with me?"

Finally, he dropped his arms and walked along the sand to her. "I suppose I have no choice, do I, Esme?"

"That's the spirit," she said, clapping him on the back.

Sefil was watching her from the front row of the church as the oath rod was placed across her hands and the crown atop her head. She knew he was uncertain and even that was a generous turn of phrase. The night before had been brief. Although as she and Sefil had gone their separate ways to their chambers, she'd noticed that he had looked uncomfortable about going to bed. As though he'd *wanted* to be around the guests, the party ambience, some more. What had she done, telling him the truth about his life? She'd thought it would stir him up, ready him for the coming days, but instead, it had taken some core part of him away. The resolute Sefil who could make decisions for himself. The one trait he had that could be considered kingly.

She chuckled at the irony of it all as the packed church looked back at her, thousands of approving, patriotic eyes happy to be led once more by one of Good King Terrens' blood. And yet, to her, this was nothing, *could be* nothing. Here she stood, applause ringing around her, as High Priest Soren concluded the Rite of the Coronation. "May the gods grant you every star in the sky." Then, to the crowd he said, "All hail the queen!"

"All hail the queen!" The cry came back at her, a wall of sound. Soren put an endearing hand on her shoulder. "Your Majesty, I am so proud. May your years be long and your reign be great." Then he took the oath rod from her hands, returning it to the altar behind him.

"Ah, Soren," she said, not loud enough for him to hear over the roar of the crowd. "How wrong you are."

TARRI

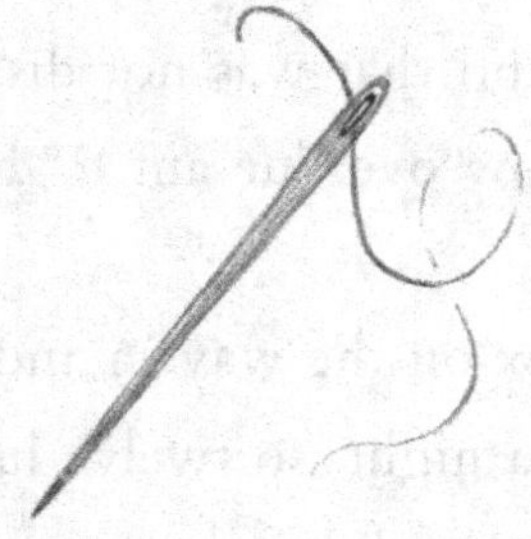

THANKFULLY, IT HADN'T BEEN hard to track Flow down. For someone who was under such close watch by the Sleepers, he gave himself up easily by being slumped over a table in the corner of The Minister's Secret. It was likely not the first night he was in such a state.

Tarri had no pity for him. She still hadn't recovered from the web of lies that he'd spun around her, but she knew this was her only chance to repair her relationship with Nischia and, in turn, any chance she had of finding Drift. She would complete this mission, even though she'd been freed from the obligation of doing so.

She walked over to the slouched male and tapped on the bracers over his shoulders.

Flow's eyes fluttered, his face crumpling. "What the…" he started, resting a hand on his newly reddened cheek. Then, with realisation, he tightened his gaze on who stood before him. "Tarri," he muttered. "What do you want?" He made a gross sound, like that of his tongue tasting the inside of his mouth, the stale breath of faint-memory ale.

"We have work to do, Flow," Tarri said.

Flow made a sound that was not dissimilar to a cat with a sore stomach. "How overdue am I?" he asked, rubbing his eyes.

"Well, I asked Vex on the way in and he said you've been out like a light for a night, so twelve hours, I'd wager." She sighed. "You're lucky he didn't throw you out onto the streets. I'd have done differently."

"Well, you aren't Vex." He eyed her. "So what do we need to do? Roots below, my head is *pounding*."

Tarri ignored that last remark. "I will request a meeting with Sedulus as soon as we arrive at the Water Management Facility. We need to convince him to tell us about the intricacies of filtration. So, whether you are the one to befriend him or I—"

"Not me, Tarri." Flow shook his head. "This is your job. *You* do it."

"And he fights like a child too!" Tarri put a sarcastic hand to her gasping mouth. "Fine. But you already know him, so I…"

Flow put up his hands. "Trust me, I *do* know him. And he isn't exactly excited about knowing me."

"I understand," Tarri gave in. "Either way, we get in, we get the most information we can about how the river is cleaned, and we leave."

Flow sighed. "No matter how water filtration is handled before it reaches Adira, *they* know how it works. They're the ones who implemented it! It's all public knowledge, Tarri."

Tarri said nothing. He did not have this power over her. He would *never* have it.

"Before this," Flow continued, calmer now, "the humans beyond Aobia would boil their water. Every other human besides those who live along the River Tomei still do. Even water without the Sickness is risky to drink. Common bacteria exist, Tarri. We had Sleepers who could do what they do and clean it up for us to source water from the river directly. The water at earlier points in the river is still contaminated. For something so monumental to occur, like this breach of the Sickness, it cannot evade the knowledge of the Magisterium. So why is Lady Nischia asking this of you?"

"Asked," Tarri replied. "It isn't in the way the water is cleaned so much as the way Sedulus knows to explain it."

Flow shook his head. "I don't… What is the difference?"

Tarri felt her confidence grow as a smile formed at the corners of her mouth. She would find the truth and either Flow or Sedulus would give it up first. "Nischia wouldn't have asked this if there wasn't a reason for it. Sedulus is hiding something, Flow. And when people try to hide things, oftentimes they hide them in the most obvious of places."

The rickety elevator down to the forest floor was long and swaying, a lofty timber shaft fixed on the sides by multiple ropes to appear like a winding staircase, not dissimilar to the grand ones Tarri recalled from the Sleepers' residences in the Mind. It wound around the limbs of the Heart before making a steady and straight drop to the forest floor, right by what seemed to be a control station. Flow showed her the locked metal door that closed over the entrance to the stairwell, built into a gnarly knot of Greatbranch in the workers' district of the Heart. Tarri played dumb, recalling the last time she was here when she'd infiltrated the elevator shaft and had come to the viaduct that overlooked the forest. With just a mention of Sedulus' name, security let them begin the unsteady journey to the forest floor.

When they reached the bottom, the sight took her breath away, just as it had the first time. A forest surrounded her unlike anything she'd seen before. Perhaps her people lived as one with nature, but the sight below them was either that of far-reaching lands or the forest directly beneath. And these days, living in the Great Tree wasn't necessarily 'natural'; instead, people relied on Luminosity for light, heat … even the longer lifespans Aobians were granted. Nobody could explain the scope of problems Luminosity solved, but it did so regardless.

Here on the forest floor, the River Tomei's rushing water providing a soothing ambience, Tarri was sure the heat from the sun wasn't something that needed defeating. Though the summertime was in its early, and suddenly warmer, months, the coolness of the clean air beneath the treetops was enough to feel entirely comfortable.

But that wasn't all that caught her. All around the forest floor, climbing up tree trunks and high in branches, was a glowing *radiance* coating everything: plants, leaf litter, fungi that grew in dark places. It was as though the forest was alive. While the glow was a mixture of warm yellow, deep violet, and cool teal, it was not unfamiliar to her and reminded her of the same glow that hung around the outlines of Nischia or Koln. The Sleepers themselves were blessed in their vocations by the Tree. While they Slept, Aobia lived. It was not hard to see the same relationship between life down here, enacted perfectly.

This was something she'd been waiting to witness and now that she was here, her curiosity grew. Did she want to see the outside world, like Drift?

Out of the corner of her eye, she saw a small unit of male and female workers approaching, all dressed in a drab grey uniform, with one superior at their head. Sedulus was here and ready to meet with them. She'd thought it would be harder than this. She'd assumed Sedulus would refuse the meeting once he realised that Flow had called for him. But here he was.

"Old friend." Sedulus reached a hand out to Flow and they shook. The tension that surrounded the three of them was not lost on Tarri.

Sedulus stepped back, gazing steadily at Tarri. "Dressmaker," he said. Tarri inclined her head toward him. He could reduce her title all he wanted, but she would not play into his hand.

"To what do I owe the pleasure?" Sedulus asked.

Flow looked at Tarri, a frown pressed into his forehead. Tarri sighed. "We are here to talk about the operations at this facility. We've been sent by the Lady Nischia and her superior, Koln, both of the Magisterium."

"You still attend to the business of the Sleepers?" Sedulus asked Flow.

Flow looked away, his mouth tight.

"Well, Sedulus, shall we start?" Tarri cut in.

"Of course," Sedulus replied, gesturing to the group behind him. "This lovely bunch are the stars to my sky, the dewdrops to my leaves; without them the facility would not operate as well as it does. This is my engineering team. They will be showing you through the place today," Sedulus went on. "Unfortunately, I have important matters to attend to. Layward?" Sedulus gestured to another male Aobian, who stepped forward from the group of engineers. He wore his long, silver hair in braids and seemed kindly.

Before he could speak, however, Tarri felt heat crawl up her throat. "Wait," she called as Sedulus turned his back on the group. "You won't be the one to deliver this tour to us?"

"Miss Tarri, there must be some misunderstanding." Sedulus' voice practically dripped with honey, sickeningly sweet. "How could you possibly expect me to have the time for something like this? At any rate, I promise you some of my time at the end." He inclined his head in a stiff bow of farewell and strode off, his gown whirling behind him.

The engineer Sedulus had introduced briefly, Layward, stepped forward and spoke. "I hope … this will still be satisfactory?"

Tarri could not bite her tongue. "You get that scheming—"

Flow stepped in front of her, cutting her off. "It's fine … Layward, is it?"

"Yes, sir."

"Could you give me a moment with my colleague?"

"Of course." Layward nodded.

Flow turned her around and walked her behind a nearby tree. "It's fine, Tarri," he hissed. "Don't you see? It's better this way!"

"Better?" she bit back. "Better for you, maybe, so you don't need to speak to him. But this was the whole point, Flow. We need to break *him!*"

"And?" Flow shrugged. "Why bother breaking him if we can exploit the innocent sharing of knowledge provided by our humble guides?" He gestured with a thumb over his shoulder at the engineers. "Come on, Tarri, they're a pack of sheep. They'll do their job to death for Sedulus. We can find out whatever we want and he'll be none the wiser. At the end, if there's anything else we need, we regroup before we speak to him one last time. It couldn't be any easier!"

"Roots below," Tarri cursed. "Let's get it done." Turning back to the engineers, she nodded to Layward. "Where to first?"

The facility was much larger than Tarri could have predicted and she found herself constantly surprised by how long the Aobian control on the River Tomei was as well as the size of the forest beneath the Canopies that the facility workers tended. There was no possible way to see all the ground the facility covered in a week, much less a day. What continued to impress her most was the forest, a spectrum of deep, rich greens and sun-soaked tree trunks draped in stringy bark. A path through the forest was made of thick chunks of timber panels pressed into the ground, some completely inundated with dirt from years of use, but each one part of a bigger whole that mapped out the facility.

Layward had been the one to show them through operations on the forest floor, where the River Tomei's flow was being managed by teams of Aobians who used odd steel lever devices called cranes to lift large rocks and dispense them in the appropriate locations, allowing them to redirect water flow and current strength. The amount of current they needed to control as the river reached the viaduct was said to be a force so large it could sweep away hundreds of people at any given time, as this part of the river resided in a basin that fell from the great heights of the Southern Ranges, which draped the background like looming, sleeping gods. Nobody went out there anymore because of the Sickness. Beyond the ranges lay the endless Janub desert, the same that the first Aobians were said to have crossed when they'd still been nomads.

Eventually, the viaduct was in sight, a strikingly tall structure of baked and rendered stone. Layward excused himself before returning with another co-worker, who wore her long hair tied up in a utilitarian bun. "This is Eamil. She'll guide you the rest of the way and then rejoin you with Sedulus." He bowed.

Tarri and Flow exchanged their thanks before saying goodbye to Layward, only to have the new guide, Eamil, begin walking towards the viaduct. "You are here on the request of the Magisterium?"

"Yes," Tarri said. "Specifically, we are here to report on the processes behind the filtration of the river water. Why is it safe for drinking after it clears the viaduct?"

"That is a multi-faceted question," Eamil said. "Let's start at the viaduct."

Eamil finally reached the top of the viaduct, where it met the edge of the waterfall that marked Aobia's border with the human lands. "Before the water passes over the waterfall, it enters a process of filtration. Part of that is because of Sleeper Luminosity, though I do not know the specifics of that. If you've come from the Magisterium, you would know more than I." She chuckled lightly.

She led them to the edge of the forest, where the water headed for the viaduct. "Of course, this water is rushing by at such a high pressure because we built a collection dam. In the water are several layers of cleansing algae that line the river's floor."

"Algae?" Flow asked.

Eamil nodded. "Algae is a collection of small lifeforms, if you will, that you cannot see unless they are clumped together in the millions. The algae here, under the Great Tree, shines with a glow not dissimilar to the Sleepers."

That made sense. All the luminous moss, toadstools, and other bits of life that lit up the forest must've shared in some part of the special nature of this 'algae'. "How is it maintained?" Tarri asked. "It can't be easy to repair a malfunction here."

"The first thing to know is malfunctions are minimal. They usually are solved so quickly that they are inconsequential. There are two main components," Eamil explained. "The first is the continued growth and control of the algae population. That's the kind of work I do. Growing algae is dependent on nutrients and mineral adjustments to the water." Eamil held up her waterskin for them to observe, undoing the cap and taking a sip. "Think about the water you drink. Since the facility opened, that water has come directly from the river. Water is naturally alkaline *or* acidic. The more acidic it is, the less chance you have of finding clean water. Whatever it was that happened thousands of years before we settled in this tree is the reason the water further south is higher in acidity and therefore provides the correct conditions for the Sickness to thrive."

Tarri, like all Aobians, was familiar with this detail about Aobian history. There were myths, stories, and recorded histories, like the great *Book of Songs*, which contained all the histories of their people dating back thousands of years. A long time ago, the Sickness had begun far in the south of Q'ara and the stories told the tale of its rise. As a result, they'd needed to migrate to a new tree, the Aobians forced back into the nomadic lifestyle they had already once escaped.

"You balance the acidity of the water so that the algae can operate and multiply?" Tarri asked.

"Indeed," Eamil replied. "The balance of minerals comes from the soilbed under the river, which is fed with the dried doses of nutrients or elementals, such as phosphor, gypsum, and calcium, as well as the feeding of *coioa* fish."

"How does a fish help?" asked Flow, furrowing his brows.

"The fish are capable of distributing the micronutrients to regulate everything happening beneath the surface. There are more studies we need to do into them to understand what causes this, but one thing we know is that the Aobians who settled in this Tree discovered that the fish were essential. They were even able to drink from the river alongside the current Tree. And so we breed them, further upstream where the water is calmer, and then we populate this pool as we see fit. We check that the water is stable as it passes beneath the viaduct." Eamil turned around, staring at the expanse of the valleys before them, which unfolded into the lands beyond Aobia and the mountain in the middle that separated the forest from Adira and Therador. Tarri felt a shiver run down her spine as she caught herself getting lost in the view. *Somewhere out there is my Drift.*

"Eamil?" she asked, beckoning the engineer to turn around and face her once again. "You mentioned two components to filtration… What's the second?"

"Something that I do not have the clearance to show you. Let me escort you back to our superior, Sedulus."

"One more thing, Eamil," Tarri said. "You said malfunctions rarely happen?"

"Yes," Eamil said.

Tarri furrowed her brows. "Well, a malfunction was reported a week ago. And the day after, it was said to be fixed. However, an engineer never returned home from work."

"I can't say I'm familiar with that, miss," Eamil said.

"It's no story, Eamil," Tarri replied. "In fact, it is the reason why—"

"Eamil! Excuse us." Flow shot an arm across Tarri's chest, stepping in front of her. "It appears Miss Tarri has gotten some aspects of our case incorrect. I apologise. We'll meet with Sedulus now. Thank you for your hospitality and for obliging our questions."

"Of course," Eamil said. "If you'll both follow me."

"What are you doing?" Flow hissed. "You're sabotaging this! Stick to the books, Tarri. Then we can be done with this and go our separate ways."

The path Eamil took them on wound back around to a rope-suspended staircase that led to the highest point of entry into the facility, a station built into the side of the Tree. "Sedulus should be waiting at the top. I hope your tour was fruitful."

Tarri looked up at the staircase, where the spiral of planks and rope seemed to reach so high, she couldn't make out where it ended. She sighed. "Chat at the top?"

Flow nodded. "The quicker we do it, the less long the pain endures."

Once they reached the top, panting and out of breath, they encountered Sedulus, a touch of a grin tugging at the side of his mouth. "Good stroll?" he asked as Flow stalked past him.

"We … wanted to … ask you … a few more … questions!" Tarri panted.

"Of course," Sedulus responded.

"Your engineer, Eamil, explained the filtration process in the pool above the viaduct. But they mentioned there is another part of the process that only you could explain."

"What I am about to show is not news to the Sleepers. In all honesty, I am surprised that you have been sent here with these questions on their request. The facility operates because of their designs and the Luminosity they are blessed with." Sedulus turned and led them down a small byway that fed into a large open-air chamber, the walls made of thick panels of furbished steel. Where Sedulus stood were two tall doors of the same steel, sealed shut and looking like an ominous frame about his body. "Beyond these doors are devices that we call generators. No common Aobian has ever seen this technology without direct clearance from the Magisterium."

Sedulus beckoned them forward, asking Flow to help him grip the handles and pulling hard on the doors so that they loosened, a soft hiss of air escaping as they opened forth.

The first thing Tarri noticed was the warm glow, the same shared between the Sleepers and the source of Luminosity she'd seen in the growing fungi throughout the forest earlier. Then she noticed Flow's jaws wide open.

In the room, the walls cast a warm light, a cosy ambience, but the source of the light was much more sinister. An uncomfortable drone began to ring audibly, bouncing between the walls like an echo chamber.

The centre of the room was filled with rows of dark metal objects bolted into the branchground, each one shaped like a cylinder with rounded ends, a whirring noise emitting from them. A deeper look revealed fans spinning evenly across the top of each unit and beneath them, rich, glowing orbs of thick, lustrous light. It was unlike anything Tarri had seen. Something about these great grey boxes filled with orbs felt … sinister, alien, clinical.

"What are they?" Tarri said over the hum of the boxes, a shiver running down her spine like a slow-moving snake.

"That's why," Flow said, letting out a long exhale.

"Why what?"

"Why the Sleepers don't need to Sleep constantly. I'd always wondered."

Sedulus nodded, gesturing for them to come closer. "These are called generators. They contain concentrated Luminosity that can be used to power all kinds of things. The lights in the city? They come from devices such as these. And when the power is depleted, it can be replenished. All it requires is one of these orbs called *cism*." Sedulus bent down, tugging open a small door on the side of a generator. He retrieved an orb from within, lifting it up to show them. It was spherical and just smaller than Sedulus' hand.

Within, light floated in waves, some aspects of it brighter than others. Some parts of the balls were dark, so dark they appeared like the night itself. Flow glanced at Tarri. They both knew what *cism* were well. "The darkness within indicates how much Luminosity is left to be converted into power," Sedulus explained. "Of course, we know the Sleepers can spend time recharging in their Orbs and then channel their Luminosity for many purposes. But generators like these are priceless.

"This is why we have moved forward as a people. Endless progress. Less time spent Sleeping, more time spent governing the people of Aobia. And the amount of power is astonishing. Each *cism* is filled with the same Luminosity as would be generated by one Sleeper in their respective Orbs. This is how we are able to control the algae in the filtration pool, cleaning vast, rushing quantities of water as quick as lightning. All with the help of fifty Sleepers' worth of power."

Tarri gulped, as astonished as she was concerned. "How is the Luminosity used?"

"That," Sedulus replied as he put back the orb, "is a question I cannot answer. The Sleepers may choose to answer any further questions once you report back to them. These generators, after all, are their design." He stiffened, standing tall. The light cutting through the fan blades moved over his face as though they were revealing aspects of him Tarri had never noticed. "I have no secrets, Miss Tarri. Perhaps the question you need to ask yourself is what secrets do the Sleepers have? I know you want the truth about your betrothed. Drift was a good worker and a hard one. If not for him, we may now have had an international incident on our hands. His sacrifice will be remembered."

"You tell her the truth, you bastard!" Flow spat.

"What truth?" Sedulus asked. "If you want to extract any further knowledge from me, you'll have to first obtain the proper permissions." With that, Sedulus stepped away from the generators, leading them back towards the doors to the chamber.

It didn't matter, Tarri realised, what Sedulus said or what she knew he had done. He had instilled a new doubt in her and it was one that she was able to rationalise, despite lacking the inclination to do so.

As they left the facility, exchanging civil farewells with the person who was responsible for the clean water in the River Tomei, the person responsible for Drift's exile, Tarri looked back at him.

It was as he stalked away, his back turned, that she swore she could see a faint glow of yellow in and around his silvery hair.

DRIFT

THE SMELL NO LONGER affected Drift. He'd vomited twice in the bag tied around his neck and both times, the mixture of liquid bile and semi-digested food had dried, glueing the bag onto his collar. *So much for new clothes,* he thought as he was dragged out the back of the caravan. He tensed his shoulders, hoping they would cushion his impact before hitting the ground with a thud. He felt hands under his arms hauling him roughly to his feet.

Without being able to see, hear, or smell properly, Drift's senses were attuned to his own body. Everything hurt. He'd been thrown into a cart that had seemed to fly over bumpy tracks all night long. The only things that told him it was now day were the change in light coming through the hairy sack that was covering his head and the incoming waves of summer heat. He couldn't recall much from the travel besides an enveloping sense of darkness and the sound of Mola's whimpers. She wouldn't talk to him during the journey at all. He'd done this. Gotten them captured by Nightingales. *An organisation aimed at exposing and containing the secrets of others,* Stag had said. *They have no true loyalties.*

They guided him and Mola along what felt like dirt road until the ground became smooth and polished and the light beyond the sack over his head diminished. A loud clank indicated the closing of a heavy door. He resisted the urge to struggle as they led him down stairs and into another room before tying his arms and legs onto a chair. Were they underground?

When the sack came off, Drift felt his neck get yanked to one side, an audible crack coming from the back of his skull. He saw stars as the room stopped spinning, his eyes finally able to see again after an entire night of darkness. Everything was black, the surfaces around him like dark mirrors. The walls mimicked the same polished feeling of the floor, as though made of obsidian.

Around him stood the hooded Nightingales that had led him here and in the middle of the room was an odd, grey box made of steel, shining with the same yellow glow of Luminosity the woman had contained in the glass sphere.

As soon as Drift noticed the box, the Nightingales all threw back their hoods. Briar Sevardson and the leader he recognised. One other, a man with olive skin and shoulder-length dark hair, stepped forward with the leader.

The woman's empty eyes bore into him and he felt he was on display with neither skin nor clothes on under her gaze. The lack of coloured pupils made him want to look away with disgust but also study her.

"Aobian," she said.

Drift looked away. "Where is she?" They had taken Mola somewhere else.

The woman chuckled. "That information is for later, husk. For now, let us introduce ourselves. You may call me Westral."

Drift clenched his teeth. He would not give her his name. If she and the Nightingales had wanted him for so long, they already knew it.

"Name, husk?" she asked, trying again. She sniffed lightly at Drift's lack of reply. "Very well."

The olive-skinned man went around the back of the chair Drift was tied to, freeing one of his hands.

Westral grabbed his hand. He felt the cool air escape from her flared nostrils in frustrated breaths. "Splitter and mallet," she called. Briar Sevardson nodded immediately and disappeared down a thin hall at the back of the room. He returned momentarily with a wooden mallet and several thin slivers of metal.

Westral snatched them from her subordinate and flashed them before Drift's eyes. The bottom of each piece of metal was rounded and the top came to a sharp, teardrop-like point.

"Why are you here, husk?" Westral asked. Before Drift could answer, however, she went on. "Because you come from the Great Tree and we want what your kind has. We want this light."

She showed him the *cism* she'd had with her when the Nightingales had invaded Mola's home. "You have this built into you. In your bones. In your mind. In your *soul*."

"I'm not a Sleeper," Drift said. Was that what they thought he was?

"And I'm no fool, husk. You may not be anything other than a normal Aobian with an abnormal name. But you can access this power. Want to know the key?" She dangled a metal strip in front of his eyes. "Trauma."

Briar Sevardson held up the wooden mallet, kneeling beside Drift's chair. The one with the dark hair stood behind Drift, two firm hands placed on his shoulders. His heart fluttered and his stomach turned from sour anticipation of what might happen next.

"You are the key, Drift of the Heart." He felt the teardrop tip of one of the metal slivers pressed up against the quick between his own fingernail and the skin of his first finger on his left hand. How did she know his name? Westral smiled at him. "You will teach us how to acquire this power, whether you like it or not."

He failed to brace himself as the pain that entered his body was unlike anything he had felt before. Tears crawled from his eyes as he felt the mallet strike the back of the metal, driving its sharp point further and further into his finger, splitting the nail away from the skin completely, nearly rubbing on bone.

He would not cry. He would not scream.

All his life, he'd been a simple worker, unexposed to violence or bodily harm of any exceptional kind. But then, he felt the next sliver of metal prepped to slide beneath his thumb, heard the *tap, tap, tap* of his own blood pattering onto the cold, hard, floor, and the beating drums that were his heartbeat resounding in his head. That was enough to send him, once again, into the dark.

Drift came to in the quiet, mirror-like room. Pain tugged at him, threatening to knock him out once more. He looked around, peeking at the dried blood, fingernails, and skin on the floor. His left hand throbbed. He couldn't even feel the individual parts of his hand, unable to tell which finger he was feeling the pain from.

Above him, Drift felt a radiance, like that of a Sleeper. "He returns to the conscious world," Westral said as she entered the room. "Our theory proved correct. You *are* someone we have been looking for."

The bald woman leaned forward, grabbing Drift's long silver hair and yanking his head forward so his face nearly touched hers. "Take a look," she said, pulling a tuft of his hair around so that he could see it.

His hair *glowed*. What had they done to him?

"What is this?" he cried. "Let me out," he begged. "Let me out!"

"Do you not see?" The woman asked, no emotion showing in her voice. "We will be the first of our kind, *humankind,* to be Luminous. You don't need a magic tree to live in, Aobian. You simply need a source and trauma." She gestured at that metal box that sat in the middle of the floor. She scooped out a *cism* filled with a collision of light and shadow, sliding around like liquid within.

"These," Westral began, "are Orbs. You know all about orbs, don't you, husk?"

Drift watched, wordless. These were not the same as the Orbs, but Drift was not going to admit he knew as much. This was a *cism*, the same sphere that Stag carried with him to communicate with the Magisterium from afar.

"The Sleepers have a symbiotic relationship with these Orbs. Is that right?"

"How would I know? That's not information shared with common people."

"You sound spiteful of your people," the woman said, evidently curious about his reaction.

"They've lied for centuries to their own," Drift said. "But I'm not here to start a war with Aobia. Clearly, that's your job." He eyed her, both of them silent for a long while. "What do you want with me?" He was exhausted, unable to determine whether he was actually able to do anything with the Luminosity they had imbued him with and no longer interested in knowing much more. He needed rest. He needed to find a way to escape this place.

"There are forces at play darker than you can imagine," she spat. "We know more about your precious Luminosity than the highest orders of your people. Once the Emperor has secured what we have on a mass scale, Theradoran dominance will be unstoppable. Therador came to this land first, tree-dweller. And they have been robbed of what they truly deserve for thousands of years. It is time for that to end."

The clang of doors opening into the chamber disrupted the rising tension of their conversation. "Westral, I trust I have not come at a cumbersome time?" asked a voice. A familiar voice.

As the person stepped into the glowing light of the grey box, Drift caught the shape of his features, the familiar furrow of his brows. Long silver hair hung about the person's neck and striking blue eyes, colder than ice, winced in recognition of Drift.

Sedulus.

ESME

"T HE THERADORANS HAVE STILL not heard our requests, my queen," Pretch said, his voice quavering. "The last we heard from any of their representatives was the morning of your father's … untimely death."

"You need not step around the issue, Pretch," Esme replied, irritated. "He's dead. I'm here. Let's just get on with it."

Pretch smiled, creases tugging at the edges of his eyes. "There is no greater leader who could walk in their father's footsteps than you, my queen. Your father would be proud."

Esme swore she could see tears forming in the old man's eyes. She touched his arm as she sat across from him at the small desk in his office. "You old fool," she said, smiling. "I could never do it without you." She stood. "Right, that's all the sentimentality you could possibly ask for from today's ration of goodwill. On to the next thing, I say."

Pretch sniffed, following her out of the room. "Of course, my queen! Though I beg of you, do not leave an old fool to chase your nimble feet!"

As they left the office, three guards appeared, kneeling before Esme. That was something she was yet to get used to. Though she'd been treated with utmost respect by all the workers at the castle, these kinds of formal greetings had been reserved for her father.

"My queen," the frontwoman for the guard bowed her head, greeting her.

"Um … stand!" Esme yelled a little too strongly and softened her tone. "Please. What can I do for you?"

"An emissary from Aobia just arrived, my queen."

"From Aobia?"

The guardswoman smiled. "Yes, my queen. They are not expected."

Pretch stepped up beside her. "Esme, they may be our allies, but we must tread with care. Let me take an escort down to meet them and if it seems desirable to bring them to you, I'll arrange it promptly."

Of course, Pretch only made these statements with her best interests in mind and after her father's death, meeting in any place besides the throne was questionable. Then again, she needed to do this herself. Though the people of Adira didn't need to see it, she knew she had herself to prove, for her father and Sefil. "No," she decided. "We do it together and at once. I won't waste time making my mark known, Pretch." She sucked back a breath as

Pretch obliged her with a nod and excused the guards. *I won't waste time,* she thought, *because there isn't much time to waste.*

Esme had known two Aobians her whole life. Flow and Stag, though young for Aobians, had been ambassadors to her father's throne since before she'd been born. They had formed a friendship with her family beyond their professional bounds and she quite honestly never could have imagined her life without their occasional visits.

She was standing in the entry to the castle, the massive stone archway that welcomed people beneath it to visit the home of the royal family. Pretch had gone along to gather the emissary and was swift to return. The tall one behind the old man stood out in a sea of humans easily and Esme smiled. There was nothing to fear. She knew this Aobian.

"Stag!" she proclaimed, smiling wide. "Back so soon?"

Stag looked at her, a morose expression across his face, though it was not unusual for him to look as such. "My queen," he knelt, bowing his head. "How much you have grown in only two weeks. Your father would be proud."

"I know you're sad, Stag," Esme said, reaching for his hand and lifting him back to stand. "But do not let my father's death leave a shadow on each day. Good things will come when they may."

"Always the strongest of us, aren't you?" Stag finally smiled.

"Maybe, but that is a learned behaviour," Esme said, winking. "Perhaps if time permits, I will tell you about those who taught it to me." She put a hand on Stag's shoulder. "Where is Flow?"

Stag's only colleague, Flow, was a different kind of person—incredibly extroverted. She'd never felt as close to him growing up, always seeking out Stag when the Aobians had been here. From Stag, she'd learned poems, songs, and mythical stories of times before the humans had arrived on the continent. From Flow, she'd learned to steal, sneak, and eventually get caught. All those lessons, however, had stuck with her through the years.

"He is … otherwise preoccupied, my queen." Stag's eyes moved from side to side, searching.

"With what?" Esme pressed. "It is not usual for only one of you to be here." Not only that, but this was not an expected visit. She noticed a weariness on Stag's face and stretched her grin wider, beckoning him into the castle. If he would not talk here, maybe he would talk in the comfort of her presence and a glass of wine alone. "It might not yet be noon here, Stag, but it is past noon somewhere else on the continent. You won't say no to wine with me, will you?"

STAG

S TAG SAT ACROSS FROM Esme, maintaining his focus despite wanting to doze off. He loved Esme like a daughter. He had spent her entire life as an ambassador to the throne and had sustained a good relationship with her father. But no joy in seeing her newly crowned as queen could keep him alert after two days straight of unstable, bumpy road travelling in the caravan. The memory of the motion sickness was so real, he feared he may feel it again as he sipped the second glass of wine Esme had handed him.

They were in her sitting room. He'd mentioned the travel, carriage-less from Providence through to Relond, and the meeting with Dayajin and Ibham at the Mountain Gate. He'd told her of their deaths, to which Esme seemed to respond with the kind of surprise he did not expect from her. Something showed in her expression that was not quite disappointment, but not far from it.

He sighed audibly through the silence that had grown between himself and Esme as his thoughts broke free of the dead Sethi couple. He knew what he had to do. "My queen," Stag started. "I haven't been entirely honest with you about this particular journey here."

Esme raised her glass to her lips. "I should think not. If you had been, it would have proved me to have a poor read on others, and that is *not* a skill a good queen should lack."

"There are two things I must recount to you about the circumstances that have led me here so soon after I last left. The first is about Flow."

"I couldn't assume this was an ordinary visit from the moment I saw you." Esme straightened her back into her chair. "So, tell me."

"Flow has been suspended from work by the Magisterium." Stag gulped. If he told her the reason he suspected for it, it might startle her enough to question Aobia's alliance. "He will not be returning here again."

Esme blinked. "I'm not sure I understand."

"I cannot say it any clearer," Stag replied. "He is to remain in Aobia. He is no longer an ambassador."

Esme raised an eyebrow. "And considering our situation, I am surprised you are not offering to tell me the reason for this."

Of course. Her father was dead and the only visitors who could've committed the crime were the Aobians and the Theradoran guest who had attended meetings earlier that day. "I would like to dispel any fears you may have, but I do not know the reason for Flow's suspension. However, if you are suggesting he had something to do with the tragic events that led us home all those days ago, I assure you that is incorrect, my queen."

Esme studied him as though for the first time ever, she was seeing a different person. Stag grew uncomfortable and averted his gaze.

"Stag, I need to know all that you know about Flow's suspension. It directly involves Adira, because he was one of two ambassadors from the Tree. Your Sleepers are so far away; they cannot hear you."

Stag cleared his throat. "When I say I do not know the reason, I am being totally honest. The Magisterium did not disclose it to me at all. However, I will tell you what I suspect caused it.

"Flow met with someone in Relond every time we were on duty for the past number of visits. Initially, I thought nothing of it. Neither of us need to live in one another's pockets. But then one night, the last night in Relond before our previous visit, I went to the same tavern that Flow did and ate there. I saw him meeting with someone in the darkest corner of the room." He looked up at Esme.

"Go on," she said simply.

"I couldn't see them, but I noticed how similarly framed they were to Flow. Somehow, I suspect Flow has been meeting with another Aobian in Relond. I don't know how it's possible. But this person, if they are who I think they are, has also been involved in the first exile case to have occurred since the war."

"Exile?" Esme asked. "This is getting rather convoluted, Stag."

Stag nodded. "This leads me to my second piece of information. I travelled with that exile," Stag said, letting out a long breath. "He joined with me just before Providence, from which we escaped with our lives and nothing else. The human that escorted us from that gods-forsaken town probably died saving us. I haven't yet lived that guilt down."

"Escaped with your lives?" Esme asked, her voice barely resonant above a breath. "From Providence?"

"Yes. With our lives, my queen. They thought we were hiding the king's death from them because we were responsible for such a tragedy."

Esme shook her head. "Ever the suspicious types are townsfolk." She studied Stag. "Well, I am glad you are here—*alive*. And I wish to know more of your mysterious colleague."

"Of course, my queen," Stag replied, hesitating.

"Please." Esme put up a hand. "Just call me by my name, Stag. You've known me since I was in the womb. It's too odd for me, I'm afraid."

Stag nodded. "If you'll permit me the formal title when we are in public, then?"

Esme smiled. "Of course. Now, what of your friend? What crime did he commit to be exiled from Aobia?"

"His name is Drift." Stag smirked. "Truthfully, Esme, if Drift is to be believed, he has not committed a crime at all. He simply left the vicinity of the Great Tree and is therefore unable to return home."

"Left the vicinity?" Esme questioned, notable sarcasm accompanying her voice. "We call that 'being away from home', Stag."

"The irony is not lost on me, Esme." Stag swirled his wine. "I feel indebted to him. I have, over the course of our travels, grown warmer to his assertion that there is more to his story than meets the eye. Now he's gone. He didn't arrive at the time I gave him when I was departing Relond. I fear the worst." He gulped audibly. "I know … you have connections in Relond that can work directly with the lawkeepers. Is there anything you can do to track him down?"

"I accept your worries are legitimate. For a start, I feel unsettled by this news about Flow. Having known you both for so long, this does not reside in me well. And I did not expect you to be here, Stag."

"I know," Stag said. "I understand this combination of events may beg more questions than answers. For what it's worth, I feel the same. I cannot help but worry that something is happening across Q'ara, something that we will discover too late, like the rumbling of a distant thunderstorm, only for the lightning to strike the moment we go out the door."

"I agree," Esme said. "There is more going on than the angry people of Providence. My father's death alone is no ordinary case. An assassination was never attempted before on any of my family. Why now? I can only assume that somebody is trying to pull Adira slowly apart and change the tides of power across the continent." She tipped her head back, swigging the last of her glass of wine. "Perhaps there are other reasons people have for intercepting you at every turn. Perhaps Flow's suspension is not so distantly related to your friend's exile, either. I'll look into it. Maybe your exiled friend and I share some common happenstance. But," Esme continued, eyes twinkling, "is that care I heard in your voice before, Stag?"

Stag grimaced. "Care and obligation are not the same thing, Esme."

"Oh?" Esme grinned. "And what is it you feel for my family or, indeed, myself? Care or obligation?"

Stag smacked his leg. "You could never say an unwise thing, child."

Esme shot him a glare like daggers. "You may address me by my name, Stag, but I would warn against infantilising me again."

Stag gulped. How she had grown since he'd seen her last and that was not even a month earlier. He could never guess again that she was in need of his advice. Before him sat an adult ready to embrace her dues in the world.

All of a sudden, Esme started laughing. First, softer, then rising in volume as the tears began to roll from her eyes and she gasped, trying to catch her breath.

"My queen?" Stag asked, confused. "What is it?"

"Oh, Stag," Esme replied, waving her hand before him as though trying to suppress her chortles. "You've never understood a single joke of mine, have you?"

Stag sat on the edge of his newly-made bed, a grand thing in an even grander room in the palace. In his hands he cradled the *cism* from his pack. Aobia needed to know he had arrived. They also needed to come quickly.

As much as he didn't wish it to be true, Esme had been undeniably suspicious of his current visit. Given the circumstances, he could understand. But the fact that a good political relationship could dissolve in the space of a day baffled him. He had worked his whole career for this family. If Aobia didn't reassure Esme that they were allies for better or worse, the plausible explanation that Stag and Flow could have killed King Terrens would not be difficult to accept.

He sighed, whipping the fabric that kept the *cism* from touching his skin out from under it. "Prime Minister," he began, "I have arrived in Adira. I am requesting political aid from Aobia. I understand the severity of this request but ask that an envoy from the Magisterium comes at once. We do not want to be caught up in any insinuations that we've participated in the murder of King Terrens."

He hesitated, noting the light emptying from the *cism*. "There are … other things, I, ahem…"

He let go of the sphere, throwing it down on the mattress and cutting the connection instantly. It went dark. "Damn it!" he yelled. He had made the call. If Staril or other Sleepers came, maybe confidence in Aobia would be renewed in the Sea Kingdom. But he would need to tell them everything else, too. About Drift and those that hunted him.

He couldn't help but feel they were on the brink of war.

TARRI

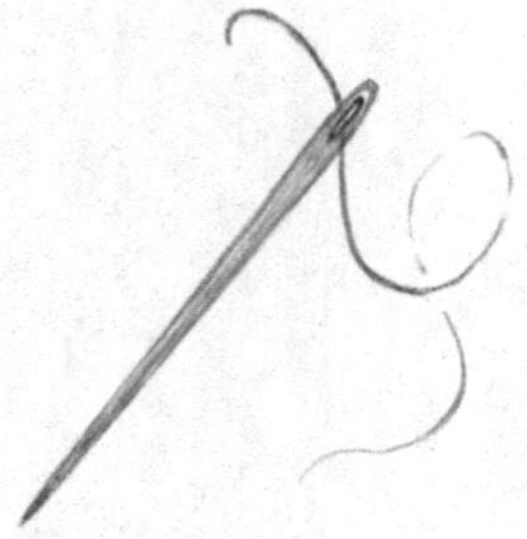

A FTER SETTING UP APRIS and Rela once more for a day at
the Tailory without her, Tarri took a cabriolet to the
Mind, thinking out what she would say to Nischia when she
arrived and sought the Sleeper out.

She had the cab come to a stop before the residential quarters
that she had been inside of not three days past, wondering
how to alert Nischia of her presence. She couldn't just go
in. What if Nischia and Koln had relayed to others that
she was untrustworthy? She couldn't wait on the roadside
either without looking suspicious. Instead, she waited in the
botanical gardens opposite Nischia's apartment.

As she waited on a bench, she further considered her options. What if she couldn't convince her that she could be
trusted, despite the work she and Flow had done the day
prior?

Additionally, her fears became more overwhelming when she thought about what she had seen at the facility: firstly, the generators, and secondly, though most importantly, Sedulus' glowing aura. He wasn't a Sleeper, so why did he seem to carry the same glow of Luminosity as them?

Her thoughts were interrupted when Nischia finally passed through the botanical gardens. Nischia looked past Tarri sitting on the bench as she walked, coming to stop right before her, though she still did not spare her a glance.

"Say what you came here to say and leave me be. I must move swiftly on my way to more important and demanding things than satisfying the whims of a liar."

Tarri felt the sting of Nischia's words and sucked in a sharp breath. "I went to the facility with Flow, as you asked."

Nischia sighed. "Why are you here, Tarri? Do you not realise you have been freed from any obligation to me ever since you broke into my home?"

"Because I must be, my lady. I cannot sleep. I cannot think properly. I dream of Drift lying dead in a human city somewhere, or lost and hungry, or…" She felt her breath pause for a moment, her heartbeat sounding in her ears. "I feel compelled to find my beloved and to do that, I must also be compelled to correct your perception of me. I must right my wrongs. I'm sorry for my deception."

"And yet, being sorry is not mutually exclusive with telling the truth, is it? Let me ask you a final time, Tarri: why did you enter my home? What was your purpose?"

"Flow told me that he needed a *cism* from your home, my lady," Tarri blurted.

"Curious," she said. "Because he already has one, doesn't he?"

"He ... said someone gave him one, my lady."

Nischia raised an eyebrow. "That's not—" She cut off, clearly thinking about her words. "Well, it doesn't matter. Go on."

Tarri wanted to push for Nischia to finish her thought but moved on. "He claimed he knew how to channel the Luminosity from a *cism* to shield his mind and said it could also be used to bi-locate, to appear in two places at once."

Nischia looked unphased. "Bi-locate? That's the stuff of children's stories."

"He insisted it was possible and told me he'd met with the same person who gave him the *cism,* who can do it."

Something changed in Nischia's eyes. A flicker of understanding perhaps. "Who?"

"Sedulus." Tarri watched Nischia as she seemed to consider what to say next.

"We were right all along. Does this mean you've known this for longer than when I suggested your job at the facility?"

Tarri stammered. "It's—it's not like that, my lady—"

"Then what is it like, Tarri? I asked you to go there to set Flow and Sedulus up and find something. But you knew the answer all along? You never trusted me." Nischia turned away, cursing under her breath. "Did you intend to use this acquired power to prevent me from entering your mind, child?"

Tarri shook her head. "No. I … was told by Flow that he tried to read my mind using a *cism* and, well, he couldn't get through. He didn't know how to explain it, but he said I was shielding him unknowingly." She took a deep breath before continuing. "My lady, I am sorry for everything. For entering your home and for not trusting you enough that I could have brought this information to you first."

Nischia nodded, her back still facing Tarri. "For now, I suppose I accept your apology. But there can be no limits between us for this to work. You want to find Drift and I want to get to the bottom of what is being shared about Luminosity where it shouldn't. Now that we know Sedulus has been breaking laws *and* inexplicably using Luminosity, I think it's safe to say these two things are correlated. And," she went on, turning back to her, "you have been shielding your mind since before we ever met, child, or, dare I say, before you could even walk. Luminosity is not for others to access, but you are not a Sleeper, yet you can access parts of what it can do. I don't fully understand it myself, but I'm willing to help you find out and teach you what I can. If you want that, you must work completely with me. Is that clear?"

Tarri felt an invigorating sense of renewed hope rush through her as she looked Nischia in the eyes. "Yes, my lady. I'll do whatever it takes. To learn what I can about Lumosity and bring my Drift home."

You have been shielding your mind since before we ever met, child, or, dare I say, before you could even walk.

Tarri leafed through the words as she walked through the botanic gardens behind Nischia. What had she meant? Was Tarri able to control this skill? Was it something gifted by the Tree, an endowment?

When they reached the building where Nischia lived, they climbed the stairwell and finally came to Nischia's apartment. "Come," she said, holding the door open. "Sit. I have something to show you."

Tarri sat in the green armchair in front of Nischia's library while the Sleeper went behind the curtains that concealed her Orb. The thrum of the mysterious Orb sounded from within, reminding Tarri of a life long since gone.

When Nischia returned, she held in her hand the very same type of glass globe that Sedulus had shown them the day before, sending a cautionary shiver down Tarri's spine.

"This is a *cism*," Nischia said. "You've seen me use one before to shield us from having our minds read. The *cism* is a Sethi globe, blown to be hollow, yet durable, using the black sands around Lake Sethiliquin. In the Sethi tongue, the word means 'sphere'. We learned from them how to replicate a similarly durable glass and now we make them here." Nischia dropped the globe on the ground and Tarri covered her mouth in habitual shock at seeing it make contact, though no breakage came. The globe rolled to Tarri's feet, still completely intact.

"Sedulus showed us mechanical boxes called generators," Tarri said. "They were filled with glowing *cism* infused with Luminosity."

"This is correct. They hold great power, Tarri. Power that *should* be unwieldable to the common person."

Tarri thought about what Nischia had said. These Luminous objects were just made of glass. "It can be broken?" she asked.

Nischia nodded. "It can, but it will not fall victim to a simple fall from an ordinary height such as this. The *cism* is able to store a full Sleep's Luminosity in it, making it a portable asset to transport the powers of the Sleepers in. This is why we do not always Sleep, Tarri. In times past, we would have to Sleep in numerous quantities for long periods of time, rotating on schedules. Between, we would be exhausted and required to rest before Sleeping once more. These days, we do not have that problem. This is the fruit of an old relationship we spawned with the Sethi people when they first came to these shores. Before the Empire of Therador grew into the titan it claims to be today."

Of course. The Sethi were the most renowned artists on the continent. But how the globe could contain Luminosity was still a mystery to Tarri. "How do you … use it? Or moreover, how do you…" She trailed off, searching for the right phrase. "Fill it?"

Nischia smiled. "Once, we Slept only to refill ourselves with the power. Since the creation of *cism*, however, we've learned that we can Sleep and then fill *cism*, allowing us to send Luminosity to places we would otherwise have to attend in person. The power of the Great Tree contained in a portable object."

"Flow suggested these *cism* could be used to weaponise Luminosity as well."

"A long time ago," Nischia began, whilst turning away to prepare the tea, "I fought in the Four-Front War. Of course, you *know* from our histories that Luminosity, and particularly Sleep, can be useful in a military situation; healing the wounded with Luminosity becomes a lot easier, for example, when you have *cism* on the field with you. Some Sleepers in the war were simply Sleeping, using the Luminosity passively, like we do now, creating lights that could outshine the human torch or accelerating the growth of edible plants or filling *cism*.

"However, a small number of us were using Luminosity differently. I was a part of this team, I'm ashamed to say. In fact, I was in charge of it. I led other Sleepers and taught them to channel the Luminosity contained in *cism* into the purest light in the world, so hot it could instantaneously burn a hole through the guts of every man in an army. I fought on the frontlines with my greatest friend."

Tarri tried to move along as Nischia's lips tightened. The Sleeper looked about to cry. "You were ashamed, my lady?"

"We Slept to fill *cism* and deploy them on the battlefield. Then we, or other Sleepers, would take them out into battle and incinerate everything in our paths," Nischia explained. "I could light a page of any book on these shelves on fire"—she gestured to her small library—"simply by touching it. But to burn a man, I could focus my *cism* on him and he would be ash before he could blink." She sighed. "Luminosity does not exist to be weaponised.

But we allowed that weaponisation in the war because without it we would've lost."

When Nischia looked up, two cups of tea in her hands, Tarri saw a shimmer of sunlight catching in a small tear in the corner of the noble lady's left eye. "What concerns me most," Nischia said, "is the reason Flow told you about these offensive uses of our Luminosity."

"My lady," Tarri began, "is what Flow said true? Can Luminosity be used to bi-locate?"

Nischia sighed. "If it can, I am not privy to the process. I might know a thousand ways to kill a man with Luminosity, but I've never heard of a Sleeper existing in multiple places at once with it."

Something wasn't adding up. "My lady, Flow explained to me that he had met with Sedulus in a human city. Sedulus told him he was there while also being at the facility." Tarri spoke slowly and methodically. "I guess I'm trying to say… What if Sedulus was meeting with others? With humans? And what if he let Drift fall as part of a deal of some kind?"

"Deal?" Nischia repeated the word. She said nothing more and Tarri watched her digest the word. Whatever she was thinking, the Sleeper would not say. But Tarri wondered whether Nischia had another piece of information about Drift that she was unwilling to share.

"There's one last thing," Tarri said, disrupting Nischia from her thoughts. "When we left the chamber where the generators were kept, I noticed something. Sedulus was glowing. Like you, my lady."

"Then he really has found a way to use *cism*," Nischia murmured in reply. "For so long, everything has seemed unconnected. But with this information, I'm starting to suspect Sedulus is the conduit between everything that's going on. If he's unlocked knowledge of Luminosity, it could only have been done with the help of one of us. If he's sharing it with others, who knows what is being planned? The king of Adira is dead and we have an exile on our hands for the first time in a century." Nischia leaned down and gripped Tarri's shoulders. "We will find the truth. Because if we do not, we could very well doom this continent and any scrap of peace it has left."

DRIFT

A DAY HAD PASSED, maybe two, judging by the hunger that was threatening to tear Drift's stomach in half. He sat in silent darkness. At least he felt some reprieve from the blasphemy of being force-fed Luminosity and blended into the darkness of the room as he should.

"Wake up, husk," someone said. This was the Nightingale who had first tied him to the chair, the man with the dark-coloured hair and olive skin.

"Light a torch and you might see my eyes are already open next time," Drift replied.

The Nightingale leaned in, breathing hot air onto Drift's cheek. "My name is Armand," he whispered. "Follow every direction I give and you'll live beyond the walls of this chamber."

"What?" Before he could ask any further questions, cold air filled the space the man had occupied and Drift sat alone in the dark once more.

The next people to enter the chamber were Westral, Sedulus, and a new man Drift didn't recognise.

The first time Drift had seen Sedulus, his old superior hadn't hung around long. In fact, they'd never spoken. Westral had led him out of the room and nobody had been back since, besides to give Drift water every now and then.

This time, Sedulus had the same imbued glow that had been forced into Drift. *So,* Drift thought, *they've done it to him too.*

Beside Sedulus stood a hulk of a man, nearly as tall as the Aobian, with long locks of hair decorated with beads. His face was scruffy with a wiry beard that covered several unhealed scars, one particularly deep across his right cheek.

"Husk," Westral said.

"Westral," Drift said.

She looked over her shoulder. "Nightingales!"

Immediately, several other Nightingales entered the room, bowing low, almost in prostration. "Your Majesty," came the abundance of voices, respectfully murmuring to the ground before them.

"You may stand," came the guttural, accented voice of the man next to Sedulus.

"My prince," Westral began. "We are ready to proceed further with our study of trauma-related acquisitions."

Drift swore he could hear Westral swallow before the man spoke. "What have you found with this specimen?"

Westral looked at Drift once more. "We have tested the process of transfer under the conditions of trauma and it was successful, albeit short-lived."

"How short-lived?" the man replied.

"A course of hours with minimal exposure, my prince."

"With maximum exposure?"

Westral hesitated. "We're not sure what that would do, my prince."

"You didn't test it?" the man said, an edge to his voice.

"We weren't prepared to waste such an invaluable resource—"

"Don't use this husk, fool! Find some lowlifes around the place and waste away, Nightingale. You're being reimbursed *very* generously for this work, you understand?"

"Of-of course, my prince," Westral said. This prince was a greater threat than her. "We did bring with us a woman who knows the husk."

"Hmm." The unnamed prince studied Drift as though he was an object only. "You could try a joint experiment. See if you can create a conduit from one to the other. If the human you captured is nobody meaningful, it will matter little if she dies."

Drift felt his face go hot but bit his tongue, remembering that other Nightingale's, Armand's, words. They were going to force Luminosity into Mola.

The man turned to Sedulus. "The current theory *you* gave us was to consider trauma as the underlying agent for taking on

Luminosity for the first time. How much trauma can we inflict on our own without killing them all?"

Sedulus shifted uncomfortably. "Your Majesty, trauma is the only thing in my research that has proved to work. It is the only thing that allowed *me* to take it on. But we are not human. I believe all Aobians are preconditioned to a certain amount of Luminosity from living in the Tree." The prince said nothing in return, and Sedulus went on. "You got the one you wanted. As long as you keep him alive, the rest of what you learn is yours to keep."

"Does this one know what he is?" the man asked.

Sedulus looked quickly to Drift, but could not sustain eye contact. "No, Your Majesty," he said, voice barely above a whisper.

The prince leaned down towards Drift. "You are special, husk. More special than you know. And for that reason, you will not die." He stood straight again, folding his hands behind his back. "But your friend may. And that is the price we must pay if we want all humans to access the power."

It was enough to set Drift in a fit of rage. He thrashed around in the chair, yelling wildly. "Leave her alone! She has done nothing to deserve—"

A swift fist connected with Drift's jaw and he felt the sound of the impact rattle inside his skull. "Do not test us, husk," Westral said, gritting her teeth. "We'll kill her for sport if you do."

"If she survives, she survives," the prince said. "But we need answers if we are to equip our forces before the siege."

Siege. Which nation did this man belong to?

"Your Majesty, may I suggest you observe the subject?" Sedulus interjected.

"I don't need to observe anything. These Nightingales will have their reward for honesty. You help my father in exchange for wealth and we tolerate that. But you're a fool," the man spat. "A fool dressed in silk is still a fool. Remember that. You are *nothing.*"

The prince stepped closer to Drift.

"This one does not seem harmed."

Westral nodded. "We discovered that the transfer from the *cism* worked easily enough for the husk by only taking fingernails. I'm not sure if the pain response would be the same in a human subject, my prince, but we'll try with the woman."

"If she dies, find more subjects to test it on. We need answers, Westral, or we risk everything. Take comprehensive notes and cross-reference the results. I need to know how different the transfer is for both subjects. And if it works on the woman, try connecting the two of them."

"Yes, my prince," Westral nodded.

"And you." The prince jabbed at Sedulus. "Do not toy with me. You know your place. You stand on the precipice of everything you want or your impending doom. Remember that, husk."

"Y-yes, Your Majesty."

Another man entered the room at that moment, dressed in a rust-coloured silk gown with a long, bushy beard that trailed down his torso, though he was still young for a human. "Prince

Rainol, the plans for the siege are underway. It is expected to proceed as normal in five days."

Prince Rainol. Drift recognised that name. He was the son of the tyrant emperor of Therador, Jurin. The one whose family line was stained with the blood of Q'ara for centuries past. Therador was planning a siege. Were they going to attack Adira or Aobia?

Rainol raised an eyebrow. "Five days? Ahem. My father moves quickly. Will that work for you, Westral?"

Westral began to speak, but the other man who just entered spoke first. "The deal must go ahead before that, my prince. If it does not, we will waste a huge number of resources. The march from Therador has already begun."

Rainol look at Sedulus. "My prince," Sedulus said, "I will ensure the deal goes ahead."

"That is good," Rainol answered, nodding at Drift. "Though I'd like to take that one too and study his … other condition." Rainol had called Drift special. What had he meant?

Sedulus grew suddenly defensive. "My prince, if the deal is to proceed and in accordance with the contract, you cannot unreasonably harm this Aobian, let alone take him. We only gave him to you for one reason. Nothing more." All along, Drift's old superior had planned his exile. Why was it that Drift specifically was needed for Therador to learn how to use stored Luminosity?

Rainol snorted. "You dare stand before me? What ground have you to stand on? This husk has already had his first share of pain."

The man in the silk robes stepped between Rainol and Sedulus as Westral looked on. "I could kill you both now, husk," he said quietly to Sedulus. "Doing so would give us everything we want, and you? You'd have nothing but ground to rot on top of."

Rainol reached out at that moment, steadying the arm of the robed man. The silence was interrupted by the looming breaths of the three who were stuck in the exchange. "The one in the chair is no use to any of us dead," he said. "And if we do not let this maggot squirm his way home, we will raise unnecessary suspicions. We are not prepared for that." He turned to look at Westral at the other end of the room. "Do as I asked, Westral, and compare your findings with some human subjects. Then bring him to the Empire and we shall study him further. If Aobia takes issue with it, I'll leave it to my father to negotiate."

Drift mimicked Sedulus' own shudder as Prince Rainol strode out of the chamber, followed by Westral. The other Nightingales around the room stayed still until long after he left and even then, they resumed their work carefully.

NISCHIA

T HE CALL CAME THROUGH while Nischia sat with Koln, discussing strategies for maintenance in the Soul's central market district, wherein much of the street's light had diminished, leaving the area desolate and unsettling to traverse at night. The complaints had been rife, yet this was one area of management Nischia could handle.

The disruption of their meeting by a young steward of the Magisterium, however, compounded some of her stress. "Master Koln and Lady Nischia," the young male Aobian said. "News comes from Prime Minister Staril. She requests you attend a meeting with her on the hour."

"News?" Koln asked, more nonchalant than Nischia would have thought possible. But then, it was Koln. An easily bored, bitter, and jaded old fellow with years of life rubbed off him like worn soles on a shoe.

"Adira has requested our help," the steward clarified.

"Do you have clearance to share what kind of help this is?" Nischia asked.

"I do, my lady." The steward nodded to her. "The request comes from the throne of Adira."

Koln stood. "Stag, the ambassador. He must've reached the city by now. It's probably a report." He clenched his teeth. "If Staril requests our audience, who am I not to oblige?"

Nischia stood and straightened her dress, shaking her head. "Koln, really, you—"

"My lady, if I might interrupt," the steward interjected. "It is pertinent that you leave immediately if at all possible."

Nischia shot the steward a look, but Koln nodded and moved for the door. "Thank you, steward. We will be on our way."

Nischia followed closely behind her superior. "A call to aid? I fear the worst."

Koln did not look at her as he spoke. "There is every chance that proper context will explain everything. Maybe we'll find out more about that exile, too."

The Magisterium was quiet aside from three figures. Prime Minister Staril was speaking with two others, yet Nichia could not piece together who they were.

"Ah, it appears we are all present," Staril said, ushering Nischia and Koln to the bottom of the auditorium and gesturing to the two wooden seats left empty in their small circle. "Thank you for coming."

"Of course, Prime Minister," Koln said, inclining his head.

Nischia bowed her head. "Of course, my lady."

To say Staril intimidated her was no exaggeration. She had spent years reporting to Koln, who in turn reported to her, whether in parliament or during the mobilisation of Aobia in the Four-Front War. But though she'd always only been at arm's length with Staril, the elder Aobian's stone-hard expression and calm yet commanding tone were not lost on her.

"You are both here because of the closeness you have to the current political situation and the pending investigation into our recent exile," Staril replied. "Our political relationship with Adira, I'm afraid, is worsening rapidly."

"We were told by your steward that a request has been made of us from the Adiran throne," Koln replied.

Staril nodded. "Not exactly. The request has been made by our ambassador, Stag, who has recently arrived there."

Nischia's ears pricked at that. Had Drift found his way to Adira by accompanying the ambassador? It was not out of the realm of possibility; Tarri had clarified that they were already well acquainted with each other through Flow.

"It is good," Nischia began, "to hear that the ambassador arrived well and safe after such a long and solitary venture."

Staril nodded. "It may not be ideal, but until we can appoint a new ambassador, his work will continue to be performed alone."

Right. Well, that took Drift out of that equation, then.

"Queen Esme has supposedly questioned Stag's current visit, because it is not regular by any account. We sent him back to reassure the new queen that we were standing with her in the wake of her father's death. It seems sending him back was a mistake and Queen Esme now has reason to further question Stag and Flow's involvement in her father's death. I believe this has been exacerbated, because she has also learned of Flow's suspension."

"Can't we simply explain *why* Flow was suspended?" Nischia asked.

Staril held up a hand. "Speak when I complete my own sentences and not a moment sooner." Koln glanced at Nischia. She hung her head as Staril continued. "I will not share confidential information like that with the head of another nation. Flow's suspension has nothing to do with her father's death."

There was silence for a moment. Of course, the Adiran queen would suspect Flow and Stag in her position. Nischia was certain she herself would, too. Every angle would need to be considered. Perhaps, the queen had been too hasty to wave off any chance of Aobia being behind the crime because of how closely the ambassadors had worked with her family for years. But from what it sounded like, Staril had ended up prompting the queen's newfound suspicion by commanding Stag to return so soon.

"The queen had already commenced official investigations without the assistance of our ambassador and has formed reason to suspect Therador is responsible for the death of the king. Though I much prefer that she finds truth in that than shuns her oldest political ally, that can only be properly determined with time. And time is a roll of the dice, especially after such a tragic event."

"That is a stern accusation the young queen makes," Koln replied. "We signed an armistice fifty years ago in case of this. Threatening Therador is unwise at the best of times. Perhaps we should encourage her to further inquire into Aobia."

"It would at least stall her pursuing Therador," Nischia agreed.

Koln went on. "Surely, we do not wish to amplify the unpredictability of the Empire? Jurin is not one to think before making a decision. He follows in his forefathers' footsteps perfectly: headstrong to death."

"The matter we are here to resolve," Staril said, "is what we are to do in all this. For what it's worth, I can see the queen's point of view. But we must squash any suspicious treatment she has of us as quickly as possible. Our combined force defeated Therador in the last war and we can do it again. But if Adira cuts us off and Therador is equipped to make an attack on them, they will be crippled. And Aobia will be tangled up in the branches of war. Of course, we can fight, take their clean water, and defend our people. But we are a peaceful nation and should cling to that ethos.

"I have decided, therefore, that for the first time in many years, an envoy of Sleepers will go to Adira and consolidate the queen's findings as well as reassure her that we are no enemy. I want you two to be the leaders of this envoy. After all, you"—she pointed at Nischia—"have been in that same position once, all those years ago. However, I need more time to reflect and consider two others who will join you in addition to a small focus group of scribes and assistants that come from the Soul."

"This is … quite the news, Prime Minister," Koln said. "I cannot say I am unsurprised or enthusiastic about the decision."

"You and Nischia are two of the most dependable Sleepers we have. Your responses to the conflicts of the past century have never gone unnoticed. I trust you utterly."

Nischia smiled. "Prime Minister, might I suggest one to accompany us?"

Koln shot her a look. "Nischia, I think the prime minister has—"

"No, Koln, I would like to hear her suggestion," Staril interjected. "Continue, child."

"Prime Minister, for the past few weeks, I've been working with a female named Tarri, a dressmaker from the Soul."

"A dressmaker?" Staril's eyes gleamed.

"She is betrothed to our unfortunate exile, the circumstance of his disappearance being the focus of our investigation."

"An interesting proposition. What can the dressmaker offer you?"

"Her ingenuity is unmatched," Nischia said. "She has single-handedly found evidence that suggests the exile's disappearance may be linked directly with King Terrens' death."

"Pardon?" Staril asked. "Koln? An update on this would've been nice prior to our meeting today."

"We are still in the preliminary stages of writing a report," Koln tried to explain. "I did not feel the need to trouble you with potentialities rather than evidence."

"I expect a summary of your findings before you leave." Staril tapped her fingers on her lap. "But until then, we must make some decisions. Koln, what are your thoughts on bringing the dressmaker?"

"I need to ponder it, as you might guess." Koln looked at Nischia.

"Of course. And yet I wonder which of us has the greater weakness: me with my quick decision-making or you with your overthinking?" Staril said. "You speak of this girl highly, Nischia. But will she attempt to reconnect with her betrothed if the chance arises? I would not want other Aobians cut off from the Tree."

"She will not, Prime Minister. I am aware that her betrothed is still out there somewhere, with his whereabouts unknown. If Tarri was to try anything, there would be serious repercussions for them both. I will have her agreement before we depart."

Staril eyed her. "I appreciate your discipline, Nischia, but do not forget: these same repercussions will fall on your shoulders if something is to occur. Have her make her agreement via *cism*-binding." Nischia shivered as Staril waved dismissively, standing. *Cism*-binding involved holding a participant's hand to a sphere and having them swear an oath with a weak flow of Luminosity running through them. Sleepers did it all the time as part of law-making processes, for example. It was irreversible and breaking the oath would send an immediate notice to the Magisterium. She couldn't help but feel like she was imprisoning Tarri by doing that. But if she wanted Tarri to go with them, she had no choice.

"Thank you, Prime Minister," Nischia stood, bowing.

"Do not thank me if you might only curse me later, Nischia," Staril said. "Koln, do you have a moment before you depart?"

"Of course," Koln replied. "Nischia can manage on her own."

Nischia left, hoping Koln would allow Tarri to come with them. Koln's need to consider everything before making a decision was both his strongest trait and his greatest infirmity. When he lacked knowledge, he lacked control, and Nischia was no stranger to the repercussions of that particular aspect of his nature.

After she gathered her shawl and satchel and trotted up the stairs to the foyer that joined the auditorium to the outside world, she stopped, picking up the low, muffled tones of an argument. Listening, she realised the sound was quickly approaching and leapt behind the wall nearest to her. Staril emerged from the auditorium beside Koln, her back straight.

"You should've known this would happen," she hissed.

"And you shouldn't?" Koln replied. "Of the ten of us, *I* was to guess that the child would eventually leave the pack?"

Staril sighed. "I hate it when you use that word. We aren't wolves."

"We act as wolves," Koln retorted, his voice bitter. "We have become what we strove to spurn when the war ended, Staril. Does this not keep you awake at night?"

"*Everything* keeps me awake at night! Always one to act as though you know the scope of all our lives, Koln. But you don't. You don't know what it takes to keep this nation moving."

They were quiet for a moment and though Nischia could not quite see them, she held her breath for fear that they would hear her.

"You devised the plan to attempt the Naming for the last time," Koln finally said, breaking the silence. "The part I played was small by comparison and you can't pretend otherwise."

Staril snorted. "Small? You're the one who Named him. You should've seen his defection coming the moment he was aware of being something else."

"Of course," Koln replied. "Why wouldn't I have seen every possible path his entire life might traverse before my very eyes?"

"It's done. We have one chance at returning him to the Tree and then we can keep him secure. Though I'm not sure that is the best idea." Staril scowled. "We never should have let him go. This plan you devised with that … *ghastly* public official should have been reviewed. I should never have let you do it. One of our own ambassadors has been removed from his post because of Sedulus. He has too much knowledge of Luminosity and the bargaining power with Therador needed to keep us from locking him up."

"Do you think I wanted this?" Koln pressed. "I put my nation first. We came out of the monarchy crumbling, divided. We fought for too long. This was a chance to fix that. But I see the Theradoran threat now. It's more real than ever. And we are not prepared, despite what you may say…"

Nischia felt a tingle spread down her arms and legs, like needles. She'd asked Koln this directly, asked whether he knew of any Naming rituals that had taken place after the tradition had been outlawed. He'd told her no.

Naming rituals, antiquated ways to keep certain members of society under the control of the monarchy in times past by fixing them to their Name with Luminosity, were outlawed in Aobia. It had never been intended to take away one's free will; rather, the idea had been that the people as a whole could be guided in an optimal direction, like a current in a river. Instead, it had created a populus of prisoners, people who'd felt compelled to act in accordance with their Names.

Of course. She should have seen it the moment Koln had put her up to investigating Drift's disappearance. Drift. To move, to never settle, to never be truly free of motion. So many still bore 'weighty' names like these, a result of Named folk and their integration into Aobia for thousands of years. The difference was that they *were not Named*.

Drift threatened every foundation that Aobia stood on, everything they had done as a nation since the end of the Aobian monarchy when they'd sworn to never Name people again as part of the alliance agreements with Adira. The reason Aobia had descended into civil war a century ago had been because of Feldra, whose Name had proved to be a much bigger problem than anyone had anticipated. Moreover, Koln had lied to her. He had not only been aware of Naming rituals taking place after the ban, but he had also taken part in them.

Tarri had been right all along. There *was* more to all of this than met the eye. And the people in power over the Great Tree were a part of the entire mess, a stew of sickness, malice, and deceit for Nischia to pick through.

She could not trust. Not in the same way she had learned after all these years. Not if she sought the truth.

Not if she wished to save them all.

TARRI

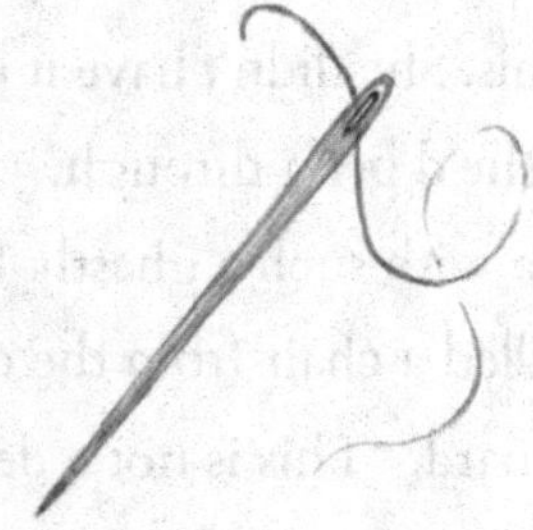

"TARRI! TARRI!"

Tarri was stitching the inner seam on a new summer dress she had been working on, a sage-green chequered number with flared sleeves and a straight-cut bosom, when the voice cried out to her from the front floor of the shop. Not Apris or Rela, but Nischia.

Tarri sighed. She was exhausted. Every facet of her being, be it her mind, her body, even her spirit, felt empty. She continued to work in the shop, because it relieved her when nothing else could. It was the only familiar thing she had. Even now, when she knew Nischia was beckoning her, she wanted to crawl under her trestle board and hide.

Before she could rise or even call out to confirm she was coming, Nischia's head appeared around the doorway that led out to the shop floor. "We need to speak."

"Of course, my lady," Tarri said.

"Stay sitting," Nischia said. "This will not be a pleasant conversation, I fear."

Tarri felt her breath catch. She'd feared the day Nischia would speak to her like that. *We've found the body and we're sorry.*

She couldn't face this. She didn't have it in her. Not right now, not after everything she'd been through.

"Do not stare at me with such a ghastly face, Tarri. It does not suit you." Nischia pulled a chair from the other side of the room across to the trestle board. "This is not a death notice, Tarri. But it is a warning. And a request."

Tarri exhaled a sigh of relief. They didn't know if he was dead until they found him. She just had to remember that. The dichotomy of it was ironic—she continued to work tirelessly to track Drift down, all the while not knowing that the worst news might be on its way to her if she succeeded at her task.

"I have met with Prime Minister Staril," Nischia said. "The ambassador has made his way to Adira and has redirected a message from their queen to us with urgency."

"So Stag has not…" Her voice trailed off.

"No," Nischia replied. "He did not encounter Drift from what he has said, though he did take much longer to reach Adira—and cost us a transportation carriage, no less."

"A message?" Tarri asked, returning to the topic. "How are messages received or sent from here?"

Nischia smiled. "It's simple. Luminosity."

Tarri frowned. "So … you *Sleep* the message to and fro?"

"Not quite," Nischia replied. "We use *cism*. One linked to another, its supply of Luminosity coming from the same stream of Sleep from the same person. Stag can provide audible messages to us nearly instantaneously; however, the risk of running out of Luminosity is very real, especially if the distances the light must travel is far. I do not suspect he could receive more than one message in response, let alone send another."

Of course. "Wait," Tarri began. "Was Flow given a *cism* by the Magisterium?" Had he lied about that, too?

"Yes," Nischia replied. "Although it would have been taken from him upon his suspension. Why?"

"What if he was never given a *cism* by Sedulus?"

Nischia shook her head. "No, child. If he told you something so severe, he had already made the decision to tell you the truth. The *cism* he was given for communicating cannot be accessed by any beside the Sleeper who first filled them. It doesn't matter what he claims he knows about Luminosity. Even I couldn't access the light within a linked *cism* if I tried. But if it was a *cism* filled with the sole intent of being used to store Luminosity for any Sleeper, and any purpose, then it would begin to make sense."

That explained why Flow wanted another *cism*. He'd already had his one taken away and the one Sedulus had given to him had been depleted. These small glass orbs were capable of so much more than she had first thought. No wonder Flow's interest in them was so precarious. "What was the message that Stag sent?"

Nischia blew cold air across the table, as though readying herself for what she was to say next. "A plea for help. A request for a political envoy of Sleepers to attend to the throne as soon as possible." She eyed Tarri. "This is no common request, Tarri. Years of peace are about to be blighted once more and Adira knows it more than anyone. The queen suspects Therador could be responsible for King Terrens' death. But she also suspects us. It is as good a declaration of war as I have heard."

"Us? Why does she suspect us?" Tarri asked, bewildered. The alliance with Adira went back centuries.

"We sent Stag to be forthcoming after his swift departure following Terrens' death. He told the new queen that Flow had been removed from work. But it seems our effort in delivering an honest explanation of what happened has only made the queen more suspicious of our two ambassadors, who were there when her father died."

"This…" Tarri breathed, "is significant, my lady. I do not know what else to say."

"Well," Nischia said, straightening out the hem of her skirt, "I hope you will have something to say, because now it is my turn to make a request of my own. Koln and I are being requested to go as part of this group. I want you there with me."

Tarri's breath caught.

"I want you to lead the scriveners; they are non-Sleeping clerks, the same who scribe sittings of parliament. Whether or not you take up this opportunity is entirely up to you. But we both know this might give you the chance to find news of Drift." Her eyes levelled with Tarri's.

"My lady," Tarri started. "My work is here, both in searching for Drift *and* with the Tailory."

"That is just as well, child, but if I am not here to assist you, how can you continue your search for your beloved?" Nischia asked.

Tarri filled her lungs, then slowly exhaled, trying to process Nischia's request. She would leave the boundaries of the Tree. Didn't those who left feel their souls tear the further they got away? What if that had already started happening to Drift, wherever he was? And what would she do out there anyway? Spend time with *humans?* In foreign places, unknown and uncomfortable, in beds that didn't accommodate her height, eating food that didn't accommodate her gut… The worries were endless. But then, maybe she would find Drift through some connection or some word in some tavern as they passed through yet another drab, overpopulated human town. And maybe they could return and start again. If they couldn't bring Drift home, she could stay with him out there in the wilds. The spark of that possibility was nearly too much to behold.

"Tarri?" Nischia whispered.

"I'm sorry!" she said. "I just…" She looked down as Nischia gripped her hand.

"This will not be easy." The older Sleeper looked nearly as mournful as she. "You will be subjected to strict rules and the obeisance of other Sleepers besides myself. You will work hard and you will need to ignore the urge to work only on finding Drift while you're out there." Then Nischia let go and looked down, leafing through her bag to reveal a *cism*.

The globe was aglow with silken waves of light, glistening against the sun coming through the window. Nischia took it out and placed her fingers on the ball. The light in the room disappeared, like candles being extinguished. They were being shielded. "I shield us for my sake, not yours. Touch the *cism* and you will see what I mean."

Tarri reached out, mimicking Nischia's fingertips on the ball. She breathed in as she felt a rush go through her and she swore she could see Luminosity leaking like light in her veins. But then, it gently rolled away from her, like the waters of the River Tomei slipping back from the shore. The light pooled around Nischia's fingertips once more, ignoring Tarri completely. Tarri lifted her hand from it.

"You see?" Nischia asked, insistent. "You are already shielding yourself. Recognising the feeling of Luminosity being channelled through your soul is the first step to being able to do it consciously.

"Now, I will speak quickly before this *cism* runs out," Nischia said, changing subjects. "Koln has cheated me. I overheard him speaking with Staril earlier. It seems some time ago, Koln and Staril were involved with a group of Sleepers who wished to test the virility of ancient Naming Rituals, for some purposes that continue to remain unclear to me. Your betrothed, as well as several others, were a part of this age-old ritual. Drift must adhere to his Name in its every meaning and contextualisation. If he does not, his life, and some of our own, could be in danger."

Naming? She knew of it but had no understanding of its place in Aobian history. The history of it was no longer taught in schools.

"Was Drift Luminous? Tell me the truth, Tarri," Nischia said. The *cism*'s last light was flowing through Nischia's arm, replacing the inside of the sphere with an opaque, nearly milky darkness.

"No," Tarri shook her head, confused. "Why would he be? He was not a Sleeper."

"Good," Nischia replied with finality. "One last question. If you decide to join me on this journey, will you swear not to betray your duty for a chance to get to Drift, should the opportunity to do so arise?"

Tarri gulped. Even if she saw him, she would have to do her duty? Could she make such a promise? Maybe if it meant getting more information about where he was and if he was okay. She would do anything to know that.

Finally, she answered in agreement after Nischia lowered Tarri's hand back down to the *cism*. The last wisp of light vanished, like a strand of hair sucked into space. Tarri looked up, taking in the ordinary room once more.

"You are bound by this *cism* now, Tarri. My own Luminosity holds you to your promise. Do not test what happens if you break it," Nischia said, standing. "If you agree to come with me to Adira, I will teach you to control your shielding. I need to know by tomorrow what you have decided." She gathered her bag, replacing the *cism* and turning to leave.

"Wait, my lady!" Tarri said, scrambling to her feet.

"Yes?"

This was the moment she decided her future. She would no longer see herself as a simple dressmaker, but something greater: someone who expected a lot and who a lot would be expected of in return.

"I'll go!" she cried. "I'll do it."

DRIFT

Two hands covered Drift's mouth from behind, waking him from the shallow state of sleep he'd been in. Panic flooded him as he tried to steady his breathing. Warm air breathed on his left ear as words cut through the darkness of the chamber like a knife. "It is Armand. Do you remember me, tree-dweller? Today is the day we leave. Do not hesitate. Do everything as I instruct it, without fault."

Armand let go of Drift's mouth but kept his head clamped between both hands. "No!" Drift replied. "I will go nowhere with you unless you tell me who you are."

"Just know that I am no Nightingale. I come from Adira."

He was Adiran. He would be able to take Drift there. "Wait!"

"What is it?" Armand hissed.

"My friend. A woman named Mola. Do you know where she is?"

Armand sidestepped the question. "She is safe enough, tree-dweller."

"I will not go without her, do you understand?" Drift threatened. "If you want to preserve what you have told me of your identity, you will bring her with us."

"Ruining my plan will not move anything in your favour," Armand retorted.

"I have nothing in my favour." It was true. What else did he have but the injuries that refused to heal, the empty pangs of hunger, and the inability to rest, here in this chair?

At that moment, Westral strode in with a captive before her, arms tied together and a bag once again over their head. They wore a familiar yet soiled collection of blue fabrics and Drift knew immediately that it was Mola.

Behind Westral was Sedulus, who stared at Drift while Armand continued to hold his head still from behind.

"Hold him tight, Armand," Westral said. "This will sting. You"—she gestured to Sedulus—"take the girl." Westral shoved Mola into Sedulus' grasp and Drift felt his heart break at her whimpers. Westral pulled out a knife no thicker than a twig, yet flat and sharp to the tip.

"The Kathani people, who belonged to the southlands of Q'ara before the Sickness eradicated them, reserved a specific torture for the most heinous of crimes," Westral announced as Armand shifted his hands to hold Drift's chest so that he could not wriggle at all. "They called it *lyn-chee*, 'the lingering death'. It involved using a knife this small to make tiny slices or incisions across the body of the offender. They would start, as was custom, with the fingernails. But you've already felt that. By the time the thousandth cut was made, the offender died. However, there was an Aobian who once survived for a length of five thousand incisions. He was protected for so long that the ones who had convicted him of his crimes and sentenced him to *lyn-chee* wavered, nearly deciding to let him go. They say he shone with the very life of the Tree from which he came so strongly that he was impervious to death."

Drift knew this story. The Aobian in question was known as The Unnamed, a defector from his Tree who'd sought to unite the many Great Trees across the southern lands. Though he'd exiled himself, he'd worked peacefully, trying to form an uprising which eventually spilled into the first Aobian Civil War, a momentous battle of one hundred years marked by the day The Unnamed perished.

"Do not talk to me about The Unnamed," Drift said, "for he was a great example to our people. As a result of his virtuous life, he absorbed Luminosity from every Tree. That was why he could not be killed. At least, not easily enough. And if you were to believe the legend that became of the story, you would also expect the ending to be different depending on who told it. In one version, The Unnamed survived the torture and exacted vengeance on the king who had sentenced him."

Drift eyed Westral. "If living peacefully is all he needed to be safe from death, what do I need? Because when we meet on the other side of these walls, I will exact my vengeance, Westral. For all those you've taken into the darkness. And all those who never saw the light again."

Westral made the first cut, a neat slice across Drift's shoulder, where the skin was thinnest. He let out a cry. "You may imagine what you will, husk," she said through gritted teeth. "But nothing will change the outcome. Our lives are only just beginning and that is owed to you and the pain you carry." Westral planted the knife in the open cut, and Drift screamed as it sliced already raw skin. Sedulus stepped forward, holding Mola in one hand and taking a *cism* from his robes with the other, thrusting the sphere before Drift's eyes as his wails continued.

"Some more for good measure." Westral shrugged, entering his skin once more just below the previous cut and peeling a long line of skin from his arm.

As Drift screamed, he felt the light from the orb warm and, strangely, calm him, numbing his mind to the pain. It seemed to erupt from the glass orb and consume him. Within the depths of the overwhelming, nearly hot-to-the-touch Luminosity, he saw himself screaming as Westral shaved another layer of skin from his arm, but it was as though he was only observing from the outside.

"*It worked!*" he heard Sedulus exclaim.

"*We knew it worked!*" Westral retorted. "*We already trialled it with less. Now that we've tested the woman too, we can try to connect them both via* cism *and see who feeds on the Luminosity more. It might hurry the process of imbuing others if we can use one person as a source.*"

While this higher awareness consumed him, he heard Armand whisper, *"Come, tree-dweller. It is our time. Follow my every word and we will escape this place. It is now or never."*

The light began to dim as he felt himself return to his body, lurching upright in his seat and gasping for air as though he had emerged from deep water. The pain hit him like a wave and he leaned forward in his seat, grunting uncontrollably.

"This is what I wanted," Sedulus said. "To know we could take from a *cism* whenever we wanted. This level of Luminosity combined with Named ones. The whole of Aobia would change…"

Westral smirked. "That is a problem for your world, husk, not ours. Now, hold the woman tight. Do not let go, no matter what. She took it once; she can take it on again. This is the real test: can the husk transfer the Luminosity to her faster if he acts as the connection between her and the orb?"

Though Sedulus complied, he reared up at Westral's words as he forced Mola to kneel beside Drift. "You speak of Aobia like it is insufferable. But you did not regard the words of your leader yesterday. The prince mentioned as much when he was here."

"If I lived in a world of husks, I would know about it—"

"You don't know a thing!" Sedulus seethed. "There were people, a century ago, who had been exposed to Luminosity so much that they nearly adopted the scope of powers our own Sleepers can access. Even the power to read minds exists in Therador, Nightingale."

"Urban myths," Westral said. "The prince made it clear that our deal with you would prove to be the first time in history that we could experiment with Luminosity and its effects on our own people. It's never been done before."

"Go and ask your emperor," Sedulus bit back. "I've seen more with my own eyes than you would dare comprehend. I've seen his worst work. I've been there, dealing with the devil he is, for longer than you have lived on this earth."

"You lie," Westral snapped. "Now let us try this connection."

I've been there, dealing with the devil he is, for longer than you have lived on this earth. It couldn't have been true. Sedulus, a traitor to the Magisterium for so long. How had he escaped the Sleepers' abilities to read minds? Then again…

Drift had always been a cynical Aobian. He'd grown up saying things he'd known he shouldn't and had never apologised for them. He'd been sceptical of the Magisterium after completing his schooling, where he'd learned that there had been a marked difference in history as it had been revealed by his educators and what he'd been able to find in his father's books. He'd spent every waking hour in his later school years cross-referencing what he'd been taught with odd material he'd found in the Grand Librarium of the Soul, questioning the Sleepers and the 'autonomy' they preached.

As a young adult, Drift had spent years relentlessly sharing this information with others, including his closest friends. He'd shared anti-Magisterium sentiments with Flow, even though Flow had been an ambassador for Adira. He had pestered the wits out of Tarri, though she'd never relented to his ideas.

He had never been investigated. He had never even met a Sleeper face to face.

It struck him all at once. How long had Drift been shielding his mind from the Sleepers?

In the distraction of his thoughts, he did not see the Theradoran prince reappear for the second time in the chamber until he caught Westral and Sedulus bowing at the front of a ring of many other Nightingales. In the prince's hand was a small stone, round and obsidian black. But Drift's gaze was cast further behind Rainol to a pair of Nightingales that carried a drooping, barely-conscious human. It was a man with long, ragged hair and unkempt stubble, barely into his middle years yet gaunt as a skeleton.

"My prince," Westral began, still on one knee. "You bring us another specimen? We already have the woman and are about to try to link her and the husk together."

Rainol grimaced. "Your fellow bruisers in black performed to the best of their abilities last night. This one was dragged in from Relond, though despite his looks he put up quite a fight … along with his unit of equally homeless crispwater addicts."

No wonder the man was in the shape he was. His eyes were sunken with purple rings around them and his skin seemed to pull into the bones, like stretched canvas. Crispwater was said to do this to people. A tea brewed from the leaves of the Tarrigrynd tree, crispwater plagued the human lands, even causing a brief ripple in Aobian society when post-war trading had been at its peak forty years prior.

Drift would never forget the night he'd finished his studies and had caught a crispwater drinker in the Soul fight like a wild dog as a team of constabularies had attempted to apprehend them. The crazed Aobian hadn't just swung limbs or lashed out; they'd clawed at their opposers, attempting to tear them to shreds, gripping skin or biting without fear or registration of their own body's pain. That kind of unhinged behaviour had sent crawling tingles throughout Drift's body as he'd watched in disbelief, unsure how to help or call for more of it.

This man, however, had been through more than a high and its subsequent comedown. He had been beaten to a near pulp, as evidenced by the bruises that had gathered across his pale arms and legs, which were nearly bulging with internal bleeding and broken vessels. His knees were not straight and Drift suspected that they had been broken in order to be able to capture him.

"Add this one on, then, Westral. Did the woman survive the first imbuing?" Rainol asked.

Westral said nothing, simply removing the bag tied about Mola's head. Drift's jaw dropped at the sight of her. The youthful beauty of her face had been stolen from her, replaced with blackened eyelids, red pupils, and the stains of tears long since past. But around her head was a warm glow, a sign that she had taken to the Luminosity they'd forced into her. What trauma had they brought upon her?

"Well then," Rainol said, satisfied. "If we can form a conduit through three people, we can begin implementing this across our forces. Proceed."

As Westral began to move her knife toward Mola, Drift felt a brute force shove his chair from behind, sending him to the floor, while still tied to it. Armand.

The Adiran man launched a kick at Westral, clipping her in the jaw as Sedulus pulled away from the scene, dropping Mola altogether.

Armand used the kick he'd planted on Westral to push back, whirling around and punching the prince's cheek as Sedulus cried for help. Westral got up, charging and leaping onto Armand's back, revealing a thin metal strap that must've been hidden in her sleeve. Using it to choke Armand, she tried to topple him.

As Armand spluttered, Drift wondered if he could just flip the chair out from under him and get it over his head so that he might be able to loosen the ropes that bound his wrists. He grunted, turning to the side and wriggling, nearly like a worm, to wrestle the chair out from behind him. A fully cloaked Nightingale saw him and raced over to stomp a fierce boot down towards his face, but he rolled to the side, breathless. Another ran up to support their comrade as Drift spun around, his lower back crunching painfully over the hump of the seat. Once over, he managed to position himself for the Nightingale's feet to get caught in the chair behind him, knocking them into other Nightingales like a series of standing tiles.

Drift exerted one last huge breath, turning as quickly as he could and launching his arms, and the chair with them, over his head. The chair collided conveniently with Sedulus, knocking him out cold. One hand loosened and Drift pulled it out. "Mola," he called to her, but she remained in the centre of the chaos, kneeling.

Armand continued to face off with Westral, trying to use her gang of goons as weighty objects against her. "Quick, tree-dweller!" he yelled, landing a fist against the side of a Nightingale's face and launching himself forward. For what these Nightingales seemed to represent, Drift couldn't help but notice how useless they worked together against the force of this one man.

Suddenly, Rainol stood and grabbed the chair that was still tied to one of Drift's hands as he tried to pull back and free it. Drift gritted through the pain as the rope twisted, contorting the direction of his hand unnaturally.

Rainol bellowed, shoving Drift into a pillar. The prince raced up to him, drawing a knife. "I will skin you, filthy husk!"

Drift threw the chair up, thwarting the first strike of Rainol's dagger and catching the blade against the ropes, enough for them to slip right off his hand.

He used both his hands to catch Rainol's free hand, turning the prince and forcing him down. As Rainol struck the ground, another Nightingale came to his aid, launching herself at Drift from the side, which forced him to crash down onto the prince.

He felt the metallic taste of blood well in his cheeks as the ring of metal on the floor sung out from beneath him. Rainol had lost the dagger. As they both came to the revelation, he shoved Rainol out from beneath him and rolled over to grab the blade.

"Nicely done," Armand wheezed, wrestling a hand from his throat. "Now, we disappear like the day into night."

"Not without Mola!" Drift said sharply. He ran to her and tried to lift her up. "Armand! Help me!"

"No!" Westral screeched, looping her metal strap around Armand's arm as he was about to run to Drift.

Armand was tugged back, his arm caught in the twisted barb. Without thinking, Drift lined up Rainol's blade with Westral's head and tossed it by the handle. The blade did enough to scare her off, leaving Armand to dash free, but it clipped the man's shoulder, causing him to cry out in pain and reach his free hand to press down on the gouge. "Let us ... be gone!" Armand cried, clearly wounded. He stumbled to Drift's side, lifting Mola from under her other arm. They got her to her feet and hauled her as hard as they could away from the commotion.

"In my cloak, tree-dweller, fetch the pouch and light it with the sconce on the wall as we exit," Armand said. "I'll hold your friend."

They ran, trying to dodge Nightingales through the narrow corridor that led to the only place he'd ever seen light leak in from. As they passed the wall sconce with barely a few metres between them and their assailants, Drift pushed Mola completely into Armand's grip. He found the small bag in Armand's cloak pocket. Undoing the knot that kept it shut, he put the sconce to it as Armand shouted, "Throw it! Throw it now!"

The sound that came next was like nothing Drift had ever heard, a deafening boom that reverberated endlessly, low frequencies overlapping with high, screeching ones, retiring his sense of hearing from assisting him at all. He noticed all too late that, as the smoke cloud consumed the corridor behind them, Armand had closed his eyes and shoved his hands up to his ears. Whatever that powder was, it had exploded, breaking the structural foundations of the earth above the chamber. The roof behind them had started to collapse, closing them off from the other Nightingales.

"Run! We must run before it all falls!" Armand yelled over the crashing cacophony that grew in their wake.

Rocks flew in many directions, smoke and dust clouding all around and filling Drift's eyes and throat, making his sight blur and his ability to breathe tight and unaccepting. All he could do was grip Mola's trailing cloak, the only connection he had to Armand, and let the man in front of them pull through the opaque mantle that had begun to thicken.

"Nearly ... there!" Armand wheezed.

Eventually, they rounded a small bank, which led to a door of black iron latched shut with a wheel-operated turnkey. Armand let Mola stand on her own feet and tried to spin the turnkey one-handed. His other arm poured blood. Drift came at once to help him push it, their combined strength getting it to shift. As the night air rushed into the space they had created, Drift felt his throat open up. They ran, gaining speed, his heart thumping. They'd done it. They'd escaped.

Behind them, the chamber entry, buried under an unassuming hill, collapsed, the outstretching claws of the dust and smoke reaching into and dying in the clean air.

TARRI

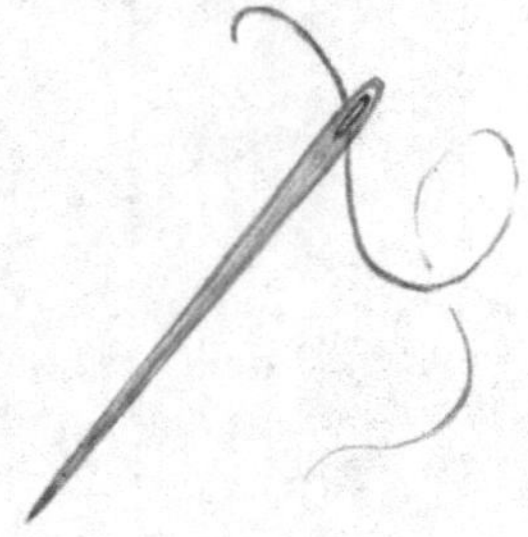

Tarri's final day in the warm embrace of the Great Canopy was near and she spent much of it aching to both leave and stay simultaneously. Sunlight clung to the world around her like a hug, the signs of early summer interrupting the bustle of everyday life as patrons began to swarm the Soul, shopping for pleasure more than need and enjoying the company of the people they roamed the streets with. This was community at its most beautiful at the best time of the year. This was home.

But aside from her feelings, one thing still tore at her. The one person she wanted to lie on the grass with, to feel the resonance of the sun on her closed eyes with, was not there. He was not home. He was lost, somewhere in the great beyond, and in the summer, no less. But she would find him if that was all that was left in her life.

She had ceded complete control of the Tailory to Apris and Rela earlier that morning. They would do a fine job. It hurt to think of people entering and then leaving happier than when they'd arrived, and not because of her. Maybe she hugged her baby too tightly. Maybe this distance from the Tailory would be good for business or good for her.

Now, she sat at her dining table, a satchel and an additional bag packed for her travels, though probably not sensibly as she'd never needed to pack a bag before. In front of her lay the huge scroll of names and connections. She'd been tempted to take it with her, but instead she decided that a couple of intensive hours might allow her to transfer smaller notes into a journal that was in her satchel. Then, she would share all she had found with Nischia.

A loud knock came at the door, accompanied by an equally loud voice. "Knock, knock!"

Flow. He looked tired with dark shadows beneath his eyes despite the lively sun beaming down from above. He was frenetic, unable to contain some boundless, unstable energy. "I hear you are leaving!"

Tarri frowned. How could he have known? "Shush! And how did you hear that?"

Flow looked past her, moving quickly into the kitchen and pouring the dregs of cold tea on the counter into a mug. "Flow hears all!" he said. "Why would you think I'd be left unaware of that, Tarri? I have connections."

"Of course," she replied, folding her arms.

"Just remember, the Sleepers only work for what they want," he said before slurping from his mug obnoxiously.

"And you?" Tarri said. "You would help me? You wouldn't be in it just for something you want?"

"It's not that simple."

"What is it then?" Tarri asked bitterly. "He was *your* friend. Your best friend! And all the while, you've been trading secrets with the one who let him fall from that waterfall. Do you not realise the consequences of that? Do you not understand why you're being so closely investigated?"

"Pfff!" Flow said. "The Magisterium has its own problems, Tarri. I'm just one part of a bigger picture."

Tarri glanced sideways, settling her gaze on the scroll on the table.

"Don't look at it so obviously," Flow spat. "I know you don't trust me. But something is happening at the Magisterium, Tarri. Something evil is stirring. It started with the death of a human king. I knew that man. He was good. And he was, until recently, the most powerful human on Q'ara."

"What are you saying, Flow?" she asked quietly.

"I … know I can't come with you. Roots below, I can't leave the Tree. But be careful out there. It's no world for an Aobian. And now, more than ever, I fear you will be living as though you are branded with a target on your back."

"I understand," Tarri nodded. "But Nischia knows the world. She will guide us through safely and keep us close."

"No." Flow shook his head. "Nobody knows the world out there as well as I. Nobody except for Stag. The Sleepers saw it in a time of chaos and war. But they did not travel needlessly or for mere political intercourse. That's been the job of people like Stag and me since the end of the monarchy. We've seen it all firsthand."

"You used to spend every minute sharing the excitement of your travels with us!" Tarri snapped. "Constantly comparing our boring lives to yours. Exploiting Drift's cynicism to make him itch for what you had!" Tarri frowned. "You are either a hypocrite, Flow, or you are scared. I think you are the latter."

"Very well." Flow turned to go. "I wish you luck, Tarri. The kind that does not expire."

When Tarri reached the Mind after crossing the road into the residential quarters, she found a large party of Sleepers and citizens mixed with Aobian high guards centred around a single person: Staril, the prime minister of the Magisterium. Tarri had seen her before, though she could count the number of times on a single hand, and each one of them was only ever from a distance. The leader of the Sleepers was said to be responsible for modern Aobia.

Through the chaos of the crowd, Tarri spotted Nischia standing towards the back. She beckoned Tarri over. "Do you have everything you need?" she asked. The wind gusting through the channel between the buildings and the Botanical Gardens swayed as though ushering them to get moving.

"Of course," Tarri replied, showing off her satchel and small pack.

"Goodness, child!" Nischia replied, aghast. "What have you packed? A single change of smallclothes?"

Tarri blushed. "I didn't think it wise to pack heavy, my lady."

"Well," Nischia sniffed. "Be that as it may, you cannot simply make yourself new clothes on the road."

"I, umm, packed some stitching essentials," Tarri said.

"You continue to astound me!" Nischia replied. "Now, we must finalise our plans with Staril. The crowd moves with her like a disease, however."

"I thought as much," Tarri replied.

"We will make sure we have all the clearances we need. Then we depart. The caravans are packed and strung together and the horses are prepared."

"How many of us are going?"

"As of an hour ago, perhaps ten. Maybe twelve." Nischia whipped her head around to look at Tarri. "Don't worry. You'll only be responsible for the Scriveners; no more than six."

"Six?" Tarri squeaked.

Nischia pursed her lips, saying nothing.

The crowd moved to the gardens tucked into the residential quarters. Staril stood before a large awning, fronted by high guards. She began her address in a large, conductive voice, the voice Tarri and many other common folk knew her for.

"Times change," she began as others settled in to listen. "And we are no strangers to change. This world has thrown its cruellest challenges at us for centuries and yet Aobia thrives to this day."

Raucous applause echoed throughout the crowd, followed by a "here, here!"

"Today marks the first of many days where we embark on a new journey. The first time in fifty years that we depart the Great Tree and travel to see our trade partners in Adira. We are not sending ambassadors. No. For the first time in a long time, a party of twelve will be leaving to offer aid and support to the queen of the Sea Kingdom.

"As I've said already: times change. We do not know what the future holds, but we can prepare for the possibilities."

As the high guards urged the crowd away, Staril stood strong. She watched most of the people leave until all that remained was a small group of Sleepers and common folk.

From behind them, Koln appeared, cool breath from his nostrils alerting Tarri and Nischia to his presence. He nodded at Nischia but grunted at Tarri.

"Thank you for accepting the call to join this group." Staril smiled. "After this brief meeting, assemble your things and make haste to Adira.

"Your objective is simple. Negotiating with the queen of Adira and supporting her is of the highest import. Now, to proceed with the details, I'd like to direct your attention to a Senior member of the Magisterium: Koln."

Koln cleared his throat. "The journey is as follows. We'll set out and make for Relond. That part of the journey is only about a day and a half, and we will stop overnight at the Mountain Gate, which is patrolled by Theradoran guards. We will stop in Relond for no more than two nights to gather supplies. From there, Adira is another day and a half. The roads between Relond and Adira are busy. They can also be dangerous late at night. We will proceed with ample caution and select places to sleep appropriately away from the roadside.

"Once in Adira, the instructions are straightforward. Provide support to the new queen and her committee, make advisory comments, and take minutes at every meeting. All Sleepers will report directly to me, and me alone. All scriveners will report to Tarri of the Soul. Tarri, raise a hand."

Tarri did so, nodding and waving to those around her. Before they knew it, Staril was thanking Koln and giving one final address. Koln indicated to a stable master behind the party as the caravans were brought over to the roadside from somewhere out of sight.

"This is our first foray as a people in many moons," Staril proclaimed. "Live as good citizens, though you will not be home. Remember where your soul belongs. Do not forget the calling of the Tree and return safely into Her merciful arms when your job is done. May the Light of Aobia bless you and grant you pardon for your leave-taking. Trust, Compassion, and Wisdom!"

STAG

T HE SHEER CURTAINS MOVED with the morning sea breeze in sunny Adira as Stag stretched his arms, yawning.

The calm he felt in Adira was something he had trained himself to feel during his time away from the Great Tree. Adira in the early summertime was beautiful. The briny yet clean saltwater smell hung in the air and the weather was always sunny.

Stag knew that the serenity he felt in the coastal city may be threatened; oddly, he was passionate about defending Adira, admitting to himself even that he would do it, even if it meant competing for the new queendom's safety against the interests of Aobia.

He changed quickly into daily garb for working, neat, sharp-edged slacks with a light linen jacket over a white silk shirt. As he pulled on his jacket, his eyes caught on a royal family portrait that hung above his door and he surprised himself a little at the tug he felt in his throat when he saw them all smiling together. King Terrens resting his hand on Esme's shoulder, her mother standing on her other side. Though the portrait was quite devoid of emotion, as most official paintings tended to be, Stag still felt touched to be as close to the family as he had been for so many years. His allegiances to Esme and her cause could not be questioned.

As though his thoughts were being heard by someone in the palace, a knock sounded, shaking him from his daydream. He answered, opening the door to the latch's point to see a young steward at the door. "My lord." The child bowed. "The queen requests your presence."

"Of course. Might I ask the reason for Her Majesty's request?"

"Uhm…" The steward hesitated. "Some visitors have arrived in the city."

Drift. Could it be? "Then take me to her at once," Stag said, shoving him aside so he could exit the room, banging the door closed behind him. "Let us be prompt, child."

At the entrance to Esme's private garden, the steward handed Stag over to Pretch, who led him through to a large, beautifully laid breakfast table, where Esme sat at one end, relaxed.

"Esme?" Stag said, confused. "Your steward requested my presence."

"Oh, Stag! Good morning. Sit and have some food," Esme said, popping a grape into her mouth, chewing louder than what seemed appropriate. "There is news that one of my intelligence agents has returned to the city from an underground job in Relond. My agent is currently being screened for entry and then will be brought to the gate."

"Is anyone with him?" Stag asked.

"Interestingly, yes," Esme said. "An Aobian and one other."

"Impossible," Stag breathed. Had Aobia heard his call for help so soon? Or was it Drift?

"The question, Stag—and that's Question with a capital 'Q'—is why there is an Aobian in the city so soon after your arrival?"

"Esme, I…" Stag began. "I don't know anything about an Aobian traveller. If I did, I would've been very transparent about it!"

"And your Magisterium?" Esme asked. "Is it transparent with you?"

"Truthfully, Esme," Stag replied, "the Magisterium does not dabble in outright subterfuge!" He felt his face grow hot.

"It could be Drift," he explained. "My companion, who I told you about when we arrived. We separated in Relond, after all."

Esme looked at him, nearly squinting, and Stag felt his heart begin to break. Despite how well he knew this woman and her family, he understood the reality they faced. The tensions that could form between Aobia and Adira were not to be taken lightly, for Stag knew that their roots were connected.

"I'm not sure what to think, Stag," she said. "Your friend, Drift… I'm just not sure whether the story you've given me is as simple as you told it."

Stag stiffened. "And you would accuse me of lying to you? I cannot offer any advice if that is the case."

"Don't close up on me, Stag," Esme snapped. "If you don't want to deal with this, you don't have to. But it's simpler if you defend yourself instead of being so fatalistic."

"I do not understand what it is you wish me to say," Stag said. He could not tell her yet that he had called upon the Magisterium for aid. If he did, her suspicions that he and Flow could've been involved in her father's death might drive her to do something shortsighted.

Esme sighed. "I wish you to tell me if this person could be anyone other than Drift," she said, dropping her voice. "Perhaps I shouldn't have been so hasty with my judgements. I'm sorry. Everything that is happening around us, Stag… It is so hard to anticipate what will happen. And I am responsible for that now. I can't do what my father—" She stopped, sucking in a breath.

"Esme," Stag said before clearing his throat. "*My queen*, you are more than capable of facing these challenges. War and peace come and go. They've traded goods with one another longer than any of us have. Your father was the perfect leader at the turn of the Four-Front War, in his own father's wake, and only he could lead us to peace. Whether you chose to or not, you have been ordained to lead Adira as safely as possible into whatever befalls her now. That is no small feat. But neither is it greater than the sum of your own parts. And I will be here for you every step of the way. I would discard my interests in my people, despite my love for the nation I represent, if it meant I would lose our friendship instead. Adira is a second home to me. I feel the most welcome and happy here that any Aobian possibly could in a human nation."

Esme squeezed his hand. "Your friendship is so valuable. But please, *never* say such things. They are promises you cannot keep, Stag. Not if you wish to follow your path with integrity. We must do what is best for our people. Let us work to keep what is best the very same between them both."

Stag let go of her hand. "Of course," he whispered. Her wisdom had outgrown his perception of her. Again, he could not see the little girl he'd once known anymore. "Well then," he said, taking a deep breath. "Child of Terrens the Great. How must we proceed from here?"

Esme giggled.

"Maybe it is not written anywhere," Stag said, smiling warmly, "but I refer to him as such whenever he crosses my mind."

"And me?" The cheeky smile spread across Esme's face once more. "What name do *I* receive, Stag?"

"Esme the Most Illustrious," Stag said, though he knew it was a far fetch the moment that Esme spat out her tea across the table, the spray of which pattered onto Stag's own plate. "Manners!" he said, chiding her as he was once able to, though she continued to laugh.

"Well," she wheezed in between laughter. "The Most Illustrious Esme has some rather illustrious details she needs to pass on to you, Stag."

"And what are they?" Stag asked drily, pushing his now tainted plate away from himself.

"My plans," Esme said. "My plans for my kingdom."

"Queendom now," Stag pointed out.

Esme shook her head. "Well, that's the thing. Listen closely, Stag."

He peered at her. "What could you possibly mean, Your Majesty?"

Esme stared deeply into his eyes, as though readying herself for what she needed to say. "I mean that this kingdom will endure, Stag. It can be no queendom without a queen. And this queen has work to do. Important work."

"And what is the nature of this work?"

"I need to find out who killed my father, Stag." Esme spoke quietly, suddenly dropping her bright tone.

Stag studied her hurt face. "I cannot imagine how much it hurts, Esme. But that is not your duty. Your father would say the same. You must stand with your people, keep them united."

Esme could not hold his gaze. "Stag, there is much that you do not know. Things I only learned in the wake of his death. Secrets he's kept for all our sakes that need to be protected. Within those secrets, there is still much to be discovered. I can't do all that *and* this." She gestured dramatically around her.

"I presume you cannot share these things with me?" Stag replied.

Esme shook her head. "They are not mine to share. Not yet." She sighed. "I know what you must be thinking. I know you think I'm being juvenile, but—"

"And how exactly do you propose you will step back from leading this nation to pursue these things?" Stag felt his cheeks grow hot.

"I must be removed entirely from the monarchy and cast out." Esme said it as plainly as she would if she were explaining what they were to eat for dinner, and Stag couldn't help but curse her silently, considering his options. How could he counsel her if this, *this,* was her plan? The immaturity that he saw in her now hung about like a bad smell. This kingdom was no plaything. This was a nation with people in it, people desperate to stay united in the wake of their former monarch's death.

"I cannot support this decision," he snapped, crossing his arms. "Irresponsible talk like this is a disease, Esme. And you are allowing it to spread across your entire person. What satisfaction will you derive from finding your father's killer? By the time you discover the answer, it could be public knowledge. And then what? You'll come back? To a people who will never accept you again?"

"I *must* do this," Esme said, rising in her seat. "I saw it, Stag. I saw the shell they made of him with my own eyes. Whoever did it will pay. And if I can be the one to enact vengeance, I will do it. Quell the brewing war before it starts. Days after his death,

I found my father's journals and notes, the discoveries he's been making about this continent. If someone wanted him dead after years of peace, they knew what he was so close to finding."

"Then tell me what it is," Stag pressed. "If it is such a great thing, I can help you manage it from the throne, like every other diplomatic job I've worked for this family."

"No, Stag," Esme said, her voice breaking. "Not if I cannot be sure of you. I know the likelihood of our alliance prevailing is great, but I need to prove it first."

"All I can do is tell you the truth," Stag said, offended. "What more can I give you? Answers that even I do not have!"

"Then let me go out and find them," Esme replied. "I will go and you can counsel Sefil. He will be a good king. A better king than anyone could give him credit for. I can take my father's knowledge with me and purge this continent of the power hungry."

"You will bring shame to this kingdom," Stag said in a low, bitter voice. "And shame to your father." He stood up emphatically. "I will await the visitors outside the palace."

Stag did not look back once as he stalked out of the gardens. What was she going to gain from leaving the kingdom? If it affected Adira as much as she hinted at, he needed to know what the secrets Terrens had been harbouring were. There were no games to be played in her position. She was not a child any longer. She was supposed to be the queen of the greatest human nation on Q'ara.

Did Esme truly doubt Stag's loyalties? He felt mad even considering the possibility, but rationality still shone through. Wouldn't he feel doubt in her shoes? With her father's death still in question and Aobia's own motivations unknown in the shifting dynamics of the continent? It was enough, in Stag's mind, to justify the way she acted. But yet again, she proved to be a mystery, a creature of perpetual motion, unable to be anticipated; that was what made Stag so uncomfortable. He was here to provide counsel to her, to help her make good decisions, and to keep her pleased with Aobia in their trade agreements and alliances across the military. How could he do his job if she wasn't willing to share her ideas with him?

As he strode to the forefront of the palace, the frustration he felt ebbed and flowed, giving and taking from him like the tides of the Adiran Sea, which one could hear from anywhere in the city. Now, he had to manage this new shift in the norm: an uninvited guest. An Aobian, no less. He had never heard of such a thing. It threatened Esme's sense of security, and for good reason. All he could hope for, the best outcome possible, was that the person he saw escorted by guards at the gate was Drift.

It was rightly so, then, that he let out an exacerbated breath of relief as he turned the corner to see the morning sun coating the fading silhouette of the very male he wished to see beside two humans, all dishevelled and haggard.

Drift was here and beside him Mola, the farmer's sister.

DRIFT

Adira was the closest Drift had come to seeing the beauty of the summer sun. Against a backdrop of friendly exchanges, chirping sea birds, and music, Adira was a clean whitestone city that presented itself impeccably.

And then there had been the guards. Armand had vouched for the three of them after confirming that he was a member of the secret intelligence in Adira. Drift hoped that the interaction was but a minor road bump in an otherwise life-altering experience.

Mola had said nothing since they'd escaped the Nightingales. At first, Drift had thought she'd merely been in a state of shock, but her silence had persisted throughout their journey. He did not poke or prod, sensing that she had to be the one to speak first.

He had realised that where they all were now was exclusively as a result of his exile. He had wondered a lot about that on the way aloud in their exchanges around the campfire (that Drift had insisted to never be kept more stoked than coals) over the two nights it had taken them to find their way here. And now, in Adira, he finally started to feel a sense of detachment from the Great Tree, that maybe Aobians were not designed to be secured in their place. All of Q'ara, in a fashion, was still supposed to be theirs to venture, thousands of years after the humans had secured and divided it. Maybe, in some odd way, the heart of Q'ara ran deep in his veins, a member of the race that had lived here for longer than the histories accounted for.

The palace at the end of the main street was the most impressive piece of architecture Drift had ever seen. Though it seemed to run in line with the sea on one side, the other fronted the city like a beacon, or the shadow of a nurturing parent, so much taller than anything else in its view. At the front were the large gates, closed into place by two defensive walls. A second layer of protection, Drift realised, as the city was surrounded with buttressed walls just like these, but on a scale even greater, running into the hills that surrounded the city. Though it was a remnant of Adira's past and Q'ara's conflict-driven recent history, he couldn't help but wonder when these defences might be tested next.

The clearance card Armand carried was shown at the gates to a host of guards ready to escort them in. "And now, on to the queen," Armand said, his voice a mixture of uncertainty and relief. The man had known the late King Terrens and was close friends with much of his personal guard. A blow, he had told Drift, that he could not yet overcome. Now they would face Terrens' daughter, the new queen. The trick, according to

Armand, was to be unafraid of humour—Esme respected a man who could make others laugh, either with him or at him. To Drift, this didn't sound like any monarch he had ever heard of. As a result, he was still unsure whether or not he would take that risk. At least he had Armand with him to steer him in the right direction.

The escort party of six guards, three halted on each side of the gate. As the doors squeaked open, Drift realised he had drawn some attention from the Adirans. Stag would've spent a large amount of his time in Adira among the locals, but that still didn't guarantee that an Aobian in the city was a regular sight.

The palace itself was another few hundred metres from the gates, though stretching out from its walls were lattices of steel that connected sheer white shadecloths together like a large hat, protecting those beneath it from the seaside summer sun. The ripples of light that pressed through the shadecloths were warming on Drift's face, though he walked through patches of shade in between, a welcome reprieve.

Then, ahead of his gaze, another welcome reprieve: Stag, alone, arms crossed, and frowning.

It was the single greatest thing Drift had seen in days.

He couldn't wipe the grin off his face as he strode forward, gripping Stag's forearm and pulling him into a hug.

"You're okay!" Stag whispered.

"Okay? Yes." Drift nodded, stepping back. "But there is much to tell you."

"Of course. And Mola, I am glad to see you safe and well."

For the first time in days, she croaked a short response. "Thank you, ambassador. Without the help of this man, we might not stand before you now."

Drift stepped aside. "This is Armand," he said. "He is the reason we are here. The reason we are alive, perhaps."

Stag shook his hand. "Then peace be upon you, friend. You are Adiran?"

Armand smiled. "I am proud to say I am. I have served the king since the moment I finished my schooling. First member of the Reef's Treasures reporting!"

"Secret intelligence," he breathed. "Well, you learn new things every day. I have been an emissary to Adira for thirty years and yet have never met a member of the Reef's Treasures." He gripped Armand's shoulder. "Come! We must talk. I moved in circles with the royal family and only heard whispers of your organisation's existence!"

"Wait, Stag!" Drift interjected. "There will be time. But for now—"

"Of course." Stag inclined his head. "I get ahead of myself. We must meet with the queen. I will warn you though that she has developed a sense of caution around strangers, and more specifically, Aobians."

The central courtyard at the heart of the palace was staggering. Drift was in awe at the perfectly laid out stone benches, rectangular strips of rock that had been cut in tessellating patterns, dotted around the clean, low-cut lawn. Their bases encased in raked sand, sturdy daisy shrubs sat out along the edges of each seat and all around the courtyard itself in dazzling violets, yellows, and pinks.

"They grow only when near the sea," came a woman's voice, light yet commanding. The queen was striding towards him. She was young, *far* too young for a human to be a monarch, but maybe that was just the difference in Aobian and human age. Her blond hair reflected the sun that hung hot and dry above them and her eyes were a steely blue. She wore near-plain clothes, a simple dress cut from cream-white linen, and wicker-woven shoes, flat to the ground. Beside her stood a shorter, older man with a stubbly face and shoulder-length white hair.

"This is Pretch, my senior advisor," she said as the man gripped Drift's hand.

"And I'm the queen, by the way, though it is refreshing to meet someone who didn't notice."

Drift felt his cheeks flush. "Your Majesty," he said, practically prostrating himself.

"Please." The young queen chuckled. "Don't lower yourself any more than that."

"Esme," Stag whinged.

He knows the queen on a first-name basis? Drift thought, bewildered.

"Drift, stand, you idiot." Stag stamped a foot. "You'll need to learn to take jokes."

"I wish him all the luck in the world." The queen laughed.

This was bizarre. Had he ever missed a moment of formal greeting for any Sleeper, let alone a monarch, in Aobia, he would've suffered a significant penalty, perhaps even serve time in confinement. Here, he was being *ridiculed* by the queen herself for being *too formal?*

"I'm sorry, Your Majesty," he said. "I'm not certain I understand."

"Are all Aobians this polite, Stag?" she asked, redirecting her reply to the other Aobian in the yard. "I recall you were just the same for many years. I've only just managed to convince you to call me by my name, now that I'm queen." She stood, waiting for some kind of response, though Stag stayed silent and Pretch, the advisor, only seemed to bow his head so as to hide a smile. Perhaps this openness was simply Adiran custom, but thus far, Drift wasn't sure of what he had stumbled into. It was as though the queen was teasing him like a life-long friend.

"Well, perhaps we should sit. I have information I should share with you and you with me. Is your friend around?" she asked as she indicated the benches. Drift and Stag both sat.

"I requested a bath for her," Stag said. "She will join us for dinner."

"Of course. To the news then. Tomorrow, the queen will be cast out. That's me, by the way," she said to Drift.

"Cast out, Your Majesty?" Drift asked. Stag smacked his own forehead.

"Everybody will say that the best work that can be done for the people can be done by the monarch that leads them. But I've had time to consider that I can't do my best work as queen."

"Yes. The 'best work' that you cannot tell us about," Stag shot back. Something must have gone on between them before Drift had arrived, he realised as Stag and the queen looked at one another with daggers in their eyes.

"It can't work without my brother, Sefil, taking the crown." The chirpy, dapper facade of the queen suddenly dropped as she let out a deep sigh. "That is not the solution I wish I had to choose, but it is the only one I think will work. The people will think I've been exiled for high treason against the nation." She looked up at Drift, her expression serious. "I understand you know something about that feeling," she said.

Drift shifted, looking away. "I do, Your Majesty."

"This is simply unfathomable, Esme!" Stag interrupted, frustration twisting his face. "I will not allow you to play games with this nation!"

"The gravity of my decisions is not lost on me, Stag!" Esme retorted. "Do not persuade me to review your position as a guest here!"

Stag stood up, stepping away. "You would do that, wouldn't you?" he said quietly, an edge to his voice. "After all my tireless years of service here? So be it, then. If you wish to continue with this ridiculous charade, don't let me convince you otherwise."

He nodded to Drift and Pretch before storming off, leaving Drift alone with the humans.

Waiting for Stag to depart the courtyard, Queen Esme continued to speak. "I apologise, tree-dweller. You may not be aware of Stag's place in this palace. Being one of two ambassadors to the city for longer than my own time on this planet practically renders him a member of our family. I will not hold his anger against him; he is a sensible advisor and the perfect counterpart to the rest of my council."

Drift nodded. "I understand," he said. "But why are you telling me this? I am not Stag's colleague."

"What are you, then?" Esme asked.

"An exile, Your Majesty, who has been caught up in so many things that still don't make sense."

Esme nodded. "Tell me then: what happened to you? Why did you find your way here with Armand?"

"He rescued me from a mercenary group known as Nightingales," Drift said. "I have my life, and Mola hers, because of Armand."

"Armand is a good man. He is also a member of our secret intelligence, an organisation called the Reef's Treasures. My father sent him to join the ranks of the Nightingales months ago. I intend to find out the whole reason for why when I meet with Armand later today." She tucked her blond hair behind her ears. "I say this carefully, tree-dweller. Though you are not an ambassador of Aobia, you are a friend to Stag, with an odd journey that seems to be coincidentally linked to my father's research. For that,

I am prepared to allow you the same knowledge of my plans that I offer Stag. I know he does not agree with me, but there are great motions underway across Q'ara that I believe are about to evolve into a continental war as tumultuous as the one we resolved fifty years ago. Please, tell me what the Nightingales wanted you for."

"I don't know the fullness of it, Your Majesty," Drift began. "But I do know they are under the employ of Therador to find a way to imbue humans with the powers of my people."

"The Luminosity of the Sleepers?" Esme asked, her eyes widening.

Drift nodded. "They wanted me specifically, but I never found out why. They did, however, have access to Luminous objects from the Great Tree, which they used to force the light into me."

"And it worked?" Esme asked, curious.

"The correlation they found was trauma. They tortured me, cut my shoulders and arms and pushed blades under my fingernails." Drift showed off his bandaged hands. "And as a result, they were able to push Luminosity into my veins."

"I am sorry," Esme said, concerned brows furrowed. "And I will ask you no more, for now. You should rest before dinner, tree-dweller. We've a chamber for you to stay in right beside Armand's in the south wing of the palace. Pretch can show you the way."

"I apologise, Your Majesty," Drift replied. "But there is more you should know before I take my leave." His bones ached just saying those words.

Esme stood. "I'll accompany you to the south wing and you can tell me on the way."

Inside the palace, glossy-clean marble tiled the walkways, ornate rugs running the length of the halls. Tapestries were mounted on the walls, a visual history of the line of succession and major events, from the Q'aran settlement to the peace treaty being signed by Esme's grandfather, Filens, ending the Four-Front War. Torches hung on the walls, lit in darker corners of the hallways, yet Drift found that in particular to be of interest. He'd always taken for granted the Luminous lamps used across Aobia, replaceable and wasteless as well as incredibly bright. It hadn't crossed his mind that this kind of technology was not accessible to humankind, but now that he'd noticed the torches, the markers of a bygone time, he couldn't help but feel it was cruel, in a sense, that what Aobia enjoyed could not be shared with the outside world.

"While I was in captivity," he said, "I met the Aobian who caused my exile: a male named Sedulus. He was taking part in some kind of deal with the prince of Therador, Rainol. The prince made it quite clear that Therador's goal was to weaponise Luminosity on a mass scale."

The queen and Pretch exchanged looks of dismay and Drift kept his mouth closed, unsure whether to continue.

"Rainol," Pretch said, as the queen rubbed her temples. "Was it definitely the prince?"

"That was the name he used and the name the Nightingales used as well," Drift said.

Queen Esme nodded. "My name for him is 'Most Vile and Pernicious Rat'—you should use it! Thank you. I fear we must let you rest. We can continue to debrief as we dine later this evening."

Pretch smiled at Drift. "Your rooms are six doors down this hall." He gestured. "Armand is next door and Stag is at the end of the wing."

Drift felt a sigh of relief. He hadn't slept in a real bed since leaving Aobia. Now, more than ever, he was ready for a bath and a nap. "Thank you, Pretch, and, of course, Your Majesty."

Drift wandered the halls, finally coming to his room when the door next to it opened, only for Mola to stride out. She was clean, the cuts on her arms inflicted upon her by the Nightingales covered with bandages. She wore a bright yellow dress and her hair carried a sheen of cleanliness unrivalled by the sun itself.

"Mola!" he exclaimed. "You look…" He let the words trail off. She looked beautiful. But in the back of his mind, a guilty reminder of his beloved led him away from finishing the sentence the way he nearly had. "Refreshed," he finished awkwardly.

"I'm fine, or at least I will be. I'm … so sorry for how I've acted. I couldn't take it all in—" She collapsed in a heap, new tears running swiftly down her cheeks as Drift caught her and held her close.

"I understand," Drift said. "I'm sorry you were caught up in my mess. Ever since the start. None of this should've happened."

"Sometimes, I feel an irrational anger towards you," she murmured. "But it is not your fault that any of this happened. And I cannot let myself believe it." She peered at him. "Who are they, Drift?"

"They are called Nightingales," Drift started. "And they are working for the Theradoran Empire to steal Aobian Luminosity and weaponise it."

Mola said nothing, shuddering.

"This will be the great leveller, Mola. A war to end all wars. To shift the tides of power in these lands in favour of Therador alone. They'll be unstoppable."

"What in the name of restful sleeping is going on here?" Stag snapped, emerging from a room on the other side of the hall.

"We need to talk," Drift said. "Now."

Stag nodded. "Fine," he said. "Let us talk. Perhaps it will spurn me on to find what I can do to stop Esme and her ridiculous plan from unfolding. A war will begin if I do not. It is inevitable. And it comes quicker than we are prepared for. Whether it begins with the enemy or within these walls, I cannot say."

"Within our own walls?" Mola asked, alert. "What is happening?"

"The queen will be exiled tomorrow," Stag whispered, leaning in close to them both. "And with her, the heart of Adira. The one that King Terrens fought so desperately to hold onto after his own father brought us to peace at the end of the war. I no longer care if it is treasonous to speak the truth. If it is the truth, it must be said. Esme will undo her father's life's work in an instant tomorrow, the ramifications of which none of us can yet see."

"Be sensible," Drift warned. "For we are safer here than anywhere else, whether the city remains standing or falls to its knees tomorrow. Do not risk that for the sake of your emotions."

"It's outrageous!" Stag hissed.

"Let me relay to you what has happened to us since we parted in Relond. Perhaps that will help you see the queen's decision from a different perspective."

"Drift is right," Mola said, standing straight. "Let us speak inside." She ushered them through her door just as the lamplight at the end of the hall was extinguished. Drift felt his skin crawl across his back as they closed the door behind themselves, wondering who had been stationed in the hallway to take the lights out and for how long.

ESME

T HE EXILE OF THE queen.

That was the name today would carry forevermore in Esme's mind. If she was to go down in the eyes of her people, however, she would go down looking the best she could. In such a manner, she wore the best dress she could find, a light blue silk dress that flowed freely behind her like the wind, and had her maids bundle her long blond hair into an ornate bun on top of her head. She wasn't convinced—there *had* to be something better she could wear.

She had spent the previous night in conversation with Armand and his reporting officer, Lyria, who had been pleased with Armand's efforts to assimilate into the Nightingales of Therador and rescue Drift.

After that tumultuous meeting, she had dined with Drift, Stag, and Mola, reviewing their story up to their arrival in Adira. She'd left the dining room satisfied and had relayed the information to both Sefil and Pretch thereafter. Pretch had confirmed that he had successfully fed the accusations of her emptying the treasury of its gold to some members of the high council and that they had begun working in the background to verify the allegations. They were going to outlaw her right before her peoples' eyes.

Sefil had tried to convince her otherwise, but she'd held fast, and even this morning, she did not feel herself waver. This had to be the truest course of help for Adira. She would find her father's killer, continue the research out on the reef, and reshape the relationship between Therador and Adira forevermore. She could be the perfect, hidden weapon. At the end of it all, she could only do what she wanted as an outcast, rather than a queen who was stuck in a palace to rule over the people.

She came to a white dress. She selected it from the stand as though without thought, instead working on instinct. How should a queen wish to be dressed on the day she was to be exiled? *No,* she thought.

She'd had a wooden box made up of her most prized possessions, including the family brooch, which was imprinted with the Adiran flag, and the jewel that sat upon her crown: two tidal waves interlocking. One in darkness, to represent the respect they carried for the grandeur of the sea, the other to represent those that lived upon and among it.

That was the city she'd inherited. One that knew, at its core, that it could belong nowhere else in the world. Then there was her father's necklace, gifted to her on her eighteenth nameday, a genteel silver chain with a pearl on the end, carved into a fine teardrop. He had worn it everywhere. He'd told her it had come from his mother, her father before her, and so on, trading places since it had first been in the hands of Esme's oldest ancestor, Brethil the Wise, the first Adiran queen.

Besides her valuables, the box contained only plain clothes. She'd happily traded some of her finer items for garments from her maidens, against which they had not at all protested. She would leave the palace today as simply Esme. Her title gone, her burden even greater, though Sefil did not see it that way.

She caught her coronation gown out of the corner of her eye. Would it be too ironic to wear such a thing? She couldn't help it. Her father had always scolded her for being such an exhibitionist. Obnoxiously loud was simply at the core of who she was, and if the queen she had been was to die today, then she would go down as loudly and intolerably as possible. Not a person in Adira would forget the day Queen Esme was exiled for high treason and she would be all the better for it. Because she could never come back, no matter how much she'd want to.

She changed, declining the services of her maids for this last day. It would all be hers, every last minute of it.

At the door, a harsh knock came and she was quick to respond. "Good morning, brother." She smiled.

Sefil shook his head, despondent. "I cannot believe you won't be talked out of this."

"What a lovely greeting," she murmured, sardonic. "Why are you here?"

"To revise the plan," Sefil said, "and to let you know it is no easy feat, hiding all this gold from the treasury's coffers so quickly. I had men working tirelessly from dusk to dawn and still some remains!"

"Enough to make a mark is all we need, brother." Esme said. "It is all in the place I said?"

"Yes." Sefil looked at her. "Esme, they'll never take you back. Not ever."

"I do not intend for them to." She shrugged, though his words stung.

"Do you really mean that?" Sefil questioned. "I will die a bastard king!"

"But you will be an amazing king, whether you are a bastard or not, my dear," she said, cupping his cheek.

"I do not know." Sefil pulled away from her. "This is all moving so fast, Esme. At least if you can't be talked out of the plan, we could move the timing of it back a little, refine the plan somewhat? Couldn't we just send you where you wish to go and announce that I'll stand in your absence?"

"You will learn quickly, brother," Esme chided, "to never put a timestamp on urgency. The rumblings of war are only the beginning. The eruption, I fear, will be on a scale the like of which we have never seen before."

Sefil scoffed. "And you would have me respond to such an eruption? A boy never trained for the job? A spare?"

"If you will not embrace the blessing of being made monarch, at least recognise that I will be enduring as much, if not worse, from behind the scenes!" Esme scowled. "I will be the one work-ing tirelessly to track down our father's killer and forwarding his research into the creatures in the reef. I will be the one trying to stamp out the embers of the Four-Front War, lest they catch aflame once more! And *I* will be the one advising you on whatever you need whenever I can! What more do you not see? Do *you* wish to be the person in charge of such tasks?" She pressed a firm finger into his chest, pushing him back into the window.

"Do not bully me!" Sefil said, but Esme feared he was scraping from the barrel of his dignity with his lofty aggression. They spent a moment in silence before he spoke again. "Please, just remind me of the plan. Then that will be all. You go your way, I go mine, and you can call on me when next you're ready to speak, the way we agreed."

The way 'they' had agreed, in fact, had been largely Sefil's idea, though Esme had no strict protest against it. The Milliner's Gusts, a primarily civilian tavern out in the Second District, was a place that Terrens had frequented all his life, happily providing public attendance in exchange for what he'd considered to be the best baked lemon haddock and olives he'd ever had the pleasure of eating. He had dined there without so much as a member of the High Guard to escort him, only with his family or friends. Sometimes, he'd even had a meeting there. Anything to be united with his favourite baked fish. The idea, though a little obvious perhaps, had Esme excited and showed her that her brother could, in fact, think as a king might; laterally and scheming when the occasion arose.

She levelled her gaze at her younger brother. When he stared back, however, she found it hard to speak. Her eyes began to sting. Was she going to … *cry?*

"Esme," Sefil said. "Please don't cry." He reached around her in an embrace that only he could give. It was the closest she'd felt to her father's own arms about her whenever she'd needed them. It instilled her with the confidence she needed to let go.

She wiped her eyes. "Neither of us will like this, and the people less so. The outrage in the streets will be damaging. So you will stay inside and let the High Guard deal with the rabble-rousers until it is safe to not do so. Is that clear?"

Sefil nodded. "They'll hate me."

"No." Esme put a finger to his mouth, silencing him. "They'll hate the fact that you're not me. That you're not Father. Once they get past that, they will love you once more as their own."

"And you? How will we do that?"

"It's simple," Esme said, unable to hide that smile of hers. "They'll put me in chains and lead me to the cells. Later, I will be released by Pretch and meet you at The Milliner's Gusts, where I will gather my things and leave by carriage."

Sefil put a hand to his face. "I don't know." He eyed her, walking to the door. "You're sick. Let's just get this over with."

Esme stood on a raised platform before the crowd, a construction that was movable on large wooden wheels but could be locked in place where it was needed. Her sentence had already been explained to the crowds with sufficient witness accounts to evidence her theft of the gold. Now, she would be exiled publicly, right within the palace gates for any bystander to witness. The gates themselves had been opened to the Second District too, as had been her request.

Behind her sat a selection of Adira's lawmakers, military generals, and noblefolk. At the centre sat her brother Sefil with Pretch on his right and General Tomas Aredon, the leader of the Adiran military, on his left. General Tomas also had direct contact with another important public official, High Council Judge Olver Brilms, an old and tired man, sour to the touch but every bit as confident a lawmaker as could come. He had presided over every high council case since the latter years of the Four-Front War, including the signing of the armistice and the War Crime Bill, an addition to the military standards of the nation. Esme had thought he might actually express an emotion today while trying the queen; however, his face was as flat and devoid of emotion as it had been the first time she'd met him as a young child.

The final person, standing directly behind her, was High Priest Soren, who awaited her fate with much more anxiety than anyone else who sat behind her. *And here I am thinking that I'm beloved by my people or that they'll miss me.*

Maybe neither was true. That would hurt. Out of all the emotions she had experienced this week, the lowest one, apart from the relentless grief for her father, was the thought that she was not as popular a monarch as she might have liked. Impostor syndrome. Maybe that was normal to feel so soon after as great a leader as King Terrens.

"For the first time, we try a queen before her own people," Judge Olver called out over the rising angst of the crowd. He stood up, supporting himself with a strong and fine cane, the handle of it shaped like a seahawk's beak. "The accusations that we received two days ago have been treated carefully. For the crime of thieving from the treasury's coffers, Esme, daughter of Terrens, is being tried. For such an act that defies every law and freedom we work and live for in Adira, the Sea Kingdom, the traitor queen must be exiled."

"Bless us, O charge of the Sea," said Soren in response, the entire crowd repeating his words in turn.

Olver coughed before speaking once more. "The conclusion of the High Court is that Queen Esme has committed a crime with the potential to raise and solidify a tyrannical government, one that would not respect the occupation or living of any civilian. The ideal punishment to be issued, in turn, can only be exile."

The sound of the crowd rose like a tidal wave, crashing with hate, anger, and protest. People wept, screamed, and even threw up. Maybe she was more popular a queen than she gave herself credit for, but that didn't matter now. A week as queen had been a week too long and Adira needed to move on. The one fear she had was that the death of a popular monarch like her father would cause substantial reactions from the civilians now. At least her father hadn't been killed by his own. This could divide the people beyond comprehension.

"Esme, daughter of Terrens," Olver proclaimed, walking to her. "You are hereby forced to abdicate the throne that you have held for eight days and seven nights. You will be succeeded, in tradition, by your brother Sefil, son of Terrens. Your punishment for the crime of high treason is decided to be exile. These are your final moments within the walls of Adira. What say you?"

The crowd roared, a commotion that nobody could be heard over. Her heart beat so loudly it competed with the collective cries of disdain. For a moment before she spoke, she wondered whether she could go through with it. This was crazy. She was going to throw her own brother in front of the vicious multitudes, and for what? For what Stag had told her was 'irresponsible'?

She inhaled sharply. No. She could prove what she needed to her wounded nation later. They would never understand how important this was until they lived through it. "For my reproach-able actions, I am sorry. To the people of Adira, my homeland; to my father Terrens, and to my half-brother, with whom I will forever be tarnished in their view." She hung her head. She *was* sorry. She was sorry for what she had to do, for the lie she had forced her loved ones to observe. She was sorry to follow through with it when the people of the nation she loved would never know the truth. She was sorry to hear the crowd roar insults as they realised their new king was actually a bastard. She was sorry that Sefil would be subjected to such hate as a result of her decision.

When she looked up, she saw Stag with Drift and Mola beside him. Stag's disappointment was not lost on her. She could only hope he would forgive her and that her actions would not cause the relationship with Aobia to fray in any way. One day, Stag would learn of her father's research and understand why she'd needed to do this. Until then, she would carry the guilt of disappointing him. "I accept my sentence," she heaved, beginning to cry authentic tears.

The guards stepped up then and put her in chains, binding her hands together and then to her chest. Only the essential people knew the truth: Sefil, Pretch, and the Aobians. Soren stepped away out of sight, as did Olver. She bent her head as they led her down from the platform, cutting a line through the crowds to the cells, an inset building wedged into the side of the palace.

The high council, as was proper, would have turned away now. They did not observe the judgement of the tried with any sense but sound. Turned around entirely, Judge Olver called out his last words. "We mourn what once was."

As they approached the cells, the guards leading her bagged her head, obstructing her vision. With the world dark and the sounds of the roaring crowd dampened, Esme felt a weight fall from her shoulders. She would not mourn. Her time, her *life,* was now.

TARRI

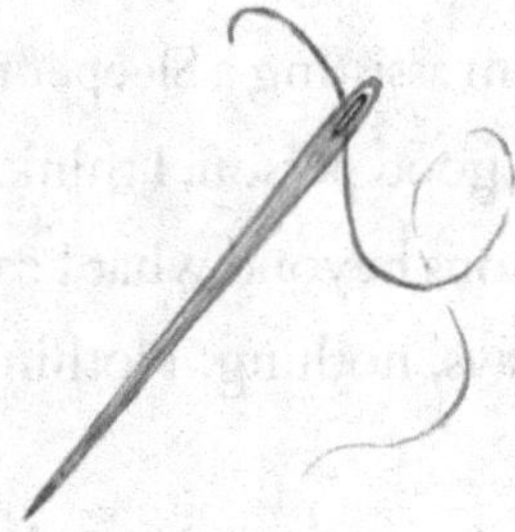

LEAVENING'S BRANCH-HOME WAS ALWAYS at its most peaceful during a long summer afternoon. Light streamed through the cracks in the wood like the fingers of the gods themselves were desperately trying to touch the one who was concealed forevermore in her Orb.

"Drift is still gone," Tarri whispered, tempted to press herself into the Orb with her mother.

She sighed. "War is coming. We thought we had found centuries of peace when the treaties were signed, but we were wrong. If ever a time was to come for you to wake up, *somehow*, it would be now. You could..." She choked back tears. "We need you. I need you, Mama."

The sobs came out messily, an anguish that cut through the room. The sniffles and heaves combined with the sound of tears falling from Tarri's cheeks to the floor like a thud, each one more obvious than the last.

"I must go," she cried, unable to open her eyes, to be disappointed once more. To be heartbroken when she inevitably had to look up at the motionless figure inside the Orb. "I do not know when I will return. I am assisting a Sleeper named Nischia. Maybe you knew her. She's a good person, I think. She wants to see Drift safe. Probably for reasons beyond what I can see before me now."

Nothing. Like always, nothing. Nothing then, nothing now. Nothing.

She stood, finally glancing at the Orb again before looking away as though it stung her eyes to keep her gaze steady. She'd done all she could do here.

She stopped at the door, hesitating. Then she spoke one last time. "I am leaving Aobia. I will travel to Adira to support the new queen. We must keep our allegiance strong. Lady Nischia thinks something is coming, so silent that we will not hear it, but so great that we will not be able to unsee it when it arrives. She thinks it will come from Therador, from the barbarian emperor. If you can hear me, Mother…"

The tears sprung one last time. "Oh, but you can't!"

Tarri could not tell whether it was the water clouding her eyes or a ripple in the outside of the Orb, but as she pulled the door closed with a final glance, she thought she caught Leavening open her eyes.

Not widely, but with purpose.

Her house was dark and quiet when Tarri got back, though the balmy air reminded her that it was summer, and with summer came life at nighttime. The streets, as a result, piped up with the choral resonance of voices, music, and celebration. But here in her home, life could not be found, *would* not be found. She was not supposed to return here; however, her tears had carried her, as though she had no autonomy, until she had landed on her own doorstep.

What was she doing? She'd packed her things in the morning before she'd met with the travelling party in the Mind. All she'd had left to do had been to see Leavening and she'd done that too. Now, she stood mute and dumb, unable to cross the precipice of the door, yet equally unsure of wavering on the other side of it. Was this her life now? Was this a life of going back and forth, like a pendulum swing moving with the wind, always uncertain of what might be around the corner? She was a planner. She was organised. She'd stacked her clothes in the same order in her wardrobes since she'd been a young child. To take that part of herself and, with abandon, embrace the ambiguity of what might come to Aobia sounded crazy.

She belonged home. She *knew* home. Could she, Tarri the dressmaker, really leave the Great Tree and stay sane enough to do good work, to contribute to the safety of her people, to find her beloved?

As the minutes ticked by, she grew tired of herself and the endless questions. It was now or not at all. She could step into the doorway and lock herself inside; or she could return to the Mind, where she would stow her pack and leave the warm embrace of the Great Tree.

She took a deep breath as though she were about to dive into water. She'd only ever heard stories of people diving into water before. Up here, who needed to?

Her breath was cut short as something hard, like metal, was pulled around her neck, the rapid breathing of a chest pressed into her back causing her to scream.

The scream didn't come. Nobody would hear her. She was tucked away at the end of her lane, nestled in branchlets, and now the sound had been squeezed out of her. Air leaking out slowly, like the final drops of water in a teapot clanging down the drain instead of going to the cup to which they belonged.

Surely the Sleepers would notice, somewhere, somehow? Criminals had no place in Aobia. That was why the jails were empty, more or less…

No. She needed to concentrate, because the world was growing wobbly and … darker? Maybe it was the night sky or maybe it was the sinister feeling of her vision being stolen from her along with her lungs' supply of air.

She felt the world spin, but in reality it was her that was spinning, turning to face her attacker.

They had no face. Maybe it was covered up with some kind of sheer cloth or maybe she simply couldn't tell which part of her reality was real or not. They pulled her close, hot breath emanating from a mouth she could not see, drying the tears that were stinging the edges of her eyes, an uncontrollable bodily response to the choking.

The attacker loosened their grip enough for Tarri to suck in air as though through a straw, a primal need overcoming her to drop, to let her legs collapse, to draw in life; but as she did so, she quickly realised she was constricting her airflow even more. "What…" she wheezed. "What do you want … with me?"

No, no, no! she panicked, her mind still alert somehow. *Stay in control. You can stay conscious. Concentrate!*

"What I want," the voice whispered, "is to remove you from the picture. Too much getting in the way, Tarri of the Soul. Your time playing detective is over."

She couldn't tell whether the voice was male or female. All she knew is they didn't intend to release her. They wanted her dead and they weren't afraid to tell her why. Because there would be no risk of their reasons being exposed. She tried to thrash but couldn't move enough to loosen her captor's grip.

"Do not press me," the voice commanded.

Tarri clawed at the metal around her neck, realising it was a link of chains wrapped around twice.

"The more you struggle," the voice threatened, "the more you will feel. That is your choice, not mine."

"Do what you will," Tarri said, teeth gritted in desperation.

The chains about her neck tightened and she choked even more, spittle spilling out from her mouth, her sense of breath fleeting.

"You will do as I say," the voice growled. The last light before the blanket of night withered from her view and Tarri panicked as her lungs were closing completely along with her consciousness. "If you do not," the voice finished grimly, "I will end you."

NISCHIA

I T WAS A JOYLESS, overcast day, defiant clouds clumped together and refusing to let the sun reach through.

Nischia rolled out of her pack, which was covered in dirt. She must've palmed the ground during her night of broken sleep, because her clothes, skin, and bedroll were stained orange.

They were a few hours' ride outside of Relond. Though they'd planned to stop in the city and find accommodations there, Nischia and her squad of Sleepers and scriveners had decided to stop off the side of the road after a storm of summer rain and the kind of hail that hit as hard as stones. The stench of petrichor was thick in the air. Humidity threatened to clump her throat together if she did not find her waterskin soon.

As she stood, her shoulders and knees cracking as if to remind her that someone her age should not lie on bare, hard ground, she glanced around. Everyone was still sound asleep, besides Koln, who was nowhere to be seen, though his pack and bedroll were entirely in disarray.

Nischia sniffled. She had not realised the difference in temperature compared to the Mountain Gate, where the group had rested the night before. There, it was freezing, its altitude so high that snow spanned its cap even at this time of year. She knew she would catch a chill from the sudden changes of the land they travelled. She'd be sure to stop in at an herbologist's once they reached Relond.

She stalked around the dusty clearing where they camped, stumbling over those still sleeping until she reached the horses tethered to the front of their caravans. A larger waterskin, mostly empty, allowed her to fill her own skin and then a bowl for the horses to share.

"Koln?" she called quietly, looking around the caravan. He was not here, either. Well, whatever had drawn him away, it was probably for good reason. She reached for the panflute strung to the front bench of the caravan and covered three holes, so one could ring loud and clear. The tone floated through the breezy air and the camp began to stir.

As the group woke, Nischia called, "Good morning. Stand to attention, please. It is time to begin the roll call." She called the names one by one: Asha, Beisel, Nadine, Iriadne, Len, Aeifi, Kean, Annat.

She didn't call the next name, which belonged to the scrivener who was already standing by her side. Freya. It had been many years since the younger Aobian had served Nischia in the war, but she was glad to have met her acquaintance once more. "My lady." Freya nodded.

The last name after Freya's sent a pulse of anger mixed with disappointment through her.

Tarri. The one who should be managing names she'd already roll-called, while Koln was to manage her and Annat. Nischia had worked so hard to repair the friendship, to rebuild the already decaying foundations of trust. And Tarri hadn't returned. Not after the debriefing in the Mind.

It was done.

"Sister," a voice came from behind her, "the ground does my old back injustice."

Nischia turned to see Annat brushing her hair using the reflection in the caravan window. "Good morning to you, too, sister. Have you seen Koln?"

"I have not," Annat replied. "Not since dinner last night."

"Well, if you see him, let him know I'm looking for him. In the meantime, let us pack our things and be gone. I'd like to be in Relond by this afternoon if possible. Then we may stay for nearly a full day and ride hard to reach Adira the following night."

"Ride hard?" Annat said. "As if my aching bones can take any more!" The thin yet ageless Sleeper, with her long neck and dimpled cheeks, strode off.

"And somehow, Staril picked *her*," Nischia said.

She turned back to the horses as Koln himself strode out from the trees. Bags hung under his eyes, his long hair an unbridled mess knotted on top of his head.

"Where have you been?" Nischia asked. "Lost in the woods?"

Koln laughed oddly. "I-I haven't been anywhere, of course. Now Nischia, have you asked for them to get a move on? And quickly!" He walked away, his gaze going to Annat.

Nischia frowned. She'd never heard Koln chuckle so awkwardly. And why the rush to move on so quickly from her? She watched him for a steady few seconds before dismissing the case entirely. Maybe he'd needed to use the … natural faculties, as it were. She certainly had been sure thus far to do the same well out of sight of anyone when the need had arisen.

The day got on well enough, and Nischia was glad to finally see the hills begin to flatten after the Mountain Gate. Every tree they drove past was dead and blackened. Remnants of fire, though to what extent, she couldn't quite tell. Colour didn't return to the earth for hours more until they could see Relond approaching.

The blackness extended over the next set of hills, a landscape devoid of light and life, and Nischia saw that, as far as her eye could see, the forest had once been flourishing. This was no old burning, as the trees that were somewhere between being charred and in full summer bloom indicated.

When they stopped to eat and water the horses, she seized a *cism* from her pack. This was one of a few that made up all the reserves of Luminosity they had, at least until they could return to the Tree and their Orbs. She would have to be sparing but could use one sphere to draw Luminosity and read the map of hot and cold on the ground. That would give her an indication of when the fire had burnt out.

Carefully, she stepped into the denser bush. She placed her fingers on the *cism*, letting light flow into her. Her fingers came alive with the radiance and she cast the light out like a net into water, seeing it scatter across the ground and the bottoms of dead trees. Before her, the Luminosity revealed a series of imprints, some hotter than others.

Footsteps, in a faintly-illuminated outline, ran along the ground from an opening in the bush that became a small clearing. Flames, too, confusing her sense of where the steps went. But one thing was certain: people had been here. She followed the prints to the clearing. Within it rested the charred remains of a campfire and atop that, the rancid, blackened smell of burned skin mixed with decay. She knew well the smell of burning death. Images of the war flashed across her mind.

She held her hands higher up, seeing handprints all over the surrounding tree trunks, some of which had not burned. The footsteps were wildly overlapping on the ground around the campfire. Perhaps a fight had happened here and someone had perished in the flames.

She looked closely at the ground, noticing the differences in the footprints. Two sets seemed closer to her own foot size. A third was much smaller, the size of a human. As she stepped back out of the clearing, the three footsteps continued all the way back to the road.

"Canopies above," she whispered. Aobians in a quarrel with a human. She clambered back through the trees towards the caravan, unveiling the *cism* from her robe and putting her hand to it. She wouldn't need to draw much, just enough to see—

Koln, Annat, and the other Aobians who were accompanying them looked at her, eyes wide and jaws dropped. They must've followed her off the road.

Her hand projected more light, catching the outline of wheels. The ground was indented beneath the heat maps, which also revealed several frenzied footsteps around them.

There were only two Aobians Nischia knew of in the human lands. She could see the truth as clearly as the heat maps before them. She snuffed them out, releasing the Luminosity she'd drawn back into the *cism*.

The exile, Drift, had found Stag, the ambassador.

And they were both alive.

ESME

THE SOOTHING ROLL OF the sea and the trill of the summer cicadas melded into an ambience of pure peace. Esme sat on the edge of the cliff, feeling long tufts of grass between her fingers like a newborn spring lamb experiencing the world for the first time. Her feet dangled over the edge. She had travelled to a secluded beach that connected with Adira's southernmost shoreline, adjacent to the vast expanse of grasslands known as the Outfields, which spanned the distance between the city of Adira and Relond. A three-hour caravan ride with Lyria, a senior agent of the Reef's Treasures, had gotten them there with a team of scientists occupying an entirely different carriage. Esme never saw them and they never saw her. Only Lyria knew she was there.

Lyria left Esme upon the clifftops as the sun set into a brilliant array of purples and oranges streaking across the sky. She'd spent several more hours stargazing, disinterested in watching the team of biologists below, who were sharing meals by their fire and discussing their work. Besides, she was so far up she could barely make out their conversations. In addition to that, she knew what they were here for. Her father had made that clear in a letter left for her, an aspect of his conveniently edited will, mere weeks before his death.

Eventually, the marine team reassembled, dressed in their leather diving suits. The bodice was designed in one large piece, made to enclose the wearer. The helmet was an ovular piece of steel with a strip of glass welded into it as an eyepiece. A simple air pump filled it with oxygen before the dive and could keep the suit airlocked and breathable for at least a quarter of an hour.

This was technology that Esme was confident nobody else had. After all, what did other nations across Q'ara want with the sea anyway? No others lived by it, besides the clans far north of Ghabbat or the Sethi Outlanders in the West, those who dwelt beyond Lake Sethiliquin and the treacherous mountains behind it.

The divers had emerged from the shining water several times now, their outfits reflecting the strange dotted lights that appeared beneath the surface only after sunset. Every time they returned to the small boat that carried them far enough out, however, they did so empty-handed. Esme crossed her fingers as the divers re-entered the rolling waves, hundreds of metres out from the shoreline. Her only marker for their whereabouts was the shimmering silver mast flag of the tiny wooden boat, kept in place by Lyria herself.

The minutes came and went and the sky was slowly combed over by thin clouds. They obscured the starlight enough to force Esme into squinting in the boat's direction. Finally, she saw the divers climbing back on deck.

She cursed. "Goddess of the Deep!" Nothing. She knew there were all manner of creatures beneath the water and yet this would be another failed attempt to retrieve anything of interest. They wouldn't be able to go out again for a week or more if the early summer wind and rain were to come as forecast.

Eventually, while the divers packed away their things and returned to their camp, the grass behind Esme rustled as footsteps sounded, edging closer to her. Lyria was mopping excess seawater out of her long red hair as she approached to sit beside her. "I'm sorry, Esme," she said. "We still have nothing."

"Three months," Esme said. "My father was no fool, Lyria. He knew the peace was coming to an end. He knew Therador were preparing their worst. We couldn't have seen his death coming, not even from around the corner. But we should've seen this."

Lyria wrapped herself in a cotton towel, drying off her skin and underclothes. Though it was a seasonally warm night, Lyria sat shaking in the balance between wet and dry. "That first specimen," she scowled. "I wish we'd kept it, preserved it somehow."

"And how? In salt, for a feast later on?" Esme replied. "No, you did all you could. We needed more time with it. Now that we have the pool, we can accrue all the specimens we need. We'll need to adjust for salinity, of course, and preserve whatever aspects of their ecosystem that we can, but it's possible.

Perhaps modelling the Aobian filtration methods could help?" She shrugged.

Lyria rested her chin on her knuckles. She had known Esme as a girl. She had followed in her mother's footsteps, becoming a marine scientist at a young age, working tirelessly to understand the science behind the sea that her people so revered, which lit up with alien blue lights every summer's night. "When your father gave me the job, I knew it would not come along as quickly as he would've wanted."

Esme sighed. "Of course. And yet we stand on thin ice, edging ourselves into the centre of a vast frozen lake more and more every day. Therador is preparing to strike. And Aobia… It's as though they wish to distance themselves from us. Any news on the envoy Stag requested?"

Lyria nodded. "They're on their way," she said. "Any day now. Are you sure you do not wish me to tell your brother? I feel as though… well, it's not my place to say. Excuse me."

"You feel as though I have thrown my brother a boulder and asked him to push it up a mountainside with one hand? Don't worry, I'm well aware." Esme peered out at the sea, its array of lights and the stars becoming one massive blanket. "He has more of a handle on his new responsibilities than many give him credit for. I always thought he'd make a better heir than I, even growing up. The difference between his blood and mine should not bear weight in the conversation."

"I agree." The two sat in silence, lost in the dazzling reflection of light coating the soft ocean. Then Lyria spoke once more. "The envoy includes a Sleeper known as Nischia. She played a crucial role in the end of the Four-Front War and she has visited our home previously, or so I am told by Logis. She might know about the filtration systems that clean the River Tomei."

Esme's eyebrows shot up. "Another scientist, then? Surely, she would—"

"Help?" Lyria cut in, before grunting. "Perhaps, but it depends on her protectiveness of the Magisterium and the Sleepers. Any information she can give will assist us, of course, but first we must be diplomatic: we need her to understand why we are researching this Luminosity. Why it is that we seek instances of it for our people."

"Well, for peace, of course," Esme murmured. "What else would they think?"

Lyria exhaled slowly. "I don't know Esme, but just a moment ago you said that you felt Aobia slipping away from us. We are all on tenterhooks and we are contributing to the mistrust. Please, whatever you must do, do not let this alliance go. Keep Sefil close, too."

"Of course," Esme relented. "I will see myself to Therador. Armand will accompany me, of course. He has his uses and he knows how to play with the Nightingales *and* the Priests of Dirt."

"Of course." Lyria stood, donning her towel like a cape. "Well, I'll turn in then. I left a spare bedroll by the caravan. You should be safe to fetch it now without the team seeing you here." She turned around to go but stood still as if concentrating deeply.

"Thank you," Esme said, looking back at her. "How deep do your divers need to go to retrieve the same specimen as the last time?"

Lyria stared, fixated on the Outfields in the distance behind them. Her hand reached for her mouth, covering a gasp.

"Lyria?" Esme said, standing. She brushed off her dress before reaching the other woman. "Lyria, what is—"

Her breath caught. In the distance, the grassy knells that were cast over the land led towards a deep, red horizon, a colour that made no sense this late after sunset. An aura slowly spreading into the sky. Esme's own sky. Adira's sky.

"Torchlight," Lyria whispered, pointing. "It looks like torch-light."

Esme watched the redness expanding. There was nothing in the Outfields. Nothing until Relond, which was at least a day's ride at a blistering pace. "Torchlight? From that far away? If that's torchlight, it's that of hundreds, if not thousands, of people."

As she said the words, she felt her skin crawl. "Goddess of the Deep," she cursed, causing Lyria's ears to prick up. "I knew this was coming. Lyria, it's them."

Her face went cold as Lyria's gaze settled on her, hard as stone, frightened as rabbits before wolves. Then she clarified what she meant, unsure if Lyria knew who she spoke of or not.

"Therador."

STAG

T HEY WERE STANDING WITH the king, exchanging good-nights, when the runner boy came, the royal sigil of the Adiran crown, the roaring waves of the sea climbing over and around it, on his chest. He couldn't have seen more than thirteen summers and was so severely out of breath that Mola had dropped to her knees with a glass of water from the massive dining table held out to his dry lips.

"What is it, boy?" Sefil asked. He'd done well to embrace the role of king these last couple days. Stag had asked him if he had heard from his sister and, of course, the answer had been no. She had leaked word of Sefil's parentage to the public before falsely dying and abandoning them. Stag feared he would feel bitter about it for so long, it might drive away the fondness he'd once had for Terrens' family. Already, he felt the call of the Great Tree louder than ever. A vice grip on his heart.

The boy spoke, puffing between words. "Travellers … Your Majesty. Many of them!"

"Travellers?" Sefil said. "What issue should I take with travellers?"

"No … Your Majesty," the boy wheezed, shaking his head. He began to cough.

Sefil knelt before him, placing a hand on the boy's shoulder. "Take your time," he said. Maybe he *could* be good at this. He might not have had the gumption of his sister, but he was trying. Stag could say no less.

"Your Majesty," the boy panted. "I have run for two days and nights, stopping only for a few hours' rest. My waterskin was empty by the morning of the second day and now I am here."

"You are a High Patrol runner?" Sefil asked, concerned. "Where is your tunic with the sigil of the Goddess?"

The boy sniffed, his bottom lip quivering. Mola took the glass of water from him and he reflexively latched his hands onto his knees. "I … cast it aside, Your Majesty. My life depended on it."

Stag felt his brows furrow. The High Patrol was an extension of the High Guard, but they watched over the other Adiran settlements including Relond, all though way as far as Providence. They hadn't sent a runner in years, at least not with this sense of urgency. "Your Majesty, if I may?"

Sefil eyed him. "Of course."

"The boy needs to catch his breath. Perhaps, we can allow him a minute? It must be important news. and important news is better received complete than indecipherable."

Sefil nodded. "You're right." He turned to the boy and said, "Sit here. Rest. There is food remaining from dinner. You'll not dine with the servants tonight. Take your time and explain everything when you can." He patted the boy's shoulder a final time before moving to the next room. Mola brought him a plate of roasted vegetables, wilted spinach, and a half fillet of haddock on top.

"What do you think?" Drift asked in a whisper.

"I don't know," Stag said. "But it unsettles me. Patrol runners like him are not a common sight. Not these days, anyway."

"It further cements that peace is about to be dismantled before us all, I think," Sefil said, putting his hands on his hips. "Fifty damned years. Could we not do better than that?"

"Your people lack the ability to remain peaceful. Most of the conflict Q'ara has seen has come at the hands and mouths of humans."

"Do not be so sharp, Stag. I did not decide to settle on this rock!" Sefil shot back. Pretch had turned away and Stag knew his words had been insulting. The pride of humans. They would never see it, he was sure. "Are you going to tell me Aobians were never at odds with one another?"

Stag bit his lip. "My lord, Aobia has had a long and complicated history. We are a nomadic people, joined to many other nomadic peoples that share a name and a spectrum of cultures. Division is natural. Forgive me, I did not mean for my words to be so cutting." Out of the corner of his eye, Stag watched Drift turn and look at Mola, head shaking. Stag didn't care. It was his job to give the king the truth and nothing but it, no matter the sting of his words.

Pretch rubbed his chin. "The boy has eaten. Let us find out what news he bears." He whirled around, waltzing back into the dining room. "Boy," Pretch started. "What is your name?"

"Sigurn, my lord," the boy replied.

"Sigurn." Pretch pulled out a seat, sitting beside him. "A good name. Sigurn, I know you have important things to disclose to us. It is time to do so."

Sigurn nodded. He pushed his plate back and turned in his seat to face the remaining adults. "I was running with other news, my lord," Sigurn explained. "But then I saw … so many soldiers, different to ours. They did not wear the stamped leathers of Adira. And they were marching over hill. I passed them by about a day or two ago. They were not far off the road from Relond, my lord."

Sefil stepped forward, alert. "Soldiers? What *were* they wearing, boy, if not our own?"

The child gulped. "Red, Your Majesty. Red and brown leather with some bronze plating. They were … fierce. They did not look like our people."

"Therador," Stag said under his breath. Pretch met his eyes but said nothing, looking back to Sigurn.

"They … raided a…" the boy trailed off, his throat lumpy, his eyes welling. "A small village just outside Relond, where I stayed my first night. They set it ablaze. Pushed through it like it was nothing, like horses stampeding through a broken gate. I could smell death on the air. Skin, hair. Blood. I was so ill from it, my lord, I had to stop as soon as I smelled it no longer. I rested and as soon as I could, I left as quick as I was able. I'm sorry I did not arrive sooner." He wept, like it had all caught up to him. Pretch looked at him with pity as Mola placed an arm around his shoulders.

Sefil stepped closer. "Sigurn, you are an admirable young man. You have made your nation proud." The boy nodded, though his eyes were shut, his chest heaving. "Did anybody hurt you?"

Sigurn shook his head. "But they saw me." He sniffed. "Patrolmen watching the outskirts of the army's camps. They chased me. All I could think to do was to cast aside my tunic, Your Majesty. I'm sorry."

"No," Sefil murmured. "You did well. Be at ease. We shall leave you alone to rest. You may stay here until I can be sure it is safe to hire a driver to take you home."

"Thank you, Your Majesty," Sigurn said, a smile spreading slowly across his young but wretchedly tired face. "If I may, Your Majesty?"

"Yes?" Sefil raised his brows.

"I… I am deeply sorry to hear of the queen, your sister."

For a moment, Sefil said nothing. Mola stepped back and Drift shifted.

"Life never prepares you for what lies around the darkest corners, Sigurn. But you can prepare yourself. I spotted my sister's treason too late. I will be taken to the depths of the sea when

I die, my soul stained with that knowledge forevermore. Your apology, however, comforts me. Thank you, Sigurn. Rest well."

Sefil turned to leave. It was moments like these, Stag had noticed, that Sefil's character came to the fore. Again, Stag was challenged to see the young man as anything *but* a king. He carried with him his father's humility, only it was greater in appearance. But now, with news of Therador marching an army towards Adira, the new king's character would be further tried and tested.

"Wait," Sefil said as they were departing. He turned around one last time. "You mentioned you were running already, didn't you, Sigurn?"

"I was, Your Majesty." The boy nodded, his mouth already filled with food again.

"Why? What was your initial task?"

Sigurn swallowed his mouthful and put down his cutlery. "It was thankfully much less dismal news, Your Majesty. An envoy from Aobia had passed through Relond the day I left. I was to get ahead of them on the High Patrol's order and let you know as quickly as I could, as it was an unusually large group of…" He turned to look at Stag and Drift as though noticing them for the first time.

"It is okay, boy." Drift spoke to him for the first time. "The sight of our kind is not common. This is no secret."

The boy stuttered. "Than-thank you, tree-dweller."

"Boy," Stag began. "Tell me, how many were in the travelling party?"

"No less than ten, my lord," Sigurn replied. "My commanding officer thought it no typical thing, my lord. I do not mean to offend."

"Of course," Stag nodded. "You have done well."

"This was not expected, Stag," the king said.

"Your Majesty," Stag began. "I must be honest. I requested aid from the Magisterium when your sister revealed her suspicions of myself and Flow. But we had *no* involvement with your father's death and I was surprised she assumed we could, given our history. I was only doing what I thought was the right thing."

"Well," Sefil said. "Over your last two visits, odder things have occurred across Adira, Stag. Now, you have an acquaintance with you of whom we know nothing, besides some strange story about a self-inflicted exile. I don't know what to make of it. But when this envoy arrives, I hope you'll have an explanation. Given the circumstances, I'm sure you can see my predicament. Do I continue this professional alliance, this political fraternising? Or do I take my people under my wing and hold fast for the storm that is to come?"

Stag opened his mouth to speak, shocked.

"No," Sefil said, spreading his arms wide. "This is *my* home, Stag. My kingdom now. I will not fail my father's legacy. I will not fail my people. And I am prepared to discard anything, or anyone, that gets in my way."

ESME

Esme quivered as she walked down the long alleyway, a terminating lane crammed between two businesses in the Second District. From her right came the sound of pleasure, a sequence of high and low moaning behind a green timber door. From the opposite direction came the sounds of different pleasures: talking, drinking, and singing. That wall also had a door carved into it, a timber-framed door that was not painted and that she had left ajar in case she needed to get the attention of the patrons within.

As a royal child, she had never had to do something like this. Now, she was well practised in her dealings with the underground. She was both excited and disgusted by it.

Eventually, a thin, middle-aged man appeared at the end of the alleyway, turning in from the quiet street it adjoined. He wore a cloak to conceal his face and keep him warm. But as he got closer, she could make out his features and smell his stale tobacco breath. He had a pencil-thin grey moustache with fluffy, malformed clumps of grey hair around his chin. His sinuses were blocked, probably from too much smoke, judging by his loud breaths.

"Well, if it isn't the old queen, as I live and breathe," the man said in a weaselly voice.

The irony of his words was not lost on Esme. "Live? Yes. Breathe? I'd stop smoking so much if I were you."

"And she's got a mouth on her!" the man exclaimed. "My kind of woman."

"Well, your kind of woman is here for only one reason," Esme replied wryly. "If you need a woman for any other reason, I believe you can head on through that green door once we're done." She gestured over her shoulder in the direction of the rolling waves of moans.

The man grunted, his humour dying as his smile dropped. "Your payment, then. And quickly so you haven't got to put up with me again."

Esme peered at him. He knew she held the box of pure gold bars from the coffers of the treasury. He could force his weight and strength on her and she might be forced to give up the goods and more if he wanted.

She spoke the riddle of his folk. "I stand amongst the fields for longer than any man. He who sweeps across my countryside will weep at the sight of me." She watched the man raise an unsure eyebrow at her words.

"You'll have me killed, won't you?" he whispered.

"No," Esme shook her head. "I might have a mouth on me, but I am not that kind of person. The point is, I *can* have you killed." She watched as the man's back tightened and he stepped backwards.

"You threaten a Scarecrow?" He spat the name. The Scarecrows were a no-good ring of criminals and Esme knew as much. But they got the job done, as they did with all their other nefarious works. The amount of them tried to death by the council was no insubstantial number. The problem of scytheweed addictions in Adira's First District was no small issue. The stuff was more prevalent here than crispwater, which plagued so many parts of the continent. This city had scars, as did any other. But many of them were dirty cuts across its limbs made by dull blades in the form of Scarecrows.

"I was queen once." Esme smirked. "I know your inimitable leaders. They'll listen to me if they are made to." She opened the box of gold bars. "Take it and go. You can see I have provided you with as much as we agreed upon. Any word of this meeting and I'll have your tongue."

The Scarecrow leaned forward, counting the bars. "Two short," he muttered.

"Pardon me?"

He looked at her. "I'm no fool. You're two short."

She looked at the box, double checking his count. So she was. Twelve had been promised and yet there were only ten. She forced on a brave face. "I'll have to pay you the remaining two another time. This is all I have for now."

The man shook his head. "Nah. Pay it now, like we agreed. I leaked the story of your bastard brother and your fake 'theft' to the people with a coordinated team. Doing that without being tried for treason was a risk beyond all rewards. And now, you offer me less than I bargained for. What ground do you have to stand on that you think you can tell a Scarecrow what to do?"

"Fight back," Esme said, trying to stand straighter, taller. "Leak the leaker. Come out of hiding. There are ways I could make your life hell, Scarecrow."

The man stood motionless. Truly, Esme began to wonder whether he would speak again or simply drop on the spot. Eventually, he glanced away, scowling. "Fine. Two less. In one week, we meet again. Here, same time. Don't be late." He seized the box of gold, trudging off.

As he neared the end of the lane, Esme remembered something. "Wait! Wait!" She ran after him. He stopped, his eyebrows nearly touching his hairline.

"Shut. *Up!*" he hissed. "What do you think you're trying to do? Have us found out?"

"I forgot something," Esme said. "Nightingales."

The man paused. "What did you say?"

"Nightingales," she puffed. "You know who I'm talking about. Do they mix with ... your lot?"

The man staggered back, growing suddenly afraid. "I don't know anything about those bastards!"

He took off at a pace quicker than street vermin, disappearing from her sight. She would need to consult with Armand. That Scarecrow knew something of the Nightingales of Therador. And it was something disturbing enough to send him reeling away from her at their mention.

Esme took a seat in the back of The Milliner's Gusts, her father's favourite place to sit amongst the people of Adira and drink. She knew that people might recognise her, so she'd worn a green cloak with the clothes of a plain lady: a gingham dress in red and beige with a loop around her waist. She'd let her hair down uncombed so that it might change the way her face appeared to all these people, who had seen her ever since she'd been a young girl that had to face the crowds regularly enough.

The food was hot, and good. She brought a fork of steaming chicken to her lips, melted cheese strung all around it. The chicken was dressed with cheese, helpings of herbs, and fresh slices of tomato. On the side of her plate was a small bowl filled with olive oil and black vinegar, accompanied by flatbread.

She tucked in and was eating when her guest took his seat across from her, his plate of food dropping to the table with a clang. Two glasses of white, petillant wine were set down with it, and Esme reached for one. "Thank you, brother," she said between mouthfuls.

"And to think all those hours of etiquette classes were not wasted on you as a child." Sefil smirked. He had agreed to meet her here at exactly three hours to midnight after she had disclosed to him that she would be making a payment to the Scarecrow who had successfully started the division in the Adiran people prior to her beheading. It was important to meet, and regularly at that, to discuss the state of the city, offer any advice she could give to her young brother, and relay the summaries of her work.

"To the first of many hot meals together in the back of an alleyway tavern," she said with a wide smile, holding up her glass. Sefil clinked his against it with a shake of the head.

"Ever the loudmouth, dear sister," he said. "I swear you'll be found out through nobody's fault but your own if you carry on as such."

"Enough about me, though I admit I enjoy hearing you praise me," Esme said. "What has changed?"

"The division, as you know, is no small thing," Sefil said. "It scares me, Esme. I had no idea our people were capable of such infighting."

"Then remember the most important advice I've given you," Esme said. "All people are capable of worse things than you could imagine. Don't let the fact that they are our own change your perspective on that. *That's* how you end up with a knife in your back. And Goddess of the Deep, don't I know how many people would like to have their hand on that handle."

Sefil seemed to shake as though her words had set his skin to crawling. "How comforting. I don't know if you recall, but this division was your doing."

Esme looked down at her plate. "I needed a distraction, Sefil. I didn't want people asking questions about my exile. There are still more than enough about Father's death."

Sefil snorted. "You acknowledge that, yet you haven't realised the greatest flaw in your plan. At some point, people will put what they have together, like many pieces from different puzzles that somehow make up a larger picture. They aren't stupid, sister."

"What do you mean?" Esme asked, affronted by the comment.

Sefil swilled his glass. "Esme, don't you think they'll find ways to blame Father's death and your exile on me? It would make sense. The jealous bastard shredding apart the monarchy from within. Why worry about Therador and pressures from the East when they have a plausible explanation before them? It would appear obvious that I'd only want a slice of the proverbial cake."

"I… I hadn't considered that," Esme said. He was right, of course. Her flair for the dramatic had once again landed her in deeper trouble than she would've liked. And now, her family would be threatened by it as a result.

Sefil sniffed. "It's okay, Esme. All of that is my responsibility now. You focus on what you need to do."

"Sefil, I'm *so sorry*. I'm still here and you know that. I'll help you however I can." She reached for his hand, but he offered nothing in return.

"Perhaps. Until you take leave of us and go gallivanting off on some secret quest. Sometimes, Esme, I can't understand when you decided to forego adulthood completely. It's like you've taken your childhood playtime and immortalised it. I can't tell if it sickens me or if it's brilliant."

What could she say to that? Just a few hours after she had last spoken with her brother, she could see their relationship fraying. Sefil sat with his shoulders back, eating more politely than her. He was a better leader already than she ever had been. Somehow, he had grown in wisdom, resoluteness, and surety, while she had embraced the very opposite. "I am going into the bear's cave, Sefil. I will not see Father's legacy dashed like a skull against the rocks. Therador is not mighty. We are. And I will do whatever it takes to bring the truth home with me."

Sefil looked away again, his eyes deep and lachrymose. Why could he not hold her gaze?

"Esme..." he began. "What you're doing, it's crazy. Crazy! This is the stuff of stories, not real life. And yet, you're obsessive to such a degree... How could any of us talk you out of your set mind? None of us could best your stubbornness, not even Mother." He sighed. "I cannot endorse your plans."

Esme laughed. "Pardon? What does that mean?"

Sefil leant across the table, crossing his hands. "If that is the path you wish to take, sister, you will walk it alone."

Esme tensed her shoulders in defence. "How dare y—"

"No." Sefil shook his head, gesturing for her to quieten. "I will not let the public glimpse us quarrelling, Esme. What must be done will be done. You go your way and I'll go mine. Be an exile, and let me manage my kingdom. If you ever find what you set out for, maybe then we can speak."

"You are casting me out of my own home?" Esme scoffed. "My 'exile' was intended to allow me to come and go as needed, meet with the Reef's Treasures and find Father's killer. It was not planned so meticulously for it to become something to which I am beholden!"

"If you cannot bring me the truth or acknowledge the stupidity that surrounds your preposterous journeying, then you will not return to Adira. Embrace your righteous exile, Esme, and let me rule in peace. Give me the chance I need to get my people on my side, to bring them together again. We cannot go on rioting. A home divided is no home at all, Esme. I must reunite us, and that requires you to either forfeit this childishness or leave. It is your decision."

Suddenly, the room shook, a deep rumble running through it. People all over the tavern stood up from their tables, unsure of what was happening. Some dropped glasses, others clung to the bar for stability. The rumbling continued, growing louder. "What was that?" Sefil asked, concern crossing his face. Then the screaming began outside, voices wailing hopelessly.

Esme leapt out of her seat, snatching Sefil's hand as they ran to the door and burst out into the street.

People were running in one direction, like a stampede of bulls, towards the walls of the next district. "What's going on?" she cried as members of the High Guard, in their steel-plated suits, scampered past her and Sefil at the pace of frightened rabbits, tearing through the crowd towards the mighty gates that closed the Second District off from the first.

"Stay here," Sefil said. "Stay inside!"

"No!" Esme grabbed his arm, pulling. "We will not break apart from each other, not now!" She whirled around, tugging on a nearby woman running past them, a stricken look in her eyes. "What is happening?" she cried.

"The enemy!" the woman said, her voice shaky. "They have arrived. The Outfields are filled with them, all coming under the light of the moon. We are under siege!" She shook herself free from Esme's grasp and Esme watched her rejoin the crowd.

Hands reached for Esme from behind, taking her own and holding them behind her back. She twisted but could not see her captor. She looked at Sefil, eyes wide, but he did not show the same degree of concern. "Brother?"

"Take her!" commanded Sefil.

She stared in horror at him. "Sefil, no! What are you doing?"

"It is only I, my lady," came a rich voice. They turned her to face them. Armand, the same member of the Reef's Treasures that had recently returned from a stint as a double agent in the Nightingales. "Armand, please let me stay. Let me—"

"Esme, go!" Sefil breathed, pushing on her.

All around them, above their world, the sky lit on fire, tongues of flame raining down on them.

Therador had, indeed, arrived.

TARRI

“T HE SIEGE IS PREPARED. The first strike should happen
sometime tonight.”

“Everything is as planned. The greatest risk is if the envoy
appears in time. They have significant power amongst them.
Several *cism* and two Sleepers. That is enough for the Theradoran
force to collapse, especially without sufficient knowledge of how
Luminosity can be channelled.”

This was what Tarri heard when she first came to. It was dark
and the air felt thinner, like she was drawing it through a straw.
She could not count the number of times she moved to and
from consciousness. The voices were also muffled, as though they
spoke through layers of cloth.

That was because they did. As she sucked in a breath, she realised her head was contained in a roughshod black bag. Her arms
were restrained about her waist and she was lying on something

neither hard nor soft, though she felt something poking into her back, causing her to shuffle around.

"Of course, Superior," came the first voice. "And what of this one?"

A pause before the second voice cut back in. "I do not yet know. My instincts tell me to discard her once we have asked all we can, but the siege demands our attention for now." She knew that voice.

Koln? The name of the Senior Sleeper bounced around like an unceasing chorus. How could *he* be behind this? What did he know of Tarri's past or her family? What did he know of *Drift*?

Then it struck her. He probably knew everything. Tarri lacked the ability to control how she shielded her mind.

The greatest risk is if the envoy appears in time. Her breath caught. That was what he'd said a moment ago, wasn't it? He had sent Nischia and the other Aobians to their death. Adira was to be besieged. Who would be at the helm of the opposition's forces? Not her people, surely.

"I will be back later to address the young one," Koln's voice returned, further away now. "Let her sleep. Remove the bag too. What difference does it make what she can see if she will never see beyond these walls again?"

Tarri shivered.

"Of course, Superior. Where can I find you if the need arises?"

"The Emperor's Temple. Jurin himself will not ride against the walls of Adira tonight. He sends his son. In the meantime, he and I have much to discuss. I need to undo this breach of peace. It was never the plan for things to happen so quickly. A siege I fear will do greater damage than we think."

"And the Magisterium?"

What did the Magisterium have to do with any of this?

"Make sure Staril knows to destroy the records. The range is fifty-four to thirty-eight years ago. Be very specific about that. If we do not remove them, I fear I will not be able to revive the armistice. Time is essential. We must adapt quicker than ever before."

"Of course."

Tarri let her neck and shoulders ease as the sounds of diverging footsteps moved about, one set closer to her and one far enough away that they disappeared. She began to panic as the rough bag was yanked upwards, loosening off her neck.

She shut her eyes, trying to appear asleep, trying to slow her heartbeat. Exhale through the nose. Pretend to survive.

"You take us for fools," the male murmured. "Do not pretend. Your shielding is not as constant as you may think."

His heavy hands grabbed her collar, pulling her to her feet from the bed she lay on.

"Please!" she sputtered, her words half-choked, a consequence of staying silent for so long.

"You were listening!" the faceless one spat. "What did you hear?" He shoved her back down onto the bed, which was a tangled mess of branches and twigs that grew out of the floor and walls.

She was inside a room within a burrow cut out directly from the Great Tree. A branch-home, like her mother's.

"Where have you brought me?" she asked, sitting up.

The faceless remained with his back to her. "Somewhere you will never be found. The branch-homes are numerous and there are many that have not contained people for centuries. You are lost to the tree. At least your life will end in an inspiring place. Take from that what you will." He turned around so she could see him and she sucked in a breath. It was not just his face that was missing. His arms, hands, and more beneath his clothing were void, as though each were a hole cut out from physical space entirely. If she focused on his visage for too long, she felt lost, as though his hollowness stole all her knowledge of the world, of herself.

"Who are you?" she breathed.

The faceless male turned away. "Those who are filled with too much light eventually expire into darkness. I am nothing, though I was not always that. But to say I am something… Well, all those who exist as I do would struggle to agree with such a statement."

He stayed still, heavy breaths causing his back to rise and fall. He was dressed, she noticed, in common Aobian clothes. Nothing on him signified that he was a part of the Magisterium: no steel, no emblem of the sun with an eye at its centre stamped on his garb, no bright colours. Just the drab, common brown and green mantle of an Aobian male. He represented the kind of homogenous dress Tarri had always sought to destroy.

Yet, for the basic quality of his clothing, the male seemed to embody something more transcendental than any other person she'd come across in Aobia before. The void of his form reminded her of the night sky and she wondered whether this male was somehow tethered to both the earth and another place altogether. Perhaps, he'd once been a Sleeper who had endured the same thing that threatened to steal Tarri's mother from her. A nova event.

"You said you … expired?" Tarri asked, quiet as the breeze that whistled past the branch-home.

"Enough." He tugged his hood over his head.

"Please," she said. "Just tell me what you want."

"What I want?" The faceless one chuckled. "I serve the Magisterium. I do as I am instructed. What more do I have in this form?" He picked up the black bag, gripping a large tuft of Tarri's hair in his other hand and stuffing it over her head. She tried to protest but gave in, going limp. If she wanted any chance of escape, she would need to be careful.

There were threads of his story she could pull on now, like those she'd learned to make into beautiful clothes. She was a tailor, after all, and she knew how to repair torn fabric. The fabric of this being's soul, it seemed, was damaged. She knew he had some connection to the Magisterium and that he had a command to be here. If she took it slow and spoke carefully, maybe she could convince him to let her go or use what he'd shared with her against him.

She studied him. Was he a Sleeper? He'd seemed to read her mind before when she'd first been 'woken'. Now, he walked off without as much as a grunt, leaving her alone. Panic. Nerves. Anxiety. When her heart had taken over her mind before, he'd read her like an open book. Maybe that was the key to shielding.

Memories came flooding back, the wrong kind of memories from her childhood. What happened to her mother…

No. She steeled herself against her evolving thoughts. She felt the tear of old unhealed heartbreak, a remembered pain of her mother's final moments, alive in the same sense as everyone else.

Her captor was the kind of person her mother had nearly become before she'd locked herself in her Orb forever. A broken Sleeper who'd taken in too much Luminosity.

DRIFT

T HE CALL TO ACTION of the Adiran people was unlike anything Drift could have imagined, having only read the histories of the Four-Front War, all of which were dry and studious. This, on the other hand, was real life.

Women clutching babies, lost children running through the streets; Drift and Stag could see it from atop the palace balustrade, an outcropping beneath which was mounted a great clock. It was so high up that he could see as far as the gates between the Second and First District. The panicking people moved like ants. He felt comfortable this high above the city; it reminded him of home.

The military had risen to attention. People in full leather cuirasses, helmets, and pads moved in preconfigured units through the streets, carrying blazing torches to light their way. The high guards in their steel plates were split up to lead each group. Drift could see, even from this far away, the nervous energy of the armed forces below as they scrambled around, uncertain of the directions they moved, as fire-lit arrows flew over the walls from the outside of the city. These people might be part of the military, but they did not fight regularly. There had been peace for fifty years—long enough that none of these men or women would have had any experience in a real battle.

The same nerves troubled him and he felt sick as he looked past Adira towards the Outfields that met the bottom of the Theradoran Ranges, where the enemy had settled. This beautiful city could be forever changed before dawn.

"This city hasn't been touched in fifty years," Stag said. "The separation between the two districts might make it more defensible, but Therador has the advantage of surprise. We should've known about this, Drift. These people are broken enough as it is. They have put their forces together quickly enough."

He turned to Drift. "It would be ironic, wouldn't it? To die in a place we don't belong."

Drift snorted. "You would stay if given the chance. You're practically part of the family."

Stag shook his head. "No. Esme changed that. I've realised where my duty lies." He sounded hurt.

"You don't have to hide your pain, Stag. Have you thought how much easier things would be if you could say what you wanted?"

Stag chuckled. "I don't need you to preach to me." He sighed. "We may die tonight, you and I. An exile and an ambassador. Who will remember us when we are gone?"

Maybe he was right. Drift had no legacy. He had no home, no place to belong. He was only able to watch as the city braced for invasion. That wasn't good enough. That made his stomach turn. "No, Stag," he said. "That is not the point. We are here now and we owe what we can give to these people. Nothing that has come or is yet to come matters."

"So even if you could, you would change nothing?" Stag shot back. "Unwind the threads of time, bring back the king? Live the way we have for fifty years?"

"An impossible request," Drift replied. "That forces you to live with impossible standards."

Stag shrugged. "Some have told me that I'm an impossible person. Maybe I work within more logical boundaries than you think."

Below, the din of the crowd rose to an unsettling cacophony. The sky screamed with flames far in the distance, the number of arrows increasing exponentially, like a swarm of locusts. This was it. This was the moment that Adira decided to fight with everything it had.

"Let us go," Stag said, glancing at him.

"Together," said Drift. It wasn't intended as a question and a smile tugged at the corners of Stag's mouth.

"I thought it might be good," he said, glancing away from Drift, "to be alone. To do my work without interruption. Flow always made life harder, less focused. But … after all is said and done, I'm glad you were by my side."

Drift smirked. "Is that the most sentimental you've ever been?"

"Of course," Stag said, resuming his usually formal tone. "And don't count on it happening again."

Children wailed in the streets. Soldiers scooped up those who had lost their mother's grip, racing through the cobblestone streets, each stone recording their footprints in the emerging chaos. The First District still had not fallen as Drift looked up to see the sky light up around him, a new volley of flaming arrows raining down on the city. He pushed through the crowds, searching for anyone he knew. Stag and he had left the palace quickly, breaking apart. Mola was nowhere to be found and neither were the king or his advisors.

Drift became suddenly aware that he was not one of these people. He was sticking out like a long blade of grass in a field of cut ones. He moved against the wave of panicking civilians, his heartbeat thudding in his head. The world around him had him in its clutches and he could do nothing but push through the tide.

Drift ended up at the gates that marked the border between districts. Before him were squads of soldiers, some in common leather while others were members of the High Guard with their steel armour, the sigil of the Adiran Sea branded and painted onto their chest pieces. Drift latched onto one squadron led by an unhelmed High Guard officer, who was coordinating the opening of the gates. "Officer!" he called, running to the team, who quickly disbanded to complete their tasks, leaving him alone with the man.

"Tree-dweller," the officer said, inclining his head.

"My name is Drift," he replied, searching the officer's face. "I am here to help."

"Of course," the officer said, extending an arm. "My name is Mirthorn." Drift took his forearm.

"Officer Mirthorn, I am part of the ambassador's party to Adira."

Mirthorn nodded. "I am indebted, tree-dweller. How do you feel about sticking with me? I fear I will see the worst of this night, but perhaps, with another at my back, we can escape unscathed, for the most part."

Drift inhaled deeply. If he was with this man, he stood as best a chance as ever of staying alive. "Okay."

"Once my men open these gates," Mirthorn said, "a flood will come. Bodies, maybe alive, maybe dead, or hurt. But we remain here and fight." He grimaced. "Have you ever used a sword or shield?"

Drift shook his head. Mirthorn led him through a door cut into the stone wall. Inside was a small armoury. "Take these," he said, handing Drift a scabbard with a belt attached and a tall shield. "Come with me," he said, running to the gates. "These two levers open the gate. Turning them will take all the manpower we have." Several soldiers were waiting for Mirthorn, their hands gripping a different handle on the enormous wooden levers that kept the gates closed. "Go to the opposite side and pull when I say. Go!"

On Mirthorn's call, the group of six men pulled on both levers' handles, cranking the gates to the First District open.

The stench of charcoal, timber, and something that smelt like cooked meat filled his nose. Fire spread from falling, flaming arrows. Near the gate, people ran with their garments lit up like a tavern hearth, their screams ringing in his ears.

In the distance, the First District had fallen, its gates entirely broken open.

"Tree-dweller!" one of Mirthorn's men called. "You must come. There is no time!"

Drift reached out and seized the soldier's wrist, who pulled him through the gate before a sword struck out of nowhere, splitting the soldier's face in two and sending his helmet flying off. Bits of blood and brain matter splattered into Drift's eyes.

The giant, hairy-armed man who had killed the Adiran soldier charged at him, sword swinging with complete abandon. Drift fell back into the crowd behind him, losing his footing. He tried to get up, but the crowd's force pushed back on him, sending him back towards the swipe of the sword, missing it by an inch. He managed to stagger back to his feet. He instinctively put his oaken shield up before his face and swung his sword arm aimlessly.

The vacuum-like twist of the crowd pushed Drift and his opponent into each other. Drift felt his sword press into the Theradoran. It came away bloody from their chest and leather cuirass. Drift had gotten lucky.

He bent over, his body taking over as he retched, bile rising up his throat, stinging, causing his eyes to water. He watched as the sickly-green sludge splashed the legs of whoever was running past and they slipped in it. The Theradoran man's body was sucked back into the crowd, ready for trampling, as Mirthorn appeared behind him.

"I told you," he said, anger flashing across his red face, the flames that threatened to engulf the First District dancing in his pupils. "Never. Leave. My side! Stow your blade and link arms with me. Shields to the front. Now!"

Drift did as he was asked, moving through the people, shields out in front of himself and Mirthorn. They were joined on their free arms. He watched as a child was cleaved carelessly through the neck, a single swoop of a blade that did not seem to notice they were there. The boy's head rolled off his shoulders, his body falling victim to the bloody stampede.

There were no rules here. They had always been taught in their history lessons that war had rules. Maybe the greater conflict did and proceeded as such; but here, in the confines of this sacking, the rules no longer applied. Aggression, and the desire to see the opposition fall were all that carried the Theradorans, who were fighting like animals. High guards were down everywhere, dead, unconscious, or being escorted through the gates by friends and comrades, seeking some succour that might never come, to tend to their wounds. Most of the common people who had gotten caught up in the fighting were dead and those that were left were fleeing as quickly as the crowd could carry them. Drift could not see many of them surviving the night, not out here, not like this.

From above, guards fired crossbows, launching steel-tipped arrows down on their enemies from the high baileys that punctuated the balustrades that connected the gates of both districts. Mirthorn lifted his shield to cover his head every so often, as though it was a normal action for him to take. As though the whistle of dropping arrows was a sound he'd heard throughout each living day. Drift followed his lead, especially once he noticed the deaths of the High Guard's own at the hands of their own crossbows was unavoidable. Everything that was happening here was sheer luck and Drift felt cast aside as much as any other man fighting for the cause, an indeterminable variable in a mess of possible outcomes.

His gazed fixed firmly on the torn-open gates of the First District, which he and Mirthorn were moving towards slowly, fighting against the current. Then, horror filled his eyes as he saw what he had wished he would never have to see again.

"Mirthorn, there! Look at them!" A unit of a hundred or so Theradoran men and women moved with swiftness through the gates, their hands emblazoned with auras of light, their hair *glowing*. The Nightingales, Rainol… They were further along in their advancements than Drift had presumed. They had weaponised Luminosity *successfully*.

An army of human Sleepers.

Suddenly, the unit's hands came together, growing in brightness until the light became so concentrated, white and hot, that it blinded them all. The crowd seemed to stop, confused, lost. Drift squinted from behind his shield to check that he and Mirthorn were still moving in the right direction, but even that was hard to tell. The light was growing like the cloud of smoke after the forest fire he had run from that night after the Mountain Gate.

When it consumed even him, he simply had to stop. He shrunk down onto the balls of his feet, bringing Mirthorn with him, and held his shield close.

They were done. They could not see, they could not act. The injustice of it nearly made him weep. In a battle where one side could not fight at all, what else was there but to give up?

TARRI

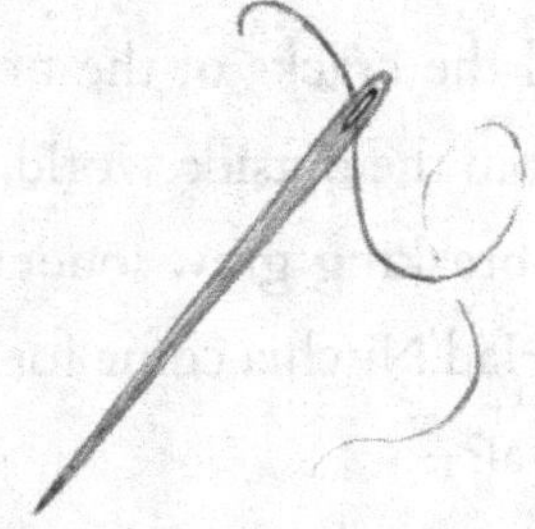

THE SOUND OF SPLITTING timber awoke Tarri from her short rest. It felt like a knife in her Aobian heart.

She could barely make out through the sack over her head her faceless captor, who lay on the floor, motionless as though asleep. "Wake up," she whispered, leaning over him. "Somebody is here!"

The faceless sprang up as though stirred from a trance. "Canopies above," he cursed. "My head." He got to his feet as the sound of tearing wood returned once more. "What is that noise?"

Tarri shrugged madly. "I don't know!"

He snatched the bag off her head and turned toward the noise, which came from the connecting room where he had been with Koln. "Nobody should know we are here," he said in genuine disbelief.

"Clearly!" Tarri snapped. If the faceless found a way to read her mind, it could ruin her chance of escape. She couldn't control her shielding, but she could control how she appeared. Why read deeper into her thoughts if what she showed on the outside was real fear?

Light began to fill the cracks of the branch-home's knotted wood, bleeding in from the outside world. Luminosity, perhaps. The sound of wood breaking grew louder, every blow causing the Tree to splinter. Had Nischia come for her? Had the Sleepers realised Koln's betrayal?

Nischia would be gone by now, maybe in Adira already. Someone else was using Luminosity and the wood was so fragile now that an axehead could be seen poking through it with every strike.

The faceless one cried out, running to where the branch-home was succumbing to the axe. The Luminosity seemed to cause the wood to creak and contract, expand and spread apart. Twigs and branches were all intersecting, widening their gaps enough for the axe to cleave them. Tarri was breathtaken at the sight.

"Someone is wielding Light," the faceless one said, running back to Tarri.

"Light?" Tarri asked. "Don't you mean Luminosity?"

"Luminosity is a gift that is only wielded for good. Light is what it becomes when you take that gift and channel it into energy. Make it hot enough, concentrate it, and it will burn. Whichever fool is channelling it, I pray they do not take it to the point of flames, for fire is the antithesis of our home." He grabbed her with a gloved hand, wrapping it around her wrist. "We must go now! The Branch can open at any end of this room with the right permissions. If you wish to survive any longer, you must do as I say!"

Tarri nodded. *Fire, the antithesis of our home,* Tarri thought, her mind racing. She'd recited that mantra her whole life. Could the Aobians on the outside of the branch-home be planning to set it ablaze?

The wood erupted completely, first revealing a set of hands clasped around a *cism*. Beside that set of the hands was another, hatcheting through the weakening limbs that knotted together to enclose the entire chamber. No, they were not burning it down. The Light revealed enough for them to get through, the heat softening the timber enough to cut it with ease.

She turned to see the faceless one parting the branch-home's limbs on another wall, speaking softly directly to the wood. Black, fluid-like smoke leaked from his hands, filling the cracks in the wall and expanding them slowly. "There's no … time," he said between haggard breaths. Whatever he was doing was quickly exhausting him. The smoke coming from his hand became like a blanket of black mist, hanging about his body like a vaporous cloud.

The final swing of the hatchet on the other side of the room cut out the remainder of the wood, allowing the two offenders to stride in. It was Flow, accompanied by … a Sleeper?

"Flow!" Tarri cried, lurching away from the faceless one. He had come here to save her. For all his flaws, something in him had compelled him to find her.

He caught her, the weight of her body sending him reeling. "How did you find me?" she asked. Then she took in the other person beside him. The female was tall, taller than she, with glowing, silver hair. She was older, but not much older than either Tarri or Flow. "I am Tiun," she said, extending a hand.

Flow let go of Tarri, seeing the faceless one at the other wall. "A remnant core," Flow breathed.

"You know what that is?" Tarri said, indicating the faceless one.

"A Sleeper that has survived a nova event. Burned out like a dead star," Tiun said. "We cannot face this creature. Whatever you do, Miss Tarri, do not let go of my hand."

The *cism* Tiun held in her other hand exploded with light, flowing out of the globe like a wave. Raw, unbound Luminosity flashed across the faceless one, who writhed in pain, screaming with a sound like hundreds of voices dying all at once.

"I've got her!" Flow cried, grabbing Tarri's other hand. "Do what you must, Tiun!"

The Sleeper gripped the *cism* with her second hand. The *cism* continued to shoot light forth like a beam. It became loud, a crackling sound coming from it, which increased in volume as the light was concentrated even more into a thinner, denser streak.

The faceless one resembled less of an Aobian figure now and more of a crumpling assembly of darkness. The outline that defined him was now blurred. Even his clothes were abandoned as the creature thrashed about. Smoke started to form, slowly replacing the faceless one's figure entirely, and the *cism* went dark, its final light exiting its centre.

Silence penetrated the hollowed-out branch-home as Tiun knelt, bowing a head in the direction of the formless smoke, which was quickly dissipating, looking more like steam now. "May the earth reclaim your broken power. May your shine be born again."

After a moment, Tiun nodded and turned, gesturing for them to leave. "Let's go."

"What happened to him?" was all Tarri could manage in reply.

"He was a Remnant Core," Tiun said. "I helped him to finally let go. Do you know, Miss Tarri, what happens when a star forms?"

Tarri shook her head.

"A supernova." Tiun's eyes widened, a startling silver. "An explosion unlike anything you could imagine. The kind of death that takes millions of years.

"When a Sleeper succumbs to the forces of their Orb, to the temptation of Luminosity, they are slowly replaced with light itself. Eventually, they burn out. They become an absence of light. A contortion of the very gift the Tree has given them. That is what a Remnant Core is. This one was just stuck between forms. Now, his soul is where it belongs."

Tarri quickly quelled thoughts of her mother. It was not the time for that, not now. Her duty now was to leave the Tree and find Nischia. Koln had betrayed them and Flow… She didn't know what to think about Flow or this new Sleeper, Tiun. Her mind raced.

"We will take you to Adira, Tarri," Flow whispered. "I see the greater picture now. I'm sorry I let you down time and time again."

Tarri looked up at him. Her eyes stung. "What is it you see?"

Flow looked over to Tiun. "Tiun showed me the impact of my actions, working with Sedulus and trying to steal knowledge of Luminosity. The Magisterium has sold us out. They have been at the heart of this blackened deal with Therador all along. Staril, Koln, and many of the other Senior Sleepers… They are the ones who have handed Luminosity to the enemy."

Tarri tried to swallow but the lump in her throat wouldn't budge. "The Magisterium… Nischia!"

"No," Tiun interjected. "Not Nischia. She won't know a thing about this, as I did not. Now, it is up to us to deliver the truth to her at any cost. Forget the risk of breaking the law or exile. Let us leave this place. We were always a nomadic people before anyway."

Tarri let the words settle. This was real. This is what they had to do: defect before they were found out. She clenched her jaw and closed her eyes, breathing deep. *We are all Aobia has, though Aobia itself does not know it.*

"Okay," she said. "We must go, my lady."

"Do not address me as such," Tiun said. "I am your sister in this Great Tree, nothing more. That, I fear, is where we have gotten all of this wrong."

DRIFT

THE LUMINOUS THERADORAN fighters were such a spectacle that the frontlines of the siege froze, both enemy and friend alike.

"Goddess below," breathed Mirthorn. Sweat ran down his face from the heat of the fire, from the weight of armour and weapons. Theradoran soldiers were stepping to the side, allowing civilians a window of time in which they could flee.

Mirthorn turned to Drift. "Tree-dweller, are these your people?"

Drift shook his head. "Do they look like my people? They are Theradorans."

"And yet they glow." Mirthorn hooked a steel-gloved hand under Drift's arm, hauling him back. "Come with me," he said through gritted teeth. "I'll believe you when I see one with my own eyes."

"Where are we going?" Drift asked.

"To the gate," Mirthorn replied. "There are walkways within the walls. They connect up to a tunnel system that we can take to the First District. While we move, you will explain who these people are. If Therador breaches the Second District, the city will be overrun."

Mirthorn let Drift put his sword back into the scabbard at his hip before gripping his arm and walking through the crowd. They walked to the far wall and entered a small doorway cut into the stone. Drift struggled to keep from hitting his head as they entered into a stone hallway that seemed to go on forever.

"These tunnels have been here since the walls were built," Mirthorn said. "Our kings and queens were proofing the city's layout for the future."

"Incredible," Drift said. A vertical maze made of hallways and ladders contained within the walls that divided Adira's three zones. Every now and then, the way diverted into a lower, darker tunnel, the beginning of a horizontal maze that joined the districts together below the ground. These humans had worked to create a place for their children, and their children's children. Generations contributing to a common cause they would never see the fullness of in their lifetime. He suddenly understood Mirthorn's patriotism. This man truly wanted the best for his people.

"If we can get to the top of the First District's walls, we can stifle the Theradorans from above."

"With what?" Drift asked.

"Wait and see."

"Mirthorn," Drift said. "I'm sorry. I promise, those Luminous people are not mine. Before I came here, I learned that Therador has found a way to weaponise Luminosity."

"The same Luminosity that your Sleepers are infused with?" Mirthorn asked in disbelief.

"Yes," Drift replied.

Mirthorn nodded stiffly. "Let's keep moving."

Outside the walls, the sounds of the battle grew. Drift felt a renewed sense of urgency. He tailed Mirthorn as closely as possible, stumbling on the uneven ground often.

"Tree-dweller," Mirthorn began. "What can they do with the light?"

"I'm not sure. I've never seen Luminosity used for anything but simple matters in Aobia. Lighting streets, warming homes in the winter… I've never known how it could be used offensively."

"And yet you call Aobia home?"

Drift wasn't sure he did. "Aobia is an … interesting place, Officer. I am Aobian in my blood and perhaps in my soul. If Aobia is home, it is because of those I love, not those who govern it."

Tarri. His heart stung. The further he went from the Tree, the less he felt its pull, and the less he felt … her. Would they ever make their way back to one another? The pain of the possibility caused his heart to ache.

He wasn't sure what he would do if he saw her again. If he would run to her or from her. If he would feel love or oddly …

nothing at all. Why did it hurt to admit that the distance might have severed them forever?

"We are nearly there," Mirthorn called. "A steel ladder will carry us up to the top of the First District walls. But before we get there, I must give you something. Hold out your hand." Drift did as instructed. Mirthorn dumped a sack into his palm.

"This is fulmin powder, also known as Serpentine," he said.

Mirthorn handed Drift a box of matches. Drift felt his throat clench. This was the same stuff that Armand had saved him and Mola with, which had caused the entrance to the Nightingale hideout to explode. With the powder in his hands, he felt a deep sadness, as flashes of the fire that had consumed Ibham and Dayajin flashed through his mind. Fire was the antithesis of life. This stuff made it all too easy to conjure it up. "One day, I hope you'll never need to light a match again in this country. A way to burn an entire forest down, kept in the palm of your hands."

"I am sorry that you must be the bearer of them, tree-dweller." Mirthorn grimaced. "But you and I are the only ones who stand a chance to change the tide of this siege and we must do so now. To the top, and when I say, cast the fulmin powder over the wall. Try to catch some of those Luminous soldiers if you can."

They reached the steel ladder, a trapdoor above it leaking light from the outside world. "Let us go and may whichever of your sea gods that hear us deliver us from harm," Drift said.

As they threw the trapdoor open, the sound of the siege filled Drift's ears. Below the wall, leather-clad Theradoran fighters, both Luminous and not, fought their way through the light Adiran force.

Drift studied the Luminous ones. They might have been glowing like Sleepers, but they were *not* at all like the Sleepers of Aobia. Instead of their hair finely glowing and silver in colour, these people were radiating a fierce yellow, nearly gold, glow across their entire body. Their hands, in particular, rippled behind a wall of light. Whatever they were doing with Luminosity, it wasn't natural.

Drift pulled his head back from the wall as forks of lightning flashed across the sky. A storm was coming, while another had already arrived.

"Drift!" Mirthorn called out. "Try not to get the Serpentine wet. We have one chance to make a dent in their army!" He hopped across the portion of the battlement that acted as an awning over the gates. "Stay where you are! We need to cover both angles. When I say, light the bag and toss it within the walls of the city!"

Drift shook his head. "The walls! They'll fall!"

Mirthorn steadied his gaze on Drift. "Yes, tree-dweller. The walls will fall. With any luck, I'll see you on the other side."

Thunder came like a dirge for the dead as the wind kicked up the beginning flecks of rain, sending thick sheets of it sideways against them. The night sky was cloaked with billows of smoke from burning buildings and glowed with the red echo of flames. "Mirthorn, will this work?"

The high guard either couldn't hear him over the sound of nature clashing with man-made disaster or he ignored him. Instead, he watched as Luminous fighters walked through the gates, clumped together as though ready to take a united stand against Adira's dwindling forces.

The Luminous soldiers' hands began to glow, the light around them burning hot and white. "Drift!" Mirthorn cried as the aura of the enemy's collective heat grew in size, becoming nearly blinding. "What is happening?"

"Mirthorn! The powder! Throw it now!" He lit his small pouch, hands quivering.

"Three!" Mirthorn called.

"Two!" The sound of the enemy's burning radiated like a mighty furnace.

"One!" As they tossed over the bags, a wave of flame followed. The walls broke like a dam in a flood and Drift fell with the debris. Light enveloped him, heat singed his face, and he felt his lungs seize.

All went dark.

ESME

THE WALLS ARE CRASHING down. The thought raced through Esme's mind, round and round, as she watched Therador's approach.

She had left Sefil's side not long ago, exiting the city through the High Guard's tunnel system that ran within the walls. Somewhere out there, her brother was amidst the chaos. The Theradorans were uncontainable, the Adiran forces too light in number, too unprepared.

She watched in horror as the Luminous Theradoran soldiers began to make their way from the Outfields into the First District, where they would encounter an Adiran force that could be squashed like bugs. They hadn't been ready. And she, the fallen, traitorous queen of Adira, was to blame.

She could never go back. This home her family had built, created from love and duty, was no longer hers. And now, it was crumbling, buckling at its knees.

Armand had taken her to this hill, where she lay in wet tufts of long grass, soaked from the short-lived rain, overlooking the First District. Then he had ridden off on the horse they had managed to obtain as they'd departed the city. He'd said he would come back for her, but if not, she would need to get moving.

That was her only plan. She stood in ragged clothing, torn pants and battered, second-hand shoes, watching the few bodies littered around the outskirts of the city walls to make sure they would not rise again. The dead were the key to her success. If she wanted to find her father's killer and help her people beat Therador in the coming months, she would need to be convincingly dead, just like the bodies on the ground.

One body at the bottom of the hill had belonged to a woman, nerves still causing the arms to twitch unnaturally. An arrow shaft poked out of the neck. It was Esme's best chance of escape, to become the dead Theradoran soldier.

She darted down the hill, hoping none of the remaining Theradoran forces on the outside of the city walls glanced in her direction. She dove as she approached the body dressed in red and brown leathers, a poor-fitting leather helmet a short distance away from it.

A hundred metres away, a group of Theradorans were scrambling to check some injured fighters beneath the shadow of the First District's walls. Esme stifled her breathing, trying to press her body deeper into the patchy grass as she quietly began to undress the dead body, removing the corpse's cloak before layers of armour, bracers, and shin greaves. She tried to suck in a breath as the discussion between the soldiers quietened and they began to spread out. The yeoman officers were out here to clean up, Esme realised, and would only be called into the city to fight if worse came to worst. There was little chance she could avoid their gazes now.

There was no time. She removed her buckskin breeches and her roughshod top, her skin cold against the sodden earth. She glanced over, only to realise a soldier was coming towards her as she finished putting the rest on. He'd obviously seen her sitting up in the thicket as she changed. Though he did not run, he did not pause either. Esme's heart pounded. *You're a good liar,* she told herself. *Make it count for something.*

"Over here! Another one alive!" cried the approaching soldier. The rest turned their heads in her direction.

Goddess of the Deep, she swore. She struggled to get the chest plate around her neck, tugging on the bracers as footsteps swiftly approached. "You alive, comrade?"

"Yes," she said. "I'm alive, I suppose. Comrade, my helmet is by your boots. Could you pick it up?" The man still hadn't noticed the body, nearly nude, lying in the grass.

"Here," he said, holding out her helmet. "You look like you've taken a beating."

"One moment I was awake, the next, I wasn't. Something must've hit me."

She could see the man's face now, covered in pocked skin and a scraggly, peppercorn-grey beard. He settled his cold, pale eyes on her, frowning. "Come with me for now, battle-sister. The Priests will be expecting our report in the coming hour before we need to ready up again."

"Again?" she gulped. She could not go back into the city.

"If the rest get overwhelmed, yes." He stopped. "Say, what's your name?"

She inhaled, stalling. She hadn't thought of that. "I … hit my head, I think."

"Your head? Explains why your helmet wasn't with you." He reached for her, lifting her chin with a calloused hand. "Your eyes look okay. But we can't take any chances. Let's get you to the infirmary. Maybe they'll withhold you from the fight if we all get called up. My name's Roish." He let go of her.

Roish. A Theradoran name. She spat out the first one that came to mind, the only one she could recall from those of the mountain people she'd met before in her life. "Eishi," she breathed, feigning an accent. "My name is Eishi."

DRIFT

D RIFT DREW DIRTY, POWDER-COATED air into his lungs. He saw only dark when he awoke, but the muffled sounds of warfare told him the conflict had gone on while he had been unconscious. He must've hit his head, as the pain shooting through the back of his skull burned worse the more he came to. Before him, a hand reached through the debris. He gripped it, hoping it would grip him back, but it came free, completely torn from whatever body it had previously belonged to. He threw it away, jaw aghast with shock.

He kicked his legs free of debris and was able to clear some pieces, but the mound he was stuck beneath was too heavy to shift and even if he could manage it, doing so might cause whatever was above him to topple and crush him.

The sound of coughing somewhere in the dark caused his ears to prick up. "Is anyone there?" came a voice.

"Don't move!" Drift wheezed. "Whatever is on top of us could come crashing down."

"Rightly so," returned the voice. Then, cautiously, "You do not sound Theradoran, though I cannot place your accent."

A tingle ran across Drift's shoulders. "I am not Theradoran."

Silence. Finally, they replied, "Well, whatever you are and whatever I am, we are both stuck beneath a wall of stone and somehow alive. The rest does not matter. Please, let me come closer and maybe we can find a way out."

The shuffling resumed and a fine glow shone through the rubble, reminding him of dappled patches of light in Aobia. One of the Theradorans that was Luminous. *No,* he thought. *I must get out.* Panic caused his heart to race and he sucked in enough dirty air that he worked himself into a violent, hacking fit. They could not be trusted. They were an abomination. They were the enemy who threatened to bring down the First District of Adira under sudden siege and lay claim to the throne that had existed here for centuries. He could not sit with such a person and escape with their help.

He wriggled around some more and the rocks above came loose, clattering down. Dust swirled in the small space before him, catching on the light that seeped through from outside.

"What is it?" the Luminous one called out. "Are you all right?"

"Y-yes," Drift stammered, trying not to alert them further. "Do not worry. I fear you cannot get through to me. We need to work at this slowly to stop the rubble from coming down on us."

He worked quickly, the man leaving him without a reply as he tunnelled through the gap that had just been made. Moonlight poked through, enough for him to get a glimpse at what lay before him, and he felt his throat grow dry, somehow more than it already had been. "Mirthorn!"

The name escaped him like a puff of air as he saw the leader of the High Guard caught below several chunks of stone, his face pressed into the floor. Drift held a hand under the high guard's nose and sighed with relief as he felt cool yet slow air from his nostrils.

Drift reached through the gap, getting onto all fours like a crippled dog and slipping through it until he was beside Mirthorn. He pushed a tiny rock away from his face and the sound of battle rose suddenly, leeching through the debris. He could see now, too, though his field of vision was narrow.

The rain had ceased, the smell of it settling pungent enough to seep through the debris. Several people lay crushed beneath sprawling masses of broken rock, some alive but screaming for death to come. Others tried to drag themselves free, clawing their way through the dirt.

Luminous Theradorans charged the streets, swallowing people into their light so fast that they seemed to be consumed entirely by it.

"Mirthorn!" he hissed, slapping the officer's face. "Wake up! They are taking the city!"

Mirthorn lay unstirring and Drift returned his eyes to the outside. Ahead of the Theradorans, a large force of Adirans pushed through the streets from the direction of the palace, a sentry line of shieldbearers covering archers at the front. In the centre of the crowd was Stag, his forehead wrinkled with anxiety.

Drift felt tears sting his eyes as he felt Stag's fear from a distance. He wanted to reach out and tell him it would be fine; they would not die; they would not lose this fight. But all he could do was watch.

Beside Stag was a royal envoy of soldiers holding up the king. Sefil was held in place by rails that extended upwards on the platform's sides, holding a sword and shield.

He could not hear their cries, but he watched as Sefil spoke to his soldiers before another woman stepped to the platform. It was another Aobian female, a Sleeper with long, silver hair tied in a bun and a midnight blue gown decorated with steel plating. She produced a small globe filled with light from within her gown. The Aobian touched her fingers to the orb, reaching out and touching Sefil's neck with her free arm. Then, Drift could hear everything the king said, as though his voice had been multiplied to be as loud as the old gods themselves: the very air, the very earth, the very sea.

"May the Goddess below bless us this night with the might of the Sea at our defence!" he started as the crowd roared back their response. "For we will fight until our last drop, until our final well of blood runs dry, until the waters rise up from the ocean and swallow us whole. Adira, stand as one and show our foes WHO WE ARE!"

The Sleeper took her hand from Sefil's neck and tucked the globe away, appearing exhausted, before hopping down from the platform. Aobia had come, against all odds. Two forces against one. And all Drift could do was watch.

As the Adiran line charged, the light of the Theradorans swelled to a crescendo, the whirring sound filling every aspect of the world, so much that Drift heard it vibrating in the stones themselves and in the floor beneath his feet. The front line fired arrows into the Theradorans, which somehow dissolved in their thick, smoggy glow. The Luminosity that Therador carried was becoming so opaque it seemed alive, as though *it* was the enemy.

Adira continued to run towards the enemy, its first lines being taken out in the light as the envoy carrying Sefil turned back, not in retreat, but in search of a different approach. Stag, however, proceeded with the army towards the foe. "Stag!" Drift tried to call from the debris.

He could do nothing but watch as even Stag was swallowed into the aura of light that hung about the enemy.

Then, in the blink of an eye, all the light in the world was snuffed out. The Theradorans shone with Luminosity no more. The sound of rain presided over the battleground as every fighter went quiet. "Roots below," Drift swore under his breath.

Smoke began to rise off of the Theradorans, coating the sky. The Adiran soldiers watched in horror as their enemies fell one by one, dying.

Limbs, then torsos, then faces, all became as dark as charcoal and the Theradorans who'd been Luminous moments before now howled in agony at their grotesque transformations. One staggered in front of the debris that housed Drift and Mirthorn, and Drift struggled to pull his gaze away. What had once been a man became a sinewy, decaying shell. Hollowed eye sockets peeled and cracked, bony hands clawing at the night as though trying to hold on to what once had been. The creature's dying breaths became odd and reverberating as though there were many voices contained in the single body. Then it bent over and fell into the dirt.

Horns rose from the First District and the Outfields of Adira beyond it as enemy soldiers cried, "Retreat!"

A cough rang out from beside Drift. "Mirthorn!" Drift exclaimed.

"Tree … tree-dweller," Mirthorn said on wispy, weak breaths. "What is happening?"

"Mirthorn, don't move! We are trapped, but I'll find a way out of this." He put a comforting hand to the man's cheek.

"I fear that I am finished, tree-dweller," Mirthorn said, coughing again. "Below my shoulders, I feel nothing. Not even a stab of pain."

"No, Mirthorn," Drift said. "You'll be fine. Just fine. Let me get you out of here and then we can find you help at the hospice or a-at—"

"If you get me out of here," Mirthorn said, "I'll owe you more than I can give for the rest of my days. If you do not, you might just survive yourself." He hacked up a cough once more and blood flecked the ground, sticky and dark. "Please, just help me breathe easier."

"Of—" Drift stopped. That lump of sadness, of defeat, rose from his chest and sat in his throat like a plug. Raegan, the Sethi couple, and now this honourable officer. Why did so many end up hurt or dead because of Drift?

"Your name," Mirthorn murmured, his eyes closing. "Your name…"

"It's okay, Mirthorn," Drift managed.

"Your name… Drift. You are not…" A cough again, like a final try, a final attempt at living. "You are not to die. Not here. You must go, escape." Mirthorn opened his eyes with a light flutter. "My name … is nothing. 'Rose of the Thorn' my mother called me. Because it sounded"—he wheezed—"poetic." A light chuckle rang from his sand-dry lips. "But you… Your people are named … with purpose in mind."

Drift shoved a rock off the man, freeing up his chest plate before diving in and over Mirthorn's head to try and move some more. Above him, crunching and clattering rang out. He looked at Mirthorn, using his back to press upwards and shift what was on top of them aside. With any luck, it might lead to the outside world.

The rock moved enough for Drift to see what had pinned Mirthorn down. The officer's arm lay in a mangled state, draped across the ground, torn at the shoulder. Sticky blood coated the openings, pooling all over the dirt. Mirthorn groaned and Drift reflexively shoved a hand on the man's mouth to quieten him. "What can you feel?" he asked the officer.

"Nothing," Mirthorn said bitterly. "Nothing at all."

"We'll fix it," Drift insisted. He didn't know how, but he'd get this man to safety, with his arm and all.

"Drift!" Mirthorn quipped with a sudden sting. "Listen to me. Leave me!"

"No!" Drift said. "I will not leave you!"

"Your name—"

"Names mean nothing, Mirthorn. That's old stuff, lost to time. There is nothing more to my name than that. Now, let me concentrate!"

The officer went silent, gritting his teeth.

With a roar, Drift felt the stone above him slip enough for him to get purchase on its sides, his hands above him. The stone wriggled in place before moving aside.

Enough to see the aftermath of the siege. Enough to see the dead.

Enough to see that there was nobody to help him or to check that he was alive.

He shook his head, found a way to step out of the rubble, and hauled Mirthorn along with him. He would keep his promise and deliver this man to his people. To someone who knew where he belonged. After all that had happened to Drift these past few weeks, he was not sure he could say the same for himself. Maybe there was truth to Mirthorn's words, that he *was* as his name suggested. He did not belong. He never had, anywhere. And now, life moved on without him.

He flung Mirthorn's limp body across his arms and looked around. The First District had been abandoned. Now, the true clean-up began. Whether he was there for it or not… Perhaps that did not matter.

Perhaps all he could do, instead, was drift.

NISCHIA

T HE WRECKAGE SILENCED HER in more ways than one. She had not seen a calamity such as this since the end of the Four-Front War, when the bodies of her people had been found frozen upon the mountain pass for months after the treaties had been signed. Now, Adira was a wasteland, a drowning victim who had not yet died.

Nischia sat in a balcony that looked out over the city and the rolling hills of the Outfields beyond. She held a hot cup of tea in her hands—jasmine—and waited for the others to arrive.

Nischia recalled the Theradorans who had fled with their lives just days before, their Luminous fighters lost to nova events. Remnant Cores could exist, it seemed, in humans as well as Aobians. *Lyria better have a good explanation for that,* she thought, biting her nails. This was a changing world and adapting to it was not easy. She had learned that as a Sleeper. But now… Now it was changing so quickly that perhaps Aobia would be left behind. Perhaps she and her people were no longer made for this world.

The glass doors creaked open as the three humans walked onto the balcony to meet her. They sat around the small table and poured themselves cups of tea, looking at her expectantly. She sighed before saying with formality, "Thank you for coming."

The three inclined their heads in reply, but only one looked back up at her directly, signalling to speak. "My lady Sleeper, there is much to discuss." Logis was old now and not suited to meeting like this. If she was present, then what was to be said was of the highest import.

"All-Mother, I wish to know more than I fear we can address. I wish to know how to fix the mess we have made."

Logis smiled, but it was resigned, like she knew that Nischia's hope was misplaced. "Let us address what we can. You have met Lyria?" She gestured to the young human woman beside her. Nischia nodded, smiling. She knew Lyria. She knew she was fiercely loyal to Adira and that she was also a commander of the intelligence organisation known as the Reef's Treasures.

"And this is Armand." Logis pointed at the man on her right, who wore a brown hood pulled over his head, although the morning was already hot.

"My lady Sleeper," he said, though he did not offer her a hand to shake. A good man. At least he understood some Aobian social rules.

"Armand also joins us from the Reef's Treasures, but he has not been heavily involved in the studies that Lyria and her team have led. He has spent time as of late integrating into a mercenary group known as Nightingales." Logis paused, lowering her gaze. "But more on that later. Lyria, will you begin?"

"Certainly, All-Mother," Lyria said, bringing out a small satchel to the tabletop. "Lady Nischia, the first specimen we found was discovered and analysed before King Terrens' passing. He got to see most of our findings and wrote down many of his thoughts in this journal." Lyria handed a small leather-bound booklet to Nischia, its pages worn and frayed but filled with delicate handwriting. Terrens had always been a perfectionist, whether with his handwriting, his children, or his people. "The exiled queen Esme read this journal days before his death, after we gave the king permission to inform her of the assessments we had been making. I believe it will be of benefit to us all to include her in any further discussions we may have after today."

The pages were filled with notes, of course, which would take Nischia a lot longer than she had now to parse. However, she eventually turned to a new page with a sketch of the specimen in question: a long, spiky back ran the length of an odd-looking fish that seemed to be partially transparent, its guts visible from the outside. Upon its head sat the most curious thing, a long line of antenna with a kind of shining globe flickering on the end of it. Luminosity. This creature was able to create light from within itself.

"This first specimen… It produced natural Luminosity? That was the conclusion?" Nischia asked the question slowly, apprehension tugging at her. She was not sure how far down this path of knowledge she wanted to go, but after Therador's siege, she felt there was no choice.

"It did." Lyria nodded. "There was a chemical reaction happening within its body, a result of many natural bacteria capable of making the fish luminesce as a response to danger and as a way to lure its own prey. We examined this with some samples of other species and watched the specimen use its light as a mechanism for attraction. A single overnight stay in the tank with the specimen led to all the smaller creatures' deaths."

"These bacteria," Nischia began. "They are similar to what you think the Tree produces, are they not?"

"They are," Lyria said. "I know it is not my place to reduce your culture and your home to a scientific explanation, but—"

"It is necessary," Nischia said abruptly. "I fear we linger enough in the past as it is."

Lyria sighed and Nischia turned to look out over Adira once more, taking in what she had learned. Eventually, the scientist continued, looking to Logis and Armand. "The sample that your ambassador brought on his last trip to Adira... We believe it acts the way it does due to a symbiotic relationship, a mutually exclusive existence where one matter cannot persist without the other."

"That *is* significant," Nischia agreed. "Though I'm not pleased about that particular ambassador being the conduit between us and your discovery."

"If I might, my lady," Armand offered. "Flow was very acquainted with our work. There were several times where he could have been removed from meetings, but the King thought otherwise."

"Yes," Nischia muttered. "Even after death, Terrens has left us with a major inconvenience. A final piece of work for us to have to deal with."

"Now, Nischia," Logis said, putting up a hand. "This is not the time to bicker. Answers are what we must seek, and as quickly and diligently as we can. Lyria, you must tell Nischia the rest."

Nischia felt her chest tighten as the faces at the table around her shifted from conversational to stern, maybe even dire. Lyria flashed a worried look at her before adjusting her tone.

"My lady," she began. "The sample you provided to us suggests that the Tree itself is changing. Of course, we will need to see more samples and collect more data, but—"

"Changing? How?" Nischia cut her off. An urgency fell upon the table like a dark cloud.

"The reason why your Sleep seems less potent, the reason why the River Tomei needs more regular maintenance, and maybe even the reason for the Sickness in the first place are linked."

Nischia raised a brow. "Go on."

"Every plant on the planet competes for survival, just like animals do. They compete for sunlight. Imagine you are a plant: the taller you stand, the less likely you are to fall to disease or starvation. It seems like for hundreds of years, the Great Tree has been winning that battle."

Nischia's frown deepened.

"The fungi and its dependents are losing Luminosity as well. At best, the situation dictates that a rapid evolution is happening and that the fungi is filled with whatever feeds Luminosity into the Great Tree."

"You're saying the plants and fungi beneath us are inherently Luminous, like the Tree itself? Or like this specimen you caught in the sea?" Nischia asked. All this time, they'd thought the Tree bestowed the glow of Luminosity upon whatever grew in its shade.

"It's a relationship we are still learning about, my lady," Lyria said. "We do not yet know enough about these things. It's as though we've come across a new scientific frontier."

It was enough to rethink her identity as a Sleeper, to consider the access to Luminosity that Therador had found so suddenly, and to stop attributing her own Luminosity to some spiritual nature. It was harder to rethink how the Great Tree itself was fed by what it crippled beneath the dark shades of its canopies. "At worst?"

"Pardon, my lady?"

"You said 'at best' before, Lyria. At worst, what is your hypothesis?"

Lyria looked at her with a face as hard as stone. Armand looked away and Logis put a hand to her mouth. "That the Great Tree is dying, my lady."

REMEMBRANCE II

TARRI

S HE HELD HER MOTHER'S hand for the last time on the morning of her thirteenth birthday. Barely entering adolescence, Tarri felt the illusion of control as she hid behind her mother's skirt when the two glowing figures arrived at the door of their small, cosy branch-home.

Tarri's throat felt like a rough stone lodged between her head and her heart. She wanted to understand what was happening, but she couldn't. Why must she be taken away? Her mother screamed at the Sleepers as they stepped forward, one of them trying to hold her thrashing arms, the other reaching around to grab the child.

"It's my fault!" Mother wailed. "It's my fault!"

No! Tarri wanted to scream. *It is not your fault. I was the problem and you noticed it.* But no voice came.

"Tree-sister," one of the glowing figures said. "You must let us take the child. It is only for her own g—"

"Get away from her!" she screamed. "You'll come no further." Her eyes lit up. "I will incinerate the skin you wear until it peels from your bones like leather."

Tarri had never heard Mother talk like this and tucked herself further into the folds of her mother's skirt. This fury unsettled her. Would Mother hurt her by accident?

She whimpered, but nobody could hear her. Nobody could see her either, tucked away in that once-safe space. She wanted to retreat, flee into the dark crevice beneath her bed, where she had hidden as a child, a sign that the Fever was returning once more. But things had gone too far now; her hair was ablaze, like fire. Her mother was an ember in her spark.

Mother toppled forward as one of the Sleepers grabbed at her arm. Tarri sat, exposed to the other Sleeper, a female with shining silver hair. She felt the shivers beginning again, the same symptoms of Fever that had caused her to pass out on occasion and that her mother was losing the strength to heal with Luminosity.

But she would try one more time. As long as they didn't take her child. Tarri whimpered on the ground like a baby, unable to move, unable to close her jaw and keep her teeth steady. Her mother thrashed in the arms of the male Sleeper. "Please, Sister, you must under—"

Mother snarled, a new sound that caused Tarri to question how much of her mother had produced it. Mother's eyes were ablaze, her fingertips growing red with concentrated light. It burst from her like lightning in a thunderstorm, striking the Sleeper down.

Tarri covered her ears as the male's screams echoed around the room, a tortured series of wails that died down to a childlike sob as he fell to the floor, crying over the black stumps that smoked away where his hands had once been.

The female cautiously put one hand beneath her cloak as the other lit up like Mother's had. "Now, Leavening," the Sleeper said, gritting her teeth. "This is your final chance to come quietly and let us take the child."

"Never!" Mother seethed. "Not after all I've done to stop the Fever!" The manic glance she gave her daughter sent shockwaves through her.

"I…" Mother heaved. "I will not … let my child go!" With that a burst of cooler, paler light flew forth like the healing ripples of a clean river, washing over Tarri. She felt the Fever immediately sag within her, like a failing enemy with nowhere to run. She felt herself growing stronger again, more … normal.

The Sleeper was shielding her eyes with her wrists, gasping at the beast that was Tarri's mother. Mother's eyes became like flames, reaching over her face and engulfing her. She grew blackened, like charcoal, her limbs and head burning, and she screeched in agony. Light flew from her, enveloping Tarri in cleansing washes while equally blasting the two Sleepers with pure, concentrated heat. The female Sleeper joined in the male's cries, flailing about as she perished, flame consuming her. Tarri recoiled at the smell of burning flesh.

The flames died as soon as Mother fell to the floor. Mother had killed two Sleepers. The Magisterium would find out. They would not let her get away with this atrocity. Tarri felt a lump in her throat as she ran to her.

"Mother!" Tarri grabbed her shoulders and pushed her upright so she could see her face. The face of the only one who had loved her, the only one who had fought for her. Smoke streamed out of Mother's eyes, the burning scent causing Tarri to cough. "Mother, what's wrong?"

She slumped forward, a dead weight too heavy for Tarri to carry. She gasped as she clambered backwards, her heart racing. Was Mother dead, too? All of that conflict, for nothing. "N-no!" she stammered. "You can't be gone. You can't be!"

She grabbed her mother's wrists, turning her onto her back. Nothing. No resistance. No life in the black wells where once bright shining eyes had hung, suspended like stars. The only stars in Tarri's sky, extinguished in moments.

The next thought that struck her was her only chance to bring her mother back. Cutting through the silence, from a curtained-off section of the room, was the constant thrum, deep and resonant, of the Orb. She'd lived with it so long, she never noticed it anymore. It didn't sing for her, anyway. She was a normal child. She had never been allowed to go beyond the break of the Fever, where she would either die or be blessed with the new life of a Sleeper. But her mother knew the Orb's tempting call well and worked to manage it, a constant tug of war.

Tarri had little choice but to try it. She moved her mother's limp body to the edge of the Orb's shimmering surface, pushing it in slowly, careful not to touch it herself. She knew not what would happen if she did.

She used the handle of a broom to get the last inch of her mother's fingertips inside, watching to see if anything would happen. Mother's body rose up, animated like a puppet so that it was sitting cross-legged in a meditative position. Her hands were pressed together. She was breathing shallowly, but there was no further movement. Helpless, shocked into silence, and unsure of what to do next, Tarri closed the curtains around the Orb and tried to let go of what had happened. There was nothing for her to do now but wait.

Tarri cleaned the bodies that night, sweeping their ashen chunks into a cane basket and dumping its contents out into the limbs outside. She slept little, the whir of the Orb growing louder than she was used to. The next day, she waited for Magisterium officials to come and try to claim her and her mother.

Nobody ever came.

THE END *of*
AN EXILE OF WATER & GOLD

Thank you, Fellow Tree-Dweller

Well, here we are. Thank you, thank you, *thank you* for reading An Exile of Water & Gold! This is my proudest work to date, and offers only a glimpse of the tumultuous happenings on Q'ara. To stay up to date with me and my work, please check out my mailing list at:

www.joshuawalkerauthor.com/subscribe

You'll find the prequel novella to this story, *The Rest of the Gods,* over there, too.

Nothing fulfils me more than getting my work into the hands of readers. If you wouldn't mind leaving me a review on Goodreads and Amazon, (or if you can't, a star rating would also be fabulous), I can do exactly that.

In the current state of publishing, a review goes a long way to getting my writing out there and in front of more readers!

Josh

July 2024

Acknowledgements

An Exile of Water & Gold is my proudest accomplishment as a writer to-date; but it's only in your hands because of several other people.

At the beginning of it all, I must thank my Creator, without whom I would not have been gifted these talents I've worked to improve over the course of my life.

To my family, who shaped me with good literature, and a deep appreciation for stories, thank you. From the moment I read The Hobbit, to tearing through Dad's comic cupboard, to the first time I watched Indiana Jones on VHS (which came with a Maccas Happy Meal, don't ask me why), I was set upon this path.

To my wife for always backing me, even when it's hard to see the return on investment in this author journey. I have to be away from you a lot more than either of us want to be able to write books, and you make it possible and always cheer me on. I love you.

To my best friends, Sam and Christian, who put in the hard yards to give me feedback as alpha readers: I don't know how you got through the book when it was in that state, let alone find things to compliment about it. You guys are the best, and honestly, this book might not be in reader's hands without you both.

To the Break-Ins, who form the single greatest group to have come out of this writing thing. Scott Palmer, Rob Leigh, Isaac Hill, Kaden Love, Adrian M Gibson, Louise Holland, Calum Lott, Jonathan Weiss, Sam Paisley, Bryan Wilson, Francisca Liliana, Andrew Watson, ZS Diamanti, and Nicholas W Fuller—you are all so great, and you will always have my love and thanks.

To my editor, Sarah Chorn for bringing out the best of this novel. I cannot believe how far this story's come since the draft I first sent you. Your ideas are magic, and your attention to detail (or the lack thereof in my case) is incomparable. Thank you, and I can't wait to work with you again soon.

To my proofreader, Isabelle: your skill was the perfect complement to Sarah's, and you have really made this book stand out for its polish and shine. Thank you.

To the king of fantasy cover art, Jeff Brown: I cannot believe the work you did for this novel, and I'm so excited to see what you create for Book Two. Thank you for putting up with my annoying emails, each one along the lines of, "Just one more thing, I promise." The same goes for my wonderful cartographer Josh Hoskins, chapter heading designer Anna Maslennikova, and interior artist Joe Requeza. Thank you all.

Ahh, the indie community. I can't possibly fit all the names of those who have supported me over the last year, but I will try to. Taking a deep breath for this one: Boe Kelley, Kristen Shafer, Bob from BlueSmokeFire and the entirety of the SFF Insiders team; Charlie Cavendish and David Walters from FanFi Addict; Abel Montero; Aaron M Payne from BiblioTheory; Esmay Rosalyne; Kayla from Kay's Hidden Shelf; Kris the Fictional Escapist; Livia J Elliot; Petrik Leo; Dr Philip Chase; Mark Timmony; Ainy Cormac; Noah's Brisk Reviews; Julianna Caro; Brenden Pugh from Writing Quest; The Empty Bookshelf ... There are so many more people I have interacted with that I can't possibly list here, but just know I appreciate you all.

Lastly, dear reader, thank you. I could write these stories for myself, but I choose to share them with you to inspire, provoke thought, and provide imaginative stories to behold. For as long as you support my work by reading it, I'll write more and more. There is much to come in this Luminous world, and this is just the beginning.

ABOUT THE AUTHOR

Joshua Walker is a fantasy author currently residing in Melbourne, Australia. He currently works as a primary school English teacher, and likes to read, brew beer, and hang out with his wife and BFD (Big Fluffy Dog), Otis, in his free time. He will not apologise for writing in British English.

To find out more about The Song of the Sleepers series, head to www.joshuawalkerauthor.com.